JASPER SPRINGS OMNIBUS VOLUME ONE

BOOKS 1-3

EVIE RILEY

Jasper Springs
Series Omnibus
Volume One
Books 1-3
Copyright © 2024
Evie Riley
ISBN: 978-1-77357-731-9
978-1-77357-732-6
Published by Naughty Nights Press LLC
Cover Art By Willsin Rowe

CADE

AN MM OPPOSITES ATTRACT
ROMANCE

Cade
An MM Opposites Attract Romance
Jasper Springs
Book One

Copyright © 2024
Evie Riley
Second Edition
ISBN: 978-1-77357-717-3
Published by Naughty Nights Press LLC
Cover Art By Willsin Rowe

CADE

Home is where the heart is…

Life in Jasper Springs may look perfect, but for Cade Green there's one thing still missing… a hunky billionaire to whisk him away, just like in the movies he can't stop binge watching after his latest break up. But life isn't some romantic tale for guys like him. That is, until the man of his dreams shows up at the local bar's karaoke night.

Can Cade's small-town heart handle the whirlwind that Weston brings?

Famed bachelor Weston Rhodes reluctantly returns to his hometown, planning on nothing more than a fleeting visit. The last thing he expects to find is a reason to stay. However, after one intense night, he soon discovers himself falling for the small town's adorable veterinarian.

Can Weston, used to city lights and endless possibilities, embrace a fairy-tale romance in his quaint hometown?

Readers seeking a small town good boy/bad boy billionaire, opposites attract romance set in a cozy little town may find this story hits those buttons.

While Cade and Weston may have cameos in future stories, each book in this series can be read as a standalone.

CHAPTER 1

CADE

THE DRIVE through Jasper Springs was always the prettiest early in the morning. The sunrise colored the skies in various rich tones, from blush to ochre to lavender like some picturesque postcard, which was one of the things I had always loved about this town.

It was always warm, a comfortable seventy degrees even in the winter, which wasn't a terrible thing. I could have only imagined driving in snow, sleet and ice when there was an emergency at the Jasper Springs Pet Hospital, beholden to snow plow trucks and whatnot. In truth, I wasn't made for the cold, clearly.

I drove past Jasper Springs High and turned up the radio. My heart ached at hearing the familiar melodic tones of Ariana Grande, if only because it reminded me of *him*. My ex.

I knew then in my heart we weren't meant to be. Hell, I knew when I started dating Bill, we were probably going to go up in flames, so I absolutely knew that I shouldn't have been so worked up over everything, but I thought... I thought maybe, just possibly I'd be proven wrong. And when we had passed that six-month mark, I thought maybe I was right. Maybe this one was different. But it turned out Bill was, in fact, not much different from any of my former flames.

The "it's not you, it's me" shit? Yeah, I'm a magnet for that.

Most of the men I met were fun for a little while, but eventually my "small town charm" became less refreshing, and more of a thorn in everyone's sides.

Just because I don't see myself leaving Jasper Springs any time doesn't mean I don't have value, or that I'm not willing to make something long-distance work.

Ariana's voice on the radio droned on about letting go.

But life wasn't a Hallmark movie, either. There weren't exactly many big city boys coming to tiny little Jasper Springs looking for a small town guy wearing flannel to sweep them off their feet.

A man can dream, right?

Just as I pulled into my usual parking space in front of the pet hospital, my phone went off, that annoying siren ringtone somehow knowing just the exact moment to pull me from my thoughts.

Out of all the men I'd loved before, Dawson was the only one I could actually wholeheartedly agree that we made better friends than we ever did as lovers.

Granted the sex wasn't half bad, but we're both way too different for things to have ever worked on a non-platonic level.

As it was our relationship didn't last long before we both realized that we just didn't feel the way we probably should have.

It was the most mutual "it's not you, it's me" I'd ever been in, because for once I actually delivered the speech, and Dawson just shrugged, as if it didn't matter. And then he asked me if I wanted pepperoni on the pizza.

And of course, I had agreed.

Is there anything better than a pepperoni pizza?

It's classic.

Punching the green icon and silencing the

trill, I sighed upon answering, knowing if I didn't, Dawson would just keep calling until I would inevitably lose my shit, despite the fact he knew I was working.

"Yes, Dawson?" I deadpanned.

The man is natural cocaine, I swear to God. His energy can be felt before he even speaks.

"M's Place put up their Bar Bingo & Karaoke schedule today," Dawson said with absolute delight as I let out a sigh.

It never bothered me, living in a small town, but there wasn't much to do around Jasper Springs other than hang out at M's Place or one of the coffee shops or few restaurants that exist. Of course there was a movie theater, a gym, a baseball field...

But entertainment was still pretty minimal. Most of the folks from Jasper Springs liked it that way, but for the social butterflies like Dawson, there was always M's Place.

Our friend Mitchell's brother, Miguel, owned the bar, and while they were most definitely classified as a "dive bar", they hosted a good amount of events. Everything from holiday parties to trivia nights, to Bar Bingo and karaoke.

And they're not douchebags when it comes to being openly queer either, being as Mitchell is about as openly gay as one can get.

I pursed my lips. I wished I could have the confidence that Mitchell and Dawson had when it came to social situations like that, but I was about as social as a clam at a clambake.

"And?" I huffed.

"And, it's *tonight*. You work until four, right?" Dawson pressed.

I knew exactly what he was getting at, and I also knew I should say no. That I should just put in my hours, go home, eat some ice cream and call it a night.

But I hadn't seen Mitch or Dawson since Bill and I broke up right before Christmas...

Who breaks up right before Christmas?

Worst holiday movie ever...

"I do, but that doesn't mean—"

"What? Like you have something better to do? Stay home in your fluffy bunny slippers eating your weight in Rocky Road?" Dawson drawled sarcastically.

I was both aggravated at the fact that the firefighter knew me so well, and offended that Dawson didn't think that was precisely my idea of a good time.

I just wish I didn't have to do it alone.

"Way to be harsh, Dawson."

"I'm sorry, man, but it's for your own good. You're just nursing the wound at this point. Time to take off the band-aid. Get back out there. Catch some bigger fish to make you forget all about Billiard-No-Brains," Dawson encouraged.

I rolled my eyes at my friend's nickname for my most recent ex.

Dawson had given him the nickname when Bill lost a game of pool to him and Mitch. Ultimately, it was a shitty call. Bill shot for a higher ball, when he clearly could have had an easy point, and it cost us the game. Dawson had taken it upon himself to refer to him as nothing else since, except, of course, in his actual presence. Though I did always worry that he was going to slip up eventually.

Guess I don't have to worry about that anymore.

I rolled my eyes again at Dawson's tone, running my hand over my face and let out a deep sigh.

I knew without a doubt that I wouldn't say no, because whether I liked it or not, Dawson was right.

I need to get out, to get myself back on track and put Billiard-No-Brains behind me.

"Yeah, okay." I conceded. "I got to go, Diane is probably wondering why I'm still sitting in the car," I said quickly.

"Excellent!" Dawson said, his tone something between a cartoon villain and a man who just won the lottery. I hung up, breathing a sigh of defeat.

It was just an evening out with friends, catching up.

What was the worst that could happen?

CHAPTER 2

Cade

The bar was packed, as was typical for Bar Bingo & karaoke. Jasper Springs wasn't exactly the biggest town on the map by far, but it wasn't uncommon for some of the folks from the neighboring towns of Paradise and Deer Hills to mosey on over to M's for the Bar Bingo nights.

Dawson slammed down his beer, rolling his eyes.

"Come on, Cade. Live a little, have some fun for once," he taunted me.

Dawson had been trying to get me up on stage to karaoke for the last hour, despite the fact he knew how much I despised that kind of thing.

It's not that I couldn't sing, because I very well could. I just didn't normally do that sort of thing outside of my house or car, and I wasn't the type to seek out attention. Everyone's eyes on me would make me nervous, but Dawson told me no one would be paying any real attention to me.

I'm not sure if that made it better or worse, to be honest.

"Leave the boy alone, Dawson," Mitchell said, taking pity on me as usual. I'd known Mitch since the sixth grade, though I'd never really considered him a best friend or anything, but nowadays I felt differently. Though I knew many people, I was closest to Dawson and Mitch, and did consider them my best friends.

They have definitely been the most consistent men in my life.

"Ya'll are lame. I'm going up," Dawson said as he left us at the high-top table.

My gaze danced around the room, taking in the sight of plenty of the other men, and even the women who all seemed like they were having a blast. A part of me wondered if I'd ever feel that vibrant again. Like I was on top of the world. Because as I watched them all, I couldn't help but feel forever stuck in the bottom of the world.

As I people watched, I noticed a man I had

certainly never seen before. While I'd never been the biggest social butterfly, I did know a good bit of folks from Paradise and Deer Hills, if only through treating their pets. A natural observer, I knew without a doubt that I had never seen this guy before.

For starters, he looked a little too… nice to be in M's Place. A perfectly tailored, rather expensive looking suit like his would stick out in any bar whose idea of fancy is putting a tiny umbrella in the frozen drinks.

I started at the man's feet, noticing the perfectly shined leather shoes that looked like they cost more than my car. My eyes widened as my gaze traveled up slender legs that looked like they went on for miles by the posture of how he straddled his bar stool. I watched intently as the attractive stranger pushed back the bottom of his suit jacket, his long, lithe fingers sliding along the top of his thigh. Instantly, I found myself imagining what that would feel like, those fingers brushing *my thighs*. I blushed from the immediate thoughts, but couldn't turn away. When my roving gaze finally made it to the man's face, I thought maybe I *had* imagined him completely.

Maybe the two beers I'd had were getting to me.

Because I swore this man looked like someone straight out of a Hallmark movie.

What were the chances he was gay?

Probably slim, but I could dream, right?

No rules against fantasizing...

Instantly, my cock twitched as I watched him shift his stance. The way this man held himself, so sure, and confident.

Not to mention that sexy smile.

I knew he was out of my league.

If he's even batting for the same team, that is.

His demeanor alone screamed "rich asshole", which should have deterred me, but only made me want him that much more because that's how fucked up *I* was.

Why am I always attracted to assholes?

What is my problem?

I chastised myself as I fought the urge to stare.

Assholes will always treat you like shit, Cade. You need a gentleman. Someone like you.

My mother's words echoed in my head. I couldn't blame the woman for trying to impart some sense in me, but I didn't think she understood that the selection pool for me wasn't exactly full of the men she read about in her romance books.

That's when I saw that Hottie-McSuit was staring back at *me* with a smirk.

Right at me.

His dark eyes sparkled with a fire that called

to my twitching cock, and I knew I should look away, but I was powerless to do so.

Nope, I was truly frozen in this man's gaze, my skin feeling suddenly flushed as his delicious lips curved into a smile and he winked at me.

Oh fuck.

Fuck fuck, fuckity fuck.

Well, that cleared some things up, I supposed. But he was still out of my league. He was probably out of my ballpark entirely.

I could hear the end of Dawson's song, Nickelback's Photograph, just as the man from my absolute dreams climbed off his barstool, sliding his hands in his suit jacket pockets. He sauntered toward me, his gaze never breaking, and I felt the world around me still.

Why did we have to pick a table in the center of the room, damn it?

CHAPTER 3

I LOATHED COMING HOME to Jasper Springs. I'd never really felt like I fit in, in the quaint, charming little town. Part of that surely had to do with the fact that I'd never spent more than the summer there, despite it being the town my family's business had been a part of for practically my entire life.

But being as my mother insisted on sending me to the highest accredited private schools my father's money could buy, that probably had a lot to do with such things, and my father only saw it as a means to an end.

Because to him, one day I'd take his place as CEO of Rhodes Enterprises, whether I wanted to or not. This company, this legacy, belonged to me.

Not to mention all the money that came with it...

But to me, the town of Jasper Springs was just so... idyllic. Like something out of a damn rom-com movie.

The only thing to really do in the town was go to the damn bar. Nightlife was non-existent in Jasper Springs, and I'm pretty sure the closest club was at least an hour away in the city. At least the bartender could make a good Manhattan.

I was about to throw in the towel and ask for the check, because quite frankly, if I had to listen to the asshole on stage screeching along to Nickelback a second longer, I would have gone insane. I noticed the man across from the bar, the one who was sitting with Nickelback's rejected soloist, was staring at me.

I was used to being stared at, quite honestly. At the risk of sounding like an ass, I knew I was in fact, the best of both worlds when it came to my inherited good looks. My mother's pedigree was very visible in my bone structure and my dark green eyes, while I got all of my father's swagger and his full, thick chestnut hair.

Though the way this California-surfer cutie was looking at me went far beyond appreciation.

His pretty little blue peepers stared at me with *hunger* and longing, and I couldn't help but smile.

Perhaps a good roll in the hay was just what I needed to get through this god-forsaken trip.

Hometown Heartthrob was actually pretty cute, if I was being honest.

I trailed my gaze over his form. I could tell by the polo shirt he was wearing, which looked a little tight around his arms, that Pretty-Blue-Eyes took good care of himself, went to the gym at least. But the way he sat on his barstool, how he hunched over just a bit, and blushed when he realized I had caught him looking, told me that he wasn't overly confident in himself.

I've always loved a good, shy boy. They're usually the dirtiest bastards in bed.

The screeching man finally finished his song, and not a moment too soon, breaking the adorable target out of his daze. I did make it a point to slowly saunter over in his direction, deciding on the way exactly which song I would select to make the damn fool drop to his knees.

Then I'd buy him a drink, and take him back to my hotel so he could really drop to his knees and suck my cock like a good, dirty boy.

As I walked past him, I made a point to get as close as possible, shooting him my telltale look that I was well aware made men like him weak.

The look that told them without a single

word that they were mine for the night and they'd do as I asked.

It wasn't like anyone usually lasted longer than that anyway, and by the time the sun came up, I would be off somewhere new. Long-term relationships didn't typically work for me.

My father liked to remind me that he was the same until he and my mom had set up shop in Jasper Springs. Until he'd met my mother, he had also been content with 'being a bachelor' as he called it. But after moving to Jasper Springs, and meeting my mom, they'd both settled down here after my mother got pregnant with me. Some people hated the constant traveling and jet-set life, like her. But business called for more jet setting after I was born, and the city was more manageable when we traveled so much.

Though I never hated it, in fact, it had been the only constant in my life. I didn't know how to stay in one place, because I'd never had to and there was a sort of poetry to that. New experiences, new men, new ways for me to pretend I was someone else...

But I'd be lying if I said I didn't think about the contrast sometimes.

Putting down roots, waking up to the same man every day, pushing a cart at the nearest Whole Foods while I drink my wheatgrass shake.

But was that really who Weston Rhodes was

beneath the veneer of expensive suits and top notch clubs?

I shoved the thought aside as I grabbed the microphone from the DJ, whispering my song choice in his ear. I didn't see the point in shouting in the loud, god-forsaken place.

My father always told me you didn't need to be loud to make people listen. Whispering forced them to listen to you, they couldn't be distracted that way or some shit.

The intro beats filled the space and the stage lights were bright, but I didn't blink. Instead, I only focused on finding Pretty-Blue-Eyes where he sat, and gave the best karaoke performance of my damn life.

Of course, I wouldn't have settled for anything less, and neither should he.

Something happened as the song droned on, as our eyes fell on one another. I knew halfway through as I watched his chest rise and fall, as I watched that hunger in the man's eyes turn into a starving need, that I had him.

I always got what I wanted, and that night I wanted him.

I graciously handed back the microphone to the DJ, and took my sweet old time approaching the object of my current desire.

"You were amazing up there," the other man said hurriedly as I leaned my hand on the table, steadying myself and standing in front of him like the piece of meat I knew that I was.

Grade A, baby.

"I know. I also know it'd be *amazing* if you let me buy you a drink. You look quite thirsty.," I said, flashing him a grin.

One of the other men at the table rolled his eyes, while the one that was screeching along before on stage just shoved Pretty-Blue-Eyes in front of me.

"Annnd this is where you say 'yes sir'," the screeching man said with a laugh.

I wasn't sure if he was taunting the object of my flirtation, or giving him a push of encouragement, but either way, something shifted in the man's gaze and he nodded quickly.

"Um, yeah... I mean, yes... I mean... sure. A drink sounds great," he said and I knew I had him. Hook, line, and sinker.

Yeah, I was definitely getting my dick sucked after this.

This trip was looking better already.

CHAPTER 4

CADE

It's just a drink, Cade. Not like you've never done this before or anything...

Though, I had to admit, something about Smooth-Suit-McGee buying me a drink felt drastically different from any other "let me buy you a drink's" I'd experienced.

If it wasn't for Dawson nearly shoving me off my damn barstool, I would have probably been a staring, speechless mess at the mountain of sex that stood in front of me. Up close, I could smell his rich, heady cologne and appreciate the finer details of his GQ-Model face. He was literally the hottest man I'd ever laid eyes on.

So I followed the man of my dreams to the bar like a moth to a flame, making our way through the crowd. When we finally got up to the bar, the patrons split like the Red Sea for us.

Well, him, technically. I'd always been about as invisible as they come, but for the moment I was riding the coattails of stardust, more than happy to bask in his starry glow.

God, he's really fucking gorgeous.

"What'll it be, darling?" he drawled as he leaned his long arms on the counter, the fabric of his jacket pulling at all the right places to showcase his form. He propped his foot up on the silver bar at the base, elongating the silhouette of his legs, and I couldn't help but get a good glance at his firm, tight ass.

I'm so out of my league.

"Well, usually I'm a Sam Adams guy," I said, trying to keep the shakiness out of my voice.

He nodded in response as he called Max, Miguel and Mitchell's sister, over. While the bar may have belonged to Miguel, it truly was a family affair. Max had been serving cocktails since the place opened, and the woman could make a mean Manhattan.

"Noted. Do you have a name or should I just call you Sam on account of your taste in beer?" He smirked, accompanied by a quick wink.

I couldn't help but shake my head at his

sarcasm. Even his words were smooth, despite the fact they were sarcastic as hell.

I knew I should have been put off by his attitude, the fancy suit and the looks he kept throwing my way as he licked his lips, but damn it if I'm not an absolute sucker for an asshole.

If all you ever want is an asshole Cade, don't be surprised when they act like an asshole.

I sighed, looking up at the man in question, mesmerized by the pure fire in his dark green eyes.

I hate that I'm like this.

Why can't I just lust after normal, nice guys?

"It's Cade," I answered, as Max finally reached us and my dreamboat mystery man barked out an order of one Sam Adams and one glass of Oban on the rocks.

Max shot me a look I could only describe as judgmental, much like the one an older sister would give when you bring home the captain of the Lacrosse team for "study time."

Give me a break, Max!

Like you wouldn't accept a drink from a guy like...

Shit, I didn't even know his name. Either the alcohol was already getting to me, or Dawson was right, and I'd been cooped up too long mourning a breakup to the point I'd forgotten how to people.

"Should I call you *Oban-Wan Kenobi* or..." I

regretted the words the minute they were out of my mouth, realizing how utterly stupid they sounded in reality. I'd always been terrible when it came to pick up lines. I thanked the stars every day for the invention of the dating app.

Truly, this shit is for the birds.

Max slid me my beer, shaking her head.

A little support would be nice, Max.

"I regret to inform you, young Padawan, I am not the Ewan McGregor you seek. Unfortunately," Hottie McSuit said with a sly grin.

"Although I can destroy that precious mouth of yours like the Phantom Menace..." He winked at me, those delicious lips curving into a delectable smile, and my insides heated at the very sight.

Max rolled her eyes as she slid him his drink.

I knew then I should walk away. Take my drink, say thanks, and get the hell away from this selfish, sexy pile of sin who was causing my damn cock to twitch.

But I just didn't know how to say no to pretty assholes like him.

Just as I opened my mouth to speak, the man took a sip of his drink, appraising me with an endearing gaze.

"It's Weston."

"Well, *Weston*, I appreciate the drink," I said,

flashing him with a cheeky grin of my own as I watched him take a sip of his drink.

"Well, perhaps you can pay me back?" he said with a raised eyebrow and I half thought he was going to ask me right then and there if I'd like to go home with him, and not even bother with pleasantries.

Weston didn't exactly seem like the type to beat around the bush, and I knew even though I shouldn't I'd probably say yes. After all, I knew Weston wasn't from around Jasper Springs, and maybe a dreamy, once in a lifetime fuck was just what I needed to move on from Billiard-No-Brains and get back to being a functional, stable adult.

Instead of the isolated, Netflix-binging, ice cream-eating hermit I've become. That's how it always works in the movies, anyway.

"Oh yeah, and how exactly do you expect me to... pay you back..." I nearly choked, thanks to swallowing a little too much beer.

I'm freaking hopeless...

Weston had the audacity to look at me like a little orphaned puppy as he drained his drink, pointing to the stage.

"Sing with me."

"You've got to be kidding me," I said, feeling a sense of panic. Karaoke really wasn't my thing, but something about the way Weston looked at me, his dark green eyes full of mischief, I felt... tempted. Comfortable, even.

"I'll make it easy. You can even pick the song," Weston said as he ran a hand over his shirt, smoothing out the miniscule wrinkles that probably only he could see.

Either that or he's just trying to get me to look at his chest, at the buttons he'd popped.

Which I'm powerless to resist...

"I'm not a very good singer," I said as I watched him set down his beer.

"Who said anything about being good? This isn't American Idol. I just want us to have some... fun."

The way Weston's voice hung on that last word, *fun...* made my insides turn to lava. And when he flashed his dark eyes at me, that look of mischief called to my soul in a way I'd never felt before.

It was just one song, what was the worst that could happen?

Right?

CHAPTER 5

I'd lost track of how many songs Weston and I had sung that night. How many songs *Weston* had sung...

I giggled as the beginning riffs of *Don't Go Breaking My Heart* filled the speakers, as Weston rolled up his sleeves, shaking his head.

At some point in the night—a point that I couldn't place to save my life—Weston had lost his suit jacket. His shirt sleeves were rolled up to the elbow to showcase his tanned, toned arms, and he'd popped more than a few buttons on his button up shirt. Under the lights of the stage, sweat gleamed off his exposed skin, and I felt *fantastic.* Better than I had in a long time.

Weston shook his hips as he brought the microphone to his lips, doing his best Elton John impression while I waited for my turn. He was hot as hell up there too, and I was fairly certain we were both sweating through our shirts, but I didn't care.

For the first time in what felt like forever, I didn't *care*. I was having a blast, and I didn't want it to end.

Like I knew it was going to.

"Don't go breaking my heart..." Weston sang, his perfectly pearly white smile making me feel even hotter under the damn lights.

"I won't go breaking your heart!" I sang in return as I pointed to Weston, but I only half sang-half laughed, because I couldn't control myself anymore, either.

I'd lost count of how many beers I'd knocked back with Weston, Dawson, and even Mitchell.

I haven't felt this good since before I met Bill...

Dawson burst out laughing as he threw on his jacket. The place was starting to clear out finally, and Max already announced last call.

Weston sauntered his way over to me, throwing one sweat-slicked arm around my shoulders as he pulled me close. The heat between us was damn near hellish from the lights and our combined sweat, and I leaned my head back against his warm shoulder as I wailed out the last bits of the song.

Weston's dark eyes sparkled with mischief, and up close like that I thought they kind of looked like semi-precious stones. My insides twisted and melted, and he smiled. A light chuckle made his chest vibrate against me. Through my hazy vision, I thought I could get lost there, staring at Weston, at his jeweled irises and perfect face.

Almost as if Weston could somehow sense my absolute mind meltdown, he whispered, "It's your turn."

I could not find the words to speak, so I did the next best thing.

I slid my hand beneath Weston's collar, feeling the heat of his flesh on my palm, and pulled him close, crushing my lips against his.

Weston startled for a moment, and then I heard the faint sound of the microphone dropping to the floor, screeching through the speakers.

Weston's mouth moved smoothly against my own, and he tasted like expensive scotch and broken promises. Somewhere in the back of my mind, I could hear Dawson hollering in the crowd, but I wasn't able to make out what he was saying. I couldn't focus on anything but Weston's tongue in my mouth.

When I broke away, watching as Weston's dark eyes gazed down at me, he steadied me in his arms. The stage lights shone directly in my eyes, and before I could get my full bearings, the DJ called, "That's a wrap!"

"Did I do a good job?" I asked, out of breath.

Though I wasn't sure I was talking about the song anymore.

"You were the best Kiki Dee I've ever seen," Weston said, flashing me a smirk. "Now how about you and I take this show elsewhere," he purred, his voice dark, inviting.

I succumbed to it without question, without hesitation.

"Okay," I breathed as Weston straightened me, patting me on the back as he pulled his phone out of his pocket, queuing up a ride no doubt.

My heart was in my throat as my pulse raced. I watched as Weston slapped down a wad of bills on the bar, nodding for me to follow him, my heart thudding in my chest.

This is it.

This is where I fall for the man I'll never have.

CHAPTER 6

WESTON

WE BARELY MADE it up the steps, and not because of the alcohol.

Somewhere between the bar and the car ride back to the hotel, Cade flipped a switch. Though I was not complaining one bit, because quite frankly, no one had accosted *me* like that in ages. Usually I'm the one in charge, but I have to say it was kind of nice to be in the spotlight for once.

Cade's mouth worked hungrily on my neck, his tongue sliding against my flesh as he sucked at the tender, taut skin there and I knew he was going to leave a mark, but for the moment, I didn't give a shit. It felt too good, and if Cade's lips on my neck were any indication at how he could work that pretty little mouth, I would have been more than happy to let him suck me like a damn vampire.

I swiped my watch over the hotel lock and it beeped, the mechanism clicking to let us in. I managed to open the door as Cade's lips found their way back to mine, and we barely got two feet in the door before I let my walls down, and finally let myself have a piece of this man.

I slammed Cade's back up against the back of the door with a thud. His eyes were hazy and full of fire and he stared back at me, his golden hair all disheveled, lips all swollen from kissing me, and I took two, slow steps toward him, boxing him against the door with my arms.

"On your knees," I said, my voice thick, and full of lustful command.

Cade stared back at me, pausing for a moment, and a deep growl escaped my throat. I was never a patient man, and the sight of a sweaty, messy Cade only stirred an equal hunger in me.

I slid my right hand up Cade's neck, feeling his pulse, his heated skin, until the edges of my fingers slid into his silky hair. I gripped the locks tightly, showing just a hint of force, a feat that was rather difficult. But I wasn't sure how Cade would respond to such things, and the last thing

I wanted to do was scare this perfect man away and go to bed alone.

In my experience, most of the men I'd been with liked the *idea* of power exchange, getting dicked down by the big boss man in charge, but when push came to shove—or more accurately, when I shoved them to the ground and told them who was boss—they usually went soft on me.

This is it. He's either going to hightail his ass out of here or he's going to double down on this cock until I really do make a mess of him.

I dared to hope that he would stay and keep stoking my fire. That he'd be willing to *play*.

Cade's back arched off the door, leaning into my touch as he brought his body against mine, the feel of his rigid hardness against my own was a most welcome answer.

To my surprise, Cade only licked his pouty lips, breathing his words like a prayer.

"Yes, sir." he said haughtily as he took his time sliding down the floor, his glassy eyes never leaving mine as he did so.

I braced myself as Cade reached for my slacks, wasting no time as he quickly unbuckled my belt and unzipped my pants, shoving them and my briefs down to my ankles in one desperate motion.

"Take off your shirt," I ordered.

Cade looked up at me in question, but did as I asked without hesitation. The hotel light shone down on his fair skin, casting shadows over his defined chest and delicious hipbones. He gazed up at me with glassy, needy eyes, swollen lips begging to be filled with my cock.

I like how he listens to me.

I brought one hand to my freed cock, squeezing and stroking myself slowly, making a show of the motions as I held Cade in place with my gaze. He sat there, perched back on his heels, his knees a fist length apart, frozen to his spot.

Waiting.

Wanting.

This man's a natural sub if I ever saw one.

"Is this what you want, Cade, hmm? Want me to wreck that pretty little mouth of yours until you're singing my name?" I taunted him, watching the heat come alive in his eyes, not missing the way he licked his lips as his gaze settled on my cock.

Cade didn't miss a beat, and I watched as he palmed his own cock through his jeans. The sight flared desire in my blood as his words echoed in the heated silence.

"Yes," he panted. "God, yes."

The desperation in his voice sang to my own hunger, and I groaned in response, a dark chuckle escaping my mouth as I stepped forward, brushing the head of my cock against his swollen, plush lips. Naturally, Cade parted them for me like the hungry man he was, his eyes closing in ecstasy as I teased him, dragging my head over his lips.

I watched in delight as he closed his lips around the tip, kissing, licking me underneath my shaft until I was moaning with pleasure. Normally, I liked to edge myself a bit, but something about the way Cade's lips felt, how his tongue slowly stroked my cock, and the sounds he made as he did so, pushed me into overdrive.

I threaded my hands through his hair, pushing my cock in further, faster, and like the perfect, good boy he was, he opened for me.

Tonight, I don't want to wait.

I want all Cade is willing to give me, and I want it all now.

I thrust my cock through Cade's parted lips, the force only starling him a bit before he eased. Within seconds he was groaning too, licking and sucking me like a damn popsicle on a ninety degree day in the middle of July.

I thrust myself slowly in and out of Cade's warm mouth, feeling the familiar tightening in my balls, and I knew it wouldn't be long.

I could barely contain myself, needing to feel more of the wet, warm sensation of his sweet tortuous mouth, and somehow, almost instinctively, he picked up his pace immediately. I thrust myself with heated force toward the back of Cade's throat as desire took over, taking my right hand and threading my fingers through his soft locks until I'd found my spot behind his head, grasping onto his hair with both hands. All the while coaxing him forward until my cock lodged in the back of his throat and his mouth was flush with my base, until I could hear Cade gag. Stealing a look down at the man choking on my cock, I could see his eyes watering, a bit of drool dripping down his chin, a most wonderful sight.

Fuck, fuck, fuck...

I'm so close...

"That's a good boy," I purred as I watched my cock disappear down Cade's throat once more, hitting that spot that made him gag again, and I was powerless against the sound, the warm, slick feel of his tongue. The sight, the way he looked up at me at that very moment, pushed me over the edge.

I came without warning, gripping him by the hair, holding his head still as I emptied myself down his throat. I watched as his Adams apple bobbed as he swallowed my cum without hesitation, his breathing rapid as he groaned around my cock.

He really is fucking perfect.

A deep rumble escaped my chest as I slowly pulled my cock out of Cade's mouth, letting the remains of my cum coat his beautiful lips, watching as a little bit dripped out of the corners of his precious mouth. A smile formed on my face as I took in my accomplishment.

I wrecked his mouth, just as I promised. But I'm not done with him. Not by a long shot. Good boys deserve rewards after a job well done.

"Stand up," I ordered, watching as Cade licked my cream off his lips, obeying me without question. The vision of him shirtless, his hands behind his back as he stood in front of me, showcasing the enormous bulge protruding from beneath his tight jeans, was a sight I would never forget.

I pulled him close, wrapping my arm around Cade's exposed waist, feeling the heat of his flesh against my palm. I brought my lips to his ear, whispered my praise.

"You took my cock so good in your mouth, I bet you'd take it even better in that sweet ass."

Cade groaned in response, telling me all I needed to know.

I took his lips without warning, licking him clean of the last bits of myself that clung to his delicious mouth. I slid my hands beneath the waistband of Cade's jeans and boxers, gripping the flesh of his ass tightly, causing him to yelp in my mouth. I rubbed the soft skin for a moment before sliding my hand back out, looping my fingers through the loopholes of Cade's jeans as I tugged him toward me, making our way backward to the bed.

Cade stumbled forward until I caught him, wrapping my arms around his waist as I turned him around until the back of his knees hit the bed. He fell back against the bed with ease, watching me as I removed my shirt, letting it fall to the floor before I hurriedly worked at his jeans. I didn't miss the way his hungry eyes took in my naked form, but this wasn't about *me*. This was about giving Cade the reward he deserved.

I practically ripped the jeans off his body, getting them off so quickly it should have been a damn crime.

But then again, I've had plenty of practice with this sort of thing.

Cade's swollen cock bounced like a spring from the freedom, and I didn't think twice about wrapping my hand around him, feeling the wetness pebbling at his head as he let a groan slip from his lips.

My own cock hardened at the sound, coming back to life slowly but surely, despite the fact I'd just unloaded a round.

But something about this man, this peachy,

sweet as apple pie dream made me want more. I wanted to make him scream my name.

"Please," Cade breathed, his breaths rapid and hot as hell. His cock throbbed in my hand as he thrust his hips desperately against my hand. He flashed his bright eyes at me, pleading for mercy. "Please... let... me..."

"Say it," I egged him on as I continued to spread his wetness over his shaft before bending down to lick the salty liquid leaking out of him, watching his eyes fall shut, his back arching again from my tease.

"Tell me how bad you want to come for me," I said as I continued to lick and kiss his swollen head, angling him further up the bed, so his back was against the headboard.

Cade's knees buckled easily as I nudged them apart, forcing him backward. I took my time as I crawled up the bed, between his legs, my cock suddenly alive and well again, wanting more of this beautiful man begging me to let him come.

Cade's cock throbbed in my hand as I lazily stroked him, the wet, slick sound of my hand sliding over his self-lubricated cock echoing in the silent air.

His head fell back against the pillows as he brought his knees up, planting his feet on the edge of the bed, pushing himself back to give me better access, and a pretty good view of his tight hole.

I took my free hand, sliding my fingers in my mouth one at a time until they'd gathered enough spit, then brought the slick digits to his rim, teasing his entrance.

"Fuck!" He moaned heatedly, his breath starting to turn rapid.

"Wes, please, I—" Cade arched his back off the bed, the way he was panting, begging...

I knew what he wanted.

I slid another finger in, feeling him soften and expand, his dick throbbing as he thrust his hips forward of his own volition, desperate, needing the friction.

I knew exactly what he wanted, and I knew I would give it to him, but a part of me wanted to hear him beg for it.

Beg for *me* to fuck him.

"Say it," I demanded, my tone firm, my voice hitching a octave. "I need to hear you say it," I instructed.

"I need you to make me come, Wes. Please... Fuck..." Cade's voice pleaded, a throaty moan escaping him, causing me to stop for a moment, to take in the sight of him like this. Fingers grasping at the sheets, face all screwed up in agony, pale, sweat-slicked skin glistening in the low incandescent light.

I let go of his cock for the moment, watching as it bobbed back and forth, beads of precum glittering like diamonds in the light as he thrust himself against the air.

I growled, catching Cade's glassy eyes before I dove back in, burying my head between his thighs as I licked him, slathering his clammy skin in a mixture of saliva and sweat, tasting his saltiness mixed with the tartness of his rim until he was writhing beneath me.

"F... fuck... me... I can't... Wes..." he struggled to form words, his voice tinged in unbridled desire.

Please," he huffed out as I lined myself up with his hole.

"Please, I want to come so bad, I—"

I kept my gaze trained on Cade's eyes as I pushed myself in an inch, letting his body acclimate to me. Like the good boy I knew he was, his body welcomed me, gripping my head like a vice and I groaned in response, inching myself in slowly as not to lose my own load. Again.

The sight of Cade's face going slack as I breached his entrance, one torturous inch at a time, was like a religious experience. Or at least it's what I'd imagine a religious experience would be, because I wouldn't know firsthand.

Mama always said I need Jesus. Think I found him in good old Jasper Springs of all places...

When I finally bottomed out, I ran my hand up and down Cade's sweaty chest, feeling his heartbeat as I found my rhythm, as I ground my hips into his. Cade's wet, slick cock left sticky trails along my heated skin as he thrust himself torturously against my stomach.

"Then be a good boy and come for me, Cade," I ordered through my teeth. After my previous orgasm, I knew I wouldn't be able to hold off much longer, either. I'd been with men, and before realizing I was gay, I'd been with a couple women too. But nothing, and no one ever hugged my cock the way Cade's body did, never felt this fucking good. Like he was made for me.

"Come for me," I ordered again, my voice getting just as tight as his insides clutching my cock.

His eyes squinted closed as his face screwed up, and he let out a ragged moan that pushed me over the edge. Cade tightened his thighs around me, and the feel of his warm release coated my abdomen with warmth.

My thrusts came to a halt as I growled out my own groan of satisfaction, spilling myself again as I filled him, all my muscles going soft from the exertion of multiple orgasms. It was no use, and I collapsed on Cade's chest, trying to catch my breath. Elation mixed with alcohol mixed with exhaustion hit me, and I closed my eyes. The faint touch of fingertips grazed along my back, the rhythmic rise and fall of Cade's chest like a lullaby, the sound of his slow and steady breath pulled me into some sort of post-fuck trance. I wasn't certain how long we stayed like that, neither of us moving. When I finally slid out of him, rolling over onto my back, I let sleep overtake me, feeling a sense of wholeness I'd never felt before.

CHAPTER 7

CADE

I woke up to a pounding headache, a sore ass, and an overwhelming need to piss.

A deep, groggy groan escaped me as I reached out my arm to stretch the achy muscles, but my entire body froze when I hit something warm and solid. The touch was like a bucket of cold water as I turned my head in slow motion, my eyes opening wide as my gaze settled on Weston, who was laying on his stomach, naked, with his firm ass on display like a prize-winning statue in a museum. The sunlight that filtered in through the window shone a beam directly on him, and panic settled in.

I lifted up the covers quickly, my suspicions

soon confirmed when I saw that I was also naked, and covered in...

Oh, good gravy...

My breath caught in my throat as anxiety flooded me, and I nearly fell over from the shock as I jumped out of bed, in search of the bathroom.

To pee, of course, but also because I needed a moment to process... well, everything.

And because life was apparently as big a fan of Hallmark movies as my mother was, my movement stirred the sleeping, naked man beside me, and just as I made it to the door, his sleepy voice stopped me dead in my tracks, all piss be damned.

"You're up," Weston groaned groggily.

"Uh huh..." I responded, like I'd altogether forgotten the ability to speak like a functional human.

I watched as Weston sat up, noting how the beam of sunlight glistened on his skin, how he ran his hand over his face and through his disheveled, dark hair. My cock twitched, bringing me back to the here and now, reminding me of the magnitude of everything converging on me at once and I jumped into the bathroom, locking the door. In there, I could breathe.

It's fine. You're fine.

Everything's fine...

I made my way to the toilet, realizing as I shook the last bits of piss out, that I was truthfully a sticky, gross mess. My gaze drifted to the stone shower, the door one big see-through pane of glass, and I had to admit a hot shower sounded like just the thing to help clear my head. Just as I was about to turn on the faucet, a slew of images flashed in my brain. Of karaoke kisses, of making out in the car, of Weston's fingers gripping my hair, holding me still while...

I sucked in a breath as the last image came to me, of Weston above me, staring down at me while he...

Oh God.

Did we...

The memory of his tongue, his fingers, his cock filling me made my heart stop.

We did. I let him top me.

Without a condom.

Oh fuck, this... this is not good.

I never sleep with a guy on the first date!

My psyche spiraled as that sarcastic, bitter part of me chastised myself.

Drinks at Bar Bingo the night you met does not actually count as a date.

"Cade?" Weston's voice pulled me from my thoughts.

"You... okay in there?" he asked, and I could

hear the caution in his voice. "I, uh, kind of need to you know—"

I shook my head, turning on the shower, if only because I didn't know what else to do. The sound of his voice alone made me want to melt, to hide until all the doubt and concern dissipated into his warm chest and spicy scent, but I could not face him like this—a god damn anxious mess—not now. Not after…

"Yeah, fine. I'll, uh… be out in a sec," I said as I stepped in the shower, closing the shower curtain. "Just, uh, getting cleaned up," I added, regretting the words immediately, feeling foolish.

God, he must think I'm an idiot...

It didn't take long for me to wash up, as it never did. I never understood how some men could take so long in the shower, when all they had to do was run some shampoo through their hair and some soap over their body.

I watched as the water circled the drain, feeling the effects of the night of drinking and sex hit me like a sack of potatoes. My stomach flipped as I remembered everything all at once.

Like stumbling like a newborn fawn over Weston as he dragged me through the hotel room, or how I nearly mauled him in the backseat of the car.

You can do this. It isn't like it's your first time. You've got this. Just grab a towel, get dressed, and be on your way. Preserve your dignity.

I nodded to myself as I finished my business, grabbing a towel, and wrapping it around my waist. In the mirror, I could see my own reflection, my messy hair, eyes slightly puffy from a night of bad decisions.

I knew on the other side of the door everything was going to change, and reality would finally sweep in and remind me of the harsh truth that what was arguably the most fun I'd had in a long time, had come to an end.

Still, a part of me wished it could go on a little longer, albeit without the addition of a throbbing headache. For a moment, I thought perhaps I could just stay in the bathroom.

But I knew better.

So instead of hiding in the gorgeous bathroom of Weston's hotel suite, I bravely opened the door to see him standing before me, looking somehow even more delicious with his hair all rumpled, hanging in his jeweled eyes. I didn't want to give in and look at him, because a part of me knew the minute I did, I'd be a goner. I'd never forget him, or the taste of his kiss, the feel of his cock.

I failed miserably as my gaze caught his, and I had to remember to breathe.

Weston sidled past me to do his business,

shutting the door and leaving me alone in the light of day. The hotel room didn't look quite as unkempt as one would expect after a night of hot, drunk sex. Though the hurricane inside of me felt every bit unkempt.

I cleared my throat as I took in the sight of the clothes strewn about the floor, like breadcrumbs leading to the bed we'd ended up in. Within seconds, the toilet flushed, and the water echoed, a ticking time bomb to me.

Weston brushed past me once more, grabbing a pair of pants from his suitcase on the way, wasting no time getting dressed. The world around me seemed in slow motion as I gripped my towel around my waist. I watched for a moment as Weston slid his briefs and the tailored pants up over his taut ass, and my cock twitched beneath my towel at the memory of his skin, warm against his own.

I had to look away. If I didn't, I knew somehow I'd make an even bigger fool of myself, so I slowly moved across the room, picking up my discarded clothes as I went, fighting not to steal any more glances at Weston.

If I look at him, I'll see the regret in his eyes, and I don't want to sour this. It's already difficult enough.

Weston must have sensed my anxiety however, because he stopped in front of me just as I was fastening the buttons on my jeans. He dipped his head, catching my gaze from under his lashes.

"Hey," he said calmly, cautiously. The candor of his voice was smooth like chocolate, and just as sinful. The desire to look at him was too hard to fight, and I lost the battle.

"What?" I asked, a lot harsher than I'd meant to. I did not want to see the regret, or the nonchalance on this beautiful man's face as I suffered my own torment. Not when I was spiraling inside over everything that had transpired between us.

The karaoke, the drinks, the sex, the aftermath where we seemed to dance in twilight, buried in the depths of one another for a perfect, blissful moment until we fell asleep.

Together.

"You okay?" Weston asked, his eyebrows furrowed.

An overwhelming desire to soothe the man broiled beneath the surface, despite the fact I felt as if maybe I could use some soothing of my own. The sight of his gaze elicited the truth from my lips. Obeying this man came as second nature, and I knew that should scare me.

So why didn't it?

"I'm fine. I just... don't normally do this... sort of thing," I admitted honestly.

Weston's eyebrows knit together and he

looked utterly confused at my words. Like I was speaking French or something.

"What do you mean?" he questioned, legitimately awestruck.

"This," I motioned around the room, between the two of us, who were standing only a hair's breadth away from one another.

When did we get so close...

"The one-night stand thing. I don't normally sleep with men I just met. I, uh… I mean, we, uh... I don't even know if you're—"

"If I'm what?" He looked back at me with confusion.

I could feel my cheeks flush with embarrassment. I forced the word that was on the top of my tongue, out, knowing I was about to completely shatter everything and make it awkward as hell.

"Um... clean."

I watched Weston's eyes widen, as understanding must have dawned on him. He ran a hand over his face, breathing out a sigh.

Fuck, that does it. I've officially ruined the moment.

"I can assure you I take my health more seriously than most," Weston bit out defensively. His response and tone made me feel like a complete idiot, realizing how shitty I must have sounded, how accusatory my tone was, and before I could apologize, tell Weston I wasn't *trying* to be a dick, that I just wanted some reassurance, he looked me dead in the eyes and said, "It's just sex, Cade. It's not like we're getting married, or anything." His tone was even, simple, nonchalant. And all at once, the illusion was broken, along with my weary heart.

Of course, he wouldn't understand. I'm probably just guy number whatever in his travels.

"Obviously," I said, turning away from Weston's smooth, jeweled gaze, feeling like an absolute pile of shit. My head was throbbing, all fantasies and dreams dissolved into thin air.

Reality was a cruel mistress.

The silence between the two of us was deafening as I pulled my shirt back on. Weston looked at me for a moment, before breaking the silence.

"Are you hungry?" he asked warily, as if I were nothing more than a caged animal.

"I'll be fine," I told him, feigning a solidarity I certainly did not feel at the moment.

Last night my walls came down, albeit due to the alcohol, but I'd be damned if I prolonged this only for Weston to pretend he wanted to talk to me, when really he just wanted this awkward moment to be over too.

I pursed my lips as Weston nodded in understanding.

So he can get back to his Sexy Suit Life, doing what-ever assholes in sexy suits do.

Drink coffee, run some board meetings. Pick up locals for a night of smoking hot sex.

The memory of Weston's lips at my ear, his words echoing in my brain, 'such a good boy,' echoed like warnings, making my cock twitch and I had to ignore it.

Absolutely not! That is not happening again...

"Do you need a ride?" he questioned as I watched him pull a fresh suit jacket on. He did not look at me directly again, instead just focused on putting on his watch, which looked like a brand new Movado.

Just because I live in Jasper Springs doesn't mean I don't fashion. I've been oogling one of those since Christmas.

"No, I'm good, thanks," I answered as I pulled out my phone.

Six missed calls and texts from Dawson.

Did James Bond murder you?

I tapped out a reply quickly, focusing for the moment on something that wasn't Weston.

The only thing he murdered is my dreams.

I kept my gaze trained on the screen as the bubbles popped up, and Dawson responded immediately.

That bad huh? You need me to call you? Pretend there's a family emergency?

His words made me feel a little better. It wouldn't be the first time Dawson would have had to come pick me up from a night of bad ideas with bad for me assholes.

Not to mention, he was one of them at one time.

I tapped out my reply almost immediately, thankful for the save.

Actually can you give me a ride to work?

Dawson answered fast, clearly prepared.

Of course. Not like I have any cats in trees to save.

He added some cat emojis for good measure.

I tapped back a thumbs up with the address of the Palisades Hotel.

"Well, it's been fun, but... I, uh... gotta go. Work... and stuff," I said quietly.

Weston slid his hand in his jacket pocket, his expression emotionless. He shrugged. "I get it. See you around, Cade."

"See ya," I answered as I headed out the door and down toward the lobby in search of something sweet to soak up all the shame, guilt, and sadness in my system while I waited for Dawson to get me.

CHAPTER 8

Cade

When Dawson's candy apple red truck pulled up to the curb, I crawled in, waiting for the judgment I knew was coming.

Better to just get it over with.

But instead, Dawson only handed me a clean *Jasper Springs Fire Co.* long-sleeve, a large iced coffee, and a bag with a donut.

Chocolate glazed, my favorite.

"You're a lifesaver," I breathed with relief as my stomach growled.

You'd think the Palisades would have had something unhealthy, but the cafe was stocked with nothing but Nutrigrain bars.

"Figured you'd need to eat your feelings a

little bit, you sounded a little stressed. Plus, I'm sure you feel like shit."

"You don't know the half of it," I mumbled as I took a long drink of iced coffee. The sweetness was overpowering, but it made me feel a little better at the moment.

"Did you at least have fun?" Dawson asked with that annoying tone of his, the one that used to get on my nerves, but now I'd become numb to hearing.

I stared out the window, chewing my straw as we took off. Jasper Springs was already bustling as the shops opened and the traffic had started. Stealing a glance at the clock, I noted it was nearly nine thirty.

I usually don't sleep so late...

Thank God I'm working the afternoon shift today.

"Yeah, I guess," I answered with a sigh as I shifted in the passenger seat.

It wasn't a lie. I *did* have fun. A little too much fun.

"I mean, when I left, you two were practically dry humping each other on stage, and you were giggling up a storm, so..." Dawson teased me, raising his eyebrows.

I knew he wouldn't stop until he'd gotten every sordid detail like the pain in the ass he was, but after my disaster of a morning, I just didn't have the spoons to rehash everything and feel worse than I already did.

"I don't want to talk about it, Dawson," I said, my heart breaking a little as the memories hazily replayed in my brain on repeat. In truth, I didn't want to talk about it, or even think about it.

The memory of Weston's lips, of his salacious tongue, and his cock would be tattooed on my damn brain for eternity.

Along with my stupidity.

Real smooth, Cade.

I half expected Dawson to push for details like he always did, forgoing boundaries altogether, but to my surprise he did no such thing. Instead, his gaze softened.

"Maybe you should take the day off," he suggested.

It wasn't a bad idea, but I knew being at home all cooped up would have only given my anxiety full reign to focus on all the spots I'd fucked everything up. No, I needed to move. To keep my mind busy so I wouldn't think of Weston and his gorgeous green eyes and sweet, chocolatey voice. Plus, there was the fundraiser the hospital was doing with Rhodes Enterprises, which we'd been planning for months and the hospital would be understaffed today because of it.

"I can't," I responded, watching the world pass me by. "The pet hospital is spread thin as it is today with the fundraiser, and a hangover with a side of guilt isn't exactly a reason to call off. At least, it isn't to me."

I expected Dawson to refute, to argue with me about how a hangover most certainly counted as a sick day, but he didn't. Instead, he just turned up the radio and left me to wallow in my own self-pity like the loser I felt I truly was at the moment.

Just once, I'd like things to work out instead of blowing up in my face.

CHAPTER 9

Cade

I sucked down another pull of my iced coffee as I headed into work, only to see my boss, Diane, flustered at the main desk. The ever-present cacophony of meows and barks was like music to my ears, and the caffeine was doing a bit to lift my spirits. I didn't feel a hundred percent better, but I did feel functional.

That had to count for something, right?

"Afternoon, Diane," I said in my best, chipper, customer service voice. Somewhere in the distance, a cockatoo cawed loudly.

"Oh, thank goodness you're here, Cade," she exclaimed with exasperation as she looked at the clock. 'And you're early! Bless you!" she said, rounding to the front of the desk, appraising me with a look that made my blood chill.

Oh no, I know that look.

"Ricardo had to leave early this morning, with a stomach bug," she said, batting her eyelashes at me.

No, no, no...

"Oh, that sucks," I deadpanned, even though my mind was screaming, "back away from the boss... slowly... find something to stock... fast."

"I need you to head down to Charlestown Street and work the booth." She clasped her fists together, doing her best impression of a puppy dog from those awful Sarah McLachlan commercials.

"Diane, you know I don't do events..." I started to say, but she pouted.

Of course she knew that, but the use of puppy dog eyes meant she was screwed and had no other option.

Fuck.

"Please, Cade, I don't have anyone else. Terri's worked six days this week and it's her daughter's school play today," Diane said, laying on the whining real thick.

I hated to say no, especially when my five foot two frazzled gremlin boss looked at me like I was her damn knight in shining armor.

Maybe the fresh air will do me good...

I sighed, admitting defeat.

"Fine." I huffed regrettably. "But I'm going to need to go home first and get my car. Dawson dropped me off," I touted. Diane didn't miss a beat.

"Oh! You are the best Cade! Thank you so much!" she said with so much appreciation I almost felt bad for wanting to decline. Almost.

I nodded, forcing a smile as I pulled out my phone and texted Dawson once more, telling him everything that had transpired in the ten minutes since he dropped me off.

He's going to kill me.

Like the best wingman he was though, Dawson tapped back a reply within seconds.

Lucky for you, I didn't make it very far. I ran into Lois at the post office and she talked my fucking head off for five minutes straight. I just walked out the door. Coming to get you."

For the second time in an hour, Dawson had saved my ass, and so I sent another thumbs up.

It was going to be a long day.

CHAPTER 10

Weston

I sighed as the door closed with a resounding echo. This was the part I loathed the most, the thing that I couldn't seem to change about my life.

The lonely morning when everyone walked away.

I'd been single for far too long, grown accustomed to the way of life of a bachelor, and on most days with enough alcohol and enough money, I could pretend it was all fine, that I was content with the way things were. But as I watched Cade's delicious ass leave the hotel room, I felt the petulant void inside of me grow.

Can't even keep them for breakfast anymore.

The phone rang, pulling me from my misery. I didn't even have to look to know who was calling, as the Darth Vader march sounded in the cavernous room.

I answered regrettably, clearly not in the mood to deal with anything but my own wallowing.

"What?" I growled, my tone much harsher than I truly meant it to be.

"Please, tell me you've left the hotel already," my mother said dryly.

"I'm leaving in five minutes, mother," I huffed whilst straightening my suit, running a hand through my hair to even it out.

The sunlight filtered in through the window, lighting up the room in its sweet, golden glow. Though despite all its golden rays, I couldn't help but feel gloomy in comparison.

Shitty way to start the day, but I guess I shouldn't be surprised.

"Where are you staying?" she pressed.

"It doesn't matter. This damn town is tinier than shit. I'll be there in fifteen minutes, tops."

"That doesn't answer my question," she huffed.

"If you must know, I'm staying at the Palisades."

"That's at least a twenty-five minute drive, Weston!"

I waved my hand at the air as I took my time grabbing my wallet, sliding it into my pants.

"It's going to be a thirty minute drive if you don't get off this phone with me and let me call an Uber."

"Do take this seriously, dear. This event is important to the company," she said with a sigh.

And the guilt trip starts. Barely been here twenty-four hours, that's got to be a record.

"It's important you understand we do more than just sell products, honey. Our strength is with this community."

"Of course, I wouldn't want to put a damper on the *company*," I drawled sarcastically.

"It is important to your father, too. And me," she said quietly.

"Uh huh, of course," I responded, hurrying to put an end to the conversation before it became the one I always dreaded hearing.

Because no matter how many times I told my parents, it never seemed to sink in.

I didn't *want* to run Rhodes Enterprises. The very idea of being cooped up in board meetings and overseeing spreadsheets sounded like the opposite of living to me.

It wasn't like I'd never worked before. In fact, up until a year ago I would have rather loved to stay at my job at the Men's Warehouse, even though it wasn't my family's idea of a genuine job. It was just shitty timing. We'd all been downright shocked when the place closed, or 'relocated', and I hadn't been asked to move with the staff I'd grown close to.

Ever since I'd been in limbo, trying to find something, anything—or someone—to pull me out of the stasis my life had become. It seemed almost as if there was nothing truly constant in my life except the inevitable change I did not seek, and a future I didn't ask for.

"Weston—"

"Leaving now, mother. See you soon," I said, not bothering to wait for her to chime in and say her goodbyes before hanging up on her as I walked out the door of the lonely, silent room, and into the overwhelmingly beige hallway of the Palisades, dreading the stupid fundraiser I'd been tasked with.

CHAPTER 11

THE SUN WAS at its peak as I strolled through the blocked off streets of town. Jasper Springs itself wasn't a large town, but the Main Street stretch alongside Charleston Street was big enough to make even the occasional passerby wonder if Jasper Springs was larger than it looked.

There were several tents strewn along the streets, everything from vegan food trucks and popsicle stands, to a multitude of small businesses like Taylor Made Bouquets and Penn's Bakery, the bakery my mother loves, as well as the local community staples such as the Jasper Springs Volunteer Fire Co. and the Jasper Springs Pet Hospital.

"Don't be such a stick in the mud," my mother nipped as we strolled down Main Street, stopping in front of a food truck selling donut holes and homemade poptarts.

"I am not a stick in the mud," I retorted, wrinkling my face at her tone.

"You've been scowling ever since you showed up, my dear. If your skincare routine wasn't handpicked by Francesca, I'd worry about you getting wrinkles from that incessant frown."

I rolled my eyes. Nothing ever got past this woman, I swear.

"I'm just... it was a rough morning." I chewed on my lip, wishing I hadn't said anything the moment the words left my mouth.

My mother's eyes lit up with resounding judgment. She'd snared me in her trap, again.

"Stay out past your bedtime again?" she nipped, her tone sweet yet full of venom at the same time.

My mother, Hilaria Rhodes, was quite capable of getting even the toughest soldier to dispel their secrets. I'd watched her on many occasions when we'd attended a plethora of events.

"I haven't had a bedtime since the third grade, mother."

Her phone rang, dissolving the moment and

her attention, and I thanked my lucky stars. She answered her phone immediately, holding up a hand to me, if only to brush me off for something far more pressing. Perhaps someone had a more dramatic situation that needed judgment than just her reluctant son.

I was more than familiar with the life of my socialite mother though, and therefore, I knew there would be no better time to exit than the one moment I'd been given. So I smiled and nodded as she turned away, spouting off "No, Cynthia', and 'that will not do', and 'please ask Mr. Lammie."

I did not waste my moment, taking my leave as I ambled down Charleston Street alone, checking out the booths one by one. The sun beat down on my back, causing steam to heat my skin beneath my shirt.

And that was when I saw him, though to be fair I wasn't entirely sure I hadn't imagined a mirage from the dire heat.

Cade stood behind one of the booths, dressed in a pink polo shirt, smiling that bright Jasper Springs smile. *Jasper Springs Pet Hospital* was sprawled across the banner in stark white font, little pawprints bespeckling the bright blue tablecloth. A part of me wanted to casually stroll over and strike up a conversation, even though Cade had made it clear he wanted nothing to do with me after this morning.

But there was also a part of me that was terrified of being caught staring, at being caught wishing for something more.

Just this once.

CHAPTER 12

CADE

I HAD JUST GOTTEN done setting up the Jasper Springs Pet Hospital booth, when Regina, one of the firewomen from Dawson's firehouse—who was conveniently set up next to me—whacked me in the arm.

"What the hell, Gina..."

"The prodigal son returns," she deadpanned, and I huffed in annoyance.

"What the hell are you talking about?" I asked. Being as close to Dawson as I was, I was more than familiar with a handful of the firefighters from the firehouse, though I didn't consider many of them my friends like I did with Dawson. However, Gina Corolla didn't seem to be phased by my lack of social skills.

What were the odds the firehouse would be set up next to the pet hospital booth anyway?

"Haven't you heard about the Rhodes' very hot, very single, and very gay son?" She looked at me with question.

I avoided her gaze, choosing instead to straighten out some brochures on my table.

"You know I don't keep up on town gossip," I said. And it was true. I'd never cared for the secret whispers and looks, the currency of small town suburbia, and I certainly didn't want to end up a whisper on someone's tongue myself.

No, I preferred to keep my life more than private, and I respected others rights to do the same.

"Well, since you've been living under a damn rock, he's coming this way so you can get a good look at him."

"Gina..." I protested, but all she did was turn my head in the direction of...

Holy shit.

Is that Weston?

"Twelve o'clock sharp. With the blue shirt, rolled up sleeves."

I felt my entire body freeze on sight.

Weston strolled down the street lazily, hands in his pockets, his blue shirt sleeves rolled up to the elbow only showcasing his fresh sun-kissed glow. His dark hair blew about in the wind, and I could have sworn I heard angels singing.

Or demons, more accurately given the state of things.

"He's..."

"Hotter than a fucking rack of ribs straight from the grill, I know," Gina said with excitement as my mind short circuited.

Rhodes.

Weston.

Weston Rhodes.

Heir to Rhodes Enterprises.

This can't be happening!

At that very moment, our eyes met just like in the movies. Weston stopped dead in his tracks, a light smirk coursing over his lips.

"You should totally ask him out," Gina cooed behind me.

I swallowed nervously as the memories of the previous night of passion flooded my brain, causing my damn cock to spring to life.

Again.

I cleared my throat as I turned away from Weston's smoldering gaze, fussing over anything else I could to try and regain a semblance of order once again. Because at the moment, all I could think about was how badly I'd messed up that morning, noting that Weston would likely want nothing to do with me now.

Now, I was just an embarrassment.

"Yeah, I don't think so. Weston is so far out of my league we're not even in the same ballpark," I chided.

Gina's lips curled into a smile. "I never said his name was Weston..."

And that was the moment Mitchell and Dawson arrived at the firehouse booth.

Perfect timing, as always.

I watched as Weston talked to a group of women, smiling genuinely and schmoozing like the unabashed rich kid he obviously was, feeling a pang in my heart. I forcibly tore my gaze from him, if only to try and put the beautiful man—and the memory of his cock down my throat—out of my mind.

"You look good for hungover," Mitchell said as he snapped a photo of me, not giving a shit if I was ready or not.

I swatted at my 'friend with camera', as Dawson let out a laugh.

"What the hell are you doing here?" I asked, with about as much venom as a daddy-long-legger. They are actually venomous, but their fangs are too short to actually hurt anyone.

What can I say, arachnids are my spirit animal.

Dawson smiled with mischief. "Sarge said I should come down here to sign calendars."

Gina rolled her eyes. "Please, like anyone would actually want you to sign anything."

Dawson opened his arms wide, motioning to himself like he was some great, Herculean hero.

To be fair, in his own brain he probably is.

"Want to take a wager on that, G?" he asked as some girls walked past, giggling as they took a gander at him. Against the bright red banner, he looked every bit Mister March, and he liked to remind everyone he was the *hottest* fireman on the calendar every chance he got.

Gina shook her head. "You're a fucking idiot."

"I am, but... I'm a hot idiot," he chimed as Mitchell snapped another photo.

"Any new recruits yet, G?" Dawson asked as he shifted his stance, brushing off his charm and turning to business.

"Not yet, but the day is still young," she said with a shrug.

Dawson nodded at me, glancing at Weston with that look that I knew was trouble.

"What are the odds..." he said with a smile.

"Dawson, don't..." I begged. I knew Dawson well enough to know he would make a scene just to get Weston over here, just so he could push my buttons.

Even if he thought he was helping.

"Isn't that the guy you were singing with last

night at karaoke?" Mitchell asked as he snapped a photograph of Weston, who was now checking out Sandra's Homemade Candles & Candies booth.

"It is," Dawson answered before I could even speak for myself.

"Shut up! You did not karaoke with *Weston freaking Rhodes?*" Gina said in mock-shock.

Instantly, anxiety flooded me and I felt as if I wanted to crawl under the table to avoid this whole conversation.

"Wait... that's Weston *Rhodes?*" Mitchell asked in surprise.

"Who?" Dawson asked, clueless as usual. For a man who loved to know everything, he was always somehow the last to know the town gossip, despite being in the middle of it all the time.

"The heir to Rhodes Enterprises, Dawson. You know, the tech guys who upgraded our entire security system, the very company whose idea it was to *put* this fundraiser together..." Gina gaped at him.

Dawson only had to audacity to blink like a sleepy kitten, the gears in his head obviously working overtime.

I felt as if I was truly going to be sick. But perhaps it was just the fact I hadn't eaten anything more than a donut and twenty ounces of iced coffee this morning.

Dawson whistled, a laugh escaping his throat. "Nice catch, Cade." he said, flashing me a wink.

"Does he have a big dick?" Mitchell teased, cracking a smile.

"Oh my God, Cade, did you two—" Gina chimed in, and the heat rose up my neck into my cheeks, betraying any words I might say to try and save my dignity.

I was rather flustered and all I could do was shift my stance, trying my hardest not to focus on the fact that Weston was walking over to *my booth.*

"I do not kiss and tell," I snapped.

Mitchell let out a laugh as Dawson childishly taunted him, Gina's 'oh my God's' coming out more like guinea pig squeals.

Kill me now.

"That is a resounding yes!" she teased, and the mortification set in as the blood rushed to my cheeks.

I need to change this conversation right now, or I need to—

"Mr. Rhodes, so nice to meet you!" Mitchell said far too cheerfully in my opinion, pulling me from my internal meltdown.

Weston stood only a few feet away, all long legs and tailored suits, his dark hair hanging in his dark, sexy eyes, and I couldn't help but stare at the *hot as hell* heir to one of the most successful businesses in Jasper Springs, feeling frozen in place once again.

No one made the world fall away around me quite like this man, and that made me feel both alarmed and... hopeful.

Weston turned his head only slightly, smirking at me before turning to Mitchell, shaking his hand firmly.

"Good to meet you too, sir," he said politely, with that same decadent smoothness that made my insides melt.

"Mind if I get some pictures of you for the paper?" Mitchell said with a grin that was far too mischievous for my liking.

Oh no, I know that look...

"Of course, just tell me where you'd—"

"Cade you can stand here, and Mr. Rhodes —" Mitchell had gone into photographer mode as he ordered about, pointing to the spots and structuring his photo. My blood ran cold, and a part of me wanted to murder him.

"You can stand here," Mitchell said with a smile as he placed me next to Weston.

I shot him a murderous gaze, if only to let

him know I knew exactly what he was doing. He and Dawson were so meddlesome sometimes, but I knew I wouldn't refuse him. Whether or not he really was going to use this photograph for the paper or not, I knew Mitchell *did* in fact need photos for the paper, which would no doubt be running an article on this fundraiser. Not to mention, I would look like an asshole if I protested, and I didn't want Weston to think I was an even bigger asshole.

Why does that bother me?

Sure, we had spent the night together, but Weston had been more than clear it didn't mean anything to him.

I didn't mean anything to him.

Except, it *did* mean something to me, but I couldn't show that. At best, I'd just look like an overly needy stage five clinger, which is just as bad if not worst than being an asshole.

So if it meant nothing to him, I should act as if it meant nothing to me, too.

No, I wouldn't let my inner clinger out in front of Weston Rhodes, the man whose gaze made my damn cock twitch from just his proximity, and certainly not in front of the firehouse gossipers, and a meddling photographer.

So I swallowed my pride and my feelings as I stood where Mitchell directed, on the left in front of the banner. There was a small modicum of space between Weston and I, which I pretended not to notice.

Even though I could feel the heat steaming between us...

Mitchell snapped his picture, taking a moment to review it before looking up with a smile and winking at me.

I'm totally going to murder him for this later.

"Okay, that's good, but this time I'm going to need you two to get a little closer. A little more... comfortable," he said.

Dawson giggled in the background, and Gina smacked him.

"Of course," Weston said smoothly as he scooted closer to me, leaving just a hair of space between us. The scent of his cologne invaded my airways, and made my stomach do a little flip.

I'm so fucked.

"Cade, move in a little bit," Mitchell instructed, and my jaw immediately tensed. Yet I did as Mitchell asked. The movement put Weston and I side by side, and I had to fight the desire to look at him.

To look up into his beautiful gem-like eyes and fall under his spell yet again.

But I didn't *have* to look at him to fall under

his spell, apparently. Just being close to him was enough.

Just as Mitchell set to take his picture, Weston's smooth, velveteen voice purred in my ear, "Such a good boy," and I knew I was was absolutely doomed.

CHAPTER 13

"THANKS, MR. RHODES," the photographer said, but I could not entirely focus on the paparazzi at the moment. Growing up under my mother's socialite arm meant I could pose and smile and deal with photographers in my damn sleep, even on my worst days.

But all I could do was replay the last twelve or so hours in my brain, to remember to breathe, as standing next to Cade was driving me and my unruly dick bananas.

"Of course," I said politely, noticing that Cade had not moved from my side.

It's a start...

I watched the photographer make his way

over to the booth next to us, chatting up the two firefighters he obviously knew, likely for a picture.

For the moment, I had Cade to myself.

"Feeling better?" I asked smoothly. Almost as if Cade had suddenly remembered my presence, he shook his head, a blush creeping onto his cheeks that reminded me of his flushed cheeks during our initial karaoke session.

His pale skin looked quite beautiful with such tones, making me think of plenty of other areas of skin I'd like to see tinged pink. My dick twitched at the thought, but I managed to keep my face plain, even.

Cool as a cucumber.

"I, um... guess you could say that," Cade said as he leaned against the table, his gaze dancing around the busy streets, focusing on anything but me.

It's almost as if I make him nervous...

At that very moment, Cade's stomach let out a rumble that was impossible to ignore.

"You are a terrible liar, *Cade*," I said, liking the way his name sounded on my tongue. I wanted to say it as much as I could.

Cade crossed his arms. "Well, I'd feel better if you stopped staring at me like... like..."

I had to admit I liked seeing him all flustered, and I couldn't help but play his adorable game, so I leaned against the booth languidly, fighting a smile.

"Like what?" I whispered darkly, watching as his gaze dipped to my lips.

"Like I'm a damn piece of meat, for starters," Cade bristled, though his tone wasn't angry or aggravated. Instead, it was full of unspoken things, and even carried a hint of embarrassment.

Did this darling little morsel not know how delicious he actually was?

Obviously not.

I cocked my head to the side. "I can assure you, as I've tasted the best meat the world has to offer, you do not fall into the category of average meat."

I watched as Cade's eyebrows furrowed, almost as if he was somehow hurt by my words.

I don't understand...

I wasn't sure if it was something I said, or perhaps if it was just the fact that he was feeling unwell at the moment, clearly as starved as I was. The heat of this damn town would make anyone lust for sustenance.

"Although, I must say I am quite famished myself. Perhaps we could actually... grab something to eat?" I offered.

A deep part of me that was foreign until this moment bubbled up with the innate desire to *take care* of this man, show him just how prized and fine he was, because perhaps no one else had ever done such a thing.

All at once, I watched the sparkle return to Cade's eyes at my offer.

"I, uh... I am kind of hungry, but I can't exactly *leave* my post," he said, chewing his lip. The sight was somehow both endearing and hot as hell as instant images of me *biting* at that lip until he begged me to stop filled my brain.

Focus, Weston!

Of course he can't just abandon his post.

Clearly this man messes with my ability to think straight...

"I could grab you something if you tell me what you want," the words came out somehow huskier than I'd intended them, and my mouth had gone dry.

"You, uh... you don't *have* to do that," Cade said sweetly as he ran a hand through his hair.

"And why not?" I asked, confused once more. This man was sending me very mixed signals. I looked at him, puzzled.

"I know I wasn't exactly the most, um... I mean, I kind of—"

"If this is about what happened between us, I can assure you I'm not offering to grab you food just because we had sex," I insisted.

It was true. Granted, I *wanted* to have a

repeat of the other night, but this moment wasn't about that. I didn't feel an obligation to buy this man lunch just because we'd had a steamy roll in the hay. I wanted to buy this man lunch because ever since I couldn't get him out of my head, and I wanted to know more about the man who had vexed me so.

Though to be fair, it would have been something I would have done in the past to placate those I once shared my bed with—the polo riders or the designers and artists who'd often wanted to be spoiled even if it was for a night only, purely because they knew I had the means to do so and that was my reputation back home. As if there was something *wrong* with wanting someone to spoil, hoping that if I threw enough money or gifts around, maybe, just maybe one of them would want to stay with *me*.

Somehow, as Cade's words fell over me, I knew this was different, though I couldn't explain why or how I knew. It wasn't about the sex, not really. I genuinely felt a need, a desire to take care of this man, this adorable, blue-eyed darling who was almost as skittish as a mouse.

To... *comfort him.*

I wanted to make Cade feel better, wanted to see a legitimate smile on his beautiful face.

What was the harm in that?

However well meaning I'd been, Cade's shoulders tightened at my words.

How could I make this man understand, I was only trying to help?

To reassure him one thing did not equal another?

I could separate a man from his dick, even if I didn't do it often.

"I mean, we were both sort of drunk, and it was great, but... One thing doesn't have anything to do with the other, I promise," I said, trying my best to comfort him even though I was not good at such a thing.

"Oh," Cade said, his voice getting a tad quieter.

"Tell you what," I said, not liking the strange tension that had befallen us, "You stay here, and I will hunt you... er... us... down something fried and sweet, and we can put this whole... debacle behind us. Start fresh." I pushed away from the table lightly, capturing his weary gaze.

Cade looked up at me, his blue eyes searching mine for something I was not sure of.

Answers maybe?

"Yeah, sure," Cade said, but his smile did not reach his eyes, and as I wandered off in search of sustenance, only to be pulled away once more by the inevitable devil that awaited me—my father—I hoped I would find a way to make things up to Cade.

CHAPTER 14

Cade

I stepped through the front door, nearly exhausted from the events of the last twenty-four hours.

I wasn't sure why I expected Weston to come back with anything. After all, I knew assholes like Weston Rhodes didn't really do the 'nice guy' thing. They didn't treat you to a smorgasbord of breakfast or buy you coffee just because they wanted to talk to you or enjoy your company.

Which makes him no different than any other asshole you've gotten your hopes up for.

I nonchalantly tossed my keys in the bowl by the door after locking it, the silence of my humble abode thick and disheartening. The lights came on of their own accord, and it was all I could do to stand there and think that maybe this was as good as it would get. Maybe I truly was meant to be a small town man, living a small town life in my quiet, quaint house, eating rocky road ice cream on the couch forever whilst watching reruns of my favorite shows.

As if perfectly on cue, my stomach grumbled once more, and I tossed the box of pizza I had picked up at Jasper Springs Pizza on the way home on the counter. Popping the lid, the scent of salty pepperoni and sweet tomato sauce filled my senses, making my mouth water. I set about to finding myself a plate, a glass of lime seltzer soda, and of course, a pint of ice cream.

I kicked off my shoes, discarding my well-worn and sweaty shirt on the arm of the couch before curling up in the cushions with my culinary treasures, and turned on the tv. Suddenly, all the exhaustion and stress slithered off of my shoulders as I got lost in the electric light, practically inhaling my food as the comfortable air conditioning soothed my hot, tired muscles.

Though nothing seemed to erase the memory of being on stage with Weston, or the way his lips turned up in a smile as he kissed me, sliding his tongue into my mouth.

Or the way he had *commanded* me to get on

my knees, the way his words of praise made me feel.

Good boy.

The memory of the prior night danced with that of the earlier afternoon, when Mitchell had tormentingly posed us together for a picture I still wasn't entirely sure *was* for the paper, but a part of me appreciated the gesture, nonetheless, even if at the time I'd felt wary.

The memory of the heat from Weston's breath on my skin caused my blood to rush through my veins, and his whispered words incited a desire deep within me that no one else had ever been truly capable of igniting.

I wanted to be *good* for a man, but no man had ever seen me as good *enough.*

Not until...

I leaned my head back, hitting the back of my couch as my cock throbbed from the memory.

Fucking hell.

I sighed, knowing there was no use.

So instead of combating my cock, which had a mind of its own, instead, I slid my hand beneath the waistband of my pants, fully intending to adjust my erection for the moment so I could finish my damn ice cream, but the touch did nothing to soothe me. In fact, it only made the need to come that much worse.

I groaned in annoyance, my voice tinged with desperation as I focused my gaze on the ceiling.

I knew I should forget Weston Rhodes, Hottie-Mc-Hot-Suit, the man of my damn rom-com dreams. But in the privacy of my own home, I could submit to the meddlesome desire, the fantasies that shamelessly plagued me.

So I gave in.

I popped the button on my jeans, unzipping my pants if only to let my strained cock breathe. I breathed a sigh of relief as my solid cock sprung forth like a damn spring, thick and wanting, already pebbling with moisture as I let my eyelids fall shut. I licked my lips as I let Weston's smooth voice reverberate in my brain.

"Good boy."

I wrapped my hand around my sensitive head, spreading some of my moisture along my engorged shaft, letting the rest of the memories out of their cage.

"You took my cock so good in your mouth," the words echoed like a canyon as I gripped my shaft, pulling and tugging slowly, building a rhythm.

I continued to let my thoughts wander down the dark pathway of memory, remembering just how Weston's thick, solid cock felt as it hit the back of my throat, causing me to gag.

None of the men I had ever been with had ever made me *gag*.

I'd panicked only slightly at first, at the feeling of losing my breath, but when I looked up to see Weston and his dreamy eyes full of lust and pleasure, I couldn't deny the sight was most appealing.

And so I hollowed my cheeks, and slid my mouth over Weston's cock until my eyes watered and the feeling of choking prevailed, reveling in the rush of his sweet release as he gripped my hair, fists tightening as he spilled himself down my throat. And like the needy man I was, I swallowed every drop, relishing in the sound of his moans and groans.

My breath caught in my throat as the thoughts fueled me and my impending release.

"Such a good boy."

The memory of Weston's whispers on my skin from this afternoon meshed with the memory of his wet and warm tongue, laving at my tight entrance, licking, nibbling at my sensitive skin, bathing me in warm saliva.

I thrust my swollen cock into my hand, some desperate liquid escaping, coating my shaft and hand. I didn't waste a drop, taking the warm wetness, slathering it over my tip and shaft like sticky, warm lube, my hand and hips picking up a rhythm as I chased my orgasm through the clouds and haze of memory. My thrusts came harder, my hips moving faster as my breathing intensified, as I thrust my cock desperately against my warm, wet palm.

"Come for me, Cade."

I pumped my cock, feeling the release nearly instantly as I remembered just how Weston had ordered me to come, and how I had obeyed, almost as if my body understood far better than my brain did, that I would do *anything* for this man. I would do whatever he asked.

I had been *so good*.

Wet, thick ropes of warm cum sprayed onto my exposed abdomen, some sliding down over my hands as I fought to control the amount or the trajectory of my release and catch my breath. I opened my eyes and stared at the ceiling with a mixture of remorse, regret, and desire that left me both sated and hungrier than I'd ever been before.

The movie credits rolled on the television, and I basked in its artificial glow, exhaustion overcoming me with finality.

CHAPTER 15

I COULD NOT STOP THINKING about that damn fundraiser. Or more accurately, the adorable puppy-dog-eyed vet technician who caused my blood to rush just from his proximity.

I ran a hand over my face, sighing before taking a long drink of my *Oban*, remembering Cade's sweet, somehow endearing flirtations.

Oban-Wan Kenobi is pretty catchy.

Though I had to admit, the fundraiser was far from my element. When I'd agreed to show up, play the part my parents wished, I'd thought I would have endless time to waltz around, smile and kick back for a change.

But it seemed that was the furthest thing

from my parent's agenda. Once my mother had discovered me, again, she'd sunk her perfectly manicured claws into my arm for the remainder of the event, buffalo fries be damned.

Time had droned on as I was shuffled from associate to associate, and before I knew it, I was both hungry and disappointed.

When I'd finally been dismissed from my duties, the Jasper Springs Pet Hospital booth was gone, as was the firefighter's booth.

I'd been too late, and I silently cursed my parents for once again throwing a monkey wrench in my plans.

Into my entire life, if we're counting.

I'd thought perhaps maybe I just needed to get out of the damned sleepy little town. Maybe getting away from Jasper Springs would dispel the thoughts of Cade from my mind. Outside of his radius, maybe I could think straight, and so I took off to the famed Sedona, without a second thought.

The restaurant itself lay between the city and Jasper Springs and somehow blended sweet, southern home cooking and upscale gastropub meets French cuisine; a combination that should not have worked at all, but together was absolutely magical.

But not even a full-bodied Scotch and filet could fill the void I felt in my heart, my soul.

What the hell is wrong with me?

Just as I aimed to sip the remains of my second glass, my phone chirped a familiar chime.

Jamie.

"Hello?" I answered, leaning back in my chair, waiting for the onslaught that I knew was about to come.

Jamie did not disappoint as she launched off into a tirade about one of our former coworkers, who happened to be the on again, off again man in her life.

"I told you, he is an asshole, darling. I tried to warn you," I said. At this point, I felt like a broken record sometimes.

"Save it, Wes. We both know we prefer our men emotionally damaged and unavailable."

Ah, so it's off again.

"I do not *prefer* emotionally damaged men or unavailable men. I just seem to attract them like a damn magnet. It's not my fault I am who I am."

Jamie hummed on the other end of the phone. " And who are you lusting after right now? Some small town hottie who's *'never done this before'.*" She snickered.

Naturally, I guffawed at her insinuations.

One time, Jamie... one time.

"I'll have you know, Cade is not—"

"So there is someone," Jamie sing-songed.

Damn it.

Weston you are smarter than this. You walked right into that!

I rolled my eyes, chastising myself for falling into Jamie's trap. I stared at the ornate venetian glass chandelier, contemplating lying or coming clean to my former coworker slash closest thing I had to a best friend.

"There was a night, Jamie. That's all. It's hardly anything to make a fuss over." I said the words, but after two rounds of scotch, I wasn't sure I believed them entirely myself.

"But you wanted a morning, am I right? Maybe even a lunch the next day? Someone to commiserate with while you play good son to mommy and daddy?"

Why isn't this woman a shrink?

"Even if I did want those things, Jamie, the chances are slim. He... *Cade*... doesn't seem to want anything to do with me."

"You said chances were slim, Wes. Not impossible. Besides, a man who doesn't succumb to your money and model looks? Shit, I'd want him too."

I sneered in response to her taunting, and just as I was about to speak, Jamie's laughter subsided, giving way to a pregnant pause.

"Why do you think he wants nothing to do

with you? Did you say something? Was the sex bad? Did you get whiskey dick or—"

My shoulders fell, and thanks to the alcohol in my system, the words came of their own volition as I confessed my sins to a woman who was certainly not pure enough to take confession.

"No, it was... wonderful, despite the alcohol, but—"

Jamie waited for me to continue, and for once in my life, I felt the need to unload, to give some of what I'd been carrying around up.

To vent, and trust my friend with the truth.

"The next morning... *this morning*.. he seemed to be... regretful. Worried about what we'd... done. I assured him it was fine, I'm clean, and it was just sex. Nothing major, and then I saw him at the fundraiser and—"

"You told him fucking him was no big deal?" she exclaimed.

Yes, because it wasn't...

But even as my thoughts wandered, as her tone hit me, I knew somehow it must have come across in a way I hadn't intended.

"Yes, because it's *not* a big deal. Sex is just... sex, Jamie. It doesn't mean we're fated mates like in those romance books you're always reading."

Jamie huffed, sighing deeply as she chose her words.

"You are such a dense asshole sometimes, but I guess I can't blame you. You haven't exactly dated many men with substance, so let me make this crystal clear for you, Wes."

My lips tightened along with my grip on my phone.

How dare she insult my choice in men! As if she is one to talk!

Before I could launch into a "that's the pot calling the kettle black" speech, Jamie's voice softened.

"Sex might not be a big deal to *you*, but it is to some of us. Some people don't give it up as easily as you do."

"Are you calling me a manwhore, Jamie?" I deadpanned.

"Yes, Weston. I am." She tutted.

She wasn't wrong. Not entirely anyway.

Perhaps that is part of the problem. I'm too detached.

But then again, in my life, attachments usually didn't pan out well for me. It wasn't like people hung around me for my intellect, or lack thereof apparently.

"I offered to buy him lunch, and he refused." I specifically left out the part where I hadn't *actually purchased* Cade lunch, but I did not need to feed Jamie any more ammo.

"Because it probably made him feel like shit. Like you were trying to pay him for—"

Oh.

Oh...

I closed my eyes as understanding befell me. I silently ran a hand over my face. This did not bode well for me.

I'd fucked up.

"Food and sex are not mutually exclusive..." I sighed defensively.

"You like him, don't you?" she said calmly.

How was it she always knew exactly what I didn't want to hear?

Her words made me feel strange. Vulnerable even.

Or maybe it's just the drinks I've had...

"I like what I know... of him." It was the truth. I didn't know him, not really. Not like I knew his favorite color or his shoe size, or who his parents were... but I knew he preferred Sam Adams, had an apparent love of Star Wars, and that he had a good heart. The man took care of animals, for God's sake. You can't love animals and be an asshole, it's just science.

"Beyond the spicy stuff?" Jamie asked hesitantly.

"He works for a veterinary hospital, and he's terrible at karaoke," I practically whispered in defeat.

Lord, take me now.

"Well, that doesn't sound like your type at all," she teased. Before I could speak, she cut in once more.

"If you really like this guy Weston, try... getting to *know* him. I know this might come as a shock to you, but *some* of us like it when a guy puts in some effort and doesn't just treat us like we're something that can be bought."

Effort.

I had certainly put in *effort*. I'd bought him a drink, offered to buy him lunch—which I'd come up short on thanks to my parents meddling as usual—and suddenly the image Cade must have formed of me hit me square in the head like a brick as Jamie's words settled in the air.

Perhaps, my current efforts had not been the brightest.

"Right. I could say the same to you, Jamie," I rebutted softly.

"I got to go, Wes. Dante is waiting for me inside," she said quietly before hanging up.

Just as we finished our call, the waiter stopped by with the check. The man smiled slyly at me, sliding the leather book toward me with a wink.

It was harrowing as I watched the man leave

slowly, noticing the way in which he moved like a gazelle.

On any other given day, I would have let my gaze linger, but my conversation with Jamie had left me feeling a bit sour.

When I opened the book to glance at my check, I'd noticed the phone number scrawled at the bottom, and my heart sank.

Because for the first time in my too long single life, I felt different.

I ran my fingers over the ink, noting a bit smudged on my fingertips. It was fresh.

It would have been far too easy to leave a large tip, to catch this shimmering fish that was desperate to be hooked. It would have been no effort at all.

Make an effort.

Jamie's voice reverberated in my head.

I decided at that moment to leave a reasonable tip, sign the check, and get the hell out of Sedona.

What I wanted wasn't here, no.

What I wanted lay in Jasper Springs, and as I left Sedona, I barely registered as I walked past the waiter, and I did not meet his goodbye. Instead, I only focused on searching my social media for the Jasper Springs Pet Hospital, in search of a very big, sparkly fish.

CHAPTER 16

Cade

I leisurely sipped my coffee as I sat down for breakfast at my kitchen island. I'd always been a stickler for my morning routine, and as such I did not usually check my messages or peruse my social media until I'd at least showered and dressed for the day.

As I took a bite of my cherry poptart, I noticed my Facebook messenger had a new message notification.

No one ever messaged me on the app, for most of the people I regularly saw or had contact with, knew I rarely checked the thing, and that texting my cell was a hell of a lot more efficient.

Still, I could not deny my budding curiosity, and so I opened the messenger, to see a message request that made my eyes widen.

Weston Rhodes would like to send you a message.

I stopped mid-chew to contemplate how I should respond, or *if* I should respond at all.

After all, Weston had said himself that just because we had sex, that didn't mean anything. And though he'd offered to grab us both something to eat, he hadn't shown up after. I knew I shouldn't have cared, after all, Weston was no different than the other assholes of my past, but I was still disappointed. A part of me had dared to *hope* that maybe, just maybe this once, things would be different.

But I also knew that it was rude to make assumptions.

So I did the noble, polite thing. I accepted the message.

I didn't know how else to get a hold of you. I wanted to apologize for... well... everything.

I feel like we got off on the wrong foot.

I glanced at Weston's profile picture, at his GQ smile and debonair attitude, at the little green circle that told me Weston was online. His pixelated face tempted me even then to answer.

And I couldn't deny him or his little icon as my fingers typed of their own accord.

You stood me up.

I chewed and swallowed the remainder of my poptart, feeling a sense of nervousness overcome me as I watched those three little dots flash on the screen.

I was detained. Believe me, I would have much rather been eating bon-bons with you.

I chewed my bottom lip as I considered his words.

Was there an emergency?

Cat stuck in a tree?

I actually felt a tad big smug at my cheeky response.

Score one for me!

Weston responded almost immediately.

Worse. My mother needed to parade me around like some prized pony.

Surprised at his candidness, I debated his words. He could be telling the truth, or it could be a lie, a cover up constructed to make him look better and not like an asshole, but...

But what reason would Weston have to lie to me?

What would he have to gain?

You catch more flies with honey than you do vinegar.

Against my better judgment, I tapped out a response, deciding to play with fire.

I see. Well, apology accepted. I guess.

I drank the last bit of my coffee as Weston typed out another message.

I don't feel like you've gotten the best impression of me, Cade. I think we should start over.

I cocked my head to the side as a smile threatened to erupt on my lips. It felt a little like he was groveling, and I had to admit, I kind of liked that idea.

Smooth, sexy Weston Rhodes on his knees begging for *me.*

Something about his words made me feel hopeful, emboldened.

And what exactly is the impression you think you gave me?

A pompous ass. Weston texted back.

My heartstrings tightened at the self-deprecation, and I was not sure what to say, but thankfully, Weston filled in the silence while I had my brain freeze.

Give me the chance to make it up to you.

At that moment, I realized I'd gotten carried away, noting the time in the corner of my phone, which almost gave me a heart attack. I was ten minutes behind and should have already left for work by now.

Fuck!

I hurriedly got myself together, tapping out a response, hoping perhaps Weston would understand.

Sounds great, but I really have to go. I'm late for work.

CHAPTER 17

Cade

The entire drive to the pet hospital, I couldn't stop thinking about Weston and his somewhat endearing text.

Truthfully, I hadn't meant to sound so abrupt, and thought about texting him back, if only because I was now worried perhaps Weston hadn't gotten the best impression of *me.*

After all, I could admit maybe I'd been a bit forward at the bar, kissing Weston on stage, practically throwing myself at the man in the Uber, and running away after a panic attack... and then I'd brushed him off this morning, after he'd apologized.

Who's the asshole now?

The welcome sound of animals early in the morning would have deterred most, but after the last forty-eight hours, I was ready for some normalcy.

Except, once Diane shot around the corner, eyeing me up with those puppy dog eyes again, I knew I was surely doomed.

"Cade, I need you to—"

"Again?" I asked, not even bothering to hide my discomfort.

"I know it's a lot to ask, but I need someone reliable to head down to Rhodes Enterprises for the board meeting at two."

Say what now?

The name made me perk up with interest.

"What, uh... what for, exactly?" I asked as I ran a hand through my hair nervously.

"The board wants to go over last night's events, and get a plan going for the next two."

My entire body stiffened as her words hit me.

Two more events?

I was only aware of the one...

"I'm sorry, since when were there *three* events, total?" I asked, slightly panicked.

"It was always in the air, so we didn't want to get anyone's hopes up, but if the first event was successful, then Rhodes agreed to do two more across town. One in Paradise and one in Deer Park."

I breathed out a long sigh and nodded in understanding.

"So you want me to go down to Rhodes Enterprises and sell them on the idea of two more events."

Diane smiled, the sight lighting up the corners of her eyes and I knew I couldn't say no. Especially if the outcome meant more money and help for the hospital.

Maybe Weston would be there. Perhaps I could apologize for being so curt this morning.

What are the actual chances Weston will be there?

And even if he is, the place is probably huge. The chances are slim...

Still, I knew a slim chance was better than no chance at all, right?

"I mean, who can resist this face?" Diane said as she picked up the hospital's resident cat, Susie, snuggling her close. Susie had the audacity to look at me with her big, glossy kitten eyes, purring up a storm.

I pursed my lips, sighing in defeat.

Fine.

"When do I leave?" I deadpanned.

Diane smiled as Susie blinked her eyes shut.

"The meeting is at two, so I suggest you leave after I come back from lunch at one."

I sighed, nodding as I checked the book for the day.

At least I'll get some time in doing my actual job.

CHAPTER 18

Cade

When I arrived at Rhodes Enterprises, I couldn't help but feel nervous.

The building stood out like a sore thumb, all sleek and shiny against the sunlight and greenery like an ominous, super-hero villain lair.

Does Batman work here too?

But if I was being honest with myself, it wasn't the building that had my stomach doing flips. It was the thought of seeing Weston, heir to the Bat Cave I stood in front of.

The inside of Rhodes Enterprises was just as shiny and futuristic, but then again, I would expect nothing less of a tech company like Rhodes.

"Can I help you?" an even, calm voice asked.

I turned to see a woman behind the lumbering metal desk, which was so shiny I could actually see my reflection in it.

"Um, yeah, actually... I, uh... I'm here from the Jasper Springs Pet Hospital," I said, clearing my throat, hoping to dredge up some confidence or semblance of bravado like Weston.

Instead, I chewed my lip as thoughts of the man pervaded me, of him in his sexy suit, latching his expensive watch and smiling that patented aristocratic smile men like him usually had.

The thoughts did nothing to quell my nervousness; in fact, they only made me long more for the man.

Focus, Cade!

"Wonderful, you can wait over there," she said as she pointed to an area equipped with white, egg-shaped chairs amidst a bright white floor and rug, floor to ceiling windows encasing the space and bathing it in bright light.

I am so out of my league, here.

I did as I was told, taking my seat in the strangely shaped chair, which swiveled without even a squeak.

What have I gotten myself into?

CHAPTER 19

I STROLLED through the halls of Rhodes Enterprises, feeling rather bored. For starters, there was nothing I loathed more than the drudgery of board meetings, which my father always *insisted* I join him for whenever I was in town on holiday.

It's like he's trying to bore me to death on purpose, perhaps to write me out of the will.

I casually pulled my phone out of my pocket, checking my messages for the hundredth time since that morning, to contemplate if I should respond back to Cade's abrupt exit text. He had agreed to a fresh start, but the last thing I wanted to do was appear... needy, or worse...

Clingy.

The fact I was worried about how I would come across to the golden-haired sexpot was baffling in itself, and should have been red flag *numero uno* to me. After all, I'd lived nearly thirty years not giving a shit what *anyone* thought of me. My parents, my coworkers, the newspapers or social media spies who liked to report my antics to embarrass me, my family, and the company.

So why did I care all of a sudden, about what the doe-eyed little cinnamon roll thought of me?

Why was making a *good impression* suddenly so important when it seemingly wasn't before?

"Morning, Mr. Rhodes," Cynthia, the desk attendant, called in her chipper, sing-song voice.

I barely looked up from my phone. But then again, I dealt with Cynthia just as much as I dealt with either of my parents. She was their right hand, after all.

"Morning, Cynthia. Where's this stupid meeting my father wants me at today?"

"Conference Room C on the fifth floor," she said sweetly, but I could see the disdain in her eyes when I finally looked up.

I knew how most of the people in the family business felt about me, which was just another reason why I wanted nothing to do with running my family's legacy, father's wishes or not.

How was I supposed to take over a company where no one even liked me because of their own preconceived notions?

Preconceived notions you helped feed with your drama, no doubt.

It was true, I had never set the record straight for any of them, not that it would have mattered. When people saw me, they saw the heir to Rhodes Enterprises, not the man who went home alone nearly every night to an empty penthouse with nothing but his hand and a stocked bar to keep him company.

They only saw the moments I wished would have lasted longer than a moment.

"Thank you, Cynthia," I murmured, trained in the art of thanking my father's assistant practically since my birth.

Sliding my phone back in my pocket, I pressed the elevator button, waiting impatiently so as to get this damn meeting over with. The sooner I showed up, played pretend for my father, the sooner I could go back to...

Was there anything truly worthwhile to go back to?

The realization struck me, cold and hard, in the chest like an icicle of truth. But I didn't want to think about cold, hard truths, and so I shoved the thoughts aside as the doors slid open, calling me forth like a lamb to the slaughter, and perhaps that was all this song and dance really was. I could fight and refuse all I wanted, but deep in my heart, I knew one day the inevitable would come.

As I sauntered down the crisp white and grey halls of the fifth floor, I noted how quiet it was, which only made the sound of my beating heart that much louder in my own ears.

And when I'd settled on Conference Room C, I'd opened the door expecting a boardroom full of company executives and my father.

But instead, what I found was something much, much better.

Cade.

"Well, well, look what the cat dragged in," I purred, a smile forming on my face.

Cade's eyes widened in surprise, a blush creeping into his perfect, pale cheeks, and immediately my cock twitched at the sight, my pea brain throwing up images of Cade blushing before me... on his *knees.*

I let out a muffled sound as I shut the door, shifting my weight only slightly as to not draw attention to the sudden erection I'd sprung from the mere *sight* of the man.

"What are you doing here?" Cade asked, dumbfounded.

I couldn't help but widen my grin. "Well, I

thought perhaps I'd be stomaching another grueling snoozefest of a meeting, but it appears today I'll be paying better attention," I said.

Cade's blush deepened as he swiveled back and forth in his chair.

"What exactly are *you* doing here, though? I did not peg you for the stalker type," I teased.

Cade blinked, just as he was about to answer me, the door behind us opened. Both of us turned to see a string of men in suits come piling in, filling the table rather quickly, followed by the latest concierge attendant, a woman I did not recognize, who had taken to passing out bottles of water as the suits took their seats.

All blushing and flirtation dissipated in the air as a familiar hand clapped my shoulder, tightening its grip. I'd know that touch anywhere.

"Morning, son," my father cooed, causing me to break my attention away from the man I would have much rather looked at.

"Morning, Dad."

"You're early. What a nice surprise."

"Yes, well, when there's nothing to do in this God-forsaken town except stare at the damn wall..." I sighed.

My father chuckled as he motioned for me to take a seat at the long oblong table.

"Well, some would call that *relaxing,*" he said

as I took my seat. His smile was polite, but genuine.

Like a true proud papa.

"Nonetheless, the time for play has come to a close. We have business to attend to," my father's voice carried as he made his way to the front of the table, right next to Cade.

I watched as my father introduced himself, shaking Cade's hand. A surge of anxiety flooded me as I watched my father's carefully practiced business expression. I could not legitimately tell my father's impression of Cade and how he felt about him, a notion that should have been alarming to me.

I had never really sought my parent's approval, especially when it came to those I had relations with. I couldn't very well say I had ever introduced them to a serious boyfriend—not that I'd had one—or girlfriend, before I'd come out.

Not to mention, my coming out to my parents had not gone as smoothly as I had hoped. They were as supportive as wealthy, image obsessed parents could be, and they'd certainly "mellowed" out in the years since, but my father did not acknowledge my romantic liaisons at all to this day, while my mother only really let her opinions be known after a drink or two.

Or four.

Still, the burgeoning need to hear their praise was an ember that would not die inside of my scorched soul, no matter how many men I seduced.

I watched like a fly on the wall as my father, and some of the other suits, addressed Cade, asking him questions about the hospital, about how much money they'd raised at the event, and their history with fundraising in general.

Cade fired off answers confidently, like a true natural. It was more than apparent that on this particular topic, that of animal care and veterinary science, Cade was in his element, and I couldn't help but stare in awe.

While the man seemed mild-mannered and quiet at first glance, below the pretty blue eyes and California surfer hair, he was a force all his own, whether he knew it or not. He was more than just attractive. He was passionate, smart, and caring.

He's such a good person.

Like sunshine in a bottle.

So fucking good.

I couldn't help but let my thoughts wander to just how I'd like to praise him for doing such a good job selling the pitch.

The image of Cade on his knees in the board room, my fingers threaded through his hair as his cheeks hollowed while he sucked me off pushed to the forefront of my mind, and I had to bite my knuckle to keep from groaning with pleasure at the thought.

Almost as if he could sense my inner turmoil, he turned his bright blue peepers at me for just a second, causing my heart to beat faster.

The image of Cade spread across the conference room table as I filled him caught like wildfire in my brain, causing the blood to rush to my cheeks as well as my cock, and I nonchalantly palmed my throbbing cock beneath the table, adjusting myself once more.

Cade looked away, smiling genuinely at my father and nodding in agreement to whatever the hell he'd just said.

Now is not the time!

"I think we have all the information we need, Mr. Green, thank you. We'll be in touch," my father said, and I realized the meeting was over.

I hadn't really gathered a word they said, my attention focused on keeping myself steady and stable in front of my father's employees and the man who seemed to have me entirely second-guessing everything in my life.

As they said their goodbyes, shaking hands and being polite, I realized at any moment Cade would walk through the door, and I could not let him do so without at least telling him he had done so well.

And then perhaps, all praise aside, I could take the good boy out for a well-deserved and overdue lunch.

"I'll be out in a minute," I said, smiling half-heartedly at my father, who nodded in response on his way out.

When the last of the suits had gone, Cade made his way to the door, but I casually shut it, stepping in front of his exit.

"Ah, ah. Not yet. We have some more *business* to discuss," I purred smoothly.

To my surprise, Cade cocked an eyebrow at me, crossing his arms in a way that was most enticing.

"And what business might that be?" he asked sarcastically, but I did not miss the hint of a smile tugging at his lips.

Oh, you want to play, do you?

Good thing for you, I love to play...

"Well, as good businessmen do, and quite often, I may add—" I licked my lips, continuing my suave speech. "I believe we should discuss *our private business* over lunch."

"Mhmmm."

"You did very well, up there," I said as I took a step closer to him.

Cade's blue eyes gazed up at me with interest.

"You flatter me, Weston, but all I did was just... read numbers and figures. That's it. A monkey could have done it. I hardly think that's a job well done."

I stopped just in front of him, sliding my hands in my pockets, adjusting my unruly erection and to prevent me from wrapping my arms around this man and telling him what I really thought of his performance.

Or rather, what performance I *wished* I could see of him in this stuffy boardroom.

Make an effort, Wes.

Beyond the physical.

"I do owe you a lunch. After I... how did you say it? Stood you up?"

Cade leaned into my space just a fraction, close enough I could smell his sweet, intoxicating scent.

Cinnamon and cloves mixed with cedar and orange... delicious.

"Mhmm. I suppose you *do* deserve the chance to make a better... impression," he said as he looked up at me from under his lashes.

Cade was playing with me, and I wanted nothing more than to take his bait. I could not help but smile, even though my insides were clamoring with excitement.

"And I promise you, *Cade*, I will not disappoint you again."

Cade's eyes lit up with amusement as I breathed his name.

"Dear lord, I hope not," he said as he swallowed nervously, his gaze dipping to my lips for a moment, that welcome tinge of pink coloring his cheeks again.

"Do you have something you desire, Cade? Something that will please your palette?" I asked, my heartbeat in my throat. It would be so very easy for me to close the gap between us, for me to run my hands through Cade's silky locks and covet his mouth to sing him my praise.

But I wanted *more*.

I wanted more than a quick, steamy, forbidden kiss in my father's boardroom. Make no mistake, I still wanted those things, but there was something I wanted more.

I wanted a date.

With Prince Charming.

A real, honest to God date in which I could bask in Cade's golden glow for longer than a moment, hear him laugh, and listen to him wail on about the drudgery of every day life in Jasper fucking Springs.

What has happened to me?

"Um... Bernard's is good, I guess," he

breathed the name of the cafe so huskily, I had to stifle another petulant moan of my own.

I want to hear him breathe my name like that.

"I could go for something quite robust myself, right about now," I said as I caught his cerulean gaze.

"I need to make a stop first, but, uh... I'll meet you there?" he said as he moved past me for the door.

I moved instinctively, giving him the out he needed. Despite my desire to keep him locked up in here forever with me, I knew I couldn't do so. I glanced at my watch, noting the time. It was barely two thirty.

"I will be there at three thirty," I noted as I moved away, regaining my composure as I opened the door for Cade.

"See you then," Cade said as he blushed once more, exiting the building, leaving me feeling quite excited for once.

This day was turning out to be better than I'd thought.

CHAPTER 20

CADE

WHEN I FINALLY MADE IT to the sanctity of my car, I had to catch my breath. Not because the walk from the fifth floor to the lobby had been brisk, but because I was rather certain that if I hadn't left when I did, I would have kissed Weston.

Again.

What the hell is wrong with me?

I'm not usually like this!

It was like every time I got near the man, I became some wanton, needy thing. The smell of his cologne, the darkness in his gem-like eyes that called to me like a moth to a flame. The way his voice was smooth like melted chocolate and caused my stomach to flip, my cock to twitch. On the physical end of things... he was absolutely perfect. It was like he was crafted from my love of rom-coms and my darkest fantasies or something.

Weston Rhodes seemed to bring out parts of myself I'd never known existed until I met him.

And seeing him swivel back and forth in his chair, amidst the crystal chandelier and stark, sleek design of the Rhodes Enterprises conference room, only hammered it into my skull that Weston was cut from a finer cloth. Despite knowing he was out of my league, I still wanted to wrap myself in that smooth, sexy cloth.

I turned the car on, the air conditioning blasting against my warm skin as I opened my phone, dialing the number of the one person who could talk me down from a burgeoning panic attack.

"Everything okay?" Dawson asked, his voice only slightly alarmed. It wasn't as if I called him regularly. Usually, I'd shoot him a text, but I could not do such a thing when my mind was rushing a thousand miles a minute.

"I have a date. With Weston."

Dawson whistled on the other end of the phone, the cool air from the vents blowing on my face.

"Well, I'll be damned," he said with a chuckle.

"I'm freaking out," I said, hearing my voice shake a little.

"Why? It's just a date. It's not like you're marrying the guy."

"Because he's... him... and I'm... me, and you know my social skills are sorely lacking and, like, what will we even talk about? I have nothing interesting to say or—"

"Pump the brakes, Cade. Breathe. Take a deep breath, and just *breathe*, buddy."

Immediately, Dawson shifted from his cavalier, charismatic air to firefighter mode, the one where he was serious and tackled everything with stoic poise and grace; the one he reserved for settling down fights or holding it together to pull someone from a burning building.

Dawson was mostly an aloof, overconfident pain in the ass, but when push came to shove, he was the best man to be in anyone's corner. It also helped that he at least had dealt with my anxiety before, both on a friendly and not-so friendly level.

I did as he instructed, sucking in a deep breath as we counted to ten.

"You've been on dates before. It's not something you don't know how to do. And I can honestly tell you, your conversation skills are fine. Just be yourself."

I let out a dark, strangled laugh. "You mean the anxious, self-deprecating, shut-in who lives on rom-coms and ice cream?"

Dawson sighed. "You forgot the bunny slippers, but no. I mean the successful man who doesn't seem to know he's a fucking catch. You bought your own damn house, Cade. You are amazing at your job, you're bomb at karaoke, I don't care what you say, you make a mean risotto, and on a scale of one to ten, you are a fucking twenty. Don't sell yourself so short."

Dawson's words hit me like a ton of bricks. Even when we'd been together, he'd never talked to me like that. It wasn't jealousy or remorse, but rather a cold, hard truth. Dawson laid it out, and for the first time, I had the inkling to believe him.

"I guess I don't normally see myself the way you see me."

"It's not just me, Cade. Everyone who knows you, knows you deserve more than the bullshit you *think* you deserve. You're a fucking gem. So go be a *gem*. Go on the date, smile and be yourself. Have a good time. I guarantee you, that's all you'll need. The rest will fall into place, and you'll have that guy eating out of your palm in no time."

I turned to look at the looming building of Rhodes Enterprises, feeling a little better.

It's just a date. It's not forever.

And I am starving.

"Thanks, Dawson," I said as my nerves started to settle.

"Anytime, buddy," he said, his tone going soft before he hung up.

I took another deep breath and counted to ten, then drove off in the direction of Bernard's.

CHAPTER 21

CADE

I WALKED through the front door of Bernard's with one goal—to give Weston *my* best impression. And also to have fun and get a damn whiskey barbecue burger with a side of extra fries because I was starving.

I'd called Diane to tell her I'd be coming back a little late, on account that I was having lunch with one of the 'employees' of Rhodes Enterprises, as was customary for business. It wasn't a *complete* lie, Weston had assured me such luncheons were a normal thing between business partners, and as far as she knew, we were partners.

I just wasn't sure if it was business or pleasure, or perhaps both.

Maybe if things go well, Weston and I will see each other again... at the next event.

I spotted Weston before the hostess looked up from her phone. He sat off to the left of the restaurant, which at this hour during the week, the restaurant itself was practically deader that a doornail.

Still, in the midst of the place, Weston looked refined in his suit, his watch glinting in the amber light to really drive home his apparent Bruce Wayne look.

Almost instantly he caught my gaze, rising to wave me over.

You got this, Cade.

I pulled up a seat across from him as the waiter came by to take our drink orders.

"I'll have a scotch on the rocks, and my friend here will have a—" He looked at me in question for a moment, and it dawned on me he was giving me a choice.

"Ice tea with lemon, please," I said politely.

"Any appetizers for you guys, or do you need a few more minutes?" the waiter asked.

"I'd love some of your famous buffalo chicken dip," Weston said with a smile, and I had to admit I was a little surprised. I didn't exactly peg him for a buffalo chicken guy. Then again, I didn't really know him beyond the flesh, and what little interactions we had had.

Which made me feel like an asshole for assuming. Nevertheless, I pushed the melancholy aside in favor of turning a new leaf, just as Weston had.

When the waiter walked away, it was just the two of us facing off against one another.

"I worried you might have changed your mind," Weston said as he leaned back in his chair, his long, lithe fingers tapping gently on the starched linen tablecloth.

"Well, you did say you owe me, so it would be rude to refuse you a chance to how did you say it? Make a better impression?" I said as I leaned back in my chair, shooting him a smile of my own.

"That I do," he said with a grin as the waiter brought our drinks and a large bowl of buffalo chicken dip with fresh made tortilla chips.

"So are you in town long, or..."

Weston shook his head. "I came because my father *insisted* I see him and the company doing something other than what they are known for. He thinks if he shows me *all the aspects* of this business, something will take and I'll just want to up and move here tomorrow to take over."

"Is that something you want?" I ask, making polite conversation.

So far so good.

Weston's eyes dimmed, as he twisted his lips, pausing before answering.

"It's what is expected of me. I am the heir to the business. What I want doesn't factor into the equation," he said as he immediately dove in for a chip, absolutely avoiding the path this conversation was headed on. I watched as he scooped up a heaping amount of dip and I couldn't help but let out a small laugh. Mid-chew he looked at me, raising an eyebrow. I had to admit, it was a sound tactic for evading an uncomfortable discussion.

Like I've never tried to talk about something other than work before.

"What?" he said through half a mouthful of food.

"Oh nothing, its just, uh... you have a little something," I said pointing to the corner of my own mouth.

Weston's deep green eyes lit up with mischief as he swallowed his chip and dip, his tongue flicking out to lick the splash of hot sauce there. The sight alone made my cock twitch, and I cleared my throat. Weston only grinned slyly.

The waiter came back, and I half wondered if he was just rushing back to make my life that much more drawn out, or if he was just keeping his normal pace and I was the one who was antsy.

"We're still going to need a few minutes," Weston touted, before looking at me. "Unless of course, you already know what you'd like?"

His words made my stomach flip, as the look in his eyes told me he most certainly wasn't talking about food.

Two can play this game, Mr. Rhodes.

"Actually," I said as I leaned forward in my chair, stretching my arm out across the table on the opposite side of him, tapping my fingernails on the tablecloth, channeling my best Weston impression.

"I will have the whiskey barbecue cheeseburger with extra pickles and sauce, and extra fries on the side," I said, dropping my voice an octave, mimicking the smoothness of Weston's natural tone.

Weston looked a little surprised, but he hid it well. Clearly he wanted to play the big, hot alpha suit who gets to order for their sweet and subby darling, but I was feeling somewhat emboldened by Dawson's words, and my little white lie to my boss. I was breaking the rules today, and perhaps the bad boy fever was driving me over the edge.

Bad boys usually get punished after all.

Weston shrugged.

"I'll have what he's having," he said with a wink, and the waiter gathered our menus before toddling off in the direction of the kitchen, leaving us to our own devices.

Weston shook his head, his dark hair swaying from the motion as he breathed a contented sigh.

"You're refreshing, do you know that?" he said as he took a sip of his scotch, straightening the wrinkles in his button-down once more.

The sight made little flashes pop up in my memory, of just how I'd watched those fingers slide over the miniscule wrinkles, over his taut chest... shirt soaked in sweat.

I shifted in my seat, my cock jumping at the memory.

"I don't see how. You aren't the only one who's given a doozy of a first impression," I say honestly, dispelling my momentary Weston impression.

"I don't know what you mean," he said as he dug for another chip, this time taking a little less of a giant heap of the dip.

"I mean, I know I kind of came off... abrupt the other morning, maybe even a little standoff-ish. Then at the fundraiser... I... I just wasn't myself. I was kind of... stressed."

Weston took a sip of his scotch before speaking.

"Would that stress have anything to do with my... reassurances?"

It was now my turn to dive into the dip and hide my words.

"You were a little... cold."

"You seemed worried about what had happened. Remorseful. I only wanted to assure you that if it meant nothing to you..." His words disappeared as his gaze dipped to where my hand still lay, fingers curled into a fist not far from him.

Understanding befell me as I realized all at once what he meant.

"If it meant nothing to me, you wanted to reflect that."

"Stage five clinger is not a good look for me, Cade," he said as he shoved a chip in his mouth.

"I know the feeling. All my exes used to say I was too needy," I breathed, instantly regretting the moment the words left my mouth.

Why the fuck would I say that?

Even if it was true, that's like date etiquette 101! Never talk about your exes!

Weston laid his free hand on the table, fingers curled into a fist only a hair's breadth away from mine.

"I wish I could be, though. Needy. Clingy. Affectionate. But most of my affections have come with a price tag, because *that* is how my exes preferred it. They didn't want my feelings, either."

The admittance makes my heart break for this man. Weston didn't move his hand, instead he stared at it, looked at the space between us with anticipation, longing.

I slowly uncurled my fingers, which put my pinky only an inch away from his wrist.

The desire to touch him, to soothe *his* worries, to *reassure* him was so strong, it was practically magnetic.

And suddenly all the nerves I had before went up in smoke as I slid my hand closer, next to his, our skin brushing in the lightest of ways.

Teasing, asking for permission.

"Kinda sounds like you dated some assholes," I said.

Weston jumped a little from the contact, but eased up nearly instantly. His green eyes gazed back at me with a depth I'd never seen in anyone else before.

"You sound like you have experience with that," he said softly.

I felt rather on the spot at his statement, but for the first time in my life, it felt like a weight had been taken off my shoulders at the same time.

The truth for once felt... freeing. Dawson was right.

I'd gone after assholes because I thought it was what I deserved, and that truth helped me see the recognition in Weston's eyes.

He thought he deserved them too, but it was clear to me as he fought to give in to his obvious desire, that maybe he deserved more too.

He'd just never asked for it.

"Yeah, you could say that."

At that moment, the waiter decided to bring our cheeseburgers, and Weston pulled his hand back, leaving mine alone.

The strange air of vulnerability had broken, as Weston shook his head, dispelling all thoughts and confessions for the moment in favor of sweet, sticky barbecue sauce and bacon grease.

I watched as he bit into his burger, his eyes practically rolling back in his head.

"Oh fuck, Cade..." he moaned, making my cock throb.

I want to hear him say those words about me...

I cleared my throat. "Uh..."

"This is the best burger I think I've ever had," he said as some barbecue sauce dripped down his chin.

I smirked before picking up my own and diving in. The salty sweetness on my tongue was divine, and I was pretty hungry.

"You ain't kidding," I said with a light laugh

as I took another bite, practically devouring my burger in a matter of seconds.

The rest of the lunch was like that. The two of us completely annihilating our sandwiches, laughing, talking about stupid shit.

Like weird food combinations, movie recommendations. What the secret ingredient was in Sandra's homemade pralines.

Weston insisted it was espresso powder, but I didn't believe him.

By the time the check had come, I was a little shocked. Though it had been an hour, it felt like time had just flown by way too fast.

I liked talking to him.

Hell, I liked *him*.

I knew it was crazy after one lunch to think you knew someone, but I was starting to know Weston Rhodes.

Not the Weston that I'd seen in articles on the Internet, or the one who swiveled around sexily in his egg chair at Rhodes Enterprises.

But the one who knew all the words to *Don't Go Breaking My Heart*, understood my Star Wars reference, apparently had an obsession with buffalo chicken dip, and who fought me tooth and nail to pay the bill.

"At least let me pitch in," I whined.

Weston shook his head. "Absolutely not. I owe you."

I watched him sign the check and hand it off hastily. I sighed, my shoulders relaxing as I arose from my chair.

"Well, since you insisted. Thank you. But you should let me return the favor... sometime," I said as Weston came behind me, setting his hand against the small of my back. He gently touched me, pushing me toward the doors. I walked slowly, never moving to remove his hand. I liked how it felt, warm against my shirt.

Calming, soothing.

When we exited Bernard's the sun warmed my air-conditioned blood.

I turned to look at him, if only to say thank you again, make my exit. But I stopped frozen underneath his gem-like gaze, my gaze dipping to his pouty, perfect lips. I noticed a smidge of barbecue sauce in the corner of his mouth, and the innate desire in me to *lick* it off of him made me realize I was truly in over my head.

As if he could sense my sudden inkling, he reached out to brush some of my hair behind my ear, his voice dropping an octave.

"I think I'd like that, Cade," he said softly.

Instinctively, I leaned into him, against his chest. Suddenly, I felt dizzy and I knew it wasn't from the lunch or the sun.

Weston moved closer, his free hand settling at my hip, his palm warm against me.

I looked up at him for a moment, readying myself for what felt like the most right thing in the world.

Weston licked his lips, his eyes searching mine.

My eyelids fluttered, and I leaned in just an inch, expecting him to meet me halfway.

To kiss me like they do in the movies.

His fingers gripped my hair as he brought his forehead to mine, letting out a sigh.

"I had a really great time today, Cade. With you," he whispered.

"Same," I whispered back.

"But all good things must come to an end, and we must return to our dreadful nemesis. Employment."

At that moment, I realized he wasn't going to kiss me.

And why should he?

It was a date, and we had fun, but...

He was right. The real world beckoned us, popping our perfect little Bernard's Bubble.

"Right," I said as I licked my lips, nodding in understanding.

"Will, uh... talk later?" I asked, feeling the nerves starting to kick up again.

Weston slid his fingers down my jaw, resting his hand on my collarbone. He implored me with deep, sorrowful eyes.

"Absolutely," he said as he slid his hand off my neck, turning away and heading for a car that I realized had been sitting in front of us since we'd exited.

Must be his driver.

I watched as Weston languidly folded himself into the backseat, as he closed the door and sped off.

I'd wanted him to kiss me. To sweep me off my small town feet and whisk me away to his Christmas Tree farm or Italian Villa or whatever it is that men like him had in those cheesy movies.

But that wasn't the realization that shocked me, no.

I was always the one who wished to be kissed, to be swept off their feet.

But in that moment, before he set his hand on my hip, before he tugged me closer, I realized I wanted to kiss *him.*

I wanted to crush my lips to his and bring him into me tenfold, wrap my arms around him and soothe his tired, achy heart.

I wanted to be *his* prince charming, come to save *him* from all the assholes.

And I'd missed my chance.

Hopefully, I'll get the chance to make it up to him.

CHAPTER 22

WESTON

IF THERE WAS one thing I hated more than coming home, it was dinner with my parents. I knew how much of a dick that made me sound like, but I didn't care. No one could really understand the whole vibe of the Rhodes when they were off the clock.

But despite my own personal feelings of being subjected to parental gaslighting, I knew it would be easier to just play along and get it over with.

Sit down with mom and dad, have some dinner, listen to their nitpicking and take it with a smile. Dad would give the usual 'one day when

I'm gone' speech, and I could make my exit after that.

So, when I pulled up to the Rhodes house, I was already in a shit mood and I didn't anticipate a sunny, cheery dinner.

Not to mention I was still kicking myself for not leaning in and kissing Cade when it was more than apparent that was what he wanted.

What is happening to me?

I exited my Uber, the melancholy settling in as I looked up the long driveway at the colonial style mansion that I spent most of my summers in and out of. The dogwood trees framing the yard and the stark, white columns in the front of the house looked ominous. Walking through the front door was like walking through the gates of heaven, or hell, if you actually knew what lay behind them.

"Oh, hello Weston," my mother said cheerily as I opened the door. She stood in the foyer with a martini in her hand, her cheeks rosy and her eyes bright. Judging by the cavalier way she pulled me into a hug, practically sloshing her gin, I would have bet it was at least the third she'd had. *It's happy hour somewhere, dear,* she'd always say.

"Mother," I said dryly as I set my hand on her back lightly, steadying her for the moment.

"You are early, again," my father said as he

came down the hall, scotch in hand, sleeves rolled up to his elbows.

His immediate presence made me straighten my stance, made whatever miniscule feelings of contentedness I had felt disappear in the cold, bitter air of the foyer.

"Father," I said as I let go of my mother.

The scent of roast duck hit me, along with the pungent smell of garlic and I had to work to keep my face even. I never cared for the fowl, no matter how they prepared it.

Mother waved her hand, dismissing my father. "No matter what time he shows up, dear. This is his *home*."

Yup, definitely her third.

"Home is in the city, mother, but thanks."

My father's eyes met mine for a moment, a dark look passing through his. It was as if he wanted to say something, but he refused.

Odd, usually the man just says what he wants with no regard to how other people will take it.

"Pish posh, darling, you will always be a Rhodes and therefore all roads will eventually lead you *home* to Jasper Springs where you belong."

I dismissed her comment as she toddled off toward the kitchen. My father followed her without question, brushing past me with an intensity that made me feel on edge.

I'd rather he just say his piece and get on with it, so I could get on with my damn life.

I followed my parents through the oversized kitchen, past the actual chef, since my mother never touched a stove in her life, and the only time she used a cutting board was to slice her lemons and limes for her cocktails.

"Smells delicious, Margo," I said with a rueful smile as I passed by.

Margo, who'd been the family chef since I was about eight, only looked at me with a bright smile of her own and a warmth that actually settled my nerves some.

"Thank you, sir," she said sweetly.

I hated it when people did that. Called me *sir* like I was some old man, at least in the presence of my every day life.

However, I certainly didn't mind it one bit when a blue-eyed god with silky blond hair and the lips of a fucking angel called me sir. Or submitted to my commands.

That I could get used to.

The thoughts of Cade pervaded my senses again, and I let out a defeated sigh. Now was really not the time, but I couldn't help but feel guilty. The lunch had gone... well.

Too well, if I was being honest.

I found myself opening up to Cade in a way I hadn't really opened up to anyone else before.

Something about his demeanor, his presence, just made me loose-lipped. It was like I could tell him *anything.*

And when he'd gotten all dominant for the blip of a moment, shooting me that dead-sexy look as he dropped the tone of his voice, I saw the undeniable monster inside of Cade begging to come out, and I...

Liked it.

I liked it a whole fucking lot.

Reel me in, sir, I am yours.

I could only hope I hadn't completely botched my chances with the man because I didn't take the obvious opening.

The heat and attraction that existed between Cade and I was obvious, but Jamie's words clung to me like a bad rash.

Make an effort.

So that's what I did. I made the effort. I evaded kissing Cade because I knew if I kissed him, I'd fall into my old patterns. I'd wrap him up in my tentacles once more and covet him all to myself, and we'd wind up in the same place we had that night after karaoke.

And for the first time in my life, I had to admit that I wanted more than just to shove my cock down Cade's throat.

I wanted to see him again. I wanted to see him as much as I could while I was here in town.

I took my seat at the long, ornate dining table that looked like it was set for a party, despite the fact there was only the three of us. The manners that were forever ingrained in me were involuntary. I placed the napkin on my lap, reached for my glass of cold, freshly poured Icelandic water, whilst Margo set about to serving us.

"So about the meeting this afternoon..."

My father's words elicited a sigh from me and a curse from my mother, as he gingerly picked up his fork. He didn't even look at me as he said it.

"For fuck's sake, can we just enjoy a nice dinner with our son without discussing business?" my mother bit out before shaking her empty martini glass in the air.

Margo swiped it with precision, trained well in my mother's routine.

"This is a family matter, and therefore it should be discussed over family dinner," my dad touted, dismissive as usual.

I rolled my eyes as Margo refilled my mother's glass, the heavy scent of garlic making my eyes water.

"Well, I'd have to say I think this is a new record. I've barely been here fifteen minutes and you're already up my ass," I said as Margo set down a glass of home brewed tea for me. I looked up at her for a moment, taking in her kind smile. I nodded in thanks, gracious for the gesture. She'd even put two slices of lemon in it, just the way I liked. I took a strong sip as my father guffawed.

"I wouldn't have to lay into you, Weston, if you actually entertained this conversation and accepted things. But with as little as we see you, a man has to take the chances he's given."

"Gee, it's almost like I don't come around because of this very issue," I growled as I set to cutting into my tender duck breast, probably slicing a little too enthusiastically.

My mother groaned, taking a sip of her martini. "I just wanted a nice family dinner..." she complained.

"I don't understand why you are so resistant to this. The company is doing well, and you would do well to have some stability in your life. Put roots down, build a life, a—"

"I'm glad you think the life *I built* in the city isn't a life. I'll take that one to my therapist. I'm sure we can squeeze a few pricey sessions out of that," I snarked back.

Truth was I had no therapist, but he didn't need to know that.

"You haven't had a job in over a year, Weston, and I've never seen you seriously entertain finding *someone* to settle down with. All you do is mope around that damn condo and stay out till all hours of the morning doing God knows what with God knows who..." My father's face flushed with pink, his eyes getting glassy.

I hadn't seen him this worked up since I came out of the closet. I fought to look away, but it was like watching a damn train wreck. I just couldn't help myself.

"It might not be the life *you* wanted for me, dad but it is *my* life."

"Your life is here, Weston. With this company, with your family!" he yelled.

My mother sobbed into her martini glass.

"My life is with whoever I want it to be, wherever the fuck I want to be!" I yelled back as I threw my napkin down, rising from my seat. I'd had enough of this.

"I think I've lost my appetite," I said as I stormed out of the dining room, my father's angry voice bellowing beside me.

"One day you'll have to grow up and be a fucking adult, Weston!"

His words hit me like a gong. The vibration sounded through every bone, every blood-filled vein in my body.

Walking away from a situation that brought me no peace was about the most adult thing I could think of.

And sure, before I'd come to Jasper Springs,

before I met *Cade*, I would have risen to his bait. I would have bit back and yelled, and stirred the shit pot some more, but I was too tired to deal with it all that day.

So instead, I said nothing. I gave my father my back and walked out of the house, down the driveway feeling nothing but rage and frustration, and shame.

I'd never be what they wanted.

What my father wanted.

No amount of sitting in boardrooms and taking pictures would ever make me the businessman he wanted me to be.

I kept my pace quick as I turned down the road. I needed to clear my head of all this nonsense, this bullshit that my family loved to dig up every time I saw them.

I'd entertained the idea once. When I was seventeen.

I had come home from boarding school that summer, and I agreed to volunteer at the company, thinking I was going to be *in* those board meetings, helping to make decisions about the business. But instead, my father had assigned me to gopher status. Getting coffees, delivering lunches and mail, sending company emails and sorting paperwork.

Grunt work.

I'd expressed an interest, and my father

treated me like it was Take Your Kid To Work day, telling me, "Everyone starts at the bottom, son."

I quickly realized that if I was going to be stuck on the bottom of the Rhodes food chain, perhaps I didn't have the stomach or drive to build myself up to the high standards my father had obviously set for me.

That was the summer I realized maybe there were *other* options for me.

Options that didn't include working for my asshole father.

So I withdrew from the company, left home early and couch-surfed on my sort of gay fuck-buddy from school's couch until the semester started. I'd made it my goal to stay as far away from Jasper Springs and Rhodes Enterprises since.

Step by step, I walked at high pace, relishing in the air against my heated skin, my emotions flourishing through me with every stride. Stuck in my head, I didn't even see the man I'd crashed into, nearly taking us both down on the sidewalk in front of...

The Jasper Springs Pet Hospital.

Shit, how long have I been walking?

Warm palms steadied my arms, and a familiar voice pulled me from my dark thoughts.

"Wes, are you... okay?" Cade's voice was like

the sound of angels singing, soothing something in my tortured soul.

I eased in his grip as we both stood straighter, my heart catching in my throat. I looked down at him, into his pretty blue eyes. They reminded me of the ocean at night, when the waves calmly crash against the sand, smoothing the rough bits out and turning it to something softer, more pliable. Capable of building great sandcastles.

"I, uh... just needed to clear my head. Maybe, uh... grab a drink somewhere."

I cleared my throat, every ounce of my being wanted to close the gap between us.

I wanted to hide away in Cade Green's kiss, in his arms, until the sun came up and took away all this bullshit with it.

Cade seemed to understand my thoughts, like the mind reader he was.

"Okay, well, there's always M's Place..." he said carefully.

"You, uh... want to get a drink... with me?" I asked hopefully.

Cade's eyes furrowed for a moment, his lips pursing as he let out his own breath. He nodded.

"Sure. Come on, I'll drive," he said as he nodded in the direction of the parking lot. The only car left at this hour was his, and a part of me felt nervous.

It wasn't like I'd never been in a car with another man before. Hell, I've had sex in the backseat of more cars than I can probably count on one hand.

But something about letting Cade take the proverbial wheel, following him into the tiny, personal space, was both intriguing and scary.

But I did it anyway, because I've always been hell for consequences.

Live in the moment was kind of my motto.

So as Cade opened the passenger door for me, as I folded myself into his tiny little white Civic, that was what I focused on.

Cade, my prince charming with a white steed.

CHAPTER 23

WESTON

AFTER THE SECOND SCOTCH, I started to feel a little better, the edge finally taken off.

Cade leaned against the high-top table, taking a pull of his beer. He'd been nursing the one all evening, which I guess, I could ascertain why. The last time we were both here, we'd gotten sloppy drunk and ended up fucking.

Something that was clearly out of the norm for Cade, though I couldn't deny the experience hadn't been a bad one, but...

I wanted him to feel comfortable. Not just here in this bar, but... with me.

I wanted him to trust me, to *like* me... and not just the me that everyone else gets.

The real me.

The fucked up, hot mess that absolutely doesn't have his shit together and has more issues than Vogue.

I wanted someone to see my disaster and not turn away.

"So... do you want to talk about it, or..."

"My dad is a grade A dick," I said, feeling that incessant word-vomit I got around Cade rearing its ugly head.

"He wants me to take over the company, settle down. *Build a life here.*" I scoff as I took a sip of my scotch.

Cade's gaze didn't wander one bit, just stayed fixed on me like he was studying a leopard in its natural habitat or something.

It dawned on me, when he didn't speak, he was waiting for me to continue, so I did.

"I guess, I just... wish he understood that my life is what *I* make it, you know?"

Cade nodded.

"Yeah, I do know actually. I, uh... I might not have a dick dad with big expectations, but, um... I've always wanted to be the main char-acter in my own life. I built everything I have on my own. I wanted this white picket fence life, like the ones in the movies... because a lot of people told me I couldn't. Because I was..."

He didn't have to say it. I knew exactly what

he meant. People are always going to make assumptions of you, gay, straight, pan, bi, ace... and those assumptions and limitations can wear you down or they can give you the best drive, the best revenge. The need to say *I told you so* can be a great motivator in life for some people, and I guess I'd subscribed to it myself. I understood Cade with the utmost sympathy and empathy.

It's hard enough *being* gay on a good day, let alone when you have no support from others around you, when you already feel isolated and lonely.

"I made it my goal to have the house with the white picket fence and a perfect job with wonderful coworkers," he said, his lips turning up into a smile.

It was clear he did love his job, a sentiment I couldn't relate to. I'd never loved any job I'd been at, but I came close at Men's Warehouse. I did genuinely enjoy fitting people for suits and talking fashion. My coworkers were awesome too.

The sparkle in his eyes dissolved as he continued though, but he didn't look at me. Rather, he gripped his beer, picking at the waterlogged label.

"But I'm still coming up short," he said.

I frowned.

"How so?" I asked, feeling the innate desire to soothe his troubles like he did for me.

"Because none of it matters if I don't have anyone to share it *with*," he said, his voice cracking.

I didn't think twice about setting my hand on his, as his words struck a chord within my damn soul.

I didn't have anyone to share my life with either. Every time I thought I had found someone, someone *good*, they turned out to be just as selfish and materialistic as the person before. Lording things over me to get what they wanted, peacing out when they'd had their fill of cock and expensive gifts.

When the next Sugar Daddy came along with gifts far better than mine.

More than anything I'd wanted the very same thing Cade did.

Someone to go to the French Riviera with on holiday, who I could come home and curl up on the couch with to Netflix and chill, who I could bake fucking cookies with during a snowstorm and fuck senseless till the wee hours of the morning.

Someone to wake up with and have breakfast, who wouldn't walk out on me when the energy of the moment wore off.

Cade looked at my hand and then at me.

His cheeks reddened a bit, his lips betraying him, showing the ghost of a smile on his face.

Why does he hold back?

I asked myself this, wondering if I was holding back too.

"Some things are just better with another person," I said, feeling my heart in my throat.

Cade swallowed, flipping his hand so that our fingers intertwined. He studied the sight for a moment, before nodding in agreement.

"I suppose they are," he said before letting go.

"I should, uh, we should probably head out soon. The presentation must have gone well, because my boss told me we're to set up for another fundraiser tomorrow over in Deer Park around noon, so..."

My eyes widened a bit.

That was fast... my father must have really liked Cade's presentation, and the event must have made a decent amount for him to consider moving so quickly.

Suddenly, I feel a sting of guilt. Maybe that's what he wanted to discuss. The fundraiser. I'd been at the last one, and it only made sense, that if I was home under his watchful forced eye to learn about the phil-anthropic side of the business, he'd want me at the next one.

But if I'd stayed in that house I surely would

have popped my cap, and I certainly wouldn't have run into Cade...

Instinctively, I pulled my phone out of my pocket, readying to que up a driver, but Cade reached out, his hand blocking my screen as he pushed it down. I looked up, to meet his gaze, full of empathy and something else.

Desire.

"Don't worry about calling for a ride. I'll, uh... I'll drive you back to the hotel."

"Okay," I agreed, draining the last of my drink and tossing some bills on the counter for tip, even though I'd already paid and closed the tab.

CHAPTER 24

Cade

I DIDN'T KNOW what had possessed me. It was like I was truly someone else. Like some alien had invaded my body like Invasion of the Body Snatchers. And I knew the alcohol wasn't to blame, because I'd literally had only one beer.

No, the intoxication came from Weston Rhodes, who was sitting in my car, staring out my window at the blur of Jasper Springs while I was having an existential crisis.

I wasn't the guy who came on to other guys. I was the guy who liked to be chased. I was *not* the guy who did the catching, whatsoever.

But somehow I'd managed to lure Weston into my web, and I didn't want to let him go.

Ever.

His sophisticated cologne filled the tiny space of the car, and the way his sleeves were rolled up to expose his toned arms made my stomach flip again.

But I was starting to see past Weston's gem-like surface. I was starting to see the mineral compounds that made the beautiful man I didn't want to stop looking at.

I wanted to dive further in, unveil all of his secrets and thoughts. I wanted to know every-thing there was to know about Weston Rhodes.

Because as I ventured into his dark, murky waters, I realized he wasn't who I thought he was.

He was more than some rich asshole looking to add a notch on his bedpost in town whatever on his list of voyages.

When we'd pulled up to the Palisades, I didn't turn the car off.

Weston turned to me, his green eyes imploring me. "Stay," he said.

One word that held so much meaning it was as heavy as a steel beam.

His eyes pleaded with me, full of wishful desire and dreams. Of promises that others had undoubtedly broken.

I wanted to stay. I wanted to stay forever.

"I want to, but—" I admitted, feeling my throat tighten with anxiety.

But the fundraiser is tomorrow, and I should probably get some rest.

But I don't have a change of clothes.

But I don't want to be a dick.

But I want to stay.

"But what?" Weston asked, turning in his seat.

"I don't even have a change of clothes or—"

"Is that all? Cade, I can get you anything you need or want. You just say the word," Weston said, cocking his head to the side. He seemed utterly confused.

I sighed, turning off the car. I didn't want to waste gas after all, and I could tell this conversation was far from over.

"I don't need you to buy me a new wardrobe, Weston. I don't need all of this," I said as I pointed to the grandiose hotel that looked like something out of a historical drama.

The Palisades was Jasper Springs's most exquisite building. Everyone and their brother had rented the place for their wedding, or had their baby showers there, and once or twice they even filmed a movie there.

Weston nodded, pursing his lips.

"I'm sorry, Cade, I didn't mean... I just... I don't know how to do *this*."

It was my turn to act shocked and confused.

"Do what Wes?" I breathed, my voice soft in the shared space.

Weston pointed between us. "This. Not control the situation. Not shower you with every expensive toy or piece of clothing you want. Give you whatever it takes to keep you, even if it's just for a night."

He turned to look out the window, and I watched his shoulders fall, watched as he hunched himself up and refused to look at me.

My heart broke to see him like this.

Candid, honest.

So desperate for a love that he'd clearly never had.

"Hey," I said as I reached out and set my hand on his thigh.

He turned slowly, his gaze flicking to where I touched him before he looked back at me.

"I don't need all the fancy bullshit. I just need you," I said honestly, my heart thumping so loudly in my chest I thought he could surely hear it.

He smirked before answering. "And a change of clothes. Obviously."

The words forced themselves out of my mouth without warning. I was running on pure adrenaline, as I'd never felt this emboldened before.

Then again, I'd never had an actual millionaire at my feet begging me to stay the night before either, so I guess that will do wonders for anyone's self esteem.

"Give me like, a half hour, forty minutes. I'll head back to my place, grab some clothes, maybe some ice cream? We can hang out all night, eating ice cream and watching some movies to forget all the bullshit, yeah?" I asked. Hoping he would say yes.

I wasn't entirely sure how to give Weston what he needed, but damned if I didn't want to try. And the only way I knew how to shove off the stress and strain of life was to curl up on my couch and do just as I was proposing. Except, I usually did it alone.

Some things are better with another person.

Weston seemed to relax at my words, nodding.

"Okay," he said, clearly nervous.

"I'll come back, I promise," I said.

He opened the door. "Text me when you're back here?" he asked, standing in the open air, the moonlight shining down on him.

I nodded in response. "Of course," I said as my nerves started to make their way to my heart.

Weston closed the door, and I watched him walk away.

Panic tried to settle in, but I pushed it aside.

I can do this.

It's not like I've never spent the night with anyone, and it doesn't mean we have to have sex.

Did I want that, though?

The fact I couldn't answer no made my entire body flush with heat, and I turned the car on, speeding off in the direction of my house.

CHAPTER 25

Cade

I HURRIEDLY PACKED AN OVERNIGHT BAG, probably with more shit than I actually needed, and as I stared at the box of condoms in my bedside table, I felt at a crossroads.

If I brought them, it didn't mean I'd have to use them. Plus, Weston had assured me he was diligent about his health and he was clean. I didn't have any reason to believe him, but that little voice inside me did.

I trusted Weston.

I barely knew him, but I was starting to. And he hadn't lied to me yet. In fact it was quite the opposite. He'd been upfront with me since that night at M's Place.

I grabbed the box, just in case.

Better to be prepared than not, right?

I looked at the quiet, dark space of my house, for the first time really feeling the absence of another person.

It had never bothered me as much before. Men came and went in my life, and my house was constant. It would always be here, even when they weren't.

But as I looked around at the crisp, clean, and cozy living room, I wondered what it would be like... to share this place with someone.

But not just any someone...

Weston.

Would he fit in here?

Amongst the Star Wars figurines and the handmade gifts from pet parents?

Would he look just as perfect on my little grey couch with a cup of coffee as he did in Bernard's?

Would he feel at home somewhere like here?

With me?

The thoughts that assaulted me were alarming.

This was a bad idea, wasn't it?

A week ago I would have said yes. But I couldn't quite say that now, not as every inch of me felt pulled toward the Palisades, toward Weston.

So I slung the bag over my shoulder, locked the door, and headed back to my car, thinking the whole way to the hotel that this is it.

This is the moment I lose my goddamn marbles and jump off the cliff.

I could only hope that Weston would be there to catch me, and that I wasn't making a complete mistake.

CHAPTER 26

WHEN I SHOWED up to Weston's hotel room, I felt on the edge of a damn precipice. I held two pints of Rocky Road in my hand, wondering if Weston even liked ice cream, or Rocky Road for that matter, pausing before I knocked. But almost as if he could sense me, he opened the door, smiling haughtily.

"You came back."

"I told you I would," I said as I cleared my throat, showing off the ice cream.

"I hope you like Rocky Road," I said as Weston waved me in.

"I like all flavors of ice cream," he said, flashing me a smirk as he closed the door.

Holy shit, I'm actually doing this.

I dropped my bag on the floor, setting the ice cream down on the bureau.

Weston motioned to a door that connected his room to another.

"You can take the other bed tonight if you like. I don't want you to feel like certain things are... expected," he said the words carefully, clearly. Like he had that first morning when he'd told me sex didn't matter.

And suddenly I understood, that it *did* matter to him.

He just didn't know how to accurately express that, because in his mind it made him unattractive. It made him needy, clingy, and everything that would drive a person away.

Oh, Weston.

I popped open the first container and opened the plastic spoon from its wrapping on the side, handing it to Weston.

"I appreciate that. But maybe for now, we just... relax. Okay?" I asked.

Weston pulled the ice cream from me, our fingers brushing; his warm against my cold hand.

"Okay." He nodded as he dug in.

I watched him slowly pull the spoon out of his mouth, his eyes fluttering in pleasure and he groaned. Immediately, my brain pushed forth the image of him doing such a thing with my cock in place of that spoon.

Fuck, now I'm hard.

That didn't take long.

I grunted in response as I turned away, both to shift my erection and grab my ice cream. Weston plopped himself on the bed, kicking his legs out. I realized at that moment that he'd also kicked his shoes off, and his bright, "Fuck Around & Find Out" socks pulled my attention. It was a quirky thing to see, amidst his finely tailored, dark slacks and his button up shirt.

It was actually kind of cute.

"Nice socks," I teased him.

Weston only wiggled his toes and raised his eyebrows. "That's my motto in life, Cade. Fuck around and find out."

I shook my head as I took my seat next to him.

"You're something else, you know that," I said as Weston turned the tv on, channel flipping. I dove in for a bit of ice cream.

"One hundred percent. And now you know it too," he said with a smile, settling on...

Of course he'd pick Star Wars Phantom Menace.

Could this man be any more perfect?

The movie had already started, so it was in the middle, but I didn't care. I took another bite of my ice cream as Weston did the same.

I leaned in closer, just a bit as the cold set in. Weston stiffened from the contact, as if he was afraid, but of what I wasn't sure.

Instinctively, I curled a little closer, seeking his warmth, and almost immediately he eased up. He wrapped his arm around my shoulders and I yawned.

The Phantom Menace was always boring to me, and I found it hard to stay awake. The low hum of Weston's breath, the rise and fall of his chest, the droning on of the movie dialogue, and a full stomach was too much to fight.

"Go to sleep Cade," Weston whispered.

And I couldn't fight his words, his command. I was really fucking tired.

"Yes, sir," I whispered as I drifted off to sleep, warm and sated.

The last thought I had before sleep overcame me was that I was falling in love with this man, and that scared me more than any public speaking event.

Because Weston had made it abundantly clear Jasper Springs wasn't his home, but as I drifted off to sleep in his arms, I dared to dream that maybe one day it could be.

CHAPTER 27

WHEN I WOKE UP, I was aware of two things. My arm had gone numb, and Cade was wrapped around me like a damn lemur on the bed. I shifted us, careful not to jostle him too much and wake him.

His lips parted just enough that I could hear tiny soft snores, his dark eyelashes standing out against his sunlit skin. The light of morning bathed him like an angel, and I couldn't help but think that's exactly what he looked like in my arms.

I steadied my breath as I ran my fingers through his soft hair, my heart lifting as he sleepily moaned out a sound of contentment from my touch.

I want to keep you and this moment forever.

However, that was the moment my pain in the ass parents decided to call me. Or more accurately, my pain in the ass father.

The annoying call broke the spell of perfection, and Cade shifted in my arms as I regrettably pulled away.

"Yes, father?" I said probably much harsher than I'd meant to, but I was still a bit tired, and as far as I was concerned it was still too early to deal with Rhodes Family Drama.

I had just woken up, for fuck's sake.

Like the businessman he was, he didn't even address our tense *discussion* at last night's barely eaten dinner. Instead, he just steamrolled right over it, launching into his serious dad tone.

"I'm holding a meeting today on the fifth floor, conference room A. Your presence is mandatory." His tone conveyed all business, commanding and with little room for refusal.

A part of me instinctively wanted to refuse on principle, because there was nothing I hated more than being forced into anything.

Especially by my father.

Fencing lessons, boarding school, a job I didn't think I was qualified for.

But I also knew that my father rarely spoke to me like *this*.

I could count on my hand the number of times he'd sounded so serious, his tone making his order seem absolutely imperative.

Which made me sit up straighter, my muscles tightened. Everything about his words caused panic to form in the pit of my stomach.

This can't be good.

Cade groggily mumbled something beside me, but it was white noise as I tried to focus on finding my own voice.

"I understand," I said, my own voice not betraying how truly worried I was.

If my presence was *mandatory*, I knew this was probably it. The day I'd been dreading since that summer before I'd graduated.

"Be there at ten o'clock. Don't be late," he said curtly, before hanging up on me, leaving me to stew in my panic alone.

The sound of a toilet flushing in the background pulled me from my waking nightmare, reminding me I *wasn't* alone. I turned to see Cade strolling through the doorway, stopping as our eyes met.

I noted the time on the nightstand clock read eight thirty. I had exactly an hour and a half until the damn world came crashing down.

My only thought was I wished I could have

spent it with Cade. Curled up under the covers, kissing him until he begged me to stop. Ordering room service and just laying in bed watching terrible hotel movies.

But life just wasn't fucking fair, sometimes.

"Who was that?" Cade asked as I climbed off the bed, pulling off my shirt. I folded it neatly and set it on the left side of my suitcase, doing the same with my slacks until I was down to my briefs. I could feel Cade's eyes on me, the heat of his gaze. I reached for a pair of clean slacks and a lilac silk shirt.

"My father. Unfortunately, I have an early meeting today," I said without inflection.

"Oh, okay," Cade said softly, his voice full of unspoken words.

I wished I could stay and coax out his truths, but unfortunately I needed to get my shit together and get out the door as soon as possible if I wanted to make it to the Rhodes building on time, and have time to at least grab a coffee or something. The traffic here in the morning was thicker than I'd thought it would be for such a small town.

I pulled on my slacks, buckling my belt with haste. I shimmied into my shirt, buttoning the buttons in the quickest sprint, before taking a seat on the bed to put my socks and shoes on, adjusting my watch.

"I'm really sorry about this, Cade, really. I am. I just—"

"I get it, Weston. Duty calls. I have a job too," he said, but I did not miss the sadness in his voice. I grabbed my deodorant off the nightstand, sprayed myself with my signature cologne, and ran a hand through my messy hair if only to help smooth the "I'd just woken up" look over. I was ready for Rhodes Family Drama in a matter of minutes.

At least on the outside.

Cade turned to me as I headed past him for the door. I stopped, my hand on the doorknob before turning to look back at him and his puppy dog blue eyes.

He looked like someone had eaten the last cookie from the cookie jar, and I hated it.

I hated that such a look was my fault.

Damn it, dad, why couldn't you do this on any other fucking day?

I pulled away from the door for a moment, taking a step toward Cade. He didn't make any sudden movements, instead just watched me intently as I invaded his space until we were close enough I could touch him.

And because I'd always been a damn glutton for punishment, I reached out and set my hand on his hip, pulling him into my space.

He fell into me with ease, without hesitation, as his pristine irises stared into my own.

"I'll see you at the fundraiser today," I said, the words hopeful and a promise all their own.

Cade sighed, his gaze dipping to my lips as he set his hand on my hip, fingernails pushing against the soft silk of my shirt, gripping me with newfound possession.

I liked the feeling, but I didn't have time to fall into Cade's sexy touch like I wanted to.

That would have to wait for later.

Later is what I should focus on, instead of the immense guilt of abandoning this perfect man right now or this meeting.

"Yeah, yeah, of course," he said calmly, nodding.

I set my hands on the side of his face, my thumb brushing over the soft, pliable flesh of his bottom lip. Between the look of longing in his eyes, the guilt, and the overwhelming *need* to bury myself into Cade until I disappeared, I was powerless to resist him when he leaned up and kissed me.

He ran his hands up my side, heated palms burning little trails of fire along my skin through the silk fabric. I softened from his touch, my shoulders relaxing as I let him coax my tongue into his mouth, as he sucked at my lower lip with a feral heat that I wanted to taste over and over again.

I broke away, breathless.

No one had ever kissed me like *that,* man or woman.

Like I was a damn bloody diamond in the rough.

Like I was *everything.*

"Okay," I said as I pulled away, immediately hating how empty and cold I felt away from his arms, from his magnetic pull.

I opened the door without looking back, because I knew if I did, I would never leave.

CHAPTER 28

WESTON

CONFERENCE ROOM A was the biggest conference room in the whole building. While most investors and clients scheduled their meetings for one or two people, and on occasion, with a team, I'd only ever had the chance to see a meeting in Conference Room A once, and that was the summer I'd volunteered.

Then, it had a been a meeting with another firm in the city, Sandusky Security, one of our biggest competitors at the time. My father proposed a truce, a merger of sorts. Thankfully, the other company agreed, but that didn't mean it was an easy one or two person affair. Since we basically bought out the company, that day the entirety of their company, their staff, and the owners had been housed in the room that held a hundred people. Our staff, our executives and those privy to the business side of the merger were all required to be there, for negotiations and for the confirmation of announcement that Sandusky Security and Rhodes Enterprises had become one.

But that didn't compare to the amount of people in the board room today... including my mother, who looked like she was nursing a hangover, with her bug-eyed black sunglasses in a natural lighting room at ten in the morning.

I took my seat next to her begrudgingly, sliding her a bottle of Fiji from the stocked bar in the corner of the conference room.

Dad always liked to have the bar stocked for the big meetings. People were more likely to be agreeable to whatever bullshit you're throwing at them when they were drinking at ten in the morning. And even if they weren't, everyone likes a free drink.

"Thanks, sweetie," she said with a sigh as she unscrewed the cap, her perfectly manicured nails glinting in the natural light filtering in.

Maybe it was my dread, maybe it was because I'd had a good night's sleep for the first time in a long time, and maybe it was because I was just feeling candid, but whatever the reason was, I eased up next to her as the rest of the suits dwindled in one by one.

"Mom, about last night…"

"It's okay, Weston, we don't have to talk about it," she said with a defeated sigh.

I batted my Fiji water back and forth in my hands, chewing my lip. Despite the anxiety swelling in my stomach, I had the overwhelming inkling to confess the truth to her.

"I… I met someone. Recently," I spoke softly.

She turned to me, peering at me over her shades to show me bright eyes full of shock.

"Weston, honey, don't take this the wrong way, but you meet a lot of people. You're going to have to give me a little more."

I bristled in my seat, knowing this was a dangerous game to play with her. My mother, as sweet as she could be, could still be quite a gossip hound, and the last thing I wanted was for Cade to end up water cooler chit chat.

But still, I felt the burdening need to be truthful. To lay it out on the table.

My father liked to think I was some playboy asshole, dicking down men that were after our fortune and nothing else, and that was embarrassing for him and the company. And being as I'd never done a thing to correct him, nor had I ever brought anyone into our Rhodes Family Soap Opera, I supposed maybe on some level he was right and I agreed with him. He and my mother didn't know I *wanted* things to change. I wanted someone different, but money complicates things. It always has and it always will.

"I met a *guy*, mom," I said as Cynthia passed out waters to a few of the men pouring in. I noted the time on the clock said it was 9:55 am, and we had a few minutes to spare. My father wasn't there yet, but I knew he liked to be exact with things. He'd waltz in the place at ten and launch into whatever it was he had to say immediately, giving no room for buffering.

My words must have registered for her as her mouth formed a tiny 'o' and she nodded, just as my father came in and shut the door.

His scoured the room, landing on my mother and I with a soft, melancholy look.

I nearly jumped out of my seat when my mother slid her hand over mine.

CHAPTER 29

Weston

The announcement of my father's retirement shouldn't have been surprising, but I guess that maybe on some level I hadn't though he'd actually do it. My entire life, my dad's main focus was his company. He'd talked about retiring years ago, but it had fallen to the wayside. He just couldn't give up control, and he didn't *want* to leave his company in the hands of just anyone.

He wanted to leave it with me, and I was not in any way, shape, or form ready to take over a company. Nor did I want to.

I just wanted to live my life. Work my dumb

little job, fuck the pretty assholes who didn't care about me, and experience everything the world had to offer me outside of Jasper Springs.

But as my dad elaborated to the room full of men that it was simply time for him to hand over the reins, I couldn't help but feel nauseous.

He'd said he would do his best to hire the *right* person for the job, the *best* person, whoever that may be. But I think all of us in that room knew it was push come to shove.

Could I really refuse?

Could I say no now that it was really happening?

And then he looked at me. For a brief moment before he wrapped up his speech, he looked at me with a gleam in his eyes.

This wasn't just a planned retirement, no. My father was calling checkmate. He was well and truly putting the ball in my court.

I knew he would entertain the idea of hiring someone else, because my father was many things; organized and ten steps ahead were two of them. But the minute I came to him and said yes, none of those candidates would matter.

Suddenly, I felt like I couldn't breathe. The room was closing in around me and I needed to get out.

I needed to be as far away from Rhodes Enterprises as I could get.

Just as my father opened the floor for questions, I took my leave.

I calmly stood, I'm sure distracting some much better equipped employees than I, and I walked as fast as I could down the hall.

When I heard footsteps behind me, I didn't turn around. Instead, I kept my eye on the elevators, picking up my pace.

"Weston, stop!" my father hollered.

I didn't stop. Instead, I hurried toward the hall, hearing him picking up his own pace.

"I'm not doing this, right now, dad," I said with a huff.

"Then when the hell will you do it?" he growled. I stopped in front of the elevator, hitting the button with rapid aggression.

"There are a hundred people in that room who are far more qualified for this job than me, and you know that," I said boldly.

"On paper, yes. But the heart of this company isn't quarterly reports and product development, and I think somewhere deep down, you know that," he said.

I turned to look at him, that hopeful, wistful look in his eyes filling up with... tears?

My dad *never* cried.

And something about that made my heart break.

I was the worst son on the planet. I didn't

deserve any of this. The company, or his unwavering faith that I could do this if he just... *forced* my hand enough.

"I've got a fundraiser to attend," I said as the elevator door opened, and I walked away.

CADE

I LAZILY STROKED the soft fur of an orange and white striped kitten in my lap. Diane called our friends from the Deer Park Rescue, albeit very last minute, but they'd agreed to let us take some kittens to the event to help promote their adoptions.

The tiny kitten pawed at my shirt, stretching her little claws to make biscuits in the folds of the fabric, and I sighed.

I'd been at the event for a couple hours, and although I had several people stop to play with the kittens and ask about the adoptions, as well as take some flyers, stickers, and pens from the hospital, I couldn't help but feel worried for the one person I didn't see.

I knew it was probably selfish of me to expect Weston to show up like the breath of fresh air he was, especially given he'd practically run out the door this morning to make a mandatory meeting at his family's company. But something about his departure, no matter how sound the reason was, left me feeling empty.

He'd said he'd be there, and I wanted to believe him.

But there was also a part of me that knew this was par for the course for me. I'd had a history of falling for assholes who I couldn't really count on.

I gazed down at the kitten who had stopped making biscuits, and was now curled up in the folds of my shirt, snoozing away.

I guessed she was bored of waiting too.

"Why so gloomy, sunshine?" a familiar voice pulled me from my thoughts.

I looked up to see Mitch, complete with camera, as usual. I swear he never left home without the damn thing.

"I'm not gloomy..." I said, even though I knew the words were a lie.

Mitchell kneeled to take some photos of the kittens in their pen.

"You are a shit liar, Cade. Seriously."

I rolled my eyes, but decided it was better to just be honest than make something up.

It wasn't like Weston was around anyway to hear me.

"Weston said he'd be here today. At the fundraiser."

Mitchell looked up from his spot on the ground.

"You haven't seen him?" Mitchell asked, reaching in the pen to stroke a grey and white striped kitten on its head with his finger.

"No..."

"He's been schmoozing around all afternoon. I think I saw him over by the park like ten minutes ago."

My blood chilled, and I was worried maybe my anxieties were right. Maybe he was ignoring me.

Had I been wrong about him?

It wouldn't have been the first time I'd looked at a man with rose tinted glasses, but...

Last night, as we cuddled on the bed together, drowning our stress in ice cream and Star Wars, I thought that maybe he *was* different. Maybe, just maybe this time I'd gotten it right.

"Earth to Cade," Mitchell said, and I realized I'd completely spaced out.

"Sorry, Mitch, I—"

"You want me to man the desk a bit? You can walk around and grab something to eat, maybe find your new boy toy," he teased.

I couldn't help the flush of blood into my cheeks at his insinuation.

"It's not like that. It's—"

"Then what is it like, Cade? Hmmm? I've known you a long time, and I've never seen you get all doe-eyed like this over anyone. Even the assholes that came before. For God's sake, when Dawson broke up with you, you didn't even bat an eye. But this guy has you all up in arms because you just haven't *seen* him? If I didn't know any better, I'd say you were in love."

His words hit me like a freight train.

I'd only known Weston for barely three days. Surely it was impossible to fall in love with someone you hardly knew for seventy-two hours. This was real life, not a Disney movie.

But as Mitch's words settled on me, infiltrating my walls, I knew they held truth.

I was head over heels in love with Weston Rhodes, and that was terrifying.

Because giving anyone that kind of power over your heart, especially when you weren't sure where you stood... was scary.

"Okay, maybe you don't need to leave..." Mitchell said as he stood.

"One loverboy coming straight at you,

twelve o clock," Mitchell cooed as he snapped a picture of Weston amongst the crowd.

My heart lifted at the sight. Seeing his lilac sleeves rolled up, two buttons popped, his dark hair blowing in the wind. He was breathtaking set against the varied trees and flowers, looking every bit the man of my dreams.

Was I the man of his?

I didn't know.

I didn't know what I was to Weston. After all, he'd been clear he was only here on business, and eventually that business would end.

We'd been lucky the event in Jasper Springs had been so successful. Successful enough that Rhodes had decided to put on two additional events, the one today and one at the end of the week in Paradise. But the events couldn't go on forever. Eventually, Weston would have to leave, and I wasn't sure where that left us.

Would I be just a Jasper Springs fling?

Some memory he looked back fondly on?

A transition from one stage to the next?

From one bed to the next?

"Hey," he said as he approached my booth, sliding his hands in his pockets.

I stood, holding the sleepy kitten tight to my chest, letting my fingers slide over the soft fur to keep myself steady.

I looked up at his dark, green eyes, and the world around me blurred.

Yeah, I was definitely in love with Weston.

There was no question.

Fuck me.

"Hey," I said, feeling my throat go dry.

"I'm sorry I didn't come find you earlier, but things have just been... Well, it was a rough morning."

"Oh," I said, suddenly at a loss for words. My brain screamed a thousand things at me.

Tell him the truth, tell him how you feel.

Ask him how he feels.

Kiss him.

Weston's gaze fell to the kitten in my arms.

"Make a new friend?" he said, flashing me a grin.

I didn't miss how it lit up his eyes. I stroked the soft, warm kitten as I swallowed nervously.

"Let me make this morning up to you?" he asked, his gaze finally leaving my fingers and meeting mine.

There were a hundred things I wanted to say, but instead all that came out of my mouth was, "You do an awful lot of making up."

Weston's shoulders fell and instantly I felt like an asshole. I hadn't meant it to sound as harsh as it did, but I guess I was still a little melancholy from this morning. Everything had been so perfect, and then just like before, we'd both been thrust back into the world of responsibility.

Before I could speak, apologize for sounding like an absolute ass, Weston ran a hand through his hair, his eyebrows furrowing.

"I'd like to change that, you know," he said gently.

The kitten stirred in my arms, yawning and stretching.

"A fresh start?" I asked, feeling all the negativity suddenly draining from me.

Weston reached out to rub the kitten between its ears, and she purred like a damn motor from his touch.

Same kitten, same.

"You can pick the place," Weston said smoothly.

I watched his fingers gently stroke her fur, watched the sadness fall on his face, and all the disappointment, all the worry and concern faded away like it hadn't been there at all.

I'd been so busy thinking about myself and my own self-sabotaging feelings that I hadn't once thought about how Weston must have felt.

Maybe he didn't want to leave either.

Maybe he needed this, needed *me* just as bad as I needed him.

So I decided in that moment, that even if

this ended in flames, that for the time being I would be everything he needed. For however long it lasted.

Because against all odds, I loved this man.

"Fine. Grab your phone," I instructed.

Weston's lips tweaked up in the corner.

"I like you bossy, you know," he said, his voice husky as he stopped petting the little motor in my arms, sliding out his phone. He cast me a dark, sexy look that made my stomach flip.

I spouted off my address, keeping my face devoid of emotion. As far as he knew, it was just another restaurant in town, a café, or something like Bernard's. After all, Weston didn't spend much time here, so there was no way for him to know the address I'd given him was actually my house.

"Meet me there at say... seven o clock?" I asked, sternly but also just in case he actually *did* have some sort of plans or business dinner.

He smiled sexily in return.

"It's a date," he said, just as a group of teenage girls caught sight of the kittens, running over with loud, shrieking squeals.

"It's a date," I said as he walked away, smiling from ear to ear.

And it's going to be the best date ever.

CHAPTER 31

I THOUGHT there had to be some mistake. Though Cade had been secretive about where he'd picked, a part of me thought I must have genuinely misheard him. Because when my Uber showed up to a quaint, little brick house complete with a white picket fence and lawn gnomes in the front yard, I was sure I had to have missed something.

Instinctively, I pulled out my phone to double check the message, as I texted Cade to tell him I was about five minutes away. But just as I queued up my messenger to tell him I'd be a few minutes late because my driver had obviously taken a wrong turn, I saw him.

Standing on the porch in a blue polo, hands in his dark wash jeans, with a smirk.

The little brat.

He'd actually gotten one over on me, and I let out a small chuckle in the space of the car. I slid my phone back in my pocket before leaving the car, taking my time to walk up the sidewalk until I'd reached his porch.

"Are you taking me somewhere special?" I teased him.

Cade cocked his head to the side as he set his hand on my hip, tugging me closer.

"Of course. You deserve only the best, right?" Cade teased me back.

I slid my arm around his waist, pulling him closer to me. His bright blue eyes sparkled with mischief and I was powerless to resist crushing my lips against his with appreciation. He tasted like strawberries and champagne, and it was divine.

"Starting the party without me?" I purred against his soft lips.

Cade gazed up at me with intrigue.

"I can't help that every time I know I'm going to see you, I get a little nervous."

My heart lifted at his words.

They were honest, endearing, and carried a hint of vulnerability I'd never known anyone to exhibit to me romantically before.

"I make you nervous?" I asked as I brought my lips to his again.

Cade groaned into my mouth, and I could feel him hardening against me, the sensation of his arousal against my own sudden erection making me see stars.

Instinctively, I let my lips wander to his jaw, nibbling, sucking at the flesh until he was practically putty in my arms.

"Fuck yes," he breathed as he relaxed in my hold.

I pulled away suddenly, taking stock of the look on his face. His swollen lips, flushed cheeks. My blood raced beneath my skin, my stomach tying into knots as I took in the beauty and the aura of the man in front of me.

"The feeling's mutual," I said, awestruck.

Cade shook his head, dispelling the momentary lapse of sanity, sliding his hand in mine as he pulled me toward the open door.

"Come in," he said, his voice catching a little to convey he really *was* nervous.

A part of me found that endearing. That I could have such an effect on anyone, let alone someone as perfect as Cade.

Inside the house, I was immediately struck with the scent of garlic, butter, and perfectly aged parmesan reggiano. My mouth watered almost instantly.

Not to mention the cozy atmosphere. While there was a fireplace, it looked like it was walled off. Instead of logs, long stemmed metal candlesticks were strewn across the bottom, and I had to appreciate the ornate mahogany mantle that looked like something out of the forties.

The living room itself wasn't huge, but it was full of character. Little Star Wars figurines, bright, woven blankets, and candles strewn about nearly everywhere, but none lit.

The couch alone begged me to jump in and take a long needed nap. Combined with the scent of butter and cheese, I felt like I'd died and gone to heaven. I stood there like an idiot, while Cade left me to my devices, coming back with a glass of fizzy pink champagne, complete with sliced strawberry at the bottom of the flute.

"Are we celebrating something?" I asked.

Cade smirked. "The opening of Cade's Cafe, of course."

"The place seems quite promising."

"And you haven't even had the best part yet," he said as he flung a kitchen towel over his shoulder as he headed into the kitchen, and I followed him without question.

His kitchen was barely a quarter the size of the one in the Rhodes Family home, but somehow it felt more open and warm than any other I'd been in. I took a seat at the island, clutching my drink as I watched him toss food in the pan, manning a couple different pots and pans with ease. The island itself was set for two, complete with little bowls of salad in bamboo bowls that had black painted paw prints on them.

Perhaps there was a time I would have found such a thing kitchsy, or tacky even, but here in Cade's home, it was cute. Endearing, even.

I watched him in awe, as he moved about his kitchen, watched the muscles in his arm flex as he flipped things in pans, taking sight of his firm ass and the way the dark wash jeans hugged his form.

Was there anything this man couldn't do?

"I hope you like risotto, because if not, you're screwed," he said with a light laugh.

I set my drink down as I swiveled back and forth on the barstool.

"I have many acquired tastes, I can assure you," I said as I watched him spoon the mixture into a deep, white bowl. "You didn't have to do this, you know."

He walked over with a bowl of fresh risotto. It smelled *divine,* and when he sprinkled fresh herbs on top from a small dish on the island, I realized without a doubt that this man was absolutely perfect, and as he sat down across from me with his own plate, smiling genuinely at me as he picked up his fork, he said, "I know, but I wanted to."

And at that moment, I knew.

Cade was as good as they came. He was passionate, smart, attractive, and had a heart that was full of so much love it would have been hard for me to *not* fall in love with him.

Because as I watched Cade blow across the steaming hot food on his fork, I knew without a doubt, I was falling in love with this man.

This man who seemed to make the rest of the world fall away, who seemed to be able to draw out the darkest parts of me and make everything... okay.

"My dad, uh, announced his retirement today," I said as I took a stab at my food.

"Is that a good thing?" He took a sip of his champagne.

The glow of the kitchen light lit up his soft blonde hair like a halo.

"He wants me to take over the company," I said the words out loud for the first time since this morning, feeling their weight. I expected them to be heavy, like steel beams, but in the presence of Cade, they didn't feel quite as heavy.

"And that's not something you want?" he pressed, taking another bite of food.

I took a bite myself, relishing in the smooth,

buttery texture, and the taste was absolutely perfect.

"Oh my God, Cade, this is *amazing*." I groaned my pleasure as I hurriedly went for another forkful.

"Thanks. I know it's not like authentic or five star, but... sometimes a homemade meal is nice too, you know."

I didn't know. Not really. When I thought about all the homemade food I'd had, it wasn't really quite like this.

Margo made most of our food, and my parents were always obsessed with healthy foods and gourmet stuff that didn't really appeal to me. I would have been fine with a pepperoni pizza, but as it was I didn't even have cheesy, junky pizza until I'd moved into the city on my own.

No one had ever made me dinner before... romantically. I'd never gone on a date that didn't end in a large bill, up until I'd come here to Jasper Springs.

"I just don't know if I'm right for the job," I said as I took another bite of my dinner.

"And no one has ever made me dinner before, so you're definitely getting a five star Michelin review from me," I said as I finished my bowl in two more, appreciative bites.

Cade looked at me in shock.

"You're kidding, right?" he asked.

I shook my head. "Wish I was, but no. Most of my exes preferred to dine out at the swankiest restaurants and bars as opposed to sitting in and ordering room service, and my parents never cooked. We had staff for that."

"I'm sorry, I didn't mean to sound ignorant." Cade set his fork down, reaching his hand across the table to cover mine.

"You didn't. I promise. It's just... you're right, it *is* nice. This whole place is nice, and you..."

"If you say I'm nice, I'm going to have to take your drink away," Cade teased me.

"You're perfect. How in the hell are you still single?

I watched as Cade blushed six shades of red.

"Well, there is this guy..." he said shyly, avoiding my gaze, and immediately my blood ran cold.

Life had always managed to knock me on my ass when I least expected it, so in theory if Cade really was interested in someone else, that would have been my luck, but the way he looked up at me from under his lashes told me there was no one else.

There was only... me.

Oh, Cade...

"Really?" I said, deciding to play his game.

"Tell me about this guy, is he an ass?"

Cade shook his head as he collected our bowls.

"Mmm, I thought maybe he was at first, but he's kind of surprised me, actually," he said.

"Oh really? How so?" I asked as I followed him to the sink.

I watched as he set the bowls in the sink, noting he couldn't see me, or my hands that settled on the edge of his counter alongside him.

He turned around, realizing he was trapped between his counter and my body. His eyes lit up with mischief and excitement, a smile ghosting his lips.

"Well, he seems to be kind of a loyal family guy, and he's a pretty good singer, not to mention he's hot as hell and brings out a side of me I didn't know existed."

"Is that so?" I whispered as Cade settled his hands around my waist, pulling me closer, flush against him. His fingers dipped below my waistband at my back, drawing little circles against my skin.

His eyelashes fluttered as he nodded.

"And I think..." He swallowed, his gaze dipping to my lips. His breathing caught in his throat, and he seemed nervous.

"What? What do you think?" I asked, imploring his gaze with my own.

Cade looked up at me with clear, blue eyes and in them I could see a hundred unsaid words, a thousand unspoken emotions.

I'd always dreamed of someone who would look at me the way he did that night in his kitchen.

I was head over heels in love with Cade Green.

Because when I looked in his eyes, I knew that the sky was the limit.

"I think I might be falling for him," he whispered, his words shaky.

I reached out, pushing some stray strands of golden hair behind the shell of his warm ear.

"Are you scared of falling, Cade?" I whispered, even though we didn't need to. However, it felt as though the words themselves were the size of great beasts.

"I'm just scared he doesn't feel the same." Cade leaned his cheek into my palm.

"I think he does," I said as I leaned my forehead against his, taking a deep breath.

I'd never considered myself a courageous man on any account, but I'd also never been afraid of wearing my heart on my sleeve. I'd given so much of myself, my body, and my money to the wrong people in hopes of one day striking gold, that I'd never considered that love, real love, couldn't be bought.

It was unearthed beneath rubble and dirt, it was born out of fate and circumstances beyond our control.

It was found where one least expected it.

Cade's entire body relaxed as I slid a hand around his waist, pulling him close until I couldn't stand it anymore.

I leaned down and took his lips like they were the dessert I'd been waiting for, for a thousand years.

Cade sank into my hold, wrapping his arms around my neck as he kissed me back, his lips and tongue still carrying a hint of buttery cheese flavor.

And when we broke away, Cade looked at me with a happiness that made my heart want to burst.

I never thought I'd ever be capable of making someone smile like that.

"It wouldn't be a date without a movie to follow," he said sweetly as he gently pushed me back.

I couldn't help but smile in return.

CHAPTER 32

ALL THE ASSUMPTIONS I'd had about Cade's couch turned out to be true. It was the softest couch I'd ever had the pleasure of being sucked into.

Cade relaxed with his legs propped up on his ottoman, complete with adorable bunny slippers, one hand behind his head, completely in his element as he focused on the actors on screen.

I couldn't tell you what was happening or even what movie we watched.

Because I couldn't take my eyes off him.

The light of the television bathed him in an

ethereal glow, and I scooted closer to him. The motion pulled his attention away for a moment.

"You okay?" he asked, taken by the sudden movement.

Being this close to him, my arm stretched over his stomach, my head on his shoulder was too much.

I nodded as I took in the sight of him, looking down at me.

When we were upright, I had a good few inches on him, being nearly six foot one myself, but in bed, or on a couch, I could cuddle up close to Cade and look up at *him*.

Like the damn angel he was.

I nodded in response. I was better than okay. I felt amazing.

I pulled him down to my lips, taking him by surprise. I loved kissing Cade, loved how his lips felt plush against my own, how he'd slowly let his tongue breach mine, stroking it until he elicited little groans of pleasure from my mouth, just from his kiss alone.

I wanted to kiss him as much as I could, among other things.

It occurred to me at that moment, as Cade slipped his tongue in my mouth and pulled me closer with his free arm that was wrapped around my shoulders, that while our first meeting had ended with me fucking Cade until he begged me to let him come, we hadn't been physical since. Part of that was on me, because while I wanted to fuck Cade's beautiful mouth and asshole every time I saw him, I was trying to be *good*.

I was trying to be a man deserving of him.

But something in between us had shifted during that time. The tables had somehow turned.

I pulled Cade closer, wrapping my leg over his hip. The movie in the background droned on as Cade instinctually ground his cock against my stomach, as his tongue probed mine with hurried motion, as he bit at my lower lip.

"I'm better than okay," I said breathlessly as I pushed back against him, settling him against his cushions. I straddled his lap, my cock straining against my jeans. I grabbed his face in my hands, kissing him with all that I was.

"You can tell me to stop if you don't want to —" I breathed as I looked down at his face, full of emotion and desire.

He looked slightly torn, but also... *hopeful.*

"I want to," he breathed, his voice shaking again with nerves.

"But?"

"No *but*, Wes. I want you. I've wanted you since that night at M's Place, since the morning I woke up with you next to me, I just... needed some time to process everything. I didn't... I didn't know if you would stay."

Something in his voice called to my soul in a way no one else had ever done.

Did I want to stay?

Here, in Jasper Springs?

With Cade?

Running my father's company?

The fact I couldn't say no entirely made me feel like for the first time in my life, I didn't know what I was capable of.

I only knew that in the arms of Cade Green, I felt like I could do anything. So that's what I focused on.

"And now?" I asked as I gazed down at perfect, crystalline eyes.

"Will you stay?" he asked, licking his lips. "Tonight? Will you stay? With me?" His eyes searched mine for answers I wasn't sure I knew myself, but for the moment I said the one that felt the truest.

"Yes," I said, sliding my hand down his chest, resting my fingers at the hem of his pants. His cock twitched beneath me, poking my thigh from where I straddled him.

"How could I not when your couch is the coziest couch I've ever been on?" I teased him.

Cade smirked as he rested his hand on my

ass, pulling me against him with teasing force. His eyes lit up with desire.

"Besides, I don't think I'm quite done making things up to you," I said as my fingers deftly unhooked his belt. His gasp of breath gave me goosebumps. I slowly tugged his jeans and boxers down just enough that his cock could spring free.

"If you make up this much, we may need some couples counseling," he taunted me, but all laughs dissipated in the air when I stared into his beautiful eyes, never breaking his gaze.

And spit in my hand.

I lathered my saliva along my fingers before teasing his entrance as I positioned myself between his knees. His pants shimmied down his legs from the movement.

Instantly, Cade flexed and arched his back from the shock of the sensation as I let my spit-covered fingers tease him, massaging the tight skin.

"Holy fuck, Wes, I—"

"Are you okay? Do you want me to stop?" I asked, half worried I'd misread his desire.

Cade shook his head. "No, absolutely not. Please don't stop," he breathed hurriedly, desire on his tongue more than prevalent.

I continued to stroke the taut skin at his hole

with my fingertip, sliding over the puckered hole, teasing his entrance.

Cade thrust himself against me, seeking more of the friction, and I slid my forefinger in a little further.

I stole a glance at his face, which had gone a little slack as he closed his eyes, thrusting his hips, his gleaming dick in the air.

And when I took his swollen head in my mouth, he cried out a string of curses, but I didn't stop until he was in the back of my throat. His asshole clenched my finger like a vice and I started to build my pace. The sleek, wet sound of sucking melded with the slip and slide of my lubricated finger, and just when I felt I'd stretched him enough, I slid another in.

"Oh God, Wes, please, I..."

I hollowed my cheeks, knowing it wouldn't be long. I could feel his cock pulsing, throbbing in my mouth, the saltiness of his precum coating my tongue.

"I'm going to go any second, I—" His voice got all tight, all screwed up right before he came.

Warm, salty cum filled my mouth, and I swallowed it down like the desperate, thirsty son of a bitch I was. I wanted to make Cade feel as good as he made me feel on every level, including the physical.

His cock softened as he caught his breath,

and I licked the remaining drops of his sweetness from his head as I came up for air.

Cade looked down at me from where he sat, his eyes full of lust and fire.

"Okay, I think that about sums up my groveling. Think I'm done now," I said with a smirk, wiping some of his mess from the corner of my mouth.

Cade sat up, pulling me against his wet cock, smothering me in a possessive, hot kiss that knocked *me* on my ass.

I opened my mouth without warning, groaning as Cade's tongue probed mine. He moaned in response, and I thought I could see literal stars.

His hands rushed at my belt and he slid his palm down the front of my pants with a welcome aggression, grabbing at my thick, aching cock. The motion pushed my pants to my ankles, leaving me in nothing but my briefs, feeling tight and constrained.

"You don't play fair," he whispered against my lips.

I snickered against his mouth and then moaned into his kiss in response as I thrust my leaking cock against his hand, separated by the thin fabric of my briefs.

"What are you going to do about it, good boy?"

Cade shoved my briefs down to my knees before grabbing me by my hips and upending me onto the couch cushions with a forceful flip. He shook off the rest of his pants as I did the same. My cock bobbed like a beacon in the night, guiding Cade and his mouth to us like the northern star.

"Maybe I'm going to punish you," he growled, but his voice didn't shake at all.

In fact, it was the clearest, sternest tone I'd heard him take yet.

Well, damn. Color me surprised. Our good boy might have a little Dom in him after all.

I leaned back on my elbows, propping myself up so I could look at him while he licked the bead of precum off my tip. His wet, pink tongue licked me from balls to head, slowly, taking in just the tip, teasing me, taunting me. His right hand cupped my balls while his left stroked me slowly.

I thrust my throbbing cock against his lips, painting his mouth with another round of clear, wet arousal.

"Oh yeah? Joke's on you, sweetheart. I like to be the bad guy."

Cade didn't miss a beat as he slipped his right hand beneath my balls, teasing my entrance, much like I had with him, and just as I thought he was going to do the same, he pulled them away, leaving my insides wanting.

Well, that's not fair.

Instead, his heated eyes burned into mine, and he straddled my hips. My gaze dipped to his hand, which was now palming *his* already semi-hard cock.

The sight of him, naked from the waist down, pink, swollen cock in his palm as he looked at me was a beautiful torment.

I'd never wanted *anything* quite this bad. I reached for my own cock, but to my surprise, Cade swatted it away.

"I didn't say you could touch yourself," he said mischievously.

Oh, if this is the game you want to play, sweetheart, I am so in.

I can be your good boy too.

I feigned embarrassment, embellishing on the role if only for Cade and his enjoyment.

I enjoyed watching him like this, and I liked the idea of him being in control.

In all the years I'd been with men, I was always the one on top. The one calling the shots, the one commanding them to submit to me.

But looking at Cade from beneath his steel thighs, I wanted to be good.

I wanted to obey him, because I knew it would bring him so much pleasure.

And if he was happy, well...

Maybe I could find some happiness in that too.

"But I'm so full, I need to come," I embellished, playing right along. I watched his eyes dilate, watched as his cock twitched as I said the words. I had him, hook, line, and sinker.

"Not until I tell you to," he said as he let go of his cock, which was now thick and full, wetness already starting to pebble at the tip.

He was a natural.

He shifted his weight, and his position, until his length bobbed against my dick. Then he looked *me* straight in the eye, and spit into *his* hand, slapping his palms together to baste them in his spit before he wrapped both hands around our cocks.

The warmth of his palm, the wetness of his spit, and the rigidity of his hardness as he thrust his cock slowly against my own was maddening. I lifted my hips, thrusting against his hand, my aching cock needing the friction. Somewhere in the distance I heard my phone ringing, but I ignored it. Whoever it was, it could wait.

"Please," I rasped.

Cade picked up the pace, stroking us both with a hurried rhythm.

"Please, what?" he asked, licking his lips, gazing down at me with those perfect blue eyes full of lust and need, lips still swollen from kissing me.

"Please, Cade, make me come," I begged.

I kind of liked it, if I was being honest.

Being the bottom, my pleasure beholden to the golden god above me.

Though Cade didn't make it, I couldn't very well be disappointed.

Because as he erupted, his warm release spread over the both of us, only adding to the slick, wetness of his saliva.

I thrust my hips madly against him until I too came with a force that had my vision going white. Instinctively, I grabbed onto Cade, wrapping my arms around his neck and pulled him to me for a deep, passionate kiss as he let go. The motion as he leaned down trailed a mixed mess of cum along both of our stomaches, but I didn't care. I wrapped my legs around his hips, thrusting against his softening, wet cock, and I knew nothing would ever be the same again.

CHAPTER 33

Cade

I awoke on my couch to the sound of a ringtone I certainly didn't recognize.

I blinked, taking in my surroundings. Weston slept soundly beside me on the couch, under one of the many blankets. The phone vibrated and sounded against the table, and I realized it was his phone.

"Wes," I groaned as I reached for the phone, tossing it to him.

He roused, grabbing the phone as he groggily answered me.

"Cade, what..." Then his entire body stiffened as he answered.

"Yes?" His voice had gone from lazy in the morning, to serious and commanding again.

Work calls, obviously.

I swung my legs over the couch, my morning erection aching and full. I needed to take a piss, and then I needed a shower. I watched as Weston slid his briefs back on, brushing off the dried fluids of...

All the memories of last night, of our date, and our Netflix & chill session came rushing back to me. This time I didn't feel guilty or worried, though. This time when the blood rushed into my cheeks I felt... *happy.* Like I wanted to do it all over again.

The dinner, the laughing, the kissing.

The opening up of feelings.

The sex.

That first time we'd fucked, neither of us were properly coherent enough to really be present. Our inhibitions were down, sure. After all I *did* let him fuck me.

But last night was different. Not only were we both *present* for the experiences, but it felt like something deeper than that.

It didn't feel like mindless, sloppy sex with a stranger.

It felt like blinding, fulfilling sex with a *partner.*

All my lines were becoming blurred with

Weston Rhodes and I wasn't sure I wanted them to be clear anymore.

Not when there was so much beauty and love in the haze.

I made my way to the bathroom, relieving myself before washing off remnants of our dried spend that was all over my stomach. I padded out of the bathroom to my bedroom, grabbing a pair of clean grey sweatpants.

When I came back out, Weston was gone.

I called out, thinking maybe he'd just gone somewhere else to talk, there was no answer. I opened the door, catching the sight of him getting into a car, and before I could speak out, he was off.

Gone without so much as a goodbye.

Had I been wrong about Weston?

Had what we shared been in my head?

My heart broke as the negative thoughts of '*I told you so*' brushed forth and I slammed my fist against the brick, not hard enough to break, but enough that it made my knuckles sore.

At that moment, my phone went off, my alarm blaring at me to get up and get ready for work. I sighed, relenting for the moment as I headed back in the house, to my shower to wash off the pain, the sadness and the reality that I'd fucked up.

Again.

So much for a fresh start.

CHAPTER 34

Cade

At work, Diane sat at the desk, a serious look on her face.

"Everything okay?" I asked as I set my Dunkin Donuts iced coffee down. She looked pale.

"Something go wrong with the fundraiser, or..."

"No, it's, uh... the fundraiser's postponed," she said calmly.

"Oh, okay..."

"The CEO of Rhodes Enterprises had a heart attack last night. He'd announced his retirement, but no replacement has been named yet, so..."

My blood chilled.

How could I have been so selfish, so self-centered?

No wonder Weston had left without a word of goodbye.

No kid wants to get *that* call about their parents, and that's just the ones who don't have parents trying to convince them to run the family business.

Which happens to make millions.

"Oh shit, Diane, I'm sorry, I—" I slide out my phone immediately as she sighs.

"I mean, it's okay, we had two fundraisers, and while I haven't counted the donations yet from last night, I'm sure... I'm sure we'll be fine if they cancel the one on Friday."

I could hear the sadness and the disappointment in her voice. Despite the fact I didn't care for working the booths, I couldn't deny that the events had really good results. High turnouts, and the first event alone had brought in almost five thousand dollars. All that would go toward the hospital, toward care for animals who needed life saving surgeries and care credit funds as well as our rescue friends.

In fact, I'd wager that Rhodes Enterprises had helped us bring in more money in two events than we'd been capable of doing on our own in the last two years.

I texted Weston immediately, worried for him and what he must be going through.

Are you okay? I texted, immediately sending another, *I heard about your dad.*

Weston texted back, *No. I'm not.*

My heart broke for him. *Tell me what you need.*

I'd said the words because I knew he was hurting, knew he must be worried sick about his dad regardless of their personal issues.

I wasn't expecting his text back to say, *You. I need you.*

I looked up at Diane.

"Diane, I know I just came in but..."

She looked at me with a smirk.

"You think I don't know about you and the Rhodes kid?" she said, shaking her head.

I felt frozen in place. How...

She must have sensed my confusion, because she sighed. "Anyone with eyeballs can see the tension between you two in that photo in the paper. Plus all the ladies in town are talking about it. You have been seen together quite a bit..." Diane twisted her lips.

Busted.

"It just sort of... happened," I said. It wasn't a lie, but... how else could I explain who or what Weston was to me. Sure, we'd admitted that we had feelings for one another, but it wasn't like we'd declared our undying love or anything, but a part of me wished I had.

"I'm sure your boyfriend is a mess, so I'm going to be nice, just this once, Cade. You've done a lot for me this week, especially with the events. I'm more than equipped with a full staff here today. Take the day off. I know you're already off tomorrow, so just... do what you need to do and I'll see you on Saturday, yeah?" she said kindly.

I grabbed my coffee, twirling my keys in my hand.

"Thank you, Diane," I said with the utmost appreciation.

"Mhmm. Don't mention it loverboy. Go be the hero of your story today," she said with a wink and I was out the door in seconds.

When I got to the car, I texted Weston immediately.

Can you meet me at Penn's Bakery? Grab some coffee?

It was like an eternity until he'd messaged me back, and I started to fear the worst.

Be there in ten minutes.

I sped off in the direction of Penn's Bakery, my heart in my throat.

I had no idea what to do or how I was going to help.

All I knew was that I needed Weston just as

bad as he needed me, and if there was something I could do, even if it was meeting up over coffee and telling him everything would be okay, even though I didn't know it would be... that was what I would do.

Because I loved him.

I wanted to be everything he needed me to be and then some.

Because he was so much more to me.

Weston made me come alive. He inspired me, pushed me, and brought out parts of me I wanted to explore with great depth. I wasn't sure what the future held for us, but I knew as I hurried my ass over to Penn's Bakery, that I didn't care where the road led me.

As long as Weston was there too, I knew everything would be all right.

CHAPTER 35

CADE

I WALKED into Penn's Bakery to see Weston sitting in the corner booth, looking like a lost puppy. I slid into the seat across from him.

"Have you eaten anything?" I asked, noting he looked a little pale.

He shook his head. "No."

"Are you hungry?" I asked, going into crisis management mode, as Dawson would call it.

"I mean, sort of..." he said with a huff.

"Stay here," I commanded as I got up, heading over to the bakery counter.

"Cade..." Weston groaned.

I shot him a look that froze him in place.

"Hush. You need food. Preferably something

with a lot of sugar," I said, easing up on the last word. I hadn't meant to sound so tense or bossy, but that was becoming more of a thing the longer I was around Weston. It was like I'd finally found my voice.

"Yes, sir," he said with a light smile. The words warmed my very soul.

I took my time ordering us both some fruit filled croissants and coffee, and in no time we were both diving into the sweet confectionary delights and caffeine like they would heal all wounds.

"Is he going to be okay, your dad?" I asked, setting down my coffee.

Weston turned his dark eyes at me, nodding, his lips pressed in a thin line.

"Yeah. Doc thinks he'll probably make a full recovery, but he needs to stay away from stressful situations."

I nodded in response. "So, I guess that means he's not visiting the old family business any time soon."

Weston nodded. "I'm sure they're all running around like chickens today. He only announced his retirement yesterday, it was hardly any time to get *anything* in order," Weston said as he took a sip of his coffee.

"What will they do? Without a current

CEO? Is there someone they'll appoint interim, or..."

Weston shrugged. "I'm not sure, actually. But I should probably stop by at least to see if there's something I can do to make the transition easier. You know, for everyone involved..."

I realized at that moment, maybe before Weston ever did, that despite what he said, he did care.

He didn't think he was fit for the job, because in his eyes he wasn't perfect. He wasn't his father. But maybe he didn't have to be.

Maybe all he had to be was honest, caring, and compassionate.

I reached across the table, taking his hand. He didn't jump or shift. Instead, he squeezed my fingers as he interlaced his with mine.

"We're going to get through this, you know. You're going to get through this," I said, forcing him to meet my gaze. Weston's eyes looked a little glassy, as if he was on the verge of tears.

I would have wiped every one away if he needed me to.

"I don't know if I can do this," he said, breaking my gaze.

Though my own insecurities threatened to rise up at his words, I knew he wasn't talking about us.

Weston was feeling overwhelmed, anxious,

and lost. And I knew a thing or two about feeling like that.

"You can. *I* know you can. And you don't have to do it alone," I promised him. He seemed to process my words, nodding slowly as he chewed on them.

"Okay," he said shakily.

I squeezed his hand for good measure. "Okay," I said, letting go.

CHAPTER 36

I STOOD In the front foyer of Rhodes Enterprises, feeling more nervous than I'd ever been before.

Not because I knew the employees inside were probably scrambling and trying to get things smoothed out between all that had happened—the announcement, the fundraiser stuff, the hiring process and postings, the day to day operations of Rhodes.

My father had plenty of people underneath him who he trusted to man the fort while he was gone on vacation or off in another state or something on business, but this was like every employee's nightmare. The boss drops a bombshell, then disappears and there's no instructions or nothing in place to keep things running smoothly.

But still, I just felt like it was the right thing to do.

I'd never seen my dad look so... unlike himself. Pale, a little frail, and like he was exhausted. Not just from his job, but from life.

My mother assured me everything would be fine, to her best ability. Though her puffy, red eyes told me she was just as worried and concerned as I was.

You never know who you are or what you're made of until you're forced to find out. I thought I'd be the person to walk away, to run when my heart and my mind threatened to pull me under the dark, terrifying waves of doubt and worry.

But instead, I found myself channeling Cade apparently, when all I'd said was, "Tell me what you need."

I'd expected them both to tell me, "For you to take over," or something along those lines. With my dad in the hospital, it would have been the perfect time to take advantage of my vulner-ability, but... they only said they needed me.

So as I bustled through the hallways of Rhodes, checking on employees and delivering donuts and coffee to each floor, as I ran from conference room to office fetching papers from the printer, and answered calls in my father's office, even if it was only to say, "Thank you for your concerns," I couldn't stop thinking about the fundraiser, which I'd taken upon myself to reinstate. It just didn't sit right with me that the thing would be in limbo or cancelled, when our company was well within its means to continue the event. It had surprised me though, that my father was the one who oversaw all the fundraising and company events, that *he* was the one who had planned them. Thankfully, my dad's right hand man, Rob, didn't seem to mind. One less thing he had to worry about, I guess. He didn't seem particularly interested in the philanthropy division.

I'd thought about that first event, the one on the main street. Where I'd found Cade after he'd left the morning after we...

Then again, when he'd pitched the numbers and the information to my father in that board-room, how he'd been so compelling that my father greenlit the next two events.

Honestly, I couldn't stop thinking about Cade, period.

His eyes as he held my hand, as he promised me everything would be okay.

No one in my life had ever shown me the genuine kindness that Cade did. Most of the people in my life were nice enough, but it was all polite veneer. When push came to shove, aside from Jamie, I didn't have many people I felt I could actually turn to, to talk to. Who could help me sort my shit out. Who'd hold my hand and tell me it would be okay.

When Cade had asked me on the phone what I needed, I didn't even have to think. I said, "You."

And it was absolutely, one hundred percent true.

"Thanks for your help today, Weston," Cynthia said with a smile as I readied to exit the building.

It was damn nearing five o'clock.

How had the day gone by so quickly?

I nodded in return as I texted Cade.

Just finishing up at the office. Pick you up in ten?

"Of course, if there's anything else I can do, just let me know. I'll probably stop by tomorrow to make sure everything is good for the fundraiser," I said as my phone buzzed nearly instantly with a response.

Sounds good.

"I will let you know if there is anything. Have a good night." Cynthia nodded as I headed out the door, toward home.

CHAPTER 37

Weston

With my parents gone for the time being, the house felt eerily silent. Though I'd always had the option of using one of my dad's cars while in town, I usually didn't like to. Mostly because he was a bit anal and fussy about his babies, more so than he was about his human son.

But something in me was shifting. I could feel it.

I didn't want to share a car with Cade and some random stranger. I wanted him all to myself.

Okay and maybe I wanted to impress him a little. Show him a good time like he'd done with me.

So I grabbed the keys from the carport in

the garage for the Audi, which was technically *my* car. I'd just never come back to claim it after I left all those years ago.

When I rejected everything my father offered me because I didn't know if I could be who he wanted me to be. I guess I didn't know who I wanted to be then, either, and in so many ways I still didn't know who I was.

But as I got in the car, hearing that sweet, sexy purr of the engine, I felt at peace. Maybe I didn't have to be someone my father wanted.

Maybe, just maybe being myself was enough.

It certainly seemed enough for Cade.

I pulled out of the garage in search of my prince charming once more, ready to show him the best of both worlds.

Mine, and his.

Because at the end of the day, after a long and arduous day scheduling and approving, and planning this weekend's fundraiser, all I wanted was two things: a stiff glass off Oban, and the man of my fucking dreams.

WESTON

"WHEN YOU SAID DATE, I have to say I didn't expect... this," Cade said with a smirk as he got out of the car.

He'd been pleasantly surprised when I pulled up, even joking with me that he thought maybe I didn't know how to drive since I was chauffeured everywhere.

I assured him I was an excellent driver, and he only shook his head. There were many things I preferred, but more or less it was because I was just accustomed to those things from the life I'd been living.

Not to mention, the men in my life prior to Cade only responded to the overzealous displays of affection like chauffeured rides to and from the hottest clubs, where we'd be seen throwing around the luxuries that built my life.

But that wasn't who I was, not really. I'd done a damn good job of pretending to be the man they all wanted me to be, so much so that I'd convinced myself that was who I was.

But as I exited the car, smiling from ear to ear as the neon glow of M's Place's sign flickered, for the first time I felt free to just... be.

Myself.

I reached for Cade's hand, tugging him closer and he blushed from the movement, but I didn't miss the smile on his face.

"The last time I was here, I had a blast. Met this amazing man who showed me the time of my life," I purred as I pulled him against me, against the hood of the car.

Cade looked up at me from under his lashes, smirking. "Is that so?" he asked coyly.

I nodded as I settled my arms around his hips, holding him close, if only because I didn't want to let him go. Ever. I looked down into his eyes, and my heart skipped a beat.

"And I have it on good authority that it's trivia night. Specifically, Star Wars trivia night," I said with a grin.

Cade's eyes lit up with surprise. "You're serious."

"Dead serious. I thought you might like it."

Cade leaned down, taking my lips like a thief in the night.

"I love it, thank you," he said, his voice barely a whisper.

I melted against his kiss, momentarily debating if I should just scrap this idea altogether, and whisk him away from here, take him back to the Rhodes Family home and shower him with all the love he deserved.

But that could wait.

"Don't thank me yet. Not until we've beaten the other teams," I said as I nipped at his lips, causing a soft chuckle to escape his throat.

"Ah, so there it is. You just want to win cool prizes."

I seriously gazed back at him, my heart in my throat. The need to say it, those three little words was almost overwhelming. But I couldn't. They disappeared on my tongue, making my entire body acutely aware that once I did say them... I'd be crossing a threshold into the unknown.

I'd never told any of the people I'd been with, that I loved them.

Love wasn't what they wanted from me, anyway.

I reached up, brushing some soft, golden locks behind his ear, settling my hand at the base of his neck, fingertips stroking his skin and hair.

"I've already got my prize. The rest is just gravy," I said, my voice betraying no hint at how utterly terrified I was.

I was more exposed in that moment than I'd ever been before, and I watched Cade's entire body relax, felt as he melted into me like butter on a hot griddle.

"Oh, Wes," he breathed, before kissing me again, that explorative tongue of his eliciting a thousand emotions and thoughts from me.

I broke away, nodding toward the entrance.

"Lead the way, Jedi," I said teasingly.

Cade grinned wildly, grabbing my hand and pulling me toward the raucous, music-filled space, and I was happy to follow him.

CHAPTER 39

WESTON

AFTER WINNING THE TRIVIA COMPETITION, we were both on cloud nine.

I parked my car outside Cade's house, exiting to open his door and walk him up the sidewalk like a total gentlemen.

He blushed at the notion, taking my arm while using his free one to carry the Han Solo in carbonite statue he'd won as a symbol of power amidst the nerds and fans who'd shown up at the event.

Some I recognized, like the photographer who seemed to be practically everywhere in this town. I'm sure he got a picture of Cade and I with the statue, smiling ear to ear.

I stopped just in front of his door, the air suddenly thickening between us.

"I had an amazing time tonight, Wes," Cade said, setting down his statue on the little metal table beside the door, turning to me as he reached in his pocket for his house keys with his now free hand.

Something about that moment felt different. I watched as he fumbled with his keys, licking his lips.

His breathing increased slightly, as if he was... nervous.

A part of me felt vindicated, validated on a whole other level when Cade got the least bit flustered around me. It was endearing, cute, and made me feel on top of the word.

I loved the effect I had on him, but more so I loved the effect he had on me.

How just being around him made me feel at ease, like I could just... be.

Content, happy.

"Every day I spend with you is amazing," I said honestly, feeling the weight of the unspoken words hiding behind the ones I breathed into life.

Cade sighed as he turned to set his key in the door. He paused after I heard the click.

I'd meant to lean forward and quickly kiss him, tell him goodnight, and thank him for everything. It was late, nearing eleven thirty, and I had intended to be back at the office bright and early when it opened, if only to make sure everything was good to go for the fundraiser, and of course, make sure everything else was operating okay in my father's absence.

But something else happened.

I leaned down and pulled him into my arms, and I whispered, "The fundraiser isn't cancelled anymore."

Cade sank into my hold, a sigh of content leaving his chest.

"It's not?" he asked breathlessly, but the words felt heavy. Like he wanted to say something else, but thought better of it.

I shook my head. "I made sure everything went through. I took care of it myself," I said, feeling the heat between us.

Cade's fingertips grazed over my jaw as he kissed me, and suddenly it was like we had both become someone else entirely. Cade's lips moved slowly against my own, his probing tongue soft and smooth as he slid his fingers in my hair.

Our lips danced together, waltzing down a dark corridor as he spoke.

"I don't want you to go," he whispered against my lips.

His words echoed warnings in my brain, because I knew then that this, this was *it*.

I could have easily kissed him, told him duty called, and I'd see him again over the weekend for the fundraiser.

But I didn't want to go anywhere where Cade wasn't.

I wanted to stay.

With him, in his arms, his heart.

"Then I won't go," I whispered as I wrapped my arms around his waist, tugging him against me with more force than I probably meant to, and it was like a switch was flipped.

Cade turned us around as he fumbled for the door, and we both practically fell in the house. He slammed it shut, never letting up as he continued to kiss me, as his hands slid up and down my back, over my hips, my ass.

I traced my hands over his hips and found the edge of his shirt, pulling at it. Cade met my fervor as he pulled it off, showcasing his perfect toned chest, bathed in the amber light of his foyer.

I dropped the shirt over the arm of the couch, remembering the last time I'd been here. Where I'd watched his eyes fall shut as he came with ecstasy, my name on his tongue like a damn prayer.

He hurriedly popped the buttons on my shirt, and I shrugged out of it as fast as I could, his hands moving to my waistband, pulling me toward him, leading me through the darkened hallway by the kitchen.

The kitchen where I'd realized I was a goner.

Where I'd realized I was in love with him.

I turned us around, slamming his back against the hallway wall. He let out a breathy moan, as I palmed his erection through his jeans, feeling the heat of his chest against my own.

"Fuck, Wes..." he moaned, and I grinned wickedly.

I loved how he said my name.

I loved how his eyes squinted a little bit, how his pouty lips swelled after he'd been kissing me or sucking my cock.

Fuck, I loved his damn risotto and his ability to make me feel like I was on cloud nine every time he looked at me.

I loved this man, and I intended to make it known even if I couldn't say it out loud.

"You can tell me to stop," I said, giving him an out in case he needed it. I never wanted to assume anything with Cade. I wanted his complete and total consent, as well as his obedience.

He shook his head, grabbing my face in his hands.

"Don't stop," he said, his eyes glazing over.

"Your wish is my command," I said as I worked at his belt.

Cade returned the favor with hurried motion, spinning us around until my back was against the wall, until we were both completely and utterly naked, our bodies melding with the shadows in the hallway.

My cock sprang free, and Cade groaned as I ground myself against him. His hardness against my own was intoxicating. He pulled me back into a dark lit room, his lips seeking mine hurriedly before trailing off over my jaw, my neck. His hands slid up my neck and gripped my hair at the base tightly. The force was sudden, but not unwanted.

"Tell me what you want, Cade," I breathed, my cock aching as he ran his thumb over my sensitive, swollen head.

His lips found their way back to mine, and he pushed me back against something hard, making my knees buckle. I fell back onto a soft, cold cushion, rumpling blankets and sheets.

Cade straddled my legs, nudging them apart as he came up for air, his pupils dilated and full of so much love, so much heat I thought for sure I must have been dreaming.

"You, Wes. I want you," he said, his blue eyes burning into mine.

I slid my hand over his hip, my fingernails

digging into his skin as I looked up at him, as he waited for my words.

"Then fucking get on your knees like a good boy and take me," I breathed, watching as his entire body relaxed.

He did as I ordered without question, dropping between my legs and spreading them further apart to make room for him. My cock bounced with anticipation as Cade started at my balls, licking, sucking and massaging them just enough to tease me into oblivion before taking that sweet tongue of his and licking me from base to head, slowly.

It was damn right torture as I thrust my throbbing cock against his lips, seeking entrance. He obliged without words, grabbing me at the base with his hand as he pumped me while simultaneously inching down on my cock.

My legs tightened around his head as pleasure surged through me, as he groaned around me. I could feel the beginnings of my precum forming, and he licked at the saltiness with a hunger that should have damn near been criminal.

My eyes fell shut, and I heard the sound of a drawer, followed by the sound of a cap before I felt a cold wetness spreading around my hole. Instantly, I arched my back off the bed, partly from the temperature but also because I felt the sudden rush of slick, wet fingers teasing my entrance. My ass clenched around the foreign invaders. His thumb brushed the outer skin, massaging me while he moved his fingers in and out slowly, all the while never letting up on my cock.

I thrust my hips into him, the motion driving my cock deeper until I hit the back of his throat, which also pulled his fingers in as far as they could go.

It wasn't enough, I needed more.

I needed...

"Fuck me," I breathed, the words pleading and desperate. I was so close to coming already, I knew I wouldn't be able to last, but I needed to feel something much thicker and bigger than a few fingers right now.

"Please," I added, if only because my manners were ingrained in me.

I wanted to feel him.

I wanted to feel the weight of his body on top of me, the stretch as he filled me, and I wanted to taste myself and my desire on his lips. I wanted to make a mess of him as much as I wanted him to make a mess of me.

I wanted to give Cade the one thing I'd never given anyone else.

Myself.

I'd never let anyone fuck me before. Mostly

because in my head it was far more intimate to let someone else possess me like that, to be in control. I'd be at their mercy, instead of the one in control of things, and that was terrifying. In my mind, as stupid as it sounded, I'd always envisioned getting fucked as this ultimate act of love and devotion. It was a whole other thing separate from fast, hard, emotionless sex. In retrospect, I guess I wasn't ready to let anyone in that close, close enough they'd see the master-piece up front and would have realized it wasn't as beautiful as it looked from afar.

But I had the utmost belief that Cade wouldn't hurt me. That when he looked at me, he saw the mess, and he still thought it was beautiful.

Without a doubt, that's what I wanted. For Cade to *take me*, to look *me* in the eye as he filled me to the brim, to kiss me until I couldn't breathe while he brought me over that threshold into the unknown.

Together.

I trusted him. I knew somehow, though I couldn't explain it, that he'd take care of me and make me feel loved because it was who he was.

And when he looked at me for a moment, my leaking cock rubbing against his abdomen with understanding, I knew that was it.

There was no going back.

"Are you sure?" he asked, his lubricated hand reaching for his own cock, which in the shadowed light looked ominous due to its size and thickness.

I momentarily wondered if he would break me in half, but decided if that was the case, so be it.

I wanted all of Cade Green. I wanted him to ruin me and put me back together again.

"Yeah, I'm sure. If... you're okay with that, I mean," I said, feeling momentarily worried maybe Cade wasn't comfortable being a top, despite his new sudden interest of exploring his confidence, this *new side of him* as he said.

All worry and fear dissipated from his eyes when he looked at me, as he lathered himself up. The wet, slick sounds of the lube as he thrust his cock through his hand was driving me fucking bananas.

I leaned back on the bed, scooting up to give him better access as he slowly, languidly, leaned himself over me. I reached my hand up, fisting in his hair as I whispered against his lips, "I trust you."

He looked at me with vulnerability, his cock poised at my entrance, waiting, teasing me. I thrust myself against him, noting how his cock twitched as I did so.

And when I looked up at him, I knew I was doomed.

Because I was no longer the same man I was before I walked through his door, before I'd set foot in Jasper Springs.

"I love you, Cade." Surprisingly, the words came easily as I whispered them against his lips, kissing him with honesty.

Cade relaxed as I wrapped my leg around his hip, drawing him closer. I wrapped my arms around him, feeling his warmth and skin against my own.

He inched himself inside me slowly, almost torturously slow. Taking his time, acclimating to my tightness, to my warmth, and thanks to the lube on both my ass and his cock, he slid in easily, like silk.

When he bottomed out, I gasped, feeling the fullness of him in every part of me. My spine, my muscles, my heartbeat. For a moment he was still, looking down at me with glassy eyes as his voice shook, his breath heavy.

"I love you too," he said, before he kissed me once more, sliding out of me deliciously slowly, and I felt every inch of him in every part of my body as he reared his hips back. And when he snapped them against me, thrusting hard and deep, I couldn't contain my moan of pleasure or the way my cock throbbed against him. It felt *amazing*.

It didn't even hurt like I thought it would. I felt nothing but pure, blissful pleasure when he fucked me, and emptiness when he slid out of me.

I reached for myself, needing to fuck something, but Cade only swatted my hand away.

"I didn't say you could touch yourself," he said with a wicked gleam, sliding out slowly only to thrust into me with a harder, faster pace, turning me into some desperate, needy bottom.

"Please, sir." I assumed my role almost instantly, gleefully. "I need to come," I moaned against his warm, delicious lips. It wasn't just an act that night. I was practically bursting at the seams, ready to blow.

Cade wrapped his hand around my cock, squeezing and stroking me with the same rhythm as his cock.

I thrust my cock into his hand, my balls tightened and my orgasm was so fucking close. My voice shook, the need and desire thick in the air between us.

"Please, Cade," I moaned in desperation.

Cade's lips shushed me once more, and his rhythm quickened. His slow, deliberate, hard thrusts had gone erratic, and I knew he was close. He fucked me with reckless abandon, with both his hand and his cock until the muscles in my legs and back stiffened and all I knew was the absolute perfection and bliss of this man and all that we were, tangled up together.

His lips coveted my groan as I came, hard and fast in his hand, as he stilled himself, filling me with a warmth I'd never known before. I could feel some of him dripping out of me, down my thigh, and I grabbed his face in my hands, kissing him with praise and love, and everything in between.

"Such a good boy," he whispered softly, breathlessly, in my ear as I clutched his body to mine, absolutely spent before exhaustion took over the both of us.

CHAPTER 40

CADE

I WOKE up to the smelling of burning. Immediately, I jumped out of bed, worrying that something had caught fire. I threw on a pair of boxers quicker than should be humanly possibly, running out to the kitchen only to find Weston, standing there in his black briefs with his perfect ass on display, cooking.

Or more accurately, trying to cook as he jumped away from the bacon pan, cursing.

The sight alone was somehow both endearing and horrific.

I'm going to have to soak that pan for hours...

"Good morning," I said as a grin erupted on my face.

Weston turned, his deep green eyes lighting up the minute he saw me.

"Oh thank God you're up," he said as he went back to the stove.

I watched as he set about to cracking some eggs, fingering out bits of shell, no doubt since he didn't crack them lightly on the side of the pan, and I decided to step in.

He looked a little... out of his element.

But damn it if it wasn't the best way to wake up.

At least I know the house isn't burning down.

"You, uh... need some help here?" I asked as I approached him, reaching out gingerly to pull him away from the stove.

He turned in my grasp, his gaze dipping to my lips.

"That depends on your definition of help," he teased as he nipped my bottom lip, making my stomach flip and the blood rush straight to my cock.

"I mean, your bacon is burning..." I said as I pointed to the sizzling pan that looked encrusted in black char at this point.

Weston pushed me aside, turning the pieces over with a satisfied sound.

"It is not burning. It is char-grilled. It's a gourmet thing."

"Hmmm, so that's what they call it," I

teased, but decided to take his lead. Instead of pushing, trying to take over, I took a seat at my island and just... watched.

I just watched the son of a millionaire make me breakfast in his underwear and it was glorious.

Entertaining too, as I watched him bustle about my kitchen like he lived there, opening and shutting cupboards, pouring coffees and orange juices, and trying to set the table like this place was a five star restaurant.

The food itself wasn't terrible... even the char-grilled bacon.

But nothing was as delicious as the man who made it, the man who really did look like he belonged here.

With me.

Just as I finished my last piece of toast, Weston's phone rang.

"Hello?" he answered, looking a bit worried, but instantly relaxed after a moment or two.

I decided to leave him to whoever he spoke to, and instead focused on cleaning up the mess from Weston's cooking extravaganza.

"I'll be right there," he said with a sigh as he hung up.

I turned to look at him. "Everything okay?"

He nodded. "My dad's getting discharged," he said calmly.

"That's a good thing, right?" I asked, immediately heading over to him. I didn't miss how his shoulders tightened, or how his entire body locked up, the tension obviously spreading.

And so I did the only thing I could think of. I pulled Weston into my arms, and I told him it was going to be okay.

He was going to be okay.

He wrapped his arms around me, tightening his hold and nodded, leaning down to brush my lips with a gentle, whisper of a kiss, and he murmured, "I know."

"I've got to get going, but, I'll call you later?" he asked as he moved out of my arms toward the bedroom.

My heart was somehow both so full and so broken as I watched this perfect morning completely disintegrate.

The night before he'd told me he loved me.

I'd said it back because it was the truth, but as I watched him get ready to head out, it dawned on me that we hadn't really talked about what we were, or where this... connection, this love we did have... where it fit into his life.

Weston had come to Jasper Springs on business, but he hadn't agreed to stay indefinitely. In fact, despite his father's insistence he take the reins, Weston had made no move to do so.

Did he plan on heading back to the city where he lived?

Would we just become some long-distance relationship where we caught up on the weekends until it was time for him to fly off somewhere else?

I wasn't sure.

But despite the anxiety, despite the thoughts that threatened to upend this beautiful, perfect morning, I chose to believe that maybe things would work out.

After all, believing in the good things, having hope, that's a hell of a lot more difficult than believing things won't work out in your favor

And sometimes, life does give you exactly what you ask for.

Like a sexy corporate leading man who falls for a small town heartthrob and they live happily ever after.

So as I kissed Weston goodbye, and readied myself for work, I chose to believe in us.

That whatever happened, we'd figure it out. Together. And for the first time in my life, that was enough.

CHAPTER 41

MY DAD LOOKED a thousand times better than he had when I'd visited him after he'd had his heart attack.

My mother also looked a little more put together than she had been in recent days, though I couldn't be certain if that was because she'd had a facial or if she was just happy my father was doing better.

Margo had set to preparing a mid-morning meal, at my mother's request. Though my father kept asking for his chocolate chip muffins, which seemed to have been left off the menu.

"I heard you've been helping out down at the company in my absence," my father said as he took a sip of his tea. After some begging and pleading, my mother had agreed to leave us alone, though I suspect she was hovering because the doctor had blatantly told us to keep my dad's stress levels down.

I knew it was no secret I added to his stress, and the feeling was mutual, but something about that day felt different.

I felt different.

"Well, I mean you *did* just announce your retirement and dramatically had a heart attack. I don't think the ink was dry on the papers yet, so..."

"Cynthia told me you reinstated the fundraiser. Took over the calls, arranging everything."

"I did," I said, feeling a sense of accomplishment for once.

My dad stared straight on out the window, watching the birds fly to the massive feeder my mother had put in when I was a kid. I used to love sitting in the four-season room, where we were, and watching all the wildlife when I was home in the summer as a kid.

Jasper Springs was so lush and green, full of wildlife, and I guess a charm I never really appreciated.

And sitting there with my dad, I had to admit... it had a calming effect on me, and him.

For once, we weren't at one another's throats.

Perhaps Hell has frozen over.

"Now that I'm out of the hospital, I will need to move on naming my replacement. The ink has likely dried on the papers, as you say."

His words weren't all that different from what I'd heard many times, but this time, I could hear the sadness, the exhaustion in his voice. I stole a look at him, noting his profile as he stared at the birds. While my mother had a constant need to try every face cream and beauty treatment available because she didn't want to "look old" like she felt, my father had let age flourish on him. But as I looked at him that day, I realized that it was not an easy decision for him. Not because I had been so adamant, but because he truly *loved* his job. He loved getting up and going to meetings, and overseeing spreadsheets, and planning fundraisers. He loved coming home to his wife and the life they'd build together, even if it wasn't perfect because he had a pain in the ass son who never visited and argued with him all the time.

"I know I've asked you a million times, and a million times you've told me no. So this will be the last time. If you truly don't want to be a part of this company, I will accept your resignation. You can go home to your condo and live your life how you see fit, and I won't ever ask you again."

His words fell on me and for the first time, I realized I couldn't say no, entirely.

No, I don't want this. No, I don't want to be you.

When the truth of the matter was, the life I had in the city wasn't really the life I wanted at all.

In fact, it was *everything* I had never wanted, and I'd deluded myself into thinking it was mine. That I thrived and loved all the late night club dates, the pretty boys who looked good in the digs I bought them, hanging on my arm for the moment they existed in my life.

But I wasn't happy.

The alcohol always ran out, and the men always disappeared. The condo was always empty, silent, and I was just... existing. I was passing time until the next dopamine rush, until the next argument. Until the next... everything.

But I didn't feel that way in Jasper Springs.

Not anymore.

I realized at that moment, that I could have everything I wanted, if I just fucking jumped. That everything I'd been searching for was right there in Jasper Springs, all along.

"What if..." My voice shook as the reality of the truth ransacked me. "What if I fuck up?" I asked.

My father turned toward me, appraising me with his stoic gaze, his lips pulling up at the corners to show the hint of a smile.

"You think I was perfect, Weston? That I knew what I was doing when I started this company? When I met your mom? When I had you?" He chortled gruffly.

"You'll always make mistakes. You're human. But your heart is in the right place, and you show up and you do your best. That's all you have to do."

"Can I... can I... think about it?" I said, the words making me feel somehow lighter.

My dad smiled, nodding.

"You've got twenty four hours. I won't be back in the office to start the hiring process until tomorrow evening."

"Tomorrow evening is the fundraiser," I said.

"So it is," he responded, taking another sip of his tea. We both sat there, staring at the birds until my tea had gone cold.

CHAPTER 42

Cade

The Jasper Springs Pet Hospital always closed early on Fridays. With the reinstatement of the last Rhodes Enterprises event, Diane felt it was important that we all attend, not just me.

Though with my track record being pretty decent from the last two events, she wanted me to man the booth, and surprisingly, I'd jumped at the opportunity.

I'd never really liked working with the public, which was one of the reasons I loved working with animals as opposed to humans. But something in me changed over the last week. I still got nervous, sure, but after speaking at two events and in front of some very important people, I knew I could do it.

And when Diane had asked me to be the person to accept the check, the big show of it, anyway, in front of our community, I wholeheartedly agreed.

We'd raised a ton of money from the last two events that I knew would go to great use, and I'd never been more proud of the hospital, or myself.

I waited around backstage for almost an hour until things actually started moving, and Mr. Rhodes came out on stage. I knew from Weston that he'd been doing better since he got home, and had already started to transition his replacement.

Though Weston was pretty tight-lipped about the future of his family's company, and I wasn't going to press him. I knew it was a sore subject, and he'd been through a lot this week. Though I'd garnered it'd been a lot for the last few years, if not his life, even though I had no proof, just from the bits and pieces he did share with me.

I wasn't even surprised to see Weston on stage, standing next to his father, looking every bit Mr. Sexy Suit.

I tried to catch his gaze, but he refused to look my way, instead focusing out over the crowd.

Maybe he doesn't know it's me accepting the check...

His father droned on about his heart attack, the company, and what it meant to him, his family and his community. He spoke about matching *all* of our donations and what we'd raised, and my heart nearly burst.

I hadn't known that much. I knew the events were good, good enough that we'd done three, but Diane had never said anything about Rhodes matching our numbers.

Just as my musings started to spin, his father called my name, loud and clear.

Shit, that's my cue!

I took a deep breath, stilling the nerves that still threatened to rile up in me, being as I was walking out on stage in front of a sea of people. But I didn't focus on them.

I only focused on Weston, who now met my gaze and was smiling with pride.

Someone walked out to hand Weston a large posterboard-sized check, and he took it easily.

I knew it was just a show, but my heart still lifted when I read the numbers, 20,000.

We'd raised more money than I ever thought possible, and Rhodes had matched our efforts. To say I was floored and humbled was an understatement.

Weston handed me my check with a smirk and a wink.

"Such a good boy," he said in a whisper only we could hear, making me turn ten shades of red on stage in front of everyone.

And then he took the microphone from his father to make his own speech.

"Rhodes Enterprises has always been a fixture of this town and community. At the heart of this company, we are built by your compassion, your kindness, and your passion. Which is why events like this one, and the others you may or may not have attended this week are so critical. This company is nothing without its community. It's taken me a long time to understand that, but now that I do, it is my promise as the future CEO of Rhodes Enterprises that there will be more of a focus going forward on this community as a whole. Because you aren't just consumers to us. You're family."

My blood chilled and I swear I almost dropped the damn check.

Weston accepted the job.

That meant...

"I'm sure you will *all* have a lot of questions, but those will need to be saved and addressed for another time. Congratulations to Cade and the Jasper Springs Pet Hospital on raising such an extraordinary amount. No doubt this will help so many animals and the humans who care for them. Well done!" he said as he clapped, and the audience roared with applause in return.

Someone came out and grabbed the check, I think it was Diane. Weston ushered me off the stage into the wings.

I felt frozen, immobilized.

What just fucking happened?

"You're..."

"Staying," Weston said as soon as we'd gotten off the stage.

They words hit me like a thousand sacks of potatoes.

He was staying.

Here, in Jasper Springs.

"Why?" I asked, suddenly overcome with too much emotion I could barely process his words.

Weston reached out to brush my hair behind my ear, his eyes sparkling in the light.

"Because everything I've ever wanted is here, and I'd be a fool to give it all up."

"Everything?" I asked, my voice shaking.

Weston settled his free hand on my hip and pulled me close, his lips brushing mine softly.

"Everything," he whispered before he kissed me, and I melted into his arms like butter.

Sometimes things work out.

And when they do... it's the most amazing thing in the world.

"You want to get out of here?" Weston asked haughtily.

"Yeah, I think I do," I answered confidently, my smile stretching ear to ear.

"I think I know just the place."

EPILOGUE

CADE

"I WOULD LIKE to propose a toast to my matchmaking skills," Dawson said as he raised his beer glass.

I swatted at him, causing him to move and slosh some beer over the sides.

"Dawson, stop," I pleaded.

"No, no, it's fine. Let the man have his moment," Weston said with a wink.

"Thank you, Weston. Or should I call you *Mr. Rhodes?*" Dawson taunted him.

Well, it's better than a derogatory nickname...

"You can call me whatever you want, Mr. March," Weston said as he took a sip of his Oban.

"Smart man. As I was saying, a toast to my matchmaking skills. It was in this very bar that I *shoved* you two together. So, I'd like everyone to remember that when you two get married."

My cheeks flushed instantly. It wasn't like I hadn't thought about the idea, but even I knew things were still way too new and fresh, but the fact Weston didn't even balk at the mention made my heart flutter like a flock of seagulls.

"Mhmmm. Shame your skills don't carry over into your own life... or is that just because Mr. March has a tiny firehose?"

"Fuck you, Mitch. Ya'll know this *firehose* is a damn triumph."

"Funny, I don't see anyone around here limping from your *triumph.*"

Weston let out a raucous roar of laughter as I shook my head.

"Fuck, Nolan's here," Dawson said, his voice shifting from fun and relaxed to angry and annoyed.

We all turned in the direction of his gaze to see a medium height man who looked like something out of Revenge of the Nerds. White button down with pens on the pocket, khaki pants, and glasses.

"Is that the claims adjuster who's always making your life miserable?" I asked, taking in the sight of Dawson's nemesis.

Nolan Harding had a knack for showing up at almost every fire Dawson and the firehouse showed up at. He was always going over every report with a fine-toothed comb, which pissed Dawson off.

I'd heard more rants about Nolan Harding than anyone should be subjected to, and I had to admit, seeing him in the flesh in all his nerdy attire was actually comical.

This was the guy Dawson hated?

He's like Harry Potter.

Dawson's lips pulled into a tight line.

"Hold my beer. I'm about to go make *his* life a living hell for once."

Mitchell rolled his eyes.

"Remember, ladies don't start fights..." he taunted Dawson as he got up.

"No, but they fucking finish them," Dawson said in a chipper tone, leaving us to ourselves.

"Did you really date him?" Weston asked, raising an eyebrow.

I thought he would have been pissed when Dawson essentially dropped the tidbit earlier, after I'd officially introduced him to my friends as my actual boyfriend.

"Yeah, but obviously I regained my smarts."

Weston grinned.

"So, the firehose..."

"Not bad, but you're a thousand times better," I said, flashing him with a wicked grin.

"You are a smart man," Weston said as he took a sip.

Mitchell got up.

"All right, well, it's karaoke night, so I'm not sitting around here while you two get all cute and handsy and Dawson's off fucking shit up. I'm singing."

I nodded in response.

"We'll be up there sooner or later," Weston said confidently.

"Oh, we will?" I asked, raising an eyebrow, challenging him.

"Absolutely. But I believe it's my turn to pick the song," he said as he pulled me between his legs, wrapping his arms around me.

The scent of scotch on his breath mixed with his cologne was heady and made me breathless.

"Fine. But you're going to owe me later," I said, kissing him back.

"A very smart man once told me I make up very well."

His hands slid up and down my back, his gaze holding me in place. It was like the rest of the world fell away, like there was only us.

And I knew it would always be like that.

"I'll hold you to that," I said as I wrapped

my arms around his neck, and kissed him like they do in the movies, our lips, tongues, and hearts singing happily ever after in the story of our own making.

Thank you for reading Cade and Weston's story.

If you enjoyed this book, please return to your favorite retailer and leave a review. Even a few words could mean the world to an author.

Continue the series with Dawson's story, Book 2 in Jasper Springs!

DAWSON

AN MM ENEMIES TO LOVERS
ROMANCE

Dawson
An MM Enemies To Lovers Romance
Jasper Springs
Book Two

Copyright © 2024
Evie Riley
Second Edition
ISBN: 978-1-77357-718-0
Published by Naughty Nights Press LLC
Cover Art By Willsin Rowe

Things are heating up in Jasper Springs...

Dawson Richards is Jasper Springs's very own famed "Mr. March." Rescuing people—and cats—is what the hunky firefighter does best. That is, when his infuriating nemesis isn't throwing a monkey wrench into Dawson's hard work.

Claims Adjuster Nolan Harding moved to Jasper Springs seeking a fresh start, but after months of working with an annoying but sinfully delicious fireman who drives him crazy, Nolan is nearing the end of his rope.

When a fire hits home for Dawson, he and Nolan must work together to close the case correctly and on time.

Can they put aside their grievances and their undeniable attraction to get the job done? Or will the heat consume their hearts too?

Readers seeking an enemies to lovers romance set in a cozy little town may find this story checks those boxes. While

CHAPTER 1

Dawson

"Bingo!" Nolan screamed, his shrill voice nearly exploding my eardrums even though he was at least three tables away.

Instinctively, my jaw tensed, his excitement like nails on a damn chalkboard.

"Fucking hell, I was one away from winning!" I groaned, ripping the sliver of thin bingo paper in half.

"Spend all your stripper money from the calendar so soon?" Cade ribbed me, his new boyfriend, Weston, shaking his head. He was still red in the face from the last round of karaoke.

"You're not supposed to show the firehose

upfront, you know. That's what OnlyFans is for," Weston jabbed, flashing a cocky grin.

I rolled my eyes.

"No, and fuck you," I said sarcastically, throwing Mitch, Cade, and Weston into a fit of laughter.

"Sore loser," Cade said as he drained the last of his beer.

I watched in disdain as Nolan fucking Harding stumbled up to the stage, like a deer who'd been hit by a car.

What the hell has him out of his office this late, anyway?

He had the audacity to shove his black, nerdy glasses up his nose just a hair before grabbing his winnings, the light of the stage shining on him like some damn halo.

But Nolan was far from an angel.

He was, in fact, the kryptonite to my Superman, the Joker to my Batman.

He was my arch nemesis.

I watched him with a scathing look as Miguel handed him his winnings, his smile stirring some sort of hurricane inside of me.

Those pouty lips, that perfect jawline...

The thought of those lips wrapped around my cock until I'd face fucked the glasses right off his pretty face had fueled more of my fantasies than I cared to admit, but who wasn't prone to a hate-fuck fantasy every now and then? It didn't mean I *liked* the guy.

I most certainly didn't like him, and the desire to make his life a living hell was only equal to my need to run.

Run away from this damn disaster of a night.

At that moment, Nolan looked up directly at me, catching my gaze. I didn't miss the blush that spread across his nose, continuing on to his cheeks. The sight immediately caused my brain to spur those hate-fuck fantasies at the wrong time, causing my damn cock to twitch. I grunted in response, breaking his gaze, feeling hot all of a sudden.

"Fuck this, I'm out," I said as I pushed away from the table, leaving Mitch to browse his phone while Weston and Cade made out like two teenagers on prom night.

Mitchell waved a hand in the air, not looking up from his phone. "Toodles, Mr. March," he said dryly.

"Nice meeting you, Dawson," Weston said politely, between breaths. "Officially, I mean."

I waved him off with a half-smile, but he'd gone back to playing tonsil hockey with Cade.

I made my way toward the bar to pay my tab, feeling only slightly buzzed. Max saw me coming a mile away, reaching over a group of patrons to hand me my check, which I quickly paid.

"Thanks, Max," I said as I stumbled over some douchebag's big ass feet that were sticking out.

"Watch where you're going, asshole," Bigfoot spoke, turning to me with an angry expression.

"Keep all hands, arms, legs, and feet inside the airplane, asshole, and I won't have to," I nipped. Max shot me a scathing look as the man sweetly told me just where to shove his gigantic foot.

"You wish," I drawled, feeling more than irritated.

The night had been a bust. I was off my game.

I'd had a shit day at work, dealing with fucking Nolan again, questioning one of my recent claims for damages, my inbox starting to fill up at that point. Why the twat felt the need to question ninety percent of my claims was beyond me.

I had sincerely fucked up everything else in my life, but the firehouse was the one place I knew my shit. At least, I had until Nolan showed up two years ago after my ex left my ass high and dry to chase his financial dreams.

One of these days, I was going to fucking ruin Nolan for being an eternal pain in the ass.

I slapped some extra bills down on the counter for Max's tip as I turned away, charismatically flipping off Bigfoot in the process.

"Sayonara, assholes," I hollered over the chatter, heading through the bar to the shadowed corridor toward the side exit.

I knew most people didn't use it, because it was technically an emergency exit, but I didn't much care at the moment, and Max or Miguel would not stop me. Fire exits were second nature to me. I pulled my phone out of my back pocket, deciding I should probably queue up a ride, knocking into another asshole, who *stepped* on me.

"What the fuck, watch where you're—"

My entire body flared with heat when I laid eyes on the culprit blocking my exit.

"Perhaps your vision needs to be checked, *Dawson*, because lord knows if I was a snake I would have bitten you," Nolan snapped as he adjusted his crooked glasses like he was *soooo much smarter* than me.

Instinctively, I bit back, "Ain't nothing wrong with my vision, Harding. Not my fault your spineless ass blends into the fucking shadows."

Nolan had the audacity to *scoff* at me, like I was the one ruining his life.

"Besides, we both know your bite is about as hard as a toothless alligator."

Nolan scowled at me, crossing his arms as the bar lights shifted, casting stray green and blue lights our way. In the beams of colored light, I could see some slight definition in his biceps from the way his short sleeves cut against his skin.

Huh, that's new.

"You think you know me, huh? I got news for you, Dawson. You don't. You don't know what I'm capable of." Nolan's voice was full of false bravado, edged with something else I'd never heard before.

Something that made my blood heat and my cock twitch as his brown eyes roved over me before settling on my lips.

Was Nolan... was he *flirting* with me?

Maybe I'm more buzzed than I thought. Yeah, Uber is a definite.

I took a step closer to Nolan, backing him up against the wall next to the exit.

"Oh, I think I know what you're capable of. You're capable of being a giant pain in my fucking ass."

The thud of Nolan's back hitting the wall sounded as I leaned in closer. I held his fiery gaze, before I nipped my teeth at him, expecting him to jump like a scared dog, but instead, he only leaned in closer.

So close, I could feel the heat of his words on my skin, smell the sweet faint scent of lime and tequila on his breath.

And then the strangest thing happened. Nolan fucking *whimpered.*

Like some damsel in distress.

Like prey.

I snickered even as the sight of his tongue flicking out to moisten his lips caused my cock to twitch.

"Just what I thought. Snakes don't have backbones," I hissed. Then I saw something shift in his eyes, his shoulders tensing as he pushed into my space, his own lips pulled back in a snarl in retaliation.

"Maybe not, but their jaws can eat predators twice their size," Nolan answered, his deep breath full of snark like a petulant little brat.

"Is that what you want, Harding? To eat a predator twice your size?"

My head spun as my cock twitched and perked up, my entire being running on instinct.

Nolan pushed at my chest lightly with one finger, pushing me back.

"Wouldn't be the first time," he said, his voice filled with attitude as I stumbled backward.

His words fell on me like a heavy steel beam.

The unmistakable realization hit me. I'd never assumed Nolan was into guys. Hell, I'd assumed from his lack of conversation about anything outside of work and making my life a living hell, he was just another dorky asshole who'd been friend-zoned by all his chick friends, which was why I didn't feel too bad about dreaming about stuffing his mouth full with my dick as punishment during happy time.

My cock *throbbed* with interest. Clearly, it had a mind of its own.

My phone had the audacity to break up the wonderfully tense moment by sounding off the incessant rings that told me my ride had arrived.

"Saved by the bell. Lucky you," Nolan quipped, hip checking me as he slid past me, heading back toward the bar, leaving me hard, confused, and in shock.

What the fuck?

CHAPTER 2

Nolan

WHAT THE FUCK is wrong with me?

I braced my arms against the table, the room spinning as I mentally recounted the absolute meltdown I'd had on my way back from the bathroom.

Of all the people to run into, to be here in this damn bar tonight, of all nights...

I just *had* to run into the one firefighter who I'd been stupidly fantasizing about since I ended up assigned to this region.

As if moving to a new city wasn't hard enough, it became quite clear, quite fast, that I did not fit in. Not at the office, and certainly not at the firehouse that my firm worked with. Not that I fit in... well, anywhere really.

My mama used to say I was just "shy", but I'm not shy. I'm awkward. Sheldon Cooper's got nothing on me.

In my head, everything makes sense. I can say what I want, dreaming up scenarios where I blend in naturally, cool as a cucumber and the life of the party.

Where I can pretend I'm someone like Dawson Richards.

Bold, confidant. Sexy enough to be practically naked on a calendar that I jack off to after a long, boring day of numbers and figures.

Which is probably how I would have spent my twenty-eighth birthday, had my best friend Allie not convinced me to go out for once. To "let loose and have a little fun." Even if I would be doing it alone, like I had for the last couple of years since moving here. It wasn't like I hadn't *tried* to meet people, but the town of Jasper Springs wasn't really all that different from where I grew up. No one took a second glance at me. No one except Mr. March. At least when I first arrived.

Dawson seemed cool. All charisma and perfect smiles, that natural flirtatious air about him that was some cross between a used car salesman and high school prom king.

I thought maybe he was different. Maybe, just maybe, moving here wouldn't be so bad if I could make one friend.

But all thoughts of hope and happiness diminished when work called us both, and Dawson's short attention span rendered me forgotten.

Until I'd been called out on my first claim, which happened to be a local fire that Dawson had responded to.

I tried to remain professional, because what else could I do?

I'd been promoted to Jasper Springs for a reason, and that reason was there were far too many claims and not enough people to accurately investigate and close the cases. I'd always been good at my job, meeting my quotas and then some. But I'd never dreamed that I would be fought quite this hard on them by one stubborn firefighter.

Who just had you backed up against the wall like some villain from a comic book.

The memory of Dawson's piercing gaze, the way he lumbered over me, caused my cock to stiffen like a lightning rod.

It wasn't like I hadn't thought about a scenario like that before. In fact, it was one I thought about often.

It was like some other entity had possessed

me, because the minute my back hit the wall, some switch inside of me flipped.

His hot breath on me, his six foot one frame towering over my measly five foot eight inches...

The command in his voice, the way his eyes blazed as his gaze fell to my lips, causing my stomach to twist into knots.

In the presence of Dawson Richards, I was someone else, and I wasn't sure how I felt about that.

I decided that I'd had enough of all this birthday insanity and threw down some money, feeling like I needed to get as far away from M's place and the memory of Dawson and his ridiculously hot stare as I could get.

But it was no use.

I closed the door, feeling even more defeated as the lights came on to illuminate my empty apartment.

I flipped the lock, tossing my keys on the kitchen counter as I opened my fridge to pull out the oversized cupcake Allie had delivered to the office earlier. I meticulously peeled the blue wrapper back, section by section to keep the confectionery delicacy from crumbling.

"Happy birthday to me," I sighed out, feeling exhaustion kick in. I devoured the chocolate cake in less than three bites, but it did nothing to sate the emptiness I felt in my stomach.

After I'd eaten my cupcake of shame, I removed my clothes, tossing them into the wicker hamper in the hallway, relishing in the cool air of my apartment as it hit my sensitive skin. I always kept the place at sixty-eight degrees.

As I crawled into bed, my mind wandered to thoughts of darkened hallways, of a tall, sexy man who made my insides twist and my cock spring to life. I groaned as I looked at the digital clock on my nightstand. 11:30pm.

Twenty-eight years old, single, and in bed by eleven thirty. Yeah, talk about lame.

There was no chance in hell anyone would find routine and order sexy.

I closed my eyes as I let my hand slide beneath the waistband of my boxers, wrapping my fist around the head of my cock. My thumb brushed over the tip, feeling the faint beginnings of precum coat my fingertips. Slowly, I tugged at the sensitive skin, building a steady rhythm as I let my mind wander further down the darkened corridor of fantasy, to thoughts of copper eyes and broad shoulders, to fists slammed against the wall beside my head.

Of thick fingers around my neck, and fiery

lips that cursed me to high hell before they claimed mine.

Of the weight of his body on top of me as he fucking *owned me.*

The thought of his cock sliding against mine, pressed against the wall, hard and wet, threw me over the edge.

I cupped my hand over my swollen head as I came, groaning in defeat as my cock pulsed, sticky, warm wetness spreading through my fingers as I fought to catch my breath. I wished it wasn't mine.

"Holy fuck." I sighed, staring up at the ceiling as I fell back to earth.

I knew then, as I lay there, that Dawson Richards was going to be the fucking death of me.

CHAPTER 3

Dawson

The whole ride home all I could think about was Nolan. Which only irritated me. His snippy little comments, his blush on stage, the way he fucking *whimpered* and leaned into me…

Fuck.

I hated it. I hated that he pushed my buttons so easily.

Or that he is capable of pushing my buttons at all.

I angrily threw my keys down in the bowl after locking the door, knowing there was only one way to truly work out my frustrations.

It didn't take long for me to settle in on my couch, pulling up my favorite go-to porn. I let the video play while I got comfortable, letting my cock spring free from my pants as I slid out of them. Leaning back against the soft cushions, I gave myself a good smack, watching my cock bounce with vibrancy as I focused on the video in front of me, specifically the way Mr. Big Cock was pounding himself into the tight little ass of the moaning computer nerd in front of him.

"You like that don't you, you little slut?" Mr. Big Cock drawled, shoving his subject's head down into the dirt.

"Yes..." I groaned along with him as I gripped my own rigid rod, closing my eyes. The sound of Mr. Big Cock's wet, slick cock and his nerdy little slut's moans as he begged for Mr. Big Cock covered me like a blanket, making my own dick throb, eliciting a deep groan from me as I let my mind fill in the blanks.

Smooth, round, pale cheeks that I could watch my thick cock disappear into formed in my brain, the image of my fingers tangled in dark locks as I gripped tightly, yanking them to turn and look at me over their shoulder.

Deep brown eyes met mine. Nolan stared at me over his glasses, throaty moans escaping his lips as his tight ass clenched me, and I immediately opened my eyes, ceasing my hold on my cock, my thumb sliding through the steady amount of precum that had already collected at the tip.

"Fuck!" I hissed as my cock throbbed and I tried to catch my breath. My gaze diverted back to the television just in time to see Mr. Big Cock quickening his pace. My hips involuntarily thrust into my still hand, clearly not getting the message.

"I don't know how much more I can take," Computer Cum Slut cried, his arm muscles tightening, his voice shaking. "Please…"

I leaned my head back once more, a sheen of sweat breaking out as I closed my eyes. In the darkness, Nolan stared at me, begging me like Computer Cum Slut.

My cock *throbbed* in my hand and I squeezed it tightly, spreading the warm, sticky precum along my shaft as I picked up my pace again.

I needed to come so fucking bad, and I didn't want to edge myself after the fucking day I'd had.

So I figured, why the hell not. It's not like I hadn't fantasized about Nolan before. It didn't mean anything.

At least that's what I told myself as I let his image fill my brain, as I allowed myself to fantasize about driving my aching cock in Nolan's tight little ass while he begged me to fuck him faster, harder.

"That's it, come for Daddy," Mr. Big Cock grunted from my speakers.

And I did.

I came like a fucking geyser, with a frustrated growl. "Fuck!"

I don't know how long I stayed there, frozen with my hand on my weeping cock, but it felt like forever.

When I finally opened my eyes to survey the mess I'd made, I felt awash with a mix of emotions.

Shame.

Embarrassment.

Desire.

Guilt.

Sadness.

I couldn't remember coming that hard *ever*. Which is why I knew I needed to do whatever I could to forget what had just happened.

You've got to get a hold of yourself, Dawson. You've got to forget tonight, forget Nolan altogether.

And as I regrettably stopped the video, and I cleaned myself of what may have been the equivalent of the Guinness World Record's largest load ever, I promised myself I'd do just that.

I would forget Nolan Harding and his stupid, pretty face and whimper, his blush, his soulful brown eyes and nerdy glasses.

But first, I was going to make him pay for ruining my fucking life.

CHAPTER 4

NOLAN

I'D JUST GOTTEN out of a meeting with my regional boss when I entered my office and saw I had several missed calls, all from the same number.

The Jasper Springs VFD.

I sighed as I plopped down in my ergonomic chair and just as I set to pick up the phone, it rang again, JSVFD appearing on my phone screen again.

I picked up the phone. "Nolan Harding, Breisinger Insurance,"

"Where the fuck have you been?" Dawson snapped on the other end, immediately throwing me a curveball.

I mean, I had a feeling it was him who called, but there was no way to be sure.

I pulled up my email, noting he'd already sent me two emails today, and I wasn't even halfway through my shift.

What's up his ass today?

"Doing my job, Mr. Richards. Something you clearly don't understand."

"Don't get cute with me, *Mr. Harding.*"

Why his bite and the way he said my name made me blush, I didn't know, but I was thankful that I was alone, in my office, away from prying eyes.

Which also meant no one else could hear me.

"If I wanted to get cute with you, *Dawson*, I wouldn't be vague about it. Lord knows you need everything spelled out for you."

"Fuck you, Nolan."

"I see we're past pleasantries now. Is there a reason for your call, or did you just want to hear my *cute* voice?" I said.

What the fuck?

Where did that come from?

There was a pause, the only sound Dawson's breathing on the other end, which strangely caused my cock to twitch. I adjusted myself in my pants, letting out a frustrated sigh.

What was his deal?

Before I could tell him I didn't have time to deal with his bullshit because I had a thousand emails to answer and claims to investigate, he spoke.

"I submitted a claim for Jonathan Bradish two days ago and no one's even been out to the guy's house yet to check anything."

What?

Since when did Dawson keep tabs on my *job?*

Naturally, the shift in conversation made me defensive. Contrary to Dawson's belief that I did nothing but sit around on my ass and jack off all day, I had a laundry list of claims to investigate as well as a boatload of administrative tasks and meetings seeing as I was practically one promotion away from becoming the manager of this damn branch.

"I'm aware of my own case load, Dawson. I don't need you to tell me how to do my job."

"Then do *your* fucking job, Nolan. Or I'll do it for you," he said gruffly, his tone all commanding and... *hot*.

Fuck, why does he sound so hot when he's pissed off?

My cock agreed as it twitched in my pants again. I crossed my legs only to apply pressure, because I did *not* have time in my schedule to take care of an inappropriate erection.

And the object of my fantasies chastising me like a bad child, is definitely not helping matters.

I pulled up my case file for Jonathan Bradish, noting that the property wasn't all that far from the office. Glancing at the clock, I knew I'd have to go to lunch soon, but maybe, just maybe I'd be able to squeeze in a trip.

I knew I should have been honest, professional, and that I should have just told Dawson I'd take care of it.

But a part of me *liked* hearing him all worked up, liked pushing his buttons... and my cock certainly liked it.

Liked *him.*

So instead of doing what I should have done, I did the exact opposite.

I took Dawson's bait like a famished fish.

"You know, *Dawson,* you catch more flies with honey than you do with vinegar," I drawled as I swiveled in my chair, licking my lips.

"What the fuck is that supposed to mean?" Dawson griped. His reaction caused a grin to spread across my face.

He really made it so easy sometimes. He was like a whistling teapot. Let him steam long enough and he'd boil over.

"It means that if you want something out of me, you're going to have to ask me. Nicely."

"Oh, I'll give you *nice,* Harding. I'll give you a nice, swift kick in that tight ass of yours, set you in the right direction."

His words caused my cock to throb, and I could already feel a wet spot forming in my underwear.

Fuuuuuck, why is this so hot?

Wait, did he just call my ass...

"I'm waiting, Dawson," I said, my breath coming out much heavier than it should have been as I tried to stifle how fucking turned on I was at the moment.

So unprofessional.

God, what is wrong with me?

I closed my eyes as I tried to regain my sanity.

"Nolan," he breathed my name like it was a sin. Another pause, Dawson's heavy breathing in my ear hovering like some sort of spell.

"Would you *please* do me a favor?" Dawson spoke with command, but his entire tone had shifted from demanding and angry to something else.

Smooth, sexy.

Like pure silk.

My entire body loosened, and I wanted to *melt* into the sound of his voice. I could imagine him telling me to get on my knees with a voice like that, which was also not helping my current situation.

I'd never heard him speak like *that* to anyone.

"Yes, Dawson?" I said, licking my lips, stilling my voice.

"Would you *please* be a good little pencil pusher and do your fucking job so I can do mine? Thanks, sweetheart. You're a doll," he said before he hung up, leaving me breathless, with a raging hard on at eleven thirty in the morning.

The dial tone echoed in my ears as I opened my eyes, staring at the ceiling.

What the fuck just happened?

Just as I hung up the phone, my cell phone went off.

I'm never getting any work done today.

I pulled out my cell, knowing without bothering to look who was calling. Very few people actually had my cell phone number, on account because I didn't have many friends.

But I'd also set Allie's ringtone to *All The Single Ladies*, which she insisted was the best song ever made.

Well, that's one way to kill a boner.

I punched the green button and answered the call. "Hey, Allie," I said, letting out a deep breath.

"What's wrong? You sound stressed," she said immediately.

I leaned back in my chair, letting the springy bounce soothe my frustration.

"I just got off the phone with Dawson. He called about a case and I just... I guess let him get to me."

"He's such an asshole. Seriously."

"I know, but—"

That's why I like him. I like his shitty attitude, his foul mouth, and he isn't bad on the eyes either...

"I wanted to let you know that I got some time coming up I have to take, so I was thinking maybe I could come visit? Spend the weekend? Get your ass out of the house for a bit?"

I sighed. I wanted to spend time with Allie, I really did, but the last month I'd gotten swamped with work, and I knew I needed to make a dent in my workload.

"Work has been a little nuts as of late, Allie. I'm sorry, I—"

"It's fine, Nolan. I know you're working your ass off right now for that promotion. Just... remember your life doesn't have to be all work, you know."

Her words settled on me, making me feel a mixture of shame, guilt, and loneliness.

It was easy for people like Allie to say that, when they had lives outside of their jobs.

My life *was* my job. It was all I had, because I was alone.

I glanced at the clock, noting it was now nearing quarter to twelve. If I wanted to hit

Jonathan Bradish's house, I'd need to get a move on it.

"I like my job..." I said with a whine.

"Mhmmm. I think you just like being around all those sweaty, hot firefighters all day."

Maybe just one hot firefighter.

"I do not—"

"Especially... who is it? Mr. March?" She giggled. "I mean, hell, I'd become a workaholic too for those calendar boys." She whistled on the other end, throwing me into another blush.

"It's not like that, and you know it. I gotta go though. I have to actually go check out a claim... that's what Dawson called about."

"I'd love to meet the asshole who gets you all flustered someday. Maybe on the next trip you can bring me down to the firehouse and show me what I'm missing," she said sweetly.

"Deal," I promised, and I let her go, getting up from my chair and grabbing my keys.

CHAPTER 5

Dawson

I'd just made it back to the firehouse when my brother called.

"Jonathan, is everything okay?" I asked, my adrenaline still spiked from the shed fire we'd just put out across town in Deer Park.

"Yeah, everything's good, I, uh... you said to give you a call whenever one of the insurance guys showed up, so I just wanted to let you know one of them showed up."

I breathed a sigh of relief. It seemed my lighting a fire under Nolan's ass worked.

"Good. I'll be there in a bit, just getting out of my gear. Don't let them leave until I get there, okay? I don't want these idiots fucking shit up on my watch."

"Dawson..." my brother protested, but I refused to let him blow me off. It was my job as his big brother to make sure he was okay, and that those asshole adjusters made sure he was covered for his losses. I knew firsthand how they could be sticklers, having dated one of them, especially when it came to folks like my brother who operated their businesses out of their homes.

"I'll see you in a few," I said as I hung up, not giving him a chance to rebuke me.

I didn't bother hitting the showers; instead, I just hung my shit up in my locker and grabbed my keys to my truck. Thankfully, my brother's place was about fifteen minutes away, but with my skilled emergency driving, I could shave off at least five minutes.

Which is exactly what I did.

All the agents at Breisinger drove the same car, a little silver sedan with a big ass logo on the side. It stood out like a sore thumb everywhere, and it was no different parked in front of my brother's house.

From the street, you would have never been able to tell there'd been a fire, but around the back was another story. I parked my truck, hopping out with haste as I entered through the front door. I didn't need to knock, after all, we were family and I was more than expected.

My brother looked up at me from his couch, the agent turning to face me as well...

And when my eyes met surprised brown irises, I think my blood actually boiled. Nolan's eyes widened, his eyebrows shooting up like I'd just caught him with his hand in the cookie jar.

"Dawson, what..." he said as he stood up, my brother following suit.

"Afternoon, Harding," I said as I sauntered past him toward my brother, casting him one of my patented *Mr. March* smiles, if only to appear *nice.*

Truth be told, my adrenaline was still pumping and the sight of those surprised peepers and pouty lips was doing things to me that I didn't want to focus on at the moment.

For starters, my brother was standing next to Nolan... which shouldn't have bothered me as much as it did.

But it did.

"I told you, Dawson, I have it covered here..." Jonathan protested with a sigh, sliding his hands into his jean pockets. He stared at me with an annoyed expression.

"Nonsense, this is my job, Jon. I told you..."

"Isn't there like a cat in a tree somewhere that requires your attention?" Nolan said, shaking off his surprise.

Jonathan laughed. "I take it you two know one another pretty well?"

I took a step closer to Nolan, using my frame to loom ominously over him.

At least, I hoped I looked ominous and not like a stiff giraffe.

"Yeah, Harding and I are the best of buds. Aren't we, *Nolan?*" I said with a smirk.

"Uh..." I didn't miss the way Nolan's gaze dipped to my lips, or the blush forming across his nose, spreading into his cheeks. The sight made my cock twitch, and I shoved my hand in my pocket, if only to adjust myself.

I needed to remember where I was, and what I was actually supposed to be doing here...

"Sure. We'll go with that," Nolan said, his voice as polite and professional as he could muster. Though clearly I'd caused him some distress as his gaze roved over me from head to toe.

"Seriously, I got it handled. But if you are going to stay until Nolan leaves, at least take a shower. You look like hell."

"Well, that would be because I came straight here from a fire, because I didn't want to miss busting the balls of your claims adjuster," I said with a grin.

Nolan shook off whatever it was that had him flustered as he crossed his arms. "I could report you for harassment, you know," he said in a hushed voice, raising a brow.

I leaned closer by an inch, licking my lips. He made it so easy sometimes.

"But you won't, because you're a good little pencil pusher aren't you, Nolan?" I said as I stepped back, removing my shirt.

I didn't miss how his eyes widened, how his mouth dropped open in stunned annoyance, or how he gazed back at me with a fire that had nothing to do with the one we were both here about.

And seeing his eyes ablaze like that caused my cock to stiffen, and I knew I needed to get away from there before I really decided to go all in and give him something to report.

"Fine. I could use a cold shower," I said out loud for everyone to hear as I headed for the hallway bathroom, leaving Nolan and my brother to the situation at hand.

Once the door was locked, I let out a frustrated sigh as I took the rest of my clothes off, folding them neatly and setting them on the back of the toilet.

I wasn't lying about needing a cold shower, as once I was alone, and my cock was free, it could have passed as a compass with how north it was pointing.

I huffed a sigh of annoyance as I stepped in the shower, hoping the cool water would help put out the fire that had started to build inside of me from just the sight of Nolan on my brother's couch.

Images flashed in my mind that I knew I shouldn't be thinking about, given current circumstances, but I knew better than to try and fight the fantasy forming in my brain.

I'd seen the way Nolan looked at me, how he blushed and stammered. A part of me liked that I obviously made him nervous, even if it wasn't a sexual thing for him.

I liked that I could get under his skin...

Not to mention our phone call earlier had worked me up into a heat I hadn't quite expected. The last thing I wanted to do was wax one out at the firehouse, when I was on call. It was just a stroke of luck that we'd gotten called out. Well, lucky for me anyway, if only because it gave me something else to focus on other than Nolan fucking Harding.

It was like over the phone, he was someone else. His voice was different, cockier, sexier.

God what is wrong with me?

Am I admitting Nolan is sexy?

Yes, I was. But I rationalized it was easier to separate the fantasies I had about Nolan from the actual person he was.

But when he'd *demanded* that I ask him nicely, his voice taking on that dark, smooth edge, I nearly lost it.

I'd never heard Nolan talk to anyone like that. Hell, I didn't know he was capable of sounding like a phone sex operator. His words from last night rang in my memory.

You don't know what I'm capable of, Dawson.

Apparently, I didn't.

I wrapped my hand around my cock, knowing it was better to ride the wave than to swim against it.

I let my thoughts wander to dark, sexy phone operator voices, imagining putting the little brat in his place, right over the arm of my brother's couch. I imagined driving him over the edge until he apologized for his sudden, cocky new attitude, imagined bringing him right to the edge, until...

My abs clenched as warm cum sprayed out again with a force I wasn't used to.

Fuuuuck.

That was twice now. Twice, that the thought of using Nolan like my own personal cocksleeve had made me come like a damn teenager who just discovered his dick.

I really needed to get a hold of myself. I needed to quit while I was ahead. I pumped the last bits of my release as I caught my breath, swearing that once I left that shower, it would be a clean slate.

And when I had managed to cleanse my skin and my brain, only then did I turn the water off, and find my way back into my jeans so I could join baby brother and the object of my fantasies gone awry.

When I came to the basement, I could see Nolan on his hands and knees shining a little penlight on something in the corner. The angle showcased the roundness of his ass. An ass I didn't mind looking at, especially since it was clear neither of them noticed my arrival.

"This wasn't in the report," Nolan said, and immediately I tensed, readying to jump to the defense for my brother, but before I could speak, before either of them could turn to see me, he sat back on his heels, looking up at my brother with kind eyes.

"But contrary to what your brother thinks, this is why my job's important. I want to make sure we have *all the information* we need to be able to get you the coverage and reimbursement you deserve."

"I appreciate that, really," Jonathan said, sighing, "I just don't want to get reamed over some stupid detail..."

Nolan stood, brushing the dirt off his knees as he looked to one of the bikes in the corner. My old bike, the one Jonathan was fixing for me, specifically. I kept to the shadows, frozen, watching the scene unfold in front of me.

"I'm sure Dawson didn't note it, because he just didn't know. His job is to fight the fire, not the red tape or the damage it leaves. Don't worry, Mr. Bradish. I'll take care of this."

At that moment, I realized that maybe I had been a little... abrasive with Nolan. I'd assumed he questioned my claims because he was a nitpicking ass, never once considering that maybe his nitpicking actually *helped* my ass.

That was the moment a paint can crashed to the ground, falling right on my fucking foot.

"Fucking ay!" I yelped as I jumped back, causing them both to turn in my direction and notice me.

Well there goes my career in the CIA.

"You coming to wreck my garage now, Daw?" Jonathan teased me.

Nolan's demeanor shifted completely.

Gone was the nice, polite and professional man who was confident and caring regarding his knowledge and job. Instead, Nolan was replaced with the shy, quiet man I'd known for the last two years. The one who couldn't even look at me most days.

"Thought maybe I'd get the renovations started early," I said, shaking off the pain as I walked further into the garage.

"W... well, on that note," Nolan said, getting flustered again as he averted his eyes from me, brushing off some invisible dirt. "I should be getting back... my lunch only goes until... twelve thirty," he stammered.

Jonathan nodded. "Thanks again!" he said as he turned to head back toward the house.

I watched Nolan leave, in slow motion, caught between talking to my brother and apologizing to the man I'd second-guessed.

My lightning rod cock twitched and pointed me in the right direction though.

"Nolan, wait..." I called out, but he was already making a beeline through the garage door toward the side of the street. I hurried to catch him, surprised at how fast he was actually moving. I had to legit sprint to catch him, and when I did, I wrapped my hand around his biceps, stopping him in his tracks. He dug his heels into the grass, coming to a complete stop, almost making me smack right into him.

He looked up at me in surprise. "Dawson..."

His gaze flicked to where my hand wrapped

around his arm, and I realized my fingers were *gripping* him rather tightly. I flexed them, letting go, as a wash of nervousness and guilt befell me.

"I just... wanted to apologize," I said, tasting the foreign words on my tongue.

"Apologize for what?" Nolan asked, rubbing his biceps where I'd left a light indentation and a pale red mark.

"I didn't mean to hurt you, I just—"

"It's fine, I promise. You aren't like the Hulk or anything, believe me," he bit.

I wanted to rise to his bait. To fight with him, because his attitude begged for an adjustment as of late, but something told me that wasn't what was best at the moment.

I needed to set the record straight, so I could go on with my day, my life.

Apologize, then everything can go back to normal, and everyone's happy.

"I meant about earlier. On the phone. I was..." I swallowed, trying to find the strength to say the words. It wasn't often I apologized to anyone for anything.

I was a hero, a good guy. Contrary to Nolan's belief, I wasn't an asshole. At least I wasn't an asshole to *everyone.*

Just one person in particular.

"I was a dick, and I shouldn't have bitten your head off. I know you have a job to do, it's just—" I felt strangely flustered as the words poured out of me.

Nolan looked up at me with those same kind eyes he gave my brother, dropping his hand from his biceps. He took a small step closer, his gaze falling to my lips and then back to my eyes again.

"It's just what, Dawson?" he asked in a calm, smooth voice. It wasn't the same smooth and sexy phone operator voice I'd busted a nut to earlier, but it eased something inside of me.

"My brother's all I have, and I just... I just hate not being able to fix this for him. To see him struggle because his shop was his life and now..."

"Hey..." Nolan reached out and set his hand on my arm, his touch soft and warm.

I didn't dislike it. In fact, I wanted to feel his touch all over me, soothing all my worries.

But I figured it was just the adrenaline making me all emotional and weird.

"Everything will be okay, I promise," he said softly. "I'll make sure of it."

I realized somehow we'd gotten closer. Close enough that if I wanted to, I could run my fingers through his dark locks, close enough to kiss.

And that thought was the one that drove me away.

This was not getting back to normal. This was dangerously close to falling over an edge I didn't want to be on.

"I'll hold you to that, Harding," I said gruffly as I headed back to my brother's to grab my shirt I'd left hanging over the edge of his couch, leaving Nolan in my dust once more.

CHAPTER 6

NOLAN

I AM A GLUTTON FOR PUNISHMENT.

Clearly, there was no other explanation. I wasn't sure what had gotten into me earlier, except for the fact that Dawson just seemed to be able to draw out parts of me I didn't even know existed.

Flirting with him over the phone was one thing. It was easier to pretend, to channel the person I *wished* I could be when I didn't have to physically look at the man.

I told myself I was going to erase that morning's phone call from my brain completely, and I had every intention of doing so; starting with focusing on work—on the job Dawson was up my ass about—and then he had to show up fresh from a fire, his sandy blond hair all disheveled, his skin flushed and sweaty still, with smudges of ash and soot on his face, with that cocky grin...

Like some hunk out of a romance novel or something.

And then when he *grabbed* me, to apologize... it was like something had shifted in him too, and even though I knew I should have been pissed and I should have told him to back off, and get as far away from me as possible, I found myself falling further into his gravitational pull.

His dark eyes implored mine as his voice cracked just in the slightest, showing off what I gathered was probably the man beneath all the equipment and fireproof armor.

Someone not a lot of people saw, and I couldn't look away. Like a moth, I was drawn to his endearing flame, his change of character, and I couldn't stop myself from falling like a star in his orbit.

His hair was still wet, and he smelled like cedar and spice. I looked up at him through my glasses, my gaze falling over his lips as I wondered for a moment if he would taste as good as he smelled, if his kiss would be as ravaging as the fires he chased, or if it would be a slow burn, like a fine whiskey making its way down your throat.

It had taken nearly all my concentration to fight the desire to take his lips and kiss away the worry that was so evident in his voice and on his face.

But I knew kissing Dawson was both unprofessional and unwarranted.

After all, how could someone like him ever want someone like me?

Even I knew the world wasn't some romance novel. Guys like Dawson could have any man they desired, and guys like me were just the wallflowers in the background, the muted colors of a painting put there only to make brighter ones stand out.

So I did the only thing I could think of. I told him, despite my better judgment, despite the overwhelming desire to kiss him in the yard of his brother's house, that everything was going to be okay, even though I wasn't certain I believed it myself.

At least, where my job was concerned, I meant that promise.

But a part of me was also trying to convince *myself* everything would be okay. That I would walk away and forget that moment, that I'd forget shirtless Dawson standing inches away from me and his spicy scent, his fiery copper eyes, and his sculpted frame, or the way his eyelashes stood out against his tanned skin.

Fucking hell, why do I always do this?

Why do I always fall for beautiful creatures I can never have?

And then it was over, and Dawson walked away, and I let him go like an idiot because I couldn't string my words together and remember how to fucking human.

"Way to go, Nolan," I chastised myself as I started the car. The digital clock blinked to tell me I was perilously close to a late arrival, so I threw my car into gear and sped off for the office, just as my phone rang.

"Harding," I answered the car's bluetooth handsfree, willing my breath to return to normal. I needed to get Dawson Richards out of my head and focus on things that were actually tangible. Like my job, and the promotion that I'd been working toward.

"Oh, Nolan, I'm so glad I got you! I know you're still out on lunch and all, and I was hoping to catch you before you came back..."

I tensed immediately upon hearing my boss Karla's voice. "What's up?" I asked as I steered the car onto Jasper Springs's main street.

I'd always thought the main street here looked like something out of a travel blog or a

Hallmark movie. The trees are always the perfect shade of green, the fences always perfectly painted off-white, and the sun lights everything up like Heaven, giving the town an ethereal glow that is somehow both cozy and inspirational.

"Verizon finally showed up to work on the lines, which means we're out of Internet for the next day or so, so you don't need to come back this afternoon," Karla said, trying to hide the excitement in her voice.

Wait...what?

"You mean I—"

"Take the day off, Nolan. I'll call you tomorrow to let you know an update on when it'll be back and when you can come back to the office."

My blood chilled as her words fell on me like heavy stones.

I hadn't taken a day off from work since...

Well, since I moved here pretty much.

Not that I didn't think about it, but what would I do?

It wasn't like I had a group of friends to gallivant around with, not to mention the town itself was pretty sparse in regard to entertainment...

I guess I could go home and maybe go for my daily run a little earlier?

Put a little extra time in?

"Seriously. Go home. Watch some Netflix or something. Take a break for once. I mean it," she said before hanging up, leaving me stunned in silence.

Well, shit.

I casually steered away from the office, slowing my speed now that I knew I didn't have to rush back to work, passing the fire station. When I'd leased my apartment, I'd thought it was a great selling point. Being close to local first responders meant I was in safe hands if something went wrong, but now it was just another reminder that my job was my life.

Instinctually, I looked for Dawson among the crew washing the fire trucks, but he wasn't there. Probably still chatting up his brother about everything.

Must be a slow day.

A part of my brain just couldn't let sleeping dogs lie though, as I tried to picture him among Gina and Sharky, and some of the newer rookies, like Frank. My mind couldn't help but remember a freshly showered and shirtless Dawson looming over me, and of course that was why my brain decided to go spiraling into thoughts of watching him get all wet and soapy, stretching those back muscles as he cleaned the truck, loose suspenders caressing the shape of his ass...

Fuck, now I'm hard.

I groaned in defeat as the light turned green, shifting in my seat to try and quell my burgeoning erection.

The high-pitched tones of Foreigner singing *Hot Blooded* filled the speakers, making me groan all the more. I huffed out a sigh as I pulled into my parking space at Jasper Springs Towers, the apartment complex I'd called home for the last two years. I shifted myself around once more as I exited the car, feeling rather on the spot.

It was pretty early still, and thankfully, that meant there wasn't a lot of traffic, and kids weren't home from school yet, so the complex itself was pretty quiet. Something I appreciated at the time.

I made my way into my apartment, relishing in the privacy of my own home as I attempted to do just what Karla instructed, and take a break.

Which consisted of me trying to get comfortable on my couch as I slipped out of my white shirt and pants down to my boxers while I doomscrolled my tv for something, anything to get my mind off Dawson, that weird phone conversation, or the last twenty four hours, really.

I settled on some older episodes of *Rescue Me*, trying to do exactly as Karla as said and relax. But neither my mind nor my dick seemed to get the memo.

I huffed out a sigh of frustration, rolling my eyes as I leaned back into my couch cushions, knowing there was truly only one way to quiet my thoughts and get on with my day.

I closed my eyes, slid my hand in my boxers and let my mind wander, to Dawson and his dark, sexy voice over the phone, the memory of his hot, shirtless self standing above me, remembering that spicy cedar scent and those perfect, kissable lips.

Fuck.

I'd barely gotten into my fantasy before I was pulsing with need, aching to be touched. I just wished someone else other than myself could touch me.

My mind wandered to the memory of Dawson's hands on my skin, when he'd grabbed me, filling in the spaces of fantasy as I let my thoughts spiral, imagining those same warm, rough hands wrapped around my cock, squeezing, sliding...

I grunted out a frustrated sound as I came, much too soon for my own liking as ropes of warm, sticky cum coated my shaft and fingers, making me feel a mix of shame, guilt, and relief.

Well at least that's taken care of, now perhaps I can get back to being a functional human being.

If I even was functional, because I sure as hell didn't feel it at the moment.

I tugged on my cock, pumping out the last bits of my guilty spend, deciding that staying around the house wasn't as solid an idea as I had hoped it would be. So I got up, ambled to the bathroom and cleaned myself up, then decided now would probably be as good a time as ever to head out for that run, work off some of those feelings, put everything out of my mind, including the devil himself and his stupid, hot face, and then I could launch into my daily workout afterward, shower, make some dinner, and watch the latest episode of *911 Lone Star* I'd missed because I worked late last week, and call it a fucking night.

Wow, I really am boring as hell.

I changed quickly, tying on my runners, slid my keys in my shorts pocket, and took off for the walking trail. Jasper Springs Towers wasn't the biggest apartment complex in town by any means. It was nestled near the woods, which gave the place a kind of quaint, cozy atmosphere, and every day I could hear the birds out of my window tweeting away as I woke up. Mixed with the ever-present light of the sun there, it was everything I thought I could have ever wanted in a place to live. I just wished I had someone to share it with. Someone to wake up to, curled in the sheets together, while we listened to the birds sing away outside. Allie tells me it was because I'm a romantic, but I thought that sort of thing was what everyone wanted.

Wasn't it?

When I got to the trail on the side of the complex, I immediately launched into my stretches. I leaned forward, lunging to stretch my calves and legs, to limber myself up for the run. There was no one around, which made me feel a little better. Not that I minded running on the trail with other people, but there was just something about being the only one amidst the trees and plants that lined both sides of the trail. It was easier to focus, to shed whatever I needed to in my thoughts and just... be.

I stretched my arms over my head from side to side, twisting my body, pulling on my elbows as well to stretch the muscles there. I learned pretty early on, if I didn't stretch before a run, I'd be paying for it later and choking down Advil with my meals for days.

In my mindless routine, a voice cut through, breaking my concentration.

"What the hell are you doing here, Harding?"

I turned as I finished my twist, my eyes

widening immediately at the sight of Dawson, dressed in nothing but silver athletic shorts and white Nikes. His tanned, muscled chest sparkled with sweat in the sunlight, his sandy hair wet. As he pulled his earbuds out, I thought I must've done some serious shit in a former life for karma to fuck me like this.

CHAPTER 7

Dawson

THE LAST PERSON I ever thought I'd see on Jasper Springs Tower's trail was Nolan. For starters, I ran the track every day, rain or shine, and I'd seen a hell of a lot of people either in passing or because I'd responded to a call, or just because Jasper Springs was the smallest town on the fucking planet.

But I'd never seen Nolan anywhere outside of work until the other night at M's Place, and it seemed like ever since then I couldn't escape the infuriating adjuster who...

Looks kind of hot in that tight Under Armour tank... even with the glasses.

Especially with the glasses.

Fuck!

"Uh... I live here," he deadpanned, as if such a thing were common knowledge.

I closed my eyes immediately as I realized how dumb I must have looked, because *of course* he lived there. The property was private for residents of the Towers, which meant...

Nolan Harding lived in my damn complex and I had no freaking idea.

What were the odds?

I decided to make up for my stupid ass comment by covering up with some good old-fashioned competition, something I was far more comfortable with than talking.

Not to mention, I came to run, to feel the hard earth of the trail beneath my feet and the heat of the sun on my skin until I couldn't focus on anything else. Because that weird moment earlier, at my brother's house... left me feeling more worked up than I wanted to admit at the moment, especially to Nolan.

"Small town, small world, I guess," I grunted as I took a well-needed stop to breathe and take a drink from my water bottle.

Nolan gave me the cold shoulder, turning away from me to continue his sexy stretching, showcasing the actual definition in his arms like I was insignificant to him or his little yoga show, like he was better than me.

How dare he.

"You gonna stretch all day or you actually going to hit the pavement?" I taunted him.

Nolan turned, looking at me with dark eyes, his expression something between surprised and enticed, and I can't say it was a bad look for him.

"I would already be hitting the pavement, if you hadn't distracted me," he said with that *laissez faire* attitude of his that caused my insides to burn.

"Then by all means, Harding, don't let me get in your way," I said as I cast him a sly grin. "Race me."

I watched Nolan raise his eyebrows before sliding his hands on his hips, shaking his head. The sunlight streamed through the trees, lighting up his skin and casting shadows in all the right places.

"Dawson..."

"What? Unless you think you can't beat me..." I said as I capped my water bottle, hooking it back on my belt.

Nolan just smirked. He fucking smirked at me!

"Oh, I'm not worried I won't beat you. I just don't want to damage your reputation," he said darkly. "Or your ego."

"Quite sure of yourself, aren't you?" I said

as I took a step closer, leaving a hair's breadth between us as I looked down at his smirking face.

I expected to see his expression falter, for him to flip whatever switch it was that had turned him into that someone I got a glimpse of earlier, over the phone.

Cocky.

Self-assured.

Hot.

"Like I said, *Dawson,* you don't know what I'm capable of."

It's on, champ.

"Then let's sweeten the incentive. One race, loser buys the winner dinner."

Nolan licked his lips, shaking his head.

"You won't take no for an answer, will you?" he asked with a dark chuckle.

I shook my head, shifting my weight so I could loom over him ominously. I can't explain why, but I just felt like it would shake him. Throw him off his game, or whatever it was that was happening between us.

"I never do," I said as I started to bounce from foot to foot, readying for takeoff.

"Fine. But it's your funeral," he said as he walked away from me, taking his position at what I assumed to be our starting line, and I followed.

"Get ready to eat my dust, Harding," I said with a grin.

"Ready, set..." he called.

"Go," I snapped, taking off within seconds.

Nolan sprinted, his legs tightening as he built his rhythm, as he caught up to me, staying beside me. But I couldn't have that.

I sucked in a breath as I willed my legs to move faster, outrunning him. The breeze against my already heated skin was like a balm, and I chased that feeling; the cool air, my racing heart, and the burn in my muscles, like it was my salvation.

And maybe in a way, it was.

I smiled as we turned the bend, satisfied with my lead until Nolan caught up to me... again. His face was red and flushed, and I could see sweat starting to form on his brow, his heavy breath like an echo in the secluded space between us.

He ran a hand back through his hair, sucking in his own breath as he pushed past me.

The little fucker!

My heartbeat raced, thudding loudly in my chest as I mustered up my speed a bit, focusing intently on catching up to him.

On catching him.

Just a few more feet and we'd be homeward

bound. I was beside him within seconds, focusing on my breath...

Nolan never looked at me. Instead, he kept his eyes trained on his target, our finish line.

Keeping with his pace, I knew it wouldn't be long until I hit that finish, until I claimed my prize.

Yet, I was more than surprised when Nolan pulled out a wicked sprint, taking off like a bat out of hell for the finish line, leaving me in *his* dust.

Literally, because his shoes kicked up a cloud of dirt on the trail as he all but leaped to the finish line. When he got there, he hunched over quickly, his hands on his knees as he tried to catch his breath.

He fucking beat me!

I wanted to snap, make some douchey comment, after all I'd always been a competitive man, but something about the reality of the moment left me feeling not only surprised, but proud.

Because he fucking beat me.

I huffed out a breath as I snatched my water bottle again for a drink, the only sound between us Nolan's labored breathing. He stood upright, face all flushed as he removed his shirt, using it to wipe the sweat from his face.

My gaze roved over his form, my cock stiffening at the sight of his abs.

Nolan has fucking abs?

Who would have thought?

His pale skin caught the sunlight streaming through the trees, the sweat on his very delicious, very pronounced Adonis belt that dipped into his shorts like a glowing sign.

The sudden image of me running my tongue along those groves, tasting the salt of his sweat, pushed to the forefront of my mind, and I mindlessly adjusted myself as I watched him wipe the sweat from his forehand.

I offered him my water bottle.

"You look a little thirsty, there Nolan," I said, much darker than I'd intended.

Nolan looked back at me with fiery amber eyes, licking his pouty lips in thirst.

Fuuuuck.

Why is that so hot right now?

Nolan shuffled his weight as he shook his head. "I'm good, thanks."

"I promise I don't have cooties. Clean as a whistle in all ways that count," I said with a wink.

What the fuck?

Where did that come from?

"Seriously," I said, covering up my creepy ass comment as I took a step closer.

Nolan looked at my water bottle like it was a snake about to bite him. He took a deep breath, before grabbing it from me, his eyes never leaving mine.

"That makes two of us." He grunted as he took a long pull, and I half worried he'd drain the whole thing, but I didn't mind as I watched him guzzle my water down his throat, little streams pouring out the sides of his pretty little mouth.

Do not think sexy thoughts.

Do not think...

I hadn't had a race like that in a long time, and something about the sweat, the sunlight... a shirtless Nolan and his cocky attitude... had me feeling off my game.

"Looks like I'm buying you dinner," I said as he handed me back my water, using the back of his hand to wipe his mouth of any remaining streams of liquid.

"You don't have to..."

"A deal is a deal, Harding. And I'm a man of my word." I hooked the near empty bottle back onto my belt.

"Not going to take no for an answer, I take it?"

"Got somewhere you want to go tonight?" I asked nonchalantly.

"Tonight?" Nolan asked, his eyes widening in surprise. "Oh, I didn't—"

"You got plans I don't know about?" I taunted him.

Nolan shrugged.

"I mean, I was going to catch up on the latest episode of *911 Lone Star*," he said, clearing his throat. "But, uh..."

"Ouch. You really know how to dig the blade in, don't you?" I said, shaking my head.

"I didn't mean..."

"I'll pick you up tomorrow at six. Be ready," I said.

"But I—"

I smirked at him as I made my way off the trail, and just as I expected, he followed me like a good little lamb.

"Wouldn't want to get in the way of your TK and Carlos marathon," I said with a wink, which caused a blush to spread across Nolan's nose and into his cheeks.

He does that a lot, it's kind of... cute.

Though he couldn't see the grin on my face, I couldn't help myself.

Sometimes he just made things so easy.

CHAPTER 8

NOLAN

THE REALITY of the situation hit me, making my already racing heart beat faster.

I beat Dawson, which meant...

Fuck.

He's buying me dinner.

Tomorrow night.

A part of me was more than ecstatic to spend an evening with *Mr. March* himself, because in some weird, twisted way, I thought this would be the only way I *could* spend time with my two year long fireman crush.

It was just happenstance that we both lived at the Towers, some sense of serendipity or a cruel twist of fate that we'd both ended up on the same trail at the same time.

By the time I caught up to Dawson, I'd started to cool down from our run, but my heart still raced. Dawson nonchalantly held the door for me after he'd gone inside the main lobby entrance. He cast me a smirk over his tanned shoulder that warmed my insides like molten lava.

"Thanks," I said, focusing on sounding like a normal, even-toned human, even though my breath was threatening to catch in my throat again.

"Don't mention it," he said with a snicker as he headed for the elevator.

Shit, that means he's not on this floor.

I casually strolled up beside him as he pressed the up button, feeling strangely on the spot.

Say something, or it's going to get awkward.

"I got out of work early today," I said, like a weirdo, feeling an ever-present need to explain myself.

Dawson shrugged. "Surprised you aren't holed up in your apartment working. Do you even know how to relax?"

"Of course, I know how to relax..." I huffed, fully rising to his bait, noting the way the corner's of Dawson's lips turned up when I did.

He's fucking playing with me. Is he...

Is he flirting *with me?*

"Running off all that pent up frustration isn't relaxing, you know."

"Watching tv is relaxing."

"No, it's not. It's mindless. It's something to focus on because you need to fill your space."

I crossed my arms as I watched the floors light up. Three more floors.

"And just how do you relax, Dawson?"

He smiled sexily, his tongue darting out to lick his lips before he spoke, and damn if it didn't make my cock twitch.

I wonder just how many licks it'd take him to get the center of my fucking tootsie roll pop...

"I don't give up all my secrets before a first date, Nolan. You'll just have to wait and see," he said as the elevator dinged, opening for us both ominously. Dawson looked back to me with a grin as he waved forward.

"After you, champ," he taunted me. I stepped in without looking back, but the heat radiating off of Dawson could be felt like it was its own entity. I leaned over to press the second floor, feeling somewhat sheepish that I could have forgone this awkward scenario and taken the stairs, but sue me... I wanted to keep Dawson to myself just a little while longer. At least until we'd split to our humble abodes, where he could rethink everything.

When he was in, the doors closed instantly, and I watched as he pressed his floor. He was on the third floor.

My heart thudded away in my chest so loud I thought it would echo in the enclosed space, thought perhaps Dawson could hear it just from standing next to me. I kept my gaze trained on the lights.

Dawson nudged me. "I haven't had anyone give me a run for my money like that in a while. We should do this again sometime," he said the words genuinely, causing me to turn in surprise. Only then did I notice he'd somehow gotten closer. He leaned his arm out against the wall, leaning languidly as his amber eyes met mine. Everything about him exuded sex appeal—his shirtless, well-defined form, his semi-wet sandy blond hair, his dark, enticing eyes. His perfect lips that begged to be kissed.

To be ravished and owned.

I let out a shaky breath as my gaze fell to those lips, licking my own as I fought the desire to close the space between us, to put this elevator on hold and do what I'd been dreaming about for two years.

But because I'm a cursed man, that was the

exact moment the elevator dinged, opening to my floor.

"I think that's your floor, champ," he said, his gaze full of heat as it dipped to my lips, his voice suddenly quite gravelly.

"Right, my floor... 911... marathon."

"Have a good night, Nolan. I'll see you tomorrow night," he said definitively, and it took all my concentration to move my sore legs, to walk out of that elevator with my dignity.

The doors started to close, and I realized I hadn't asked where we were going.

A part of me thought maybe it was a fruitless endeavor, after all, he could change his mind by tomorrow, but maybe I just wanted one more moment, one last glance at the man of my dreams before it all went up in flames.

I stopped the doors with a palm, and Dawson shifted his stance, his gaze still full of fire.

"Where are we going? Tomorrow? I need to know so I know how to—"

"Now, now, where would the fun be in telling you? I'd rather make you sweat. Hot and bothered is a good look on you," he drawled as he gently pushed my arm away, and the doors slowly slid closed.

My mouth gaped as I watched the doors

close, taking Dawson up to third floor, leaving me stiff, hot, and full of panic.

I can't fuck this up.

This might be closest I ever get to a date with Dawson Richards.

Because it wasn't a date by any means. Dawson was a man of his word, and I'd won fair and square. It was just good sportsmanship, nothing more.

Even if I wanted it to be...

So, as I gathered myself and headed down the hall to my apartment, I promised myself I would do whatever it took to make the one shot I had absolutely perfect.

CHAPTER 9

DAWSON

I'D NEVER BEEN so relieved to be cut off by an elevator in my life.

I just couldn't seem to help myself around Nolan. I *liked* pushing his buttons, throwing him off guard and causing a little chaos to his daily routine, I could admit that at least.

But there was a moment, in that elevator where I'd forgotten who we were, where we were.

As I leaned against the wall, staring down at those pouty, perfect lips, I thought *fuck, this is it. This is my sexual harassment suit in the making.*

I sighed as the doors opened on my floor,

thanking the heavens above for the brief moment of reality.

My body was flushed, still hot, and I was certain it wasn't entirely from the run.

Once in my apartment, I could relax. Or at least, that's what I intended on doing. Shower, clean up a bit, maybe get some take out before I headed back to the firehouse. I stared at my phone on the counter, feeling a little antsy.

It'd been a weird fucking day, and a part of me wanted to call my best friend and dish about all the grade A tea. About that hot-as-hell phone call, Nolan showing up at my brother's... that hot-as-hell race, and me nearly losing all my fucking marbles in that damn elevator.

But a part of me also knew that Cade was in that new relationship haze.

Which meant for him nothing would matter except the man he was all twitterpated for at the moment; a man who was actually *good* for him. I wanted things to really work out for them.

I wasn't lying when I said what I did at M's Place the other night. I wanted to see my ex turned bestie settle down and have the life he always wanted. I sighed, shaking my head.

What about what *I wanted?*

Did I want some white picket fence, brunch on Sundays sort of life that everyone around here seemed accustomed to?

I swear, sometimes it's like the Stepford Wives up in here.

I'd always known what I *didn't* want. But knowing what I did want... I wasn't so sure what that was.

There was a sort of rhythm to being a bachelor. To living life the way I had, without attachments. I'd had boyfriends, sure, but I hadn't been on a *date* somewhere like Sedona in a while. I knew immediately I'd wanted to take Nolan there, not only because I knew it would shock him—I doubted the pencil pusher had been anywhere like the five-star restaurant in the city that's famous for its cocktails and it's flaming tower dessert—but because for some reason I couldn't explain... I wanted to *impress* him.

I wanted the chance to show this pain in the ass that I wasn't just some dumb, charismatic asshole who lived to make his life hell.

Even though I do enjoy raining hell down on him.

Why do I care what Nolan Harding thinks of me?

I slid out of my shorts, groaning in defeat as I headed for the bathroom, the cool air of my apartment kissing my skin.

I knew the answer, even if I didn't want to admit it.

Because maybe this was fate giving us a second chance.

A do-over.

Not that he remembers anyway, that's clear.

I turned the water on in the shower as I let my thoughts wander to two years ago, the day I met Nolan.

I'd just gotten out of a relationship with my ex, Vance, who worked for the same company Nolan did, Breisinger Insurance.

It had been a rocky relationship from the start, and I knew he wasn't going to stick around —after all, he was planning to move if he got his dream job at some accounting firm he'd been hard on since college. Breisinger Insurance was just a pit stop for him. Something to pay the bills until he could squirrel his pennies and get the fuck out of Jasper Springs. I knew that, and it wasn't like I was after anything serious either. Or at least, that was what I told myself.

But somewhere in my feeble, stupid, romantic brain I thought maybe, just maybe *I'd be enough.*

I wanted to be enough.

But I wasn't.

He broke it off with me and no sooner was he packed and out the door, blowing dust in my direction. I wasn't in love with the guy or anything, but it still stung. I'd become used to having another person in my bed, in my space, and suddenly... it was cold.

Lonely.

Breisinger didn't wait until the ink even dried on Vance's two weeks notice before they brought in Nolan.

A dark-haired young buck who looked like some cross between Hot Harry Potter from a B-produced porno and your little sister's math tutor.

Vance left, and there wasn't even a mourning period. He'd been replaced, and it made me feel like I'd been replaced too.

I wanted to hate Nolan Harding. And I did, for a while. I hated his doe-eyed face, his nitpicking, his refusal to talk or gossip with anyone, especially me.

His little snide comments he thought I didn't hear in passing when we'd see each other on the job.

But I was starting to realize that perhaps there was more to Nolan than I'd thought, and maybe I didn't *actually* hate the guy.

Maybe I was actually starting to... like him.

I jumped in the shower immediately upon that thought, needing the cold water to wash away my thoughts and feelings.

One thing at a time.

CHAPTER 10

DAWSON

AFTER A LONG DAY OF CALLS, I was practically butter in the shower. I wasn't sure why I was so nervous.

It wasn't like I'd never been on a date, and I certainly knew how to show a guy a good time. Yet, I found myself distracted now that I was done for the day and the hours were dwindling closer until I'd have to pick up Nolan and whisk him away to reap the reward of his winnings.

Hey…

I almost couldn't believe the text that had come through from Nolan—who I affectionately had listed in my phone as Fucking Asshole—and I did a double take.

Nolan never texted me. If he needed to reach me about anything, he usually called, albeit most of those calls where always when I was in the middle of something, so this was new.

Heyyyyy, I texted back if only to be an asshole myself and be sarcastic. *Where's the fire?* I asked cheekily.

There is no fire.

I rolled my eyes, clearly Fucking Asshole's sense of humor was hit or miss.

I know that, asshole. You just never text me, so I assumed something was of dire importance.

I watched as those three little bubbles appeared on the screen, imagining Nolan tapping away furiously.

Right, of course, I just wanted to let you know I followed up on your brother's claim.

I leaned against the fire truck as I read his message.

You couldn't just call to tell me that? I asked.

I'm not in the office today. Verizon is still working on the lines.

A part of me knew I should keep things professional. After all, we worked together and I didn't want things to get weird, especially since as far as work was concerned. Nolan was helping me out and we were somewhat getting along. The last thing I needed was to piss him off when he was the one overseeing my brother's claim.

But hell if I wasn't a glutton for punishment and bad decisions, and maybe I needed something to take the edge off of my uncharacteristic nerves regarding our date tonight.

It's not a date.

Not really...

I'd told myself that over and over since the day prior, when I'd told Nolan I was a man of my word. It wasn't a date.

But it didn't feel like a business meeting either.

Instead of falling down that rabbit hole, I decided to push thoughts of our date–not date out of my mind.

And antagonize Nerdy Nolan a bit, if only because I considered it one of my favorite hobbies.

So what you're telling me is you're home... alone. Working.

I watched the text bubbles dance in wait of his reply.

I am, I thought we established this... he texted. I could hear the exasperation in his tiny little digital letters on the screen as text bubbles popped up again.

I just wanted to let you know everything was

processed. I'll keep an eye on this claim, and let you know if anything comes up.

Suddenly, I felt like an ass. I let out a sigh as I realized he was probably just trying to help, and I'd been an asshole taking advantage of the situation to what?

Flirt?

Make him all flustered?

Like some insensitive idiot.

Thanks, I appreciate it. Really.

It seemed forever until he'd texted me back.

Work's been a little crazy as of late, but you made it pretty clear this is important to you, so it's important to me too.

I wasn't sure how to respond to that. I knew Nolan was being professional, despite my attempts to make things unprofessional by flirting, but a part of me also wanted to hope that maybe there was more to his words.

I wasn't the kind of guy to ask for help with anything. I was the guy who always swooped in and rescued other people. But the idea that someone would back me up, support the things that were important to me because it's who they were or what was right, was something I was lacking in my life.

Before I could respond, those little bubbles started to come up again.

I knew I should just let it go, thank him, and

be done with shit. But the weird hope that had somehow blossomed in my chest and my ever-present need to take something serious and make it less serious won out.

You know what else is important to me, Nolan?

The bubbles disappeared.

After a moment of no response, I thought perhaps he'd ended the conversation, or that he'd gone off to do something else, leaving me hanging on the edge.

Rude.

But soon enough a *?* came through.

A strange sense of relief flooded me.

He's still there... I thought.

Your apartment number.

Truth be told, I kind of already knew since he was one floor below me, and I had access to such knowledge because I'd been on enough cases at the Towers that finding his apartment wasn't all that difficult, but it felt sort of like an overreach if I just showed up at his door unannounced. While I saw something like that as romantic and fun, someone shy and quiet like Nolan might feel like their privacy was violated.

Boundaries and all.

So I figured now would be as good as a time as ever to ask.

Why do you need to know my apartment number? I can just meet you wherever...

A part of me wondered if Nolan regretted agreeing to this dinner. He seemed a bit skittish, or nervous even.

But I wasn't letting him off the hook. If all I had was this one chance to put this all to rest, put Nolan out of my mind entirely, I needed to see this through.

Besides who doesn't want to go to a fancy restaurant with a hot guy and enjoy themselves for a night?

I typed out my reply quickly. *Well, if you lived in a house, I'd ride up in my trusty steed and pick you up from your doorstep like a true gentlemen.*

Nolan quickly responded. *Somehow, I have a hard time believing* you *are a gentleman in any facet of life.*

My smile spread as excitement took hold.

That little fucker!

I tapped out the words in rapid pace. *I can be whoever you want me to be, baby. As long as you're dressed in something nice and ready for me to pick you up at your door at six o'clock. No takebacks.*

I hit send, then immediately sent another text after I realized how desperate I sounded.

Was I really this desperate?

Yes, yes I was.

Desperate for something different, for a chance to forget about my boring life, about my brother's claim, which apparently was 'being handled' by Nolan now, about the fact that I hadn't had a successful relationship with someone other than my hand in at least two years.

Unless all you have is twelve pairs of white shirts and khakis, which then I might have to call 911 and report a fashion emergency.

A smirk played at my lips, a chuckle forming in my throat.

Nolan took my bait. Hook, line, and sinker.

I loved how easy it was to ruffle his feathers. It was entertaining as hell.

I will have you know, I own far more than just white shirts and khakis! I can look nice *if I want to. I can look even nicer if you tell me where we are going.*

I shook my head, typing back, *Not a chance, champ. Just be ready for me. Six o'clock. I'll pick you up and we'll head there in my truck. No sense in us taking two cars anyway, since we are both going back to the same place.*

That was the moment Gina called me from across the room, nipping at me to get off my phone and get my ass in the house to help Frank, our newest rookie with something.

Gotta go. I'll see you tonight.

CHAPTER 11

Nolan

"THERE'S NO NEED TO PANIC," Allie said calmly as I paced across my bedroom.

Her disembodied voice was not helping matters as she watched me from FaceTime like I was some anxious animal.

Because I am an anxious animal.

"Of course, there is a need to panic! I haven't been on a date in like five years, Allie. I need... I need this to go well, you know. Not just because it's Dawson, but..."

Because I need to know I'm not a complete failure of a human being.

"I thought you said it *wasn't* a date. That it

was just a silly bet. That it's just you besting him and getting your reward."

I huffed out a groan of defeat. "I know what I said, but..."

Truth was, up until I'd texted Dawson, I was content to believe it was just some silly bet, nothing to get worked up over. I'd put on some nice clothes, smile, and enjoy wherever we were going solely because it was a night out with the man I've been pining over for the last two years, and quite frankly, I was starting to think Karla was right. Maybe I *did* need a break, maybe I did need to relax.

But after Dawson's weirdly flirtatious texts earlier about making sure I looked nice, how he'd called me *baby*... telling me to be ready when *he* picked me up.

Well, it kind of sounded like maybe this *was* a date, which I knew was crazy. After all, Dawson Richards could have any man he wanted. He'd only have to blink and they'd say, "Yes, Daddy, take me home and ruin me."

Myself included.

I'd won the race fair and square, but as I second-guessed everything in my closet earlier, I felt more like a loser than a winner in anything.

I'm so out of my league here.

"Then why do I feel like a high-schooler going out with the captain of the football team?" I grumbled as I smoothed the front of my light blue button down for the hundredth time in an hour.

Staring at myself in the mirror, I had to admit I did look *nice.* My shirtsleeves were rolled up to the elbows, which I felt showed off my arms nicely, especially since I'd been working out a lot more since the beginning of the year. I wasn't built like Dawson or the other firefighters, but I liked where my definition was going, and I knew if I kept it up, it would only get better.

I stared at my mirror image, my pale skin contrasting the perfectly crisp pale blue shirt and a nice tailored pair of slacks, my dark hair swept back just enough to look like I hadn't spent a half hour strategically arranging it in front of my bathroom mirror. Even my glasses looked nice with the outfit. It was a simple look, but I'd found through the years that sometimes simple was best. It's often understated, but I'd gotten through plenty of weddings, cocktail parties, and business meetings with that outfit.

As I looked at myself, I felt a pang in my heart. I wanted to look more than *nice.* I wanted to look like someone who could be on a date with *Mr. March.*

I wanted to look *sexy.*

I wanted to *feel* sexy.

Sigh.

That was when I heard the knock on my door, which made me nearly jump out of my clothes and skin as my gaze flashed to my digital clock. It was only five fifty-three.

He's a couple minutes early.

I ran to grab my phone from its stand, Allie's eyes lighting up with excitement.

"Holy shit, he's here..." I gulped, watching Allie smile ear to ear.

"You're going to have a great time, Nolan. I promise. Just be yourself."

I wished I could be anyone else, truly.

Someone whose heart wasn't ready to beat out of his chest with anxiety right about now.

"Right, I'll call you later," I said as I ended our call.

Dawson rapped on my door again, causing an involuntary reaction of annoyance.

"I'm coming, hold your horses," I bit out as I power-walked through my apartment to the door. When I got there, I took a deep breath.

It's now or never, Nolan.

I opened the door and I immediately thought I must have died.

Had a heart attack five minutes ago when the reality that I was going on a date with Dawson set in.

Because the sight of the man in front of me was damn near breath-stealing.

Dawson leaned against my doorframe, the position showcasing his sexy-as-fuck arm muscles. He was also dressed in a button down, but from the sight of it, it looked like silk, and it was a deep ochre. The color against his naturally tanned skin made him look golden, like some sun god. His brownish-blonde hair fell in his eyes a bit, in a rogue, unkempt sort of way that somehow looked both refined and chaotically beautiful. My gaze roved over his form from head to toe, noting that the slacks he was wearing were perfectly tight around his hips where his gold belt caught the light from above, glittering like a glowing sign that pointed directly to his...

"Wow," was all I could say, like a fucking idiot.

Yup, totally out of my league here.

Dawson's pretty lips curved into a wicked smile as he raised an eyebrow.

"Like what you see, Harding?" he teased.

I nodded, swallowing nervously.

"You look... nice."

Dawson smirked. "Just nice?" His voice was dark and inviting, and I had half a mind to pull him into my fucking apartment and kiss him until I couldn't breathe.

But I needed to remain cool, collected. I

couldn't afford to fuck this up. I wanted this night to be perfect.

Grabbing Dawson and sequestering him in my apartment like a creepy stalker is not perfect by any means.

I shrugged, collecting my surprise and putting on my best impression of a normal person.

"I mean, I prefer you in your uniform, but that's just me."

Why the fuck did I say that?

I'm supposed to be acting normal!

Dawson didn't miss a beat though, taking my moment of lunacy and running with it.

"Didn't peg you for a badge bunny, champ."

"I'm not," I huffed in defense. "You're early..." I said, avoiding his gaze, if only so he couldn't see my blush.

Truth was, I'd never been into service men of any kind, despite the fact I'd been working with them for a while.

I didn't really have a type, to be honest. The only men I'd ever had relationships with tended to be like me. Quiet, reserved, and most certainly not the type to run into a burning building or pose in their underwear for calendars.

"Don't do that," he admonished darkly as he

gently tugged my chin to face him, making my entire body flush with heat.

The flush in my face had to be insanely prevalent and as close to a steamed tomato as humanly possible, judging from the heat that had overtaken me.

"Do what?" I breathed, my voice much huskier than I intended it to be, my gaze downcast.

"Look at me when you talk to me."

My insides twisted as I realized he hadn't let go of me. Trapped in his fiery gaze, I felt myself crumbling like a stack of cards. My gaze flashed up to meet his.

"I'm sorry, I..."

"Don't apologize, Nolan. You clean up nice too, you know," he said softly, his thumb brushing the underside of my chin as he gazed back at me, his tongue darting out to lick his lips.

Which caused my cock to wake the fuck up.

I felt my blush spread across my cheeks, my instinct to turn away, but Dawson's fingers held me in place.

"Are you nervous, Nolan?" His voice was playful, but enticing all the same. Like yesterday when we'd talked on the phone.

The memory of that moment only made my cock twitch.

Like an idiot I said, "I'm just... hungry, I guess."

I *was* hungry. But I wasn't sure if it was for food or for... him.

Maybe a little of both.

A wicked smile graced his lips as he let go of my chin, and I hated that my skin felt colder without his touch.

"Me too, champ. Let's go," he said as he turned away, leading me down the hall to the elevator, my head spinning and my cock aching.

What the fuck have I gotten myself into?

CHAPTER 12

Nolan

I sat in Dawson's candy apple red truck, feeling like I was going to pass out. I set my hands on my thighs, if only so my pants would absorb the sweat from my palms.

Dawson crawled into the driver's seat, and cranking the ignition. Music blared from the speakers, some Nickelback song that I didn't know all the lyrics to.

"Are you going to tell me where we're going yet? Or are you going to blindfold me?" I drawled sarcastically.

Dawson flashed me a smirk. "That depends, do you want me to blindfold you?"

The darkness in his voice called to my cock

like a damn siren and I shifted in my seat, trying my hardest to quell my burgeoning erection as I looked out the window so he couldn't see my blush.

"No, thank you," I said with a cough and a swallow.

No way in hell was I walking into that trap. The last thing I needed was to come in my pants sitting next to the man of my dreams before we even got to the fucking restaurant.

Christ, I haven't felt this horny since I discovered I liked cock.

Dawson chuckled as he pulled the car out of the Towers parking lot.

And he didn't say a word. He only focused on the road, his lips pursed. Gone was the playfulness, the sexy banter, and in its place was an awkward tension that filled the space.

I looked over at him, wondering if I'd said something wrong, done something, or if maybe he was just regretting this whole situation altogether. Whatever it was, I decided to try and break the ice.

The speakers blared with *Theory Of A Deadman*, which I knew only because in high school the guy I dated was obsessed with the band. A part of me felt inclined to scoot closer, to close the space between us, but I didn't.

"Can you at least tell me if where we're going is close?" I asked.

Dawson turned briefly to look at me.

"About a half hour. Why, you got some other pressing engagement tonight? Another tv marathon?" he said, but his voice was not playful or fun. Instead, it was replaced with a bit of anger.

My eyebrows furrowed and I shook my head.

"Nope. I'm all yours this evening." I swallowed as I said the words, but they weren't as difficult to speak as I thought they would be.

Dawson's shoulders loosened a fraction as he pursed his lips.

Some band I didn't recognize came over the speakers, the singer practically screaming and making my ears ring as they sang about the sound of madness.

"How can you listen to this stuff? It's just freaking noise," I said.

Dawson huffed out a sigh of annoyance.

"*Shinedown* is not noise," Dawson said defensively.

"Well, not to you. But it's a little grating on my ears," I half-whined, following it with a pout.

Dawson shot me a look that I could only describe as domineering, and I half worried he was going to pull this car over and murder me for my disdain of what was clearly his favorite music.

Way to go, Nolan.

"You know," I started as I sat back in my seat, crossing my arms. "Technically, the winner should pick the music," I quipped.

That seemed to alter his mood a bit, replacing the moody Dawson in front of me with the charismatic Dawson I was used to.

"Bratty boys don't always get what they want. Sometimes they have to work for it," he teased back, flashing a half-smile.

I couldn't help that my mouth dropped open at his words.

Was he calling me a... brat?

The notion made me turn six shades of red, and Dawson only shook his head, a complete smile finally spreading across his face.

"Fucking hell, Nolan, you need to stop doing that," he said, chuckling.

"Doing what?"

"Being fucking cute," he said, flashing me a grin as he hit his steering wheel.

Dawson thinks I'm... cute?

The words caused me to choke on my own air.

No fucking way.

He shook his head. "Driver picks the music, champ. Maybe if you're a good boy though...

you can pick it on the way home." His voice was dark and enticing and my cock throbbed from the implications.

I shifted in my seat once more, casually adjusting myself in a way that wouldn't draw attention.

The last thing I needed was for Dawson to know just how freaking turned on I was at the moment.

Because I most definitely found Dawson Richards more than *cute*.

He was freaking perfect.

Too perfect for someone like me, and I was dancing dangerously close to the edge of Heaven. So, I decided if I was going to die on this hill, I was going to go down in style.

"Oh, I can be *very good*," I said, flashing him with a grin of my own. "With proper incentive, that is. I like rewards."

"Of course you do," he said as he continued to drive, turning up the radio.

But I didn't fight him on it. Instead, I just let myself take in the sight of him dressed like a fucking snack, the wind messing up his hair through the window, and I committed the perfect image to my memory.

Because I knew after all was said and done, that's all I'd have.

CHAPTER 13

I parked the car, my mind racing and my pulse thudding away like a steel drum. I turned to look at Nolan, to take in the sight of his face, but instead I found him staring at *me.*

"You didn't have to do this," he said, his cheeks still holding his color from the heat of the outdoors mixed with his natural demeanor.

I wasn't lying when I'd told him he needed to quit with the bashful antics. I swear, every time the man sported a blush it made my cock rise to attention, made my heart skip a beat.

Not to mention it made me think about other things... like wondering if his pale ass would brighten like his face if I took my hand to it.

Fuck, now is not the time for sexy thoughts!

I internally chastised myself as I cleared my throat.

"I told you I'm a man of my word," I said as I leaned back against my seat.

Nolan sighed. "I know, but this... this is expensive and fancy, and..."

"And what? I can't like expensive, fancy things?"

"That's not what I'm saying. It's just... I would have been fine with..."

I watched as his eyebrows furrowed, as his shoulders tightened as he looked from me to the sleek building in front of us.

"Not many people in Jasper Springs can undermine me quite like you, Nolan. You beat me, and that's not something I take lightly. Great things deserve great rewards." I shrugged as I opened my door, hurrying to his before he could open it himself. I pulled the door open to see glassy brown eyes staring at me over his glasses, and I stepped to the side, if only to give him room to get out, but also because...

Because if I stood any closer, we might not have made it into the damn restaurant.

"I do not *undermine* you," he grumbled as he crossed his arms.

I closed the door, casting him a smirk. "I know this is a difficult concept to grasp for you, but maybe I think you're worth it, champ. It's not everyday someone hands my ass to me on a silver platter."

Nolan softened a tad. "That's because not everyone can keep up with your fine ass in order to do so."

I smiled both at his words and at the way they made him blush.

Sweet Jesus, grant me the strength to make it through this dinner without busting a damn nut.

"Shall we?" I said as I slid my hands in my pockets.

Nolan sighed, nodding in approval. "Lead the way."

CHAPTER 14

Dawson

"I'm sorry Mr. Richards, but your table isn't quite ready yet," the hostess said in the most graceful tone possible. I knew we were early, but I guess I had not realized *how* early. I really put the pedal to the medal, arriving a whole *twenty minutes early.* To be fair, there was no traffic, and I guess all that nervous energy got channeled into my lead foot.

"It's fine," "Nolan said, kindly and politely as I sighed. This date was off to a terrible start. Not only had I managed to sound like an absolute ass in the car, but now we were going to have to wait around for twenty or so minutes until we could eat, and I was seriously starving.

"You can find us at the bar, when it's ready," I said with a shrug, flashing her a smile and turning to make my way to the onyx bar.

Sedona itself was pretty uppity in its design but the bar was something else entirely. Long, sleek, shimmering black onyx from one end to the other, the gemstone and resin design was one that could only be appreciated up close. The top of the bar itself looked like one of those cracked geode rocks from fourth grade science class but much sexier, and the bottles of top-shelf liquor were lit from behind with blues and purples that made even the bottles themselves look divine.

"What can I get you, sir?" the bartender asked, his vague transatlantic accent perfectly in line with the aesthetic of the place.

"What you got on tap?" I asked, noting Nolan approached the bar slowly, picking up an acrylic table sign of drink specials, looking nonplussed.

The bartender slowly rambled on, but I couldn't focus on his words. All I could focus on was Nolan. His skin lit up with the outlying glow of the lights behind the bar, biting his perfect pout. Which made me swallow hard, made my cock twitch.

"Sir?" the man asked me again, and I realized I must have completely tuned him out, so I waved my hand, nodding with a smile. "The last one," I said, hoping to hell that whatever it was I just ordered wouldn't be dry and bitter as hell.

"And for you, sir?" the bartender turned to Nolan, his lips pulling up in the corner. It was the smallest smile, but it was a smile I hadn't been given.

Oh no, you don't, asshole. This one's mine.

Immediately, I froze upon my thoughts as Nolan looked up from his drink specials, big brown eyes oblivious to the bartender's subtle flirt.

I'd never thought of Nolan as much more than a thorn in my side for the last two years— well, unless you counted my fantasies but that was different.

Because fantasy was certainly not reality, and the reality was that Nolan didn't belong to me, not even in the slightest. He drove me damn near to drink with his incessant nitpicking and oversight of the claims I filed, and aggravated the hell out of me with his uncanny way of showing up just when I didn't want him to, but it seemed like somewhere along the line, my entire brain had done a complete one eighty.

The reality was that at some point, whether it was the race, or him showing up to *take care* of my brother because it was important to me, or maybe it was the night he showed up at M's

Place and won bingo... somewhere along the line I'd changed, and I no longer wanted to make Nolan's life a living hell.

I just wanted *him*.

To make his cheeks turn scarlet, to get him so flustered he couldn't speak, to fuck him so good he wouldn't be able to leave his fucking couch.

I swallowed harshly as that reality set in, because I knew this wasn't a date.

But maybe I wanted it to be.

So, I decided if this date-not-date was going to be a disaster, I might as well make it a pretty one.

"Oh, uh, I'm not..."

"Tell the nice man what you want, baby," I taunted him, which made him flush.

Dawson 1, Nolan 10, bartender 0.

"If you have questions or would like a recommendation," the bartender said smoothly as he leaned his arms across the surface, his voice smooth and rich like the bar itself.

Nolan set the drink specials down, chewing on his lip as if contemplating what to order with great thought.

"I'll have the Elderberry Fizz. Please," he said poignantly.

"Will that be all, sir?" the bartender asked, his voice huskier than I liked.

I moved closer to Nolan, only by an inch, placing my hand at the small of his back, which made Nolan jump nearly five feet off the ground.

"See, now was that so hard?" I teased.

Nolan side-eyed me from underneath his thick, black glasses and smirked. "You are insufferable, you know that?" he said as he cocked his head to the side, blowing a stray piece of hair out of his eyes.

"It is my number one goal in life. To be an insufferable bastard," I said, flashing him with a grin as I turned to look at the bartender. "That'll be all, thanks."

Twenty minutes turned into thirty minutes, as there had been a party before us who was in our spot, who just didn't seem to want to leave. Normally, I would have argued, gotten angry that I was planning on spending good money there too, so why the hell wasn't I capable of being seated on time, but I'd already accepted this date-not-date was an epic disaster, so what else could I do? Especially after two beers of my own, knowing I needed to slow down or we'd be catching an Uber home.

Which didn't sound bad, but then again, I didn't want an audience with Nolan. In fact, I didn't want *anyone* else with Nolan but me.

Mine.

All mine.

My buzzed thoughts wandered to places they shouldn't, my little Nolan fantasies threatening to take the driver's seat.

Despite his cocky, bratty attitude at times, Nolan hadn't been the clearest on his signals. While I knew without a doubt at this point he did in fact like guys, and he'd made a few comments about me and my calendar shoots, I wasn't entirely sure if he liked... me.

He did insult your taste in music.

Whether or not he liked me—the me underneath the charisma and the humor—shouldn't have mattered to me at all.

Why did I care if he liked me?

It wasn't like every man I fucked in my life liked me for my winning personality. Sex was just that, sex.

And sometimes it was way hotter when I was balls deep in some pretty asshole that didn't respect me or like me *at all.*

But my feeble, inebriated mind warred with my heart and my hunger, desiring something more.

I wanted him to like me, because I liked him. More than I ever thought I would.

We followed the waiter, who was dressed in a get up that looked strangely reminiscent of a penguin, Nolan giggling the entire way. After the

second Elderberry Fizz, he seemed to have loosened up and I wasn't complaining.

Once we'd both ordered our meals, and the
waiter had left us once again, I had Nolan all to
myself, which I enjoyed far too much.

"Glad to see you're enjoying yourself," I said
genuinely, relishing in the smile that formed
across his face. He nodded.

God he has a nice smile.

My entire body loosened at the sight.

Shit, I definitely need to stick with water.

"I am, actually. I... I can't remember the last
time I've even done something like this."

"Like what?" I asked involuntarily, and took
a sip of my water.

"I mean, it's been awhile since I've been out
on a date in general, let alone with someone like
you," Nolan said as he spun his stir stick in his
drink.

"What do you mean, like me?" I asked,
confused.

"Confident, brave. Sexy," he said, and he
took another drink, hiding his blush behind his
glass. But I wasn't about to let him off the hook.
Not now when he seemed keen on dishing out
compliments.

I'm a sucker for a little praise, so sue me.

But something about the way he said the
words felt deeply genuine, and I couldn't help

but rise to his bait, especially because it made me feel like I'd just won bar bingo.

Well, well... maybe I should take Nolan out for a drink more often.

"Is that so?" I said as I tapped my fingers on the table, steeling my gaze on his pink cheeks. "You think I'm... sexy? Is that why you're always up my ass?" I teased him, my own smile forcing its way across my face.

Nolan shook his head. "I mean, how many times have you gotten naked for the damn calendar? Like four times?"

"You counted?" I asked coyly.

Nolan shrugged, taking another sip of his drink. "Absolutely not,"

Liar.

"You know, you're not quite what I thought you were either. For the record." The words came out of my mouth of their own volition, causing Nolan to peer up at me over his thick frames.

"Wha... what do you mean?" he stuttered.

"I mean, don't get me wrong, you're still a giant pain in my ass, but I thought... I thought I knew you. But I'm just starting to scratch the surface, I think."

Nolan looked up at me with big, bright puppy dog eyes, his entire expression shifting like I'd just told him the last piece of cake was his.

As far as I'm concerned, he can have whatever he wants tonight... and I do hope there's cake.

"I hope that's not a bad thing," he whispered, his eyebrows furrowing.

Oh you sweet, sweet man...

Who the hell burned you?

I looked him in the eye, mustering as much seriousness as I could when I said, "No, Nolan. Not at all. In fact, I—"

Before I could spill all my secrets and newfound desires out on the table like a teenage girl, the waiter came with our food, shattering the strange sort of tension that had grown between us, and neither of us had any thoughts about anything but the absolutely fantastic food in front of us.

When we'd both devoured our meals plus dessert—a delectable chocolate horchata cake—and the check came, Nolan immediately tried to grab it.

"Ah, ah... paws off, baby."

"Come on, we can split it. You don't have to—"

"I want to, Nolan. Seriously, just let..." I sighed as I watched his face intently.

"Just let me take care of *you.*"

CHAPTER 15

NOLAN

THE ELDERBERRY FIZZES must have gone to my head. There was no other way I could explain the complete disconnect that happened in my brain and body when Dawson told me he wanted to *take care of me.*

It was like an out of body experience. I'd had two serious boyfriends in my short, twenty-eight years of life. Well, one wasn't really my boyfriend, he was more or less trying to figure his shit out, but we weren't in the closet or anything, so I think it counts.

Because if it didn't, that would mean I've only ever been in one serious relationship my entire life.

Sure, I'd thought of scenarios like this one

when I was alone—usually because the crux of my thoughts were centered around what would happen *after* I'd been sufficiently wined and dined by a handsome man with eyes only for me, and usually in those thoughts, I ended up on my knees showing my praise and putting out like a homecoming queen.

God, I am so easy!

But I never thought I'd actually be here, in this situation, with Dawson Richards of all people.

Despite the alcohol, I found myself unable to speak, even though my thoughts were running a mile a minute.

Dawson's eyebrows furrowed and he narrowed his gaze at me as he handed the check and his credit card to the waiter.

"I—" I cleared my throat, finding the will to speak once more if only because I didn't want to seem rude.

"Thank... you," I managed to get the words out.

Dawson cast a smile I could only describe as dirty and wicked at me, his brown eyes lighting up with the signature golden energy that encapsulated him most of the time.

Drawing me closer, like a bug to the sun.

"Don't thank me just yet. Wait till we get

home," he said, flashing me a flirtatious wink, causing my blush to hit me like a tidal wave.

I both hated and loved that with barely a few words and a look, this man could have me so flushed and flustered, so damn desperate for more of that hot, golden light that only he could shine.

I wanted more.

Stupidly, I wanted anything Dawson was willing to give me.

I sucked down the remainder of my third fizzy drink, feeling much more relaxed than I usually did. I wasn't sure what all the bartender put in that thing, but whatever it was, it was making me feel on cloud nine, invincible almost.

Which probably accounted for my sudden influx of confidence at the moment.

Because as I watched Dawson sign his receipt and slide his credit card back into his wallet, then slide said wallet into his slacks as we rose from the table, I'd made an impulsive, split decision, and I wasn't going back.

So, I let Dawson show me out, let him walk me to his truck, stilling my breath as best I could.

When we got to the truck, he moved to open my door but I stopped him.

Realistically, he'd drive me home, forget

about this date-not-date like he forgot about me that first time we met, after we'd flirted.

We'd go back to life as normal—working together, aggravating one another, hiding our true feelings. And I just... didn't want to go back to that.

It's now or never, Nolan.

If you want things to change, change them.

I'd never been more sure of anything in my life.

"Nolan, what—"

I didn't think twice about doing what I'd wanted to do for two years, what I'd wanted to do since that night in M's Place, under his spell, what I wished I had done when we were standing in his brother's front yard.

I pulled Dawson Richards into me and I pressed my lips to his. He startled for a moment, clearly surprised by my sudden boldness, but only for a split second. Then he relaxed in my hold, setting his warm palm on my hip, tugging me closer, his lips moving unhurriedly against mine.

A deep, satisfied groan escaped my throat as his tongue breached my lips. With both hands on my hips, he pulled me tight against him; so tight I could feel his hardness against my own.

I ran my hands up his neck, letting my

fingertips play with the edges of his soft hair, and I lived in that kiss for a hundred years.

Because no one had ever kissed me the way Dawson kissed me.

He broke away, and my lips felt swollen and warm from his fiery kiss, longing to be caressed once more.

I think that was when I knew nothing would ever be the same again, and on some deeper level, I knew it was the beginning of something so much greater than I'd ever expected.

But I couldn't process all of that amidst the alcohol infusing my brain.

"Fucking brat," he said with a laugh. "I said, wait till we get home. I told you, good boys get—"

I couldn't help but smile at his words. "Maybe I don't want to be rewarded, Dawson," I said with a giggle of my own as I boldly went where I'd never gone before. "Maybe I want to be punished instead."

It was Dawson's turn to blush, and I took much pride in that.

He slid his hands down my side, licking his lips as he implored me with his gaze.

"Get. In. The. Car," he said sternly, and I wanted to argue.

To fight him, to instigate him.

It was second nature to me, but I also didn't

want to piss him off and make him regret this entire night, so for once, I did as I was told. I climbed into the car, but I didn't miss as Dawson tugged at the tent he'd pitched in his pants before he scrambled into the driver's seat.

I watched as he took a deep breath, his hands tight on the steering wheel as if he was trying to find his own confidence, or his own way out of a deep, dark place.

Back to reality.

He turned the car on, flashing me a look when Metallica came on over the radio.

"I told you, if you were good you could pick the music," he said with a smirk. "And I am a man of my word, as you know, so go ahead, champ. Have at it."

I smugly smiled, feeling like the truck was only slightly spinning, but I wasn't sure if that was because of the alcohol, or because the way Dawson was looking at me was making me seriously debate going full bad boy and straddling his lap right here.

My desires, my thoughts, my actions... everything was a hazy blur stirring within me like some cyclone.

But I managed to keep from falling apart at the seams, languidly moving forward to gently twist the knob until I'd found a station I liked, which was playing my favorite song. *Hot Blooded.*

Dawson shot me a look as he pulled out of the parking lot, shaking his head as I hummed along and murmured the words to myself. At least, I thought I was singing to myself.

The entire ride home was like that. Both of us singing along to the radio like two teenagers out late on a school night.

And I'd never felt so... free.

So unequivocally *me*.

I'd spent the majority of my life on the sidelines. By myself. My mother always said it was because I was shy, but the reality was I just wasn't comfortable being my awkward self around most people. The world expected you to be a certain way, it classified you based on what you liked, the job you did, and the things you surrounded yourself with. I knew when people looked at me what they saw, the person they'd decided I was, and quite frankly, I didn't see the point in trying to live up to their ideals and expectations, and I didn't want to disappoint anyone. So, I just... didn't open up.

But something about Dawson made me feel like for the first time, it was okay to open up. It was okay to be *me*.

The me who likes to bust out into song like it's an episode of Carpool Karaoke, the me who is sarcastic, the me who is relaxed and fun, and not wound up tighter than an Egyptian mummy most of the time.

I'd barely even noticed when Dawson parked the car at the Towers. Only when the music stopped did I realize we'd been singing and laughing for nearly thirty minutes.

We both sat there in silence for a long moment, and finally, I decided to speak.

"I had... a really great time tonight," I said, not wanting this to end.

I wanted more nights where I felt alive like I did with Dawson.

Dawson moved closer to me, turning to face me. "Me too," he said softly, his gaze roving over me, before settling on my lips.

I scooted closer to him, until our thighs were brushing against one another.

"Dawson, I—"

It was my turn to be surprised, when Dawson reached out, setting his palm against my neck as he pulled me closer, popping one of my buttons as he slid his hand beneath my collar. I shifted my weight until I was practically in his lap. His lips moved against mine with a hunger that echoed my own, and I melted into him like an ice cube on the sidewalk on the Fourth of July.

"Fuck..." I groaned as his tongue slipped

into my mouth again, my cock springing back to life.

Instinct took over, and I shifted my weight over his lap, straddling his lap with my thighs. My ass hit the steering wheel, but I didn't care.

Dawson moved his seat back a hair to give me room, but I didn't want room. I wanted to be as close to Dawson as I could get.

Dawson groaned in my mouth as I ground my rigid erection against his, both loving the friction and hating the barriers between us. My head was spinning.

"Nolan..." he purred, my name on his tongue stronger than any drink I'd ever had. His hand slid up my neck, fingers grasping at my hair with a tight grip, causing my cock to throb. Instinctively, I ground myself against him, needing to feel the friction.

His hands slid down my body in a rushed motion, over my hips, resting on my ass as I let my lips brush his jaw before landing over his neck. I could feel his pulse against my tongue as I licked his skin. His fingers squeezed my ass with a force that had it not been for clothes, would have left a mark. Dawson's touch was full of fire, and I wanted to burn within it.

"Fucking hell... Nolan—"

I stifled his words with my mouth, driven by need, by desire.

Two years.

I'd been dreaming of this man for two years, fantasizing about this cock for two years.

I didn't want to stop. I didn't want this perfect night to end.

Dawson thrust his hips upward, the motion causing his hardness to slide against mine through our slacks, and I moaned in response, already feeling a wet spot forming in my boxers.

I slid my hands down his chest to his waistband, my fingers ready to claim my prize.

Dawson's hand stopped me, which was like a splash of cold water.

"I think... I think we need..." His breath was coming in rapidly, and I could hear the lust in it, but already my nerves were shot as I realized what was happening.

I'd miscalculated. I was wrong.

Dawson didn't want this.

He didn't want *me.*

"I think we need to slow down."

And just like that, my dreams were shattered.

CHAPTER 16

DAWSON

IT TOOK every ounce of concentration, every bit of willpower I had, to tell Nolan to stop.

Because I didn't want him to stop.

Fucking hell, I wanted to unearth more of the Nolan I'd seen tonight. The one who wasn't *anything* like I thought he was. The one who blushed constantly at my flirtations, who sang the best karaoke, who knew when to be playful and when to be serious. Who was still a pain in my ass, but was now adding a whole new sort of pain.

When he kissed me outside the restaurant, I was surprised, but mostly because up until that point I didn't think he was into... me. Not like I was slowly becoming into him.

When he kissed me outside the restaurant, his tongue sliding against mine, his dick rubbing against mine, I knew I was a goner. Nolan Harding had blazed through me like a five alarm fire, and I loved it. I wanted more of it.

Which is probably why I had let things get this far to begin with. It was easier to pretend at Sedona that we weren't... us. That we were some beautiful couple on a date, enjoying one another.

But outside home, outside the Towers, reality waited for me.

Nolan wasn't just some hot guy I wanted to take back to my apartment and suck off.

He was my co-worker. He was in charge of my brother's claim.

And he's probably at least a little drunk, and might regret this come tomorrow morning.

I didn't want to be a regret. I wanted to see Nolan again, and not in the capacity I'd been used to.

I wanted *him.*

So, I knew I had to do things right this time. I had to take my time. Show Nolan that he was worth more than just some truck fuck.

The pain and sadness that registered on his face at my words damn near fucking killed me.

"I'm so sorry. I—" Nolan scrambled off of my lap, leaving my aching boner on full display, the prevalent need to come ebbing in every part of my body.

I leaned my head back against the headrest, closing my eyes as I stilled my breath, grabbing myself to try and stifle my erection. But it was no use, and I was far too sensitive from all of Nolan's dirty grinding, and I came the minute I grabbed myself.

Fuck... I breathed through my ruptured orgasm, the sound of the door slamming pulling me back to the here and now. I adjusted myself as I jumped out of the car, chasing after Nolan when I felt like I needed an eight hour nap.

I don't think I've come in my pants from fucking frotting since I was a damn teen!

"Nolan, wait!" I yelled as he stomped across the parking lot like a petulant child. I jogged to catch up to him, noting the tension in his shoulders. I reached out, grabbing his shoulder, turning him to look at me, and I could see the fire in his eyes.

"Don't," he bit out. "Just... don't make this worse."

"Nolan..." I pleaded as he opened the door, heading for the elevator. I followed him like a lamb to the slaughter.

The elevator dinged and we both tried to go

in at once, colliding with one another. I motioned for him to go in first, and he huffed in annoyance. When the elevator closed, Nolan stood there with his arms crossed, refusing to look at me.

"Would you just look at me?" I hissed breathlessly.

"I can't," he said as the elevator opened on his floor. "I'll be fine. Just, let me go."

His words were like ice, and I knew he wouldn't be. Whoever had burned this man before me left some deep wounds. That I was sure of.

My insides ached to soothe him, soothe whatever fear or bullshit he was feeding himself. I needed him to understand that he deserved more.

We deserved more.

I couldn't let him go. So, I ran out of the elevator until I got to his apartment, breathing heavily as he stood in front of his door, keys in hand.

"Nolan, just listen to me, damn it!" I barked, not caring about the volume of my voice. He turned to me with glassy eyes.

"It's not that I don't want to, I do, I just—"

"What? It's not you, it's me? Really, Dawson?" Nolan bit out, his tongue flicking out over his lips as he narrowed his wet gaze at me.

He was trying to be tough, but I could see the reality of his emotional state clear as day.

My rejection had hurt him.

I'd fucked up.

I stepped closer, reaching out to touch him because I too, was a glutton for punishment. I expected him to push me away but instead, his shoulders loosened, his eyes gazing up at me with sadness and inebriation.

"It's not you..." I said, the words somehow so clear in my mind, but so difficult to say. So I chose another route. I pulled him close, kissing him once more.

Nolan sunk into my kiss like I was the air he needed to breathe, making my heart race. He broke away, his eyes full of tears.

I pulled him into my arms, wrapping them around him like he was a damn life preserver and I was drowning.

Because in a way, I was. We both were.

Drowning in our own personal hell, in denial.

Nolan's hand settled on my hip as he brushed his face against my shirt.

"Why won't you let me be the good guy for once?" I asked, my voice barely a whisper.

I pulled away, looking at his face, at the pain in his expression.

Pain I caused.

Fuck, how do I make this right?

Nolan turned away from me for a moment, his dark lashes standing out against his pale skin, the sheen of his black frames catching the light from above in the hallway.

He turned back to me, his voice pained.

"Because that's my job, Dawson. To be the good guy. You're *supposed* to the bad guy," he chortled.

"What do you mean?" I asked, feeling my own heart break at his words.

Was that how he saw me?

Truly?

As some Bond villain?

Nolan stepped forward an inch, closing the distance between us that had formed. "You're supposed to fucking ruin me," he said, tears falling down his pale cheeks, his voice dark and full of things that made my cock twitch again.

Made my blood hot.

Nolan said the words, but I felt them in my core.

He wanted to burn.

He wanted me in the worst way, and the reality of that notion scared me more than anything else.

I slid my hands through his soft, dark hair, staring back at his beautiful, tear-stained face, and I felt on the edge of a cliff.

And that was when I decided to jump.

A part of me knew he may not remember this conversation in the morning, but if he did... I hoped he'd at least respect me for it.

"If you want this..." I breathed heavily, stroking the wet streaks on his cheek with my thumb. "If you want *me*," I started. "Then you can have me. But not like this," I whispered, planting a kiss on his forehead.

Nolan pushed me away.

"Whatever, Dawson," he said as he unlocked his door, and I watched him disappear, leaving me and my heart in ruin.

I only prayed that we could rebuild what I'd broken.

CHAPTER 17

Nolan

I woke up with a pounding headache, a dry mouth, and an overbearing need to piss. The sunlight filtered in through my window, and it was blindingly bright as I shielded my eyes from it.

I groaned as reality set in, memories of the prior night playing over in my mind like a movie. Dawson and I... We kissed.

Fuck, I kissed him!

The memory of Dawson relaxing into me, of his warm lips against mine, made my entire body flush with heat.

I'd had probably a little more than I could handle in the liquor department, but to be fair, those drinks didn't even taste like they had alcohol in them at all. It was like sucking down a Capri Sun. But the throbbing pain in my head told me those sweet, fizzy drinks packed quite a punch.

I leaned back in my bed, running my hand over my eyes as I let the hazy memories surface, as I tried to hold on to what had happened, how things had transpired.

Though I remembered kissing Dawson, everything else seemed rather vague and blurry. As if one moment bled into the next, and all I could remember was the feel of his lips on mine, of his cock against mine.

Fuck!

I want you to ruin me.

The words surfaced in my brain, and even though I was alone with no one to witness my mortification, I blushed what I would have guessed was a deep scarlet from the way my entire body heated at the memory.

Of me being pissed off because we...

Were making out in his truck!

And I told him that?

That I wanted *him to fucking ruin me?*

I groaned miserably as I grabbed the pillow next to me, feeling a slight panic attack coming on.

Breathe, Nolan, it's fine.

You can blame it on the fizzy bubbly drinks... maybe he doesn't remember anyway... or...

Honestly, I wasn't sure I *could* blame it all on the alcohol. That may have accounted for my loose lips, but it wasn't like I was lying about what I said. I *did* want Dawson to ruin me. I wanted him to destroy me in more ways than one, and then build me back up from total destruction.

The memory of his fingers gripping my ass resurfaced, only causing more of a mixture of pain and embarrassment meddled with lust and desire.

I am so fucked up.

I wanted him to forget my momentary lapse of judgment, my embarrassing, desperate attempt to lull him into my apartment and live out my stupid fantasy.

After all, I *was* practically throwing myself at him.

And his answer had been very clear, because here I was, awake and alone.

But I didn't have time to process such things. Duty called, after all. I swung my legs over the side of the bed and planted my feet on the carpet as I tried to stabilize my breath.

Of two things I was absolutely certain. One, that Dawson had kissed me back.

Which changed *everything*.

But the second thing I knew was that despite the fact he seemed into it, he left me alone on my doorstep, pissed off, horny, and rejected. He just... left.

Because I wasn't good enough.

Because I'd upset the delicate balance of the tightrope between us.

Because he wanted to be a good guy.

Maybe I'd ruined everything.

I felt a sting of guilt, but it would have to be short-lived, because not ten seconds later my phone was ringing, louder than it probably should have been.

I fumbled with my phone on the nightstand, knocking over a box of tissues as I squinted to see the screen.

Karla calling.

Great, just who I wanted to hear from at seven thirty in the morning when I was hungover.

"Hello?" I answered groggily.

"Morning sleepyhead," Karla said in a tone that was much too chipper for my liking.

"I could have used five more minutes..." I groaned as I slowly ambled my way across the floor to the hallway and down to the bathroom.

"I bet. You sound like shit. You're not sick, are you?" she asked, her tone changing to one of concern.

I easily slid my cock out of my boxers, relieving myself while I tried to focus.

"I wish," I mumbled. "But no."

"Techs should be wrapping up this morning, so you're good to come back in the office this afternoon. You should be all recharged and ready to go," she said.

"Great," I touted as I tucked myself back in my boxers.

"Sounds great, hun. See you this afternoon!" she said, her voice filled with excitement.

I'm glad one of us is in a good mood.

CHAPTER 18

Nolan

I PULLED up to the Breisinger building like a functional human being, despite feeling the exact opposite. I clutched my iced coffee, forcing a smile as I walked through the doors past Brittany, our receptionist.

"Afternoon, Mr. Harding," she said with faked enthusiasm that I couldn't even muster at the moment.

"Afternoon, Britt," I said as I headed for my office.

"Regional called about the Bradish claim."

I stopped dead in my tracks.

Bradish... That would be Dawson's brother... What could Regional possibly want?

"Did they say what it was about?" I asked, already on edge. We rarely got calls from the big guys, they usually left us alone as long as we closed our claims and met our goals, and I'd only gotten a call from them once, regarding one of Dawson's claims when I'd first started. It had been a clear misunderstanding. Something Dawson noted that wasn't listed under the right subset or something. I'd learned after that call to double check *everything* submitted by Dawson and his crew, if only because I didn't want any oversights and to have Regional breathing down my neck.

Britt shrugged. "Not really, just said they wanted you to call them back when you got in."

I nodded, my grip around my ice coffee tightening as I mustered a half-smile. Maybe when I didn't have a pounding headache I could pretend, but not today.

"Thanks, Britt," I said as I made a beeline for my door, doing my best to evade Karla's office door, which was open. I didn't dislike my boss, but sometimes she had a tendency to want to gossip and chitchat when I wanted nothing to do with the insider gossip on Jasper Springs's residents.

I tried to stay out of the drama, thank you very much.

With a hefty amount of luck, I managed to

squeeze past her door while she was otherwise engaged in something at her computer, taking refuge in my office and immediately shutting the door.

Flopping down in my chair, I let out a heavy breath.

Okay, Nolan, just take it easy. You don't know it's anything bad...

I set up at my desk, focusing on my breath.

Here goes nothing.

CHAPTER 19

Nolan

I LET OUT a sigh of frustration as I hung up the phone. Apparently, the files I'd sent electronically had gotten all fucked up, and I needed to re-evaluate the claim with brand new photos, a brand new report... and video of the location and business.

Fuck me.

Just as I contemplated crumbling into a million pieces, Karla's voice cut through my disdain.

"Guess you heard from Regional?" she asked, crossing her arms.

"Yeah," I mumbled.

"You're not the only one. Lex and Stacey

also have to go back out and do re-evals. Seems whatever was going on with our computers, you all had some serious damage to your files. I asked the techs about it and they said with the new upgrades it likely won't happen again, and it was a fluke."

Yeah, a fluke that just had to happen on the worst day of my life.

"I literally just got here..."

Karla softened her gaze. "You okay? You seem... grouchy. More so than usual," she pried, no doubt looking for gossip, and a part of me wanted to talk. But another knew whatever I had to process or say would be better left in my own mind than to be aired out for Jasper Springs's Blair Waldorf.

"I'm fine, just... I need to get caught up here. You know, get back to work..."

Karla's gaze steadied as she squinted, sizing me up.

If she could tell I was lying, she didn't show it. Instead, she nodded and said, "Okay, Nolan. But I'm watching you." She pointed between us sarcastically.

"Yeah, yeah, I get it," I said as my email started to sound, the whistle of work calling me. I stared at my inbox, a part of me hoping to see an email from Dawson. He loved to blow up my inbox with insults and nitpicks about the claims of his I'd checked.

But my shoulders sunk when I saw nothing. Nothing from anyone other than Karla and Regional, anyway.

Certainly not anything from Dawson Richards.

I let out a breath, leaning back in my chair. I wanted to reach out, apologize for what an ass I'd been... but I also didn't want to appear overbearing, or cliché.

I've never done this before, or I don't usually act like this is definitely cliché. Worse, it's juvenile. I'm a twenty-eight year old adult. I've certainly done this before.

Enough to know that it was probably better I leave Dawson alone for a day or two, let things smooth over, let him have time to forget what happened. Forget me.

And maybe I should forget him too. Be happy we'd had a decent time before I blew everything to smithereens.

I took another long pull of my iced coffee, checking the clock on my computer screen. Four more hours left in this day, surely I could manage that.

CHAPTER 20

Nolan

I stared at my phone, at the text thread that remained empty. He hadn't texted me, and I hadn't made a move to do so either. Instead, I'd only stared at that blank text bubble all day as if I could magically wield the words on screen. Words that would somehow fix this, erase my embarrassing behavior, and put us back to square one.

In the woods.

Where I could lose the race, and the chance to have ever been so close to such perfection. Where I could exist not knowing how good his lips tasted against mine.

I set the phone down on the bar as I pushed

away for a moment, grabbing my beer as I glanced around the room.

I didn't come to M's Place often, but after feeling like shit all day at work about everything —my botched date, my job, my life in general— I didn't want to go home.

When I found myself in front of the bar, I didn't question it. It wasn't the same as being with someone, or talking to someone, but it beat going home alone to wallow.

Wallowing at a bar is what normal people do anyway, isn't it?

That was when I saw him.

With someone else.

Instinctively, I felt a sting of jealousy, mixed with sadness and anger.

I knew I didn't have a claim on Dawson, that he was free to do whatever he wanted with whoever he wanted, but even knowing that I couldn't help it.

Especially when the guy he was with was absolutely gorgeous compared to me. Toned, defined form, golden blond hair... He looked like a Calvin Klein model or something. Not to mention the two seemed pretty comfortable with one another, smiling and laughing.

Which only made me feel worse.

How could I have been so stupid?

Dawson had said he hadn't been on a date

in awhile, and I wanted to believe him, but was I that easily played?

He probably told *all* the guys that. It was probably part of his charm or act.

I drained the last of my beer, feeling like I needed to get out of the place.

Away from the sight of Dawson with Mr. Perfect.

So, I threw my cash on the counter, with a nice tip of course, considering I'd only bought the one drink, but that was all I needed, and honestly, after seeing Dawson with his date, it was all I could stomach.

CHAPTER 21

Dawson

Of all the days to be slow, today was the slowest.

I leaned my head back against the couch in the living room upstairs in the firehouse, fighting to concentrate on anything except the previous night.

On the memory of my embarrassing moment.

Granted, Nolan had no idea all his grinding had caused me to explode in such a fashion, and I wasn't about to tell him that little tidbit. I'd take that to my fucking grave.

But the fact of the matter was, I knew there

was absolutely no way I'd be able to look at Nolan the same again.

Not after he'd kissed me, after he'd wriggled his way onto my lap and into my damn heart like he had.

I wanted to text him. All day I thought about it, but I didn't want to seem too forward. I wasn't sure how much he remembered, if he remembered pinning me beneath him in my truck and making my damn head spin, or if he was hungover as shit and wanted to be left alone. I knew I hated to be bothered when I drank a bit too much, when I was hungover as shit.

No, I knew I needed to give Nolan space, and I didn't want to appear... clingy.

Even though I'm dying to know his thoughts, if he remembers what happened.

If he regrets what happened.

I hated leaving Nolan like I had. I'd wanted to give into temptation, wanted to *ruin* him as he requested, but I also wanted more... I knew I had to tread carefully because the last thing I wanted was to create problems for either of us at work.

Firehouse gossip spreads fast too.

The clock chimed on three, waking me from my spell of self-loathing just as my phone buzzed.

In an awful moment of weakness earlier, I'd texted the one person who knew me better than most, because I knew I needed to talk or I'd end up doing something I regretted.

Like send a string of text messages that made me appear like a level six stalker.

I needed to get things out in the open, to be able to process what had happened and how I could fix things, and there wasn't anyone I trusted more with my secrets than Cade.

Mitch was a great friend, don't get me wrong, but his emotional capacity was only a smidge higher than an amoeba.

The man was about as anti-romance as you could get. If I needed help moving something, or new social media photos, or even to borrow twenty bucks, Mitch was the guy to ask. But if I needed advice on dick and all things centered around the dick... I was better asking a hopeless romantic like Cade.

I'd half expected him to blow me off, being as he and his new boyfriend were practically attached at the hip, and I was pleasantly surprised when he answered my angsty, emo-kid text with, '*Sure, let's meet up at M's this evening and talk about it. What time you off?*'

The instant relief that poured over me should have been embarrassing had I not felt the stress of everything melt almost immediately.

I wasn't sure what the right thing to do was, but I knew at least if I talked things out with my best friend, he'd steer me in the right direction.

CHAPTER 22

Dawson

When I walked into M's Place at five-thirty, Cade was already waiting. His bright blue eyes caught mine from across the room, and I didn't miss the smile. He'd had a rough year, before Weston showed up in town to sweep him off his feet like some knight in fine tailored armor, riding his trusty BMW steed, and I had to admit, happiness looked good on him.

I wish I could have that too.

"Hey," he said as he reached out to hug me.

I hugged him back, already feeling a little better. I'd never been an emotional person. In fact, I'd always been pretty clear-headed and level when it came to tough situations, knowing how to rein my feelings in to prevent a bigger issue, but it seemed like lately I was losing my ability to not give a fuck.

My walls were crumbling around me and I knew why. I just didn't want to admit it out loud.

"Hey," I said as we broke apart our hug and took our seats.

"So, tell me about this guy that's got you all —" He whistled, a slow smile spreading across his face.

I sighed.

Well, it's now or never.

"He's not just... some guy. Cade, he's..." I struggled to find my words, but true to his nature, Cade was as patient as a saint with me.

"It's... Nolan."

"Nolan riding your ass again at work? I told you—"

"No, Cade. The guy that's... It's Nolan. We sort of... ran into each other on the trail at the Towers, and I sort of made a bet with him, and he won, and we sort of went on a date, but it wasn't supposed to be a date, and then we kissed, and started making out in my truck, and I lost it, and he ran off, and..."

"Slow down, Dawson. One thing at a time..." Cade said, his eyebrows furrowing in concentration.

"I just, uh... I think somehow I may have fucked shit up, and I'm not sure what to do."

Cade smiled, shaking his head. "I knew it. You got it bad, huh?" he said slyly.

On instinct, I balked at his comment. After all, I'd prided myself for years on my carefree personality, the guy who just had fun without getting too involved in anything remotely serious.

It was still strange despite how I felt inside, to hear someone else say it out loud.

"I wouldn't go that far, I—"

Cade's shoulders loosened as he sat back in his chair, eyeing me like a teacher eyes the kid in class who screamed when they weren't supposed to.

"Dawson. It's me. You can be honest."

"It's complicated," I said, hating how cliché I sounded.

"It always is," Cade said as the waiter finally came by to take our order.

I opted for a beer and a basket of hot wings, while Cade opted for a spiked seltzer and some fried pickles. He briefly checked his phone, a smile gracing his lips, and I almost rolled my eyes.

"Prince Charming whispering sweet nothings in your ear again?"

Cade set his phone down, smirking. "Actually, he said he's getting out of work early, and asked if he could join us?'"

I wanted to be pissed. Really, I did, but seeing the way Cade lit up when he talked about the man made it hard to say no.

"Of course, the more the merrier," I said with a half-smile. It wasn't that I didn't like Weston, or that I felt like I deserved this alone time with Cade and selfishly wanted to keep it that way. I wanted to be supportive, not just for my friend, but also because I felt some sort of intrinsic responsibility for setting them up in the first place, for telling Cade to go after what he wanted—Weston—just like he was sitting here listening to me drone on about a very attractive complication of my own.

Besides, Weston seemed like a decent guy. Not that that meant I was going to tell him all my secrets and have a slumber party with the guy any time soon, but I wasn't about to say no to another drinking buddy and the man who clearly made my best friend happy.

Cade tapped out his response on his phone before looking back at me with his know-it-all stare.

"All I'm saying is, if you like him, you should be honest."

"It's not that easy..." I said, letting out a defeated sigh.

Cade pressed. "Why not? What's so hard about—"

"Well, for starters, we work together."

Cade raised an eyebrow in surprise. "And? When has something like that ever been an issue for you? You dated Vance, and he worked for Breisinger."

Just the mention of my ex, made me stiffen. I'd been a different person then, and I knew even though it shouldn't bother me that Nolan had replaced my ex at his job, it felt like in a way he was angling to replace him in my heart too. But that was stupid, and it wasn't like Nolan knew about my internal grudge.

However, as Cade said the words, I wondered if maybe that's what I wanted.

For Nolan to heal my broken heart.

"It's just..."

"Complicated, I know," Cade snarked.

"Dawson, you've been an upfront guy as long as I have known you. You don't mince words, and you're honest to a fault. Hell, it was one of the things that *I* was drawn to, when I met you. You're bold and confident, and that's sexy as hell. So, what exactly are you afraid of losing if you come clean with Nolan, because we both know it's not like you're going to lose your job or anything."

Cade was right, but I just didn't want to admit that.

Thankfully, I didn't have to because the waiter came with my basket of wings and Cade's pickles and the rest of the conversation died in favor of our sustenance.

I'd just finished the last hot wing when I noticed a familiar head of dark hair at the bar, thick, black glasses glinting in the light like the north star in the woods.

My pulse heated immediately, my stomach doing flips—although, I couldn't be certain if that was in part to the food I'd just inhaled, or if it was because of the attractive nerd of my damn dreams.

Mr. Complicated.

Suddenly, my agonizing over texts seemed crazy when he was just within my reach. Maybe if we could talk, I could tell him how sorry I was that I upset him. Maybe we could have a do-over.

An actual date where we were both on the same page.

"I'll be right back," I said, not able to resist the pull of Nolan Harding even if my damn life depended on it.

I wandered through the crowd until I came up to him, setting my hand on his oblivious shoulder as he rose from his seat at the bar.

"Hey," I said nervously.

Nolan turned around quickly, his eyes widening in surprise. "Hey..." he said, swallowing harshly, his gaze turning from surprised to hurt.

"I wanted to text you earlier, but I wasn't sure how you were feeling after—"

"Really? Could have fooled me," Nolan growled.

Excuse me?

"I'm not sure..."

"You know, I get it. I'm not everyone's cup of tea, but my mother always said I'd be someone's shot of whiskey. Guess I wasn't yours though, was I?" he said as he turned away.

Oh fuck no.

I grabbed him by the shoulder, this time much more harshly.

"What the fuck? Where is this coming from, I thought—"

"You thought what, Dawson? That I was fun to dick around for a night, but not enough to call the next day? Or were you too busy planning your next date with Apollo over there?" he said as he brushed me off, stomping off toward the bathroom.

And like the lovesick fool I was, I ran after him, angered and placated by his sudden bout of jealousy as I realized he must have seen me with Cade and assumed the worst.

"Who? Cade? He's not... I mean we dated once, but it's not like that. Not anymore. He's just a friend, I promise, I—"

"Save your excuses for someone who cares, Dawson," he retorted as he headed for the exit.

But I wouldn't let him get that far. Not until I said what I needed to, to clear the air, but also... because the words were on the tip of my tongue and I knew if I didn't do it then, I'd lose my nerve.

And I'd lose Nolan forever.

I blocked his exit with my body, causing him to crash up against me. He stumbled with a growl.

"Dawson get out of my way, I—"

"No," I said as I challenged his space, backing him up against the wall. "I've had enough of your mouth. It's *my* turn to talk, champ."

Nolan gazed up at me with fire in his eyes, his lips pursed into a thin line, but he didn't move a muscle.

Because I was a glutton for punishment as much as I was for laying it on thick, and because it was impossible to stand in front of this man who made my entire body heat with passion and anger, I reached my hand out, settling my palm against his neck. I tightened my fingers around the back of his head, his silky hair tickling the back of my knuckles.

There was so much I wanted to say. I knew what I *should* have said.

But instead, I found myself rising to Nolan's anger, his jealousy, blossoming like an angry lotus.

How dare he insinuate I don't give a shit about him or what happened!

"You are being a fucking brat right now," I said, my voice much darker than I intended.

Nolan opened his mouth to speak, but he never would get the words out.

Because the moment his luscious lips parted, I claimed them with mine, pouring my pent up frustration, my anger, and my wildy catching feelings into that kiss.

I expected him to fight me, to make some snide comment or get cocky, but instead, Nolan fell back against the wall, his hand snaking its way up my neck, pulling me closer.

And into his gravity I fell, like a damn meteorite crashing to earth.

Nolan Harding was the sun at the center of my universe and I had no idea how to process that, especially at that moment.

But *damn it*, I was going to try.

I pulled away, relishing in his heavy, heated

breath, in the feel of his body pressed against mine.

"I loathe your fucking attitude," I snarled.

Nolan's fingers gripped the edges of my hair as I gazed at his delicious lips, swollen from our heated kiss.

And then he said the magic words.

The words that would undoubtedly change both our lives forever.

"Then fucking do something about it, Dawson," he said calmly as he broke free from my grasp, sliding out the door like a thief in the night, leaving me alone in the dark to realize that this situation was more than just complicated.

Because without a doubt, I was falling in love with Nolan.

CHAPTER 23

Nolan

My lungs ached, and the room smelled like burnt toast. My dreams disintegrated into ash as I awoke to a thick, dense cloud of smoke blanketing me and the sound of alarms blared through my groggy consciousness.

But it took all of mere seconds for me to understand what was happening.

Fire.

Something had happened, and I was in danger, and my adrenaline immediately spiked. I didn't think twice about throwing my legs over the side of my bed, grabbing my glasses and phone from the bedside table, and dropping to the ground.

The heat from the fire ebbed like a pulse, but I didn't see any flames in my bedroom as I army crawled across the floor. Though the smoke made it hard as hell to see, and my lungs hurt to breathe, I knew I had to keep going if I wanted to make it out of there alive.

Every ounce of my being focused on finding my way to the door.

When I finally did, I fought to push it open, and made my way out into the hall, my vision still blurry from the smoke. But what I could see was tenants evacuating, firemen running into doors, and the sound of the blaring alarms made it hard to concentrate. I tried to stand, stumbling as I clutched the wall and tried to clear my vision.

Just a few more steps...

"Nolan!" a familiar voice cut through the confusion as I tried to focus my eyesight on where it was coming from. I coughed so hard my stomach twisted.

"Fuck, Nolan, it's okay, you're okay..." Steady, strong arms pulled me in, giving me the support I needed to stand. Through my smoke-clouded vision I could make out Dawson's perfect face, his copper eyes full of concern.

"Dawson... What..."

"Come on, champ, let's get you somewhere safe," he said, his voice stern and commanding.

I tried to move, but my legs felt like deadweight and I stumbled as I tried to follow his lead. "I can't... I..." My words were choked and labored, and I could barely process what had happened.

I felt my body being swept up off the ground like I was nothing more than a ragdoll. My head fell against a soft, damp shirt that smelled like cedar and spice, the fabric warm to my cheek, and like a confused, dazed idiot, I burrowed into it seeking its warmth and safety.

"It's okay, I got you. You're gonna be okay, I promise." Dawson's voice faltered only a moment, but it soothed me nonetheless.

Then darkness came, and took with it the smell of smoke, the heat of fire, and all the things I'd thought mattered, but in this moment knew they were miniscule.

I could feel my body being moved as I clutched my phone to my chest. The warmth and safety of Dawson's arms left me, and I hated it. I wanted to crawl into his hold and never leave.

"The paramedics need to check you out, okay? I'll be back, I promise," he said calmly, brushing my hair back from my face.

My eyelids fluttered as he came into my vision, the chill air kissing my skin. He was truly the most beautiful thing I'd ever seen, soot all over his face, standing there in a damp, white shirt, against the glow of a fire and smoke.

My hero.

I reached for him, to tell him I was sorry. I was wrong. For what, I wasn't sure, but the need to apologize was overwhelming.

Dawson only took my hand for a moment, nodding at me. "Promise," he said before he let me go, and I watched my hero disappear into the smoke without a moment's hesitation.

My heart ached as I watched him boldly do what it was he did every day.

The paramedics put an oxygen mask on me, taking my pulse, checking me over. Someone mentioned something or other about my rapid heartbeat, about my vitals, but it was all white noise in comparison to the realization that I was alive, and I was okay, and that Dawson had saved my life.

And I prayed to whatever God would listen to me that he would come back to me, because in that moment, I'd never seen anything clearer.

I was falling in love with Dawson Richards, and the thought of losing him—to a fire, or even to my own selfish, self-sabotaging behavior—terrified me.

I watched in silent horror as the firemen evacuated the second floor, and the first, where apparently the fire had started, according to the chatter of the paramedics.

And when the fire had been cleansed, when the threat had been diminished, I waited for what felt like an eternity as my vision returned, my breathing evened out.

"Can I make a phone call?" I asked, once I was free of my oxygen mask, my breathing stable. The paramedic shrugged.

"Probably a good idea to call someone you can stay with for awhile until this mess is sorted."

His words settled on me, and I realized he was right. There was no way I was getting back in my apartment tonight, given there would need to be an official claim for the building, not to mention individual tenant's claims about the damages incurred... including my own.

But I didn't really know anyone in Jasper Springs, and Allie wasn't close by. Still, I felt I should call her and let her know what happened. Maybe I could take up residence in the Paradise Hotel for a little while.

I checked the time; it was around two in the morning. I hated to wake her but...

In my wandering, I'd accidentally hit the Facetime button instead of call, and barely had time to register what happened before she accepted the call.

"Nolan, are you okay?" she said immediately, knowing a two am call from me was probably the worst. For goodness' sake, I was in bed by ten thirty most nights.

"I..." My voice caught as the words fell out. "I am now. There was a fire in my building, and..."

"Oh my God!" Allie said as she sat up in bed.

"I made it out okay, and then Dawson..."

The sight of Dawson walking toward me, decked out in his yellow fire suit and hat made my heart stop and my voice die on the wind.

He looked so badass it would have been impossible *not* to fall in love with the man.

"Nolan... Nolan!" Allie yelled.

I turned the phone in his direction absentmindedly, and Allie gasped.

"Is that..."

"The man who saved my life, yeah," I said softly.

"Oh, Nolan..." Allie tutted.

"I'm… going to have to call you back, Allie," I said.

"Nolan..."

"I'm okay, I promise. I just... I'll call you with any updates, okay?" I said as Dawson came closer, just a few feet away now.

"Fine. But I'm holding you to that!" she blurted and I ended our call.

Dawson stopped just inches away from me, his golden gaze roving over me.

"You're okay..." he said, his voice filled with relief, and I felt it through every part of my being.

I nodded dumbly. "Yeah, because of you..." I said.

"This one's good to go, right?" Dawson asked the paramedic beside me.

"Minor smoke inhalation, maybe a little shock, but otherwise, yeah. Vitals are stable."

"Good. Because he's coming with me," Dawson proclaimed.

"I... I need to get over to the Paradise," I said, trying to remember how to speak.

Dawson only shook his head.

"Like hell you are. I ain't letting you out of my sight, champ. You're under my watch until—"

"You don't have to do that," I said as I rubbed my arms. The cold night air was getting to me.

Dawson instinctively pulled off his fireproof jacket, throwing it over my shoulders like the hero he truly was.

"I know, but I want to," he said as he

adjusted the jacket, looking down at me. "Let me take care of you, Nolan."

Something about his words made my heart melt, decimated all the anger and the upset, and the unspoken words. Looking up at his amber eyes of fire, I couldn't resist him.

How could I tell him no, when I never wanted to leave his arms or his golden presence?

"Okay," I agreed, my voice shaky as he ran his hand along my back, guiding me toward the building stairs.

"Fire was electrical. Caught in the cafe. Second floor only sustained smoke damage, which is good, and third floors and above are all untouched. Everyone has been evacuated, and arrangements are being made," he said as he coaxed me along, never removing his hand from my back.

"Oh, okay," I said, because I wasn't sure what else to say. I guessed the paramedic was right, I was in shock.

"You can stay with me as long as you need until things get back to normal, okay?" he said as I followed him up three flights of steps and down the hall. I nodded, tugging his jacket closer. It smelled of fire and spice, and I liked it. I liked it a lot, because it made me feel warm and safe.

It made me feel *loved*.

But that was crazy, and I knew that. I blamed it on the shock, because there was no way in hell Dawson was in love with me. The man barely tolerated me, and had downright rejected my advances.

He's just doing his job.

Dawson opened the door for me, and I stepped across the threshold into the darkness once more.

CHAPTER 24

Dawson

My heart thudded away in my chest as the sound of the shower filled the otherwise silent air of my home.

I'd fought plenty of fires in my lifetime, but this one was different. I'd never been in a position where I felt so powerless before.

It was my job to go in and save people, to pull them out of burning buildings and residences, get them the help they needed.

But as I ran with Nolan in my arms, it was the first time I'd felt sincerely panicked, worried that I might have failed.

And if something happened to him, I wasn't sure I could handle it.

It had taken everything in me to leave him with Jordan and the other paramedics, and focus on my job.

But I prayed that when I returned, he'd be okay. I had to believe he would, because I couldn't stand to think otherwise.

The sight of him, alive and okay, made my damn heart feel like it was going to explode. I knew his apartment would be out of commission for the next couple days until the claims and everything settled, and maybe I offered for him to stay out of a sense of guilt, or maybe I did it because somewhere deep down where I didn't want to admit, I was scared. Scared that I'd almost lost him.

Scared that something could have happened to him and I wouldn't have been able to protect him. It was a weird tug in my chest, the thought and desire to protect this bratty, infuriating, beautiful man.

There was no way I was letting him out of my sight.

Not tonight, not ever.

"Hey," his voice cut through my wandering thoughts, bringing me back to the here and now, reality staring at me with a well-toned chest and a rather delicious Adonis belt poking out of the size too big sweatpants I'd loaned him.

Nolan's hair was still wet from his shower, his dark eyes behind his glasses full of apprehension.

"Wow," I murmured under my breath without warning, heat returning to my body to remind me I was alive, and Nolan was here.

In my apartment, dressed in my sweats, looking like my fantasy come to life.

"I, uh... appreciate your, uh... letting me stay. I promise, I'll figure things out tomorrow. I just—"

I pushed away from my counter, taking my time as I walked across the room, drawn to Nolan Harding like kerosene to a fire.

"You can stay as long as you need," I said as I stopped in front of him. Nolan's gaze searched mine, for what I wasn't sure, but I couldn't help myself in his presence.

Every time I got close to the man, I found it hard to resist touching him, to resist falling into his enchanting spell.

"Dawson, I..."

"Are you hungry?" I asked, pushing some stray strands of hair out of his glasses, watching the way his eyes sparkled in the dim light of my hallway.

"What?" Nolan asked, though his voice was soft, and he didn't break my gaze.

"I said, are you hungry?" I repeated myself, the innate desire to take care of this man overriding the rest of my ill-formed psyche that was losing its last marble.

"I... kind of... I mean..."

"Sit down on the couch," I commanded as I turned away.

"What?" he asked as he followed me, the sound of his bare feet on the tiles echoing in the small space.

"I said, sit down. Take a load off. I'll grab you something," I told him as I headed for my fridge.

"Fine," Nolan grumbled, but he did as I asked.

So, he can listen... when he wants to.

I set about to grabbing the ingredients for the one thing that always made *me* feel better. I wasn't entirely sure it would work for Nolan, but it was worth a shot. I set the chocolate and Nutella spread out, gathered my latest batch of specialty marshmallows from Penn's Bakery, and fished the graham crackers out of the cupboard.

I turned to see Nolan curling up on my couch, noting how good he looked in my clothes. Like he was well and truly *mine.*

I swallowed at the thought of the word. I wasn't the possessive type, and I'd never been.

But something about Nolan brought out a side of me I'd never known, and I didn't dislike it.

Not one bit.

I quickly slathered my graham crackers with the equal amounts of chocolate and Nutella spread, taking my time as I assembled my plate of s'mores. It didn't take long until I had four of them done, and I tossed them in the air fryer.

I turned, setting my gaze on Nolan, who was watching me intently.

"Is there anything you don't do?" he asked, his voice edged with sarcasm.

"I..."

"It's like, just when I think I know you... you find some way to keep me guessing."

It was my turn to smile. "I could say the same about you, you know."

"Me?" Nolan's eyes widened and I smirked, noting the blush that crept onto his cheeks made my cock twitch and my heart race.

"Yeah, you. For the last two years, I thought I had you pegged. Then all of a sudden, you show up to bar bingo and get all cocky with me... then you beat me running, and then you —" I swallowed, my words dying in the air as I remembered Nolan and his mouthwatering kiss, his rigid hardness against my own causing me to see stars as I came in my damn pants like a teenager.

How my heart panicked when I saw him in the hallway earlier.

The air fryer dinged, perfectly on cue to break up the tense moment.

"I, uh... hold that thought," I said as I pulled the s'mores out with my fingers quickly to avoid getting burned.

I grabbed the plate and made my way over to the couch, taking a seat next to Nolan. The cushions moved only slightly where I sat, making Nolan slope toward me in the slightest movement.

He looked at my plate with eyes as wide as saucers.

"Air fried s'mores?" he said with a raise of his eyebrow.

"Whenever I have a shit day, a little chocolate therapy usually does the trick. Unless, of course, you don't like—"

"I like it, Dawson," he said, his dark eyes focused on me intently. Something about his words felt off, like he wanted to say more but thought better of it.

I offered him the first bite, and he took it.

His eyelashes fluttered, and he groaned as he took his bite, the sound going straight to my cock, and I had to cover my own mouth to stifle a groan.

Fuuuuuck.

"Oh man, that's good," he said, licking his lips of the remains of gooey marshmallow and chocolate.

I smiled as I reached for a s'more of my own, letting the warm, smooth sweetness coat my tongue and settle my nerves a bit. I leaned back into my cushions, the motion bringing my shoulder right against Nolan's. I expected him to move away, but he didn't. In fact, he leaned a little closer.

Instinctively, I wanted to wrap my free arm around him, but I also didn't want to ruin this perfect moment.

To my surprise, he shifted his position, turning toward me. In the light of my apartment, his pale skin took on an almost angelic glow, his dark frames and eyes captivating me like the sucker I truly was in his presence.

God, was he pretty like this. Relaxed, freshly showered, lips begging to be kissed.

Fuck me sideways.

"I need to tell you something," he said with a sigh.

I slowly chewed the remainder of my smore as I nodded, completely dumbfounded under his gaze.

"Well, out with it then," I said as I swallowed the sweetness down my throat.

"I need to apologize," he said as he ran a

hand through his dark hair, his eyelashes fluttering, lips pursed in a tight line.

"Apologize for what, Nolan?" I asked as I shifted my position, turning my body to face him. The motion made us both sink into the cushions, our legs brushing one another in a soft collision.

I licked some chocolate off my thumb, watching his nose and cheeks redden as he let out a shaky breath.

"For being a dick earlier tonight, at M's Place... I..."

I wanted to stop him, tell him it didn't matter. All that mattered now was he was safe, and he was here. With me.

But something told me, that wasn't what I should do, and so I said nothing.

Nolan continued. "I think your asshole tendencies might be rubbing off on me," he said with a nervous laugh.

The sound made me smile, and instinctively I reached out and set my hand on his thigh, patting him with a gesture that was somehow both assuring, and soft all at once.

"You know what I think?" I asked with a smirk.

Nolan raised an eyebrow. "What?" he asked, pulling his pouty bottom lip in between his teeth, causing my cock to twitch again.

"I think you're just a natural brat," I said, my voice much darker than I intended.

Nolan looked back at me in question, chewing his lip. "I—" he started, just as I shook my head, placing a finger on his lips to shut him up.

"It's not a bad thing, Nolan. I kind of... like it. I..."

Nolan's soft lips against my fingertips were warm, igniting a fire in my blood that was hard to ignore.

The words fell out of my mouth without warning. "I kind of like... you."

The weight of those words left me feeling lighter after I'd said them.

Because I understood at that moment the truth they held.

I did like Nolan.

I liked him a whole hell of a lot, and on some deeper level, I needed him to know that. I needed to be clear, and honest, just like Cade had told me to be.

But first, I needed to admit the truth to myself, and that truth was that Nolan Harding was more to me than some thorn in my side, pain in the ass arch nemesis.

He was the match and I was the fuse.

Nolan leaned into my space, the couch

creaking just a bit as his motion drew me closer into him, like quicksand.

Nolan reached out a shaky hand, sliding his fingers in my hair softly, gripping as if he were afraid I would disappear at any moment.

Like he was afraid of upsetting the delicate balance of the cliff we were both on.

I slid my hand up and down his thigh, trying to reassure him the best way I knew how that this was what I wanted, because I couldn't speak. I could only focus on feeling him beneath my fingertips, because I didn't want him to disappear either.

I pulled him closer, the position once again putting him in my lap, and Nolan let out a sigh that cut straight through to my heart, my cock, and my feeble Nolan-obsessed brain.

"I kinda like you too, Dawson," he whispered, his breath warm on the edge of my lips, and I didn't wait.

I closed the space between us without warning, tasting his sweet lips and the remains of sticky sugar on my tongue.

Nolan let out a contented sigh as he relaxed into my hold, his fingertips tightening their grip in my hair. I let my tongue stroke his, exploring his mouth like it was uncharted territory.

And in a way it was, because this kiss wasn't rushed or surprising like the last time.

It was deep, and warm, and new and I never wanted to stop. I wanted to die in that kiss on my couch, with Nolan in my arms, wearing my goddamn sweatpants.

My cock throbbed, and I groaned in response, knowing if we didn't stop now, I'd fucking own this man before he'd finished his dessert, and cold s'mores did not go down as well.

I broke away, regrettably, my gaze settling on his swollen lips, on his bright eyes and the way his lips turned up in the corners into a smile.

"But I also like *warm* s'mores, not cold ones, so let's not let my grade A baking skills go to waste, okay?" I teased.

Nolan blushed a bit as he nodded. "Yeah, yeah, of course, where are my manners?" he taunted me as he languidly reached over my fucking lap, right over my throbbing cock, to grab another delicacy.

Such a fucking brat.

He shot me a dark look as he bit into his s'more, groaning louder this time, making a show of it, if only to irritate the hell out of me.

And it worked.

"Now, be a good boy and eat your dessert and maybe I'll reward you.'

Nolan stared back at me as he took another bite, some stray marshmallow fluff spreading across his lips. I shifted my position on the couch as I reached for the last s'more, if only to hide my erection at the moment. I didn't want a repeat of last time.

No this time, I'd get it right. Because Nolan was more than a good boy.

He was fucking perfect, and I wasn't going to let him forget it.

CHAPTER 25

I'D JUST TURNED off the faucet in the kitchen, after rinsing the plate our s'mores were served on, when Dawson spoke up.

"Come to bed with me," he said the words warmly.

I stopped drying my hands on the dishtowel. It hadn't been addressed exactly, where I would be sleeping. I'd assumed it would be the couch.

"I can sleep on the couch, it's fine."

"You are not sleeping on the couch," Dawson said, shaking his head. "That thing will kill your back and then some. You can sleep with me, my bed is more than big enough to fit us both, and I promise you, I don't bite, and I'm not going to try anything," he pledged as he held his hands up. "Unless, you want me to. But that's up to you, champ."

I couldn't help the smirk that formed on my lips. On one hand, I knew I should say no.

But something changed between us on that couch. Dawson had told me flat out he... liked me.

And then he fucking kissed me.

Thing was, I *wanted* to do exactly what he was asking. I wanted to crawl into bed with Dawson, and the last thing I wanted to do was sleep. But I was also sated from the sugar and tired from the drop in adrenaline from everything that had happened. So I really didn't have the energy to fight with him.

"Fine," I said, letting out a yawn.

"Really?" he said, a little surprised. "I thought you'd fight me on it, at least a little bit."

"Too tired to argue," I said as I sauntered over to him. "You going to show me where the magic happens or am I going to have to find it myself?" I asked as I stared up at him. Dawson's sexy grin spread wide on his face, making my entire body blush.

"Follow me, champ," he said as he turned to lead me down the hall. My heart beat loudly in my ears every step we took toward his bedroom, and that was when it hit me.

That this, sleeping with Dawson, was actually a reality, and that made me nervous.

Not because of his implications, or because of what I wanted, but because I'd literally fantasized about this moment for two years, and now that it was here, a reality, I wasn't sure what to actually do.

Fucking hell.

Dawson started to undress as we entered his room, the light coming on almost immediately.

He definitely wasn't kidding about the size of the bed. It looked big enough for three people, and suddenly the negative thoughts came rushing back. After all, he was *Mr. March*, how was I to know he didn't have orgies back at his place on the regular?

But something told me, that wasn't the case, and I decided to go with my gut instead of my self-sabotaging brain.

Just as he removed his shirt, his gaze caught mine.

"You okay, Harding?" he asked, pulling me from my thoughts. My gaze settled on him standing there, shirtless, in his damn *briefs*, looking like a five alarm fire all on his own, and my stomach twisted in knots.

"Yeah, I just..."

Dawson walked over to me, half naked without a care.

The way he stopped in front of me, how he set his palm against my cheek, thumb brushing along my jaw, fixing those golden eyes on me made me feel like I was about to become a puddle on the floor.

"Hey, I meant what I said. We don't... we don't have to do anything you aren't comfortable with. I don't expect anything from you. I want to take care of you."

The natural inclination to debunk his sweetness pestered me from inside my psyche, but I fought it.

I didn't want to ruin this moment with my anxiety and self-esteem issues. So instead of asking why, I nodded.

"Okay," I said as I let Dawson lead me to his bed like a lamb to the slaughter.

He pulled down the covers, waiting for me to get in. I curled up underneath them, in his sweatpants. I had opted not to borrow a pair of underwear, only because it felt weird to me to wear someone else's underwear—let alone underwear that belonged to the man I'd fantasized about—even if it was just a formality. I'd take my clothes to the Laundromat in the morning, hit up the local Target and get some new digs to hold me over until I could get back to my apartment and back to normal.

Dawson was definitely bigger than I was in

all ways that counted, so his sweatpants were a little loose on me, but not so loose they didn't fit. They hung on my hips and I half worried they would fall down, but they seemed to hold. Though I couldn't deny that under his covers, all cozy in those sweatpants, my balls felt spoiled as all hell. The minute my back hit his mattress, I felt a wave of stress melt away.

Dawson climbed in beside me, keeping his distance and I hated it. I didn't want him to be so far away. It didn't feel right. So for once, I did what *I* wanted to do. I did what felt right, despite the voice in my head telling me otherwise. I scooted closer and threw my arm over his hip, pulling him into me.

Dawson leaned over his shoulder, looking at me.

"Really? A brat like you doesn't want to be the little spoon?"

I smirked at him in return even though he couldn't see me.

"Gotta keep you guessing or else you'll get bored," I teased him, fixing my front to his back.

The brush of his ass against my cock sent a jolt right to my damn system, and my cock immediately began to swell. A dark groan escaped my throat, which I hadn't meant to happen, but I was powerless to stop it.

I was powerless against the sex appeal of Dawson Richards.

"I don't think you'd ever bore me, Nolan," he said as he arched his back, pushing back against my budding erection.

"Fuck," I hissed as I tried to breathe through the sudden flush of heat and desire.

"I can stop if—"

"Hell no," I said as I let my hand fall over his hip, across his stomach, my fingertips grazing the waistband of his briefs. "I like it. I don't want you to stop."

Dawson chuckled darkly as he slid his hand over top of mine, dragging it down beneath the waistband of his briefs, so I could feel his warm skin, his coarse hair, and his...

Holy fuck.

The memory of grinding myself against Dawson was still hazy, but I'd seen enough photographs of strategically placed items to formulate an idea of the size of his cock.

But the touch alone proved I had underestimated him, because it was definitely larger than what I was used to—if I was used to anything, really—and it was thicker than I'd expected.

Dawson slowly guided my hand up and down his cock, building a slow rhythm that caused my own dick to throb. Instinctively, I ground my erection against his clothed ass, just as my thumb brushed over the tip of his head to be met with warm, sticky precum, and I let out a strangled groan.

"You like that, don't you?" Dawson's voice egged me on.

"Yes," I breathed desperately.

"Is that what you want, Nolan?" His voice had taken on a hint of teasing, but it was entrenched in lust and was making my head spin.

"You want my cum down your throat, hmmm? Dripping out of your tight ass?"

Dawson thrust his cock into my fist, the wetness spreading, and I didn't think twice about what I wanted.

I slid my hand out of his briefs, and Dawson turned over, looking at me with worry.

"Yes," I said as I leaned over him, straddling his thighs again. In the low light of his bedroom, the shadows fell on him beautifully, and I tugged at his waistband.

Dawson looked up at me with surprise, but he let me pull his briefs down, and the sight of his cock springing free was better than anything I'd ever fantasized about.

As I looked at the sight of his swollen, pink cock bouncing back and forth, leaking salty, sweet precum, I wondered if I would die choking on his cock. His length and thickness alone made me half consider abandoning this plan altogether. Maybe that wasn't such a bad way to go.

I sucked in a deep breath before signing my death certificate as I leaned down and licked his shaft from base to tip.

"Jesus Christ, Nolan!" Dawson gasped. His entire body tensed as I took him into the back of my throat in one fell swoop.

"Oh fuck!" Dawson hissed, his hands going straight for my hair. His fingers gripped my locks tight, the surprise of the moment dissipating as Dawson found himself once again. He thrust into the back of my throat, making me nearly gag. But I didn't dislike it one bit.

In fact, I kind of loved it.

"You like that, don't you?" he asked, his voice shifting to something darker. "You like choking on this dick?" He grunted as he thrust into the back of my throat again. I answered him by hollowing my cheeks, swirling my tongue around his thick head, and humming my appreciation, which only made him hiss and grab my hair tighter. So tight it hurt but in such a delicious way.

My cock throbbed in my sweatpants, and I could feel a wet spot already forming as I mindlessly thrust my own hardness against the inside of Dawson's sweatpants.

"What's the matter, champ? You all worked up with nothing to fuck?" he taunted me as he slid his cock out of my mouth, pushing forward so that I was the one now on my back, eyes wide in surprise,

Dawson's heavy, naked form held me down, his leaking cock leaving a sticky trail down my abdomen as he grabbed me by the waistband of my borrowed sweatpants.

"Dawson, please..." I begged, wanting to finish what I started. The taste of his precum still lingered in my mouth, but I wanted more. I wanted to make him come. I wanted to feel him and his thick cock bursting like a dam in my mouth. And then I wanted to—

Dawson palmed my erection through my sweatpants, right on my wet spot.

"That's what I thought," he said, his voice husky as I involuntarily thrust against his palm, feeling a mixture of shame and desire.

"Please, I need to take care of *you*," I said weakly. It was true, I did want to make him come, but it was more than that. I needed to be able to say with my body the words that were so difficult to speak with my tongue.

I want you.

I want this.

I don't want this to end...

"No, no, we're not doing that again," he

said, and I wanted to ask what he meant. But before I could, he *yanked* my sweatpants down to my ankles, my own cock springing free, wet and wild.

"Look at that big, beautiful cock of yours," Dawson said, his voice all gravelly and sexy. I thrust into the air, from the sound of his voice alone. My cock literally *ached*. I wanted to come so fucking bad, and to hear Dawson like that... to see him like that... naked, swollen cock on display as he stared down at me with a startling intensity, I had to grab a hold of myself. I needed to be touched.

"Ah, ah..." Dawson growled as he smacked my hand away, the motion making my cock bounce and twinge from the impact.

"I didn't say you could do that," he teased.

"Dawson, please, I..." My words faded into nothing as Dawson's thick hardness pressed against mine and his hand wrapped around us both. The feel of his cock against mine, wet and slippery, made me see stars. A deep groan left my chest and bubbled from my lips as Dawson built a rhythm, stroking us together.

"I don't know if I can hold off. I—"

I couldn't hold it. With one squeeze and thrust, I was erupting like a damn volcano over both of our cocks, over his hand, and my vision had gone white.

"God, you are beautiful when you come," he purred as his thrusts came to a halt. "Fuuuu-uck..." He groaned, long and low, the sensation of his pulsing, throbbing cock against mine throwing me into rapture. We both laid there, a sticky, wet, gross mess of mutual cum, until our breathing had returned to normal, and Dawson removed himself from atop of me, falling to the other side of the bed, his limbs still tangled with mine.

Slumber crept in under the crash of adrenaline, of relief. I vaguely registered Dawson wiping me up with a towel before crawling back into bed with me, pulling me close to him.

The last thing I remember before darkness fell, was the warmth of his hold, and the whisper of one word.

Mine.

CHAPTER 26

I woke up to the sound of birds singing, like some damn Hallmark movie. Warmth surrounded me, and I burrowed into it like a rabbit hunkering down for winter, not wanting to open my eyes.

I wanted to hold onto the perfect, pre-awakening haze that held Dawson and I together like glue for the moment. His leg threaded through mine, his fingers cascading along my back slowly as he fought his own consciousness, no doubt.

I curled a little closer to his warm chest, the coarse, sparse hair there tickling my cheek. Pressed so close, I could hear his heartbeat, slow and steady.

I could also feel his semi-erect cock twitching against mine, and the memory of the previous night came flooding back to me, causing my own cock to wake up.

"Good Morning, beautiful." Dawson's half-asleep voice shouldn't have sounded *that* sexy, but damn if it didn't wake up every nerve ending in my body.

Instinctively, I ground my cock against him as I buried my head in his shoulder, the taut skin on his neck teasing my lips, baiting me to kiss and suck his flesh until I'd marked him like some teenage vampire.

Mine, mine, mine.

I opened my eyes, my vision blurry until Dawson's gorgeous face came into focus. I hadn't remembered taking my glasses off, but I was aware from the semi-blur of shapes behind Dawson that I didn't have them.

Which made me feel entirely more vulnerable.

That first time you spend the night with someone, where you let them see *you* underneath all that you present to the world is always nerve-wracking, but when you're letting the man of your literal dreams see you and your bedhead and your terrible vision first thing in the morning, it's something else completely.

"Morning," I said, letting out a yawn,

looking up at Dawson from my spot beneath him.

"You don't have to get up," he purred, his fingertips tracing lines up and down my spine, hovering just above my bare ass.

The amount of desire that flooded me, the innate *need* to feel his fingers stretching me, was almost enough to make me come on the spot. Almost.

But I knew that despite our sexual compatibility, that if I wanted Dawson—and I did *want* him—for myself, as something more than a fulfilled fantasy, I needed to rein in my horny beast. Maybe just a little.

Not to mention there were other pressing matters I needed to attend to, that would have to be dealt with sooner rather than later. Like the claim on my apartment, getting clean clothes that fit me, and of course, calling work and Allie to let them know the details and that I was okay.

Dawson moved just slightly, hooking his knuckle underneath my chin, forcing me to look up at him.

"I meant what I said. You can stay here as long as you need to. As long as you want... with me." His voice was still tinged with the remnants of sleep, but his words were bright and full of life.

I'd known Dawson for two years. In that

time, I'd only known him to be a charismatic ass, someone who didn't seem to take things or himself seriously. But in the last several days, I'd come to see the man beneath the fireproof suit, and though he was still charismatic and a bit of an ass, he was so much more.

He was commanding, relentless, and caring.

And as I looked into his beautiful eyes, I realized that I was falling in love with him.

The absolute look of wonder in his eyes made my breath catch, rendering me speechless. No man had ever looked at me like he was looking at me at that moment. And when he leaned down, bringing his soft, warm lips to mine, I knew I was absolutely doomed.

How could I *not* fall in love with him?

Dawson kissed me, and it was better than I'd ever imagined it could be.

He tasted like fire and love, like sweet sugar with an undercut of hot spice.

Why would I want to be anywhere else?

He broke away, too soon for my liking as he pushed away, throwing the blanket off of him.

"I however, need to get ready to head the firehouse and deal with this shit."

He grumbled as I watched his naked form saunter across the room, the sunlight casting an ethereal glow on his tanned skin. He absent-mindedly tugged his sizeable cock, grunting as he did so and a part of me wanted to pull him back down into the sheets and never let him out of *my sight.*

He caught my stare, winking at me sexily, a lazy smile gracing his luscious lips.

"Be a good boy and do as you're told and maybe I'll reward you," he teased.

I sighed as I watched his bare ass leave the room, heading down the hall toward the shower. When he was gone, I fell back in the sheets, running my hand over my face.

If anyone had told me the week prior that I'd be lying naked with Dawson's dried cum all over my stomach, I would never have believed them. But there I was in his bed, naked, hard, and ready for fucking round two.

I wanted to blame the fact I hadn't been with anyone in a couple years, and the fact that I had a real live human to touch and to touch me was the root of my sudden influx of desire, but I knew that wasn't entirely the case.

Sex for me had always been a way to communicate how I felt, when I found the words too difficult to say. And telling the guy you've been dreaming about for two years you are falling in love with him after one night in his bed screamed psycho clinger. But it was the truth.

The sound of the running shower pulled me from my thoughts. I knew I could lie there, in Dawson's bed, forever trying to work up the courage to tell him I wanted to stay, not just now but... I wanted to stay as long as he wanted me to. I wanted to be with *him* as long as he wanted to be with me. But lying there spinning myself into circles, trying to work up the nerve would only make me second-guess myself, and I wasn't about to let my self-doubt ruin this.

So instead, I threw my legs over the side of the mattress and climbed out of bed, padding down the hall to the bathroom. I gently pushed open the door, the steam in there budding like an impatient flower.

I took my time, relieving myself and washing my hands in the sink, if only to give myself the briefest moment to chicken out completely.

I knew what I wanted, but going after *anyone* was new to me. Normally, I preferred to be the one being chased, being pursued, because I'd never been a bold, confident man in any sense of the word. But something about Dawson sparked the side of me that *wanted* to be those things, that felt like maybe I could be that man with the right person.

I took one step and a deep breath as I moved toward an unsuspecting Dawson, who was humming to himself in the shower, his back to me.

Two steps, and another deep breath, and then...

I opened the curtain and quietly stepped in. Dawson turned around in surprise, his amber eyes looking me up and down with excitement and hunger. His lips turned up in a smirk.

"Nolan, what—"

"Conserve water, shower with a friend," I said, flashing him with a smirk of my own.

Dawson ran his hands through his hair, slicking the locks back as the water sluiced in rivulets down his neck.

"Of course. Think of the turtles," he said in a husky voice as I stepped closer, letting some of the water run over me.

"But if you're uncomfortable, I'll leave," I said, and I meant it. Maybe part of me was concerned I was being too forward, after all this was all new to me. Not the sex, I mean... I'd had shower sex before. But the coming onto a man like *this*... that was something I'd never done before and I had no idea what the fuck I was doing.

Dawson slid his hand over my stomach, his fingers brushing the remains of his release off of me with gentle scrubbing, before literally smacking my awakened cock. The motion made me jump as my cock bounced, twitching with desire from the rush of his rough touch.

Fuuuuck.

"You are such a fucking brat. You think you are gonna lie there in *my bed* and grind this—" He squeezed my swollen cock tightly, causing my hips to involuntarily thrust into his grasp, eliciting a groan from my mouth.

"Grind this pretty little cock all over me and then leave me hanging? Think you can crawl into this shower and tease me?" he said as he ran his thumb over my leaking hole, using his other hand to push me back against the tile. The motion angled him over top of me, and he slowly started to stroke me. My breath hitched as I relished the feel and the words of this man who held me at my wit's end.

I wanted more.

I wanted to give him *everything* I couldn't find the words to say.

"I'm not a fucking tease, Dawson, and I'm not a brat."

"Oh really? Then what are you? A good little boy? Because good boys do what they're told, and I told you to stay in bed."

Dawson let go of my cock, if only to palm his own. My gaze dipped to his thick, pink, swollen head, and I didn't think twice about dropping to my knees, staring up at him through my lashes as water rained down on me like a cleansing rain.

"If I'm so bad, why don't you teach me a lesson?" I purred, licking my lips.

Dawson smirked as he closed his position over top of me, using his hand to hold his cock as he teased my lips with the tip. Salty liquid graced my lips, and my own desire flared as I waited for him to take the bait.

I hoped by the sheer grace of God he understood that this... this wasn't about sex. It was, but it was more than that. I hoped somehow he knew that.

"Is that what you want, Nolan? You want Daddy to teach you a lesson?"

"Yes," I said, my throat going dry as my eyes fixated on his thick, engorged dick in front of me.

"Then open that pretty mouth of yours so I can wash it out with my cum," he growled, his dark eyes sparkling like hot coals, stoking the fire within me once more.

CHAPTER 27

NOLAN FUCKING Harding was going to kill me.

Who would have guessed that the quiet and reserved insurance nerd would be into a little praise and degradation?

Most of the men I'd held relationships with weren't exactly into exploring that sort of power dynamic with me, not that many had gotten that far to begin with, except maybe Cade.

But Cade always had to be *guided* through the scenes, which I hadn't minded at the time, but Nolan didn't need any guidance whatsoever.

Nolan didn't miss a fucking beat. He picked up exactly what I threw down, and he didn't even blink.

Nolan batted his pretty eyelashes at me as he opened his perfect mouth, leaning back on his heels. Water cascaded over us, and at this angle I had a clear sight of his cock, glimmering from the dewdrops of water and desire.

Everything about Nolan was absolute perfection. His dark hair, the way his glasses framed his face when he wore them, his luscious lips that begged to be stuffed with my cock, not to mention his sizeable member that was filling my brain with fuck fantasies that were less about me owning Nolan, and more about spearing myself over him and feeling *that* stretch until it hurt.

Which should have been my first clue I was in well over my head.

I wasn't bottom material. I liked to be in control, it gave me a sort of sense of purpose, of stability in my everyday life, and sex was no different. I preferred to be the one delivering the mind-shattering fucks.

But as I stared at Nolan and his beautiful cock as he sat on his heels, mouth open for me like a natural submissive, fuck if I didn't want to be owned by this man in every way that mattered.

But would he even be into that?

I pushed the thought from my mind if only

because I didn't want to keep my little brat waiting for his funishment.

Not to mention, I was dying to paint his lips and face with my cum. The thought alone made me shiver as I imagined my hot spend rolling down the side of his lips.

Fucking hell, Dawson, focus or you're going to blow your load early again!

I slid my cock into Nolan's warm mouth, and he moaned a sound that made my heart swell.

"Fuuuck, your mouth feels so good..." I groaned, unable to control my words. My heart raced as Nolan grabbed my ass cheeks, pulling me closer, the angle driving my cock in over his slick tongue until I hit the back of his throat.

"That's it, fuck..." I threaded my hands through Nolan's wet locks, driving him down on my dick until I heard him gag. His face reddened under my ministrations as I fucked his mouth like I wished he'd fuck my ass.

Relentlessly.

"That's it, make me come, Nolan. Be a good boy and make me——"

The surprise touch of Nolan's fingertip as it slipped into my tight pucker made me nearly jump, but I didn't dislike it one bit.

The water ran down my skin, and the sensation of his digit pushing into me was rough and I wasn't nearly lubricated enough, but something about that made it better. I could feel every stroke, every touch tenfold as he used his one hand to fuck my hole and the other to caress my balls while he wrapped his tongue around my head.

Fucking hell, that feels amazing!

Instinctively, I picked up my pace, fucking his mouth with reckless abandon as I chased my orgasm, and the world around me shifted into a hazy blur of water, heat, and blinding release. I stilled as I gripped Nolan's hair tightly in my fists as I poured myself down his throat.

I half-expected him to gag from the amount, because even for me I knew it was a lot, but he didn't. He drank me down like I was a keg of beer, groaning like a damn porn star the entire time.

He removed his fingers from my ass, sliding them over my skin and my body went limp. When he was done, he licked the remains of my release from my tip, and then stared up at me with a sly grin on his face.

"Get up," I ordered, my breath catching in my throat. Nolan did as he was told, his gaze never leaving mine.

I wrapped my hand around his fat cock,

feeling the stickiness of his excitement spreading along my fingertips.

"Good boys get rewards," I said through harsh breaths, and then I claimed his mouth with mine. Nolan startled for a moment, but relaxed against the wall, his tongue stroking mine hungrily.

I could taste myself on him, and I didn't hate it. But it wasn't what I wanted. No, I wanted to level the playing field. If Nolan was going to play dirty, I wasn't going to go down without a fight.

Nolan's eyes sparkled with fire as I squeezed him gently before dropping to my knees, an action which caused Nolan to blush redder than a tomato. Just as I knew it would.

"Dawson, wait you don't—"

I didn't wait for him to finish before I took his cock in *my* mouth, cradling his balls with one hand and stroking his shaft with the other. His entire body tensed as his eyelids fluttered closed.

"Fuck, Dawson..." he groaned. "Oh my God..." His voice was strained and that only served to egg me on more.

I moved my hand from his balls to his perineum, dragging my finger up along his seam to taunt him. I removed my mouth from his dick to look up at him and speak, using my hand to continue my strokes as I grinned wickedly.

"And you've been very good, Nolan," I said, and I happily watched his face screw up completely, once I took him back into my mouth, hollowing my cheeks as I deep-throated him.

"Oh my God, fuuuuuck!" Nolan cried in utter abandon, his cock pulsing with release as he spilled himself down my throat, fingernails scratching along the tile walls, his chest heaving with the effort to suck in stuttered breaths.

He truly was a sight to behold, and I wanted more moments like this.

I wanted all of Nolan Harding's edges and then some. I wanted to unravel him piece by piece until he was a fucking mess because of *me*.

When I was done, I rose, noticing the water had gone cold. I smiled as I leaned against Nolan, gently kissing his trembling lips. Like putty, he melted against me, and I felt on top of the world.

Nothing could ruin *this*.

"It's been fun, champ, but duty calls," I murmured, teasing his bottom lip with my teeth. I reached down and turned the now near-freezing water off.

Nolan's breaths were rapid and his pupils blown, his eyes staring at me in wonder. "Of course, don't let me stop you," he breathed heavily.

I opened the curtain, grabbing my towel as I turned to take one more look at the beautiful man in my shower, before heading to my bedroom to dress and make it to the firehouse on time.

CHAPTER 28

Dawson

"Ground control to Richards!" Gina's harsh voice snapped me out of my daze. The smell of sizzling bacon invaded my airways, reminding me it was probably time to flip it.

"Don't get your panties in a bunch, Corolla," I nipped as I used the tongs to turn the bacon slices, noting that they were fairly charred at the edges.

"What is the matter with you today? I mean, don't get me wrong, you're not exactly the brightest crayon in the box on most days, but it's like you're barely tapped into Earth today."

I sighed as I flipped the burgers on the burner next to the bacon. I'd never been the greatest cook in my own life, but at the firehouse things were different. We all took turns doing things, but somehow I'd gotten conned into being the house chef, but I didn't mind most of the time. In most ways, the firehouse was my home.

More home than my lonely apartment, anyway. Not to mention the firehouse was usually packed with my fellow firefighters on duty or coming off of it, so it was like I was always around family, which I loved. My brother was usually working, and when he wasn't, he'd make the hour and a half trek to see his girlfriend for an extended break. Since the fire though, he'd been even more scarce, hanging around if only to deal with the disaster at hand, and the minute he had an opening, he was off to spend time with the next Mrs. Bradish.

I wish I could have blamed my distraction on my brother's situation, but the truth of the matter was I couldn't stop thinking about Nolan.

About what had happened between us.

I'd been one hundred percent clear when I told him I liked him. Hell, I kissed him after that, to be one hundred percent clear... and then something crazy happened. He kissed me back and told me he liked me too, and that changed everything. The spark caught, and then ravaged us both in its flames, taking us under. And it felt *good.*

It felt more than good, actually. Being with Nolan, holding him, kissing him, tasting him... it all felt so damn right. Like that's the way it was supposed to be. And that scared me a little bit, because I'd never fallen for anyone in my life so fast before.

Sure I'd fucked on the first date before, but I'd never found myself daydreaming about being railed by any one of those guys, I can assure you.

"I'm just... tired, that's all," I lied.

Gina rolled her eyes. "I smell bullshit," she said as she opened the bag of buns, setting up the plates. The laughter from our fellow crewmembers carried from the living room, and I sighed. I didn't want to get into it all with Gina, not because I didn't trust her, but because I wasn't sure how to explain that I was falling in love with our regular claims adjuster—who I'd been more than upfront that I despised for two years.

I turned the burners off, strolling over to help Gina prepare the plates for the moment while things cooled down.

"It's not bullshit, I just—"

"Dawson, we've been working together longer than most of the assholes in this house. I know what you're like when you're tired. You don't smile from ear to ear or get a dumbass look in your eye when you need a nap. In fact, I don't think I've seen you smile like *that* since you and Cade hooked up."

She had me there.

While Cade and I had gotten off to a good start, and the sex was great, things fizzled out pretty quickly. I loved hanging out with him, and I still do, but hanging out with Cade always felt more like hanging out with my high school bestie than it did with a boyfriend. And Cade pretty much said the same thing, and we mutually agreed that being friends was probably better. But in those first few weeks, I was still riding that high of new dick, and I was pretty happy.

Did that mean that Nolan would fizzle out too?

After the haze of new dick wore off, would he get bored with me and decide we'd be better off as... friends?

God, I hoped not. To be honest, I wasn't sure if I could go back to the way things were before with Nolan, not now that I'd tasted him and let him into my heart and my bed. No, there was no way I could go back to hating Nolan, and there was no way I could just pretend he wasn't the hottest fucking nerd on the planet.

"Yeah, well... people change," I said gruffly as I laid the cheese out on the burgers.

"Whoever he is, as long as he's good to you and not an asshole—" She narrowed her eyes at me, making me feel on the spot.

"I don't know what you're talking about," I spat, even though I did.

My relationships were far and few between, but I had garnered something of a reputation for the string of *assholes* I'd collected over the years. Assholes who wanted nothing more than to get fucked by *Mr. March*, or get their firefighter fantasies out of their system.

I wasn't stupid, I knew what I was doing, and I knew those assholes weren't going to last longer than a night or two. But I wasn't looking to settle down and build a white picket fence life like Cade. I was fine with being a one night stand, or a plus one for someone's cousin's twice removed wedding.

The thought of being that now, though... where Nolan was involved, made my stomach flip.

What was happening to me?

Gina placed the pickles on top of the cheese I'd laid out.

"As long as he's good to you, treats you like a person, we're good. Because you know, that's how you *should* be treated. Not like some sex toy." She said the words quietly, which only added to their magnitude. I did know, and I hated that her words made me feel so vulnerable.

"I know," I said softly.

Gina nudged me in the shoulder. "I know you know. But you have to believe you're worth the good stuff, Dawson. Because you are."

A soft smile tugged at my lips. Gina wasn't the type to get emotional or soft. She always said things as they were, didn't mince words. Her bluntness and boldness were two of the things I loved about her and probably why I considered her my work wife above all others.

Like Cade, Gina just got me.

"I want the good stuff," I said quietly. "I just... don't know how to be the *good guy* who gets it all, you know?"

Gina and I topped the burgers with ketchup and mustard, and I felt more exposed than I had in my shower this morning with Nolan.

"What are ya waitin' for? Christmas?" Frank yelled from the living room.

Gina rolled her eyes. "We're waiting for you to grow a pair and get up off your ass and actually make yourself useful!" Gina hollered back.

It was my turn to roll my eyes, and I loaded up my arm with plates, server style.

"The natives are restless," I said with a half smile. "Come on, better get them fed before they turn to cannibalism."

Gina huffed, but she didn't argue. Instead, she followed me into the living room for another family lunch.

CHAPTER 29

Dawson

It was barely after four o'clock when I pulled up to my brother's house.

I hadn't heard anything in a couple days, and figured if I dropped by I'd know if he was home or not, and if he was, I could at least see if there was anything he needed.

Big brother habits and all.

My brother was loading his truck up.

"Headed out of town to see the misses?" I quipped as I came up to him.

"Yeah, well, it's not like I'm needed any time soon, considering that adjuster just did a re-eval of everything all over again."

"What?" I asked, confused.

Re-eval?

Nolan hadn't said anything about the claim needing to be re-evaluated.

"Yeah, apparently there was an issue, and we had to fucking start all over again. I'm just ready for my shit to be replaced, you know. Feel like these insurance assholes are just dicking me around."

My jaw tensed immediately. I wanted to believe Nolan when he said he'd make sure things were good, but it sounded like they were in fact, not good. Not at all.

Damn it!

Why didn't he say something?

I told him to keep me in the fucking loop!

I fought to keep my facial expression normal. After all, I didn't want to give my brother any more reason for alarm. I'd get to the bottom of this, and I'd take care of it.

My brother was going to get his money. I would make sure of it.

"Yeah, I know what you mean. So, uh... how long you going to be out?" I asked nonchalantly, even though my teeth ached to grind.

"Couple days. Cara has a couple days off work, so we might do a little trip up to the campground," he said with a shrug. "Get my mind off all this stupid shit, you know?"

I nodded. "Probably a good idea, I'll call

you if I hear something," I said as I tapped the hood of his truck with my hand, smiling friendly enough that I hoped he bought my display.

My brother smiled in return. "Sounds good."

When I got to my car, I immediately dialed Nolan. I tried to keep my panic in check, but it was no use. Once he picked up, I snapped.

"Dawson, hey..."

"Why didn't you tell me about the re-eval?" I asked, cutting to the chase.

Immediately, Nolan turned defensive.

"What? How the hell do you know—"

"He's my brother, Nolan. It's my job to know what's going on with his life, especially when it concerns his financial stability and job."

Nolan huffed. "I told you I would take care of it, and I'm—"

"Doesn't look like you're doing a very good job," I snarled.

Nolan actually sounded a little hurt, but he snapped back, "Maybe I could do a better job if I was focused on the task at hand and not being bitched at about every move I make! I don't come to *your* job and tell you how to fight fires, Dawson. So don't sit there and act like you know one thing about what I fucking do!"

Oh the attitude on this one grinds my fucking gears.

"Why wouldn't you tell *me*? He's my brother!" I said, feeling panic racing through my veins.

"Maybe because I didn't want to stress you out, like you clearly are now," Nolan grated, his voice full of disdain and snark.

"Since when do you get to make decisions for me, huh? This is... is my life and I am the one in charge here, not you!" I spat, the words coming of their own volition.

"Whatever, Dawson. I'm not doing this with you right now. I have a *job* to do," he nipped, hanging up on me, which only served to piss me off further. I threw the phone on the passenger seat, cursing aloud in my truck.

Fuck!

The phone buzzed immediately, and I half expected it to be Nolan, but it wasn't.

It was Cade.

Just got a table, how close are you?

I closed my eyes, sighing as I remembered I had forgotten about the plans I'd made yesterday with Cade, due to the fire last night, and my morning spent under Nolan's damn spell. I tapped out my text quickly.

Be there in 10.

I only hoped maybe a good basket of cheese fries would soak up all the anger and frustration I was feeling at the moment.

CHAPTER 30

Nolan

"I'm just glad you're okay, and there wasn't too much damage," Allie said, letting out a sigh.

I nodded briefly as I continued to chop the cucumbers on the cutting board for the salad I was making. While I probably should have been more pissed at Dawson than I was, a part of me was numb to people blowing up at me on the phone as I dealt with angry clients on the daily. And to be fair, until recently, I'd endured Dawson's unappreciative customer service gripes for the last two years. Dawson yelling at me didn't phase me anymore.

But what really did me in was hearing his voice *shake* when he claimed it was his life, and he was in control. He sounded like me, or the me I was before all of this—whatever *this* was —happened.

I hated disruption, disorder. I prided myself on always doing what was right, keeping to the status quo, and keeping my nose down. I liked routine better than anyone, and I understood feeling helpless when things were out of my control.

It was just barely twenty-four hours since I'd felt that way, since I'd woken up in the middle of a literal fire and Dawson had come to *my* rescue with s'mores and sweet whispers of wanting to take care of me. So, instead of rising to his anger, instead of feeding into his need to control the situation, I did the only thing I could think of to do.

I tried to take care of *him*. Which for me, meant making my calls on the Bradish claim in between filing my own, and hitting the market to grab some stuff to make dinner.

I wasn't stupid, I knew given the situation, I'd probably be gone afterward, taking up residence at the Paradise until my apartment was ready for me to inhabit it again. So, at the very least, it was a thank you. I'd probably overstayed my welcome, anyway.

I sprinkled the cucumber wedges in the salad bowls as Allie continued.

"Still though, you have to admit it is sort of ironic that *Mr. March* came to *your* rescue like some knight in shining armor. I mean, you can't make that kind of stuff up. It's like, Hallmark material."

"It would be Hallmark material if it ended happily ever after, but we both know that's not happening."

"And why not?" Allie pressed. "I'd kill to have a hot guy make *me* dinner when I've had a shit day."

I tossed the cutting board and knife in the sink as I turned to her.

Her eyes sparkled even through Facetime, her lips smirking with smugness.

"Because that would mean I actually did something right for once," I grumbled as the timer went off for the pasta.

"You don't give yourself enough credit, Nolan. You're a damn gem, and one argument does not mean you're toast. If Dawson has any brains, he'll be groveling after tasting your damn cooking. What are you making anyway?" she said as she tried to peer around me.

I emptied the pasta into the strainer. "Chicken Alfredo and salad. Not exactly fancy, but..."

The sound of the door unlocking alerted me, and Allie's eyes widened.

"Fuck, I gotta go, Allie. I'll call you later," I said, and I hung up quickly. It wasn't like I was embarrassed or anything, but some things I liked to keep to myself. And Allie was one of those things. We'd been friends since high school, and she was the closest thing I had to a sister. I told her everything, and I mean *everything*. Something my exes didn't particularly care for.

I'd just added the cooked pasta to the sauce pot as Dawson walked through the door.

"I didn't think you'd be here," Dawson said, his entire body freezing upon the sight of me.

"Expecting someone else?" I growled, a little harsher than I'd meant to. I tossed the pasta in the pot, making sure it was coated well with sauce.

Dawson let out a sigh. "No, I just..."

"Sit down," I said briskly as I set the bowls out. A part of me worried Dawson might find my exploration of his kitchen cabinets invasive, but I hoped the scent of overpowering parmesan and bacon distracted him from the fact I'd gone through his stuff.

I had a good reason though...

I braced myself for an argument. After all, last I'd spoken to him he'd been pretty upset, and Dawson wasn't the type to take commands without a little rebuttal. I'd seen him around the firehouse. True to what he'd claimed earlier, he was usually the one in charge, telling others what to do.

So, when he did as I asked without question, sitting his ass on his barstool, eyes wide and focused on me like a kid in a candy store, I couldn't help but be surprised.

And maybe a little smug. So sue me.

"Did you actually make all this from scratch?" Dawson asked carefully.

I set the bowls of salad and pasta in front of him before sliding him a fork.

"It's the least I could do," I said as I sat across from him, focusing on my bowl of pasta because I knew if I looked at him, I'd lose my nerve.

I'd never fucking leave.

"Nolan, listen..."

I held up my hand and shook my head. "Food first. Then we can fight."

I didn't miss the small smirk that fell across Dawson's lips.

"Is that an order?" he asked, his voice edged in sarcasm.

"Just shut up and eat your damn dinner," I said, half-chuckling because he truly was a pain in the ass.

A pain in the ass that I knew I was most definitely falling in love with.

When we'd finally finished eating, Dawson moved to help me clean up.

"It's fine, I—"

"Nope, not gonna let you win this one. You cooked, I clean. Those are the rules."

I huffed in annoyance, but figured if he was in a better mood, I could let it go. It was his place after all, and I was just a guest. A guest on their way out.

"Dawson, listen... I really appreciate you letting me stay, but I think I should go. I'll grab a room at the Paradise—"

"No," Dawson said, turning to look at me with concerned eyes as he set the dishes in the sink. "Don't go on account of my being as asshole... I didn't mean, I just—"

Watching Dawson, a man who was usually so bold and confident, struggle over his words was somehow equally endearing as it was painful. And that melted my damn resolve, if I'd had any to begin with. I sighed.

"I was an ass. Earlier, I know I was, and I didn't mean to be, really. I just..."

I took one small step toward him, noting how his entire body *relaxed* when I did. Almost as if he really didn't want me to leave.

Dawson looked down at me with those fiery amber eyes, his gaze full of unspoken things and uncharted territory.

Full of hope.

But what did Dawson hope for?

"At the risk of sounding like an absolute idiot, I... I like you Nolan. I like you *a lot*, and I really like you being here, with me, but it's more than that..."

Suddenly, I was the one who felt like the rug had been pulled out underneath me, despite the fact I was standing on it. My throat instantly tightened, my heart skipping a beat, my blood starting to rush with the onslaught of panic and anxiety. I know what I wanted him to say, but that didn't mean he was going to say it.

Because the truth was, I liked being with Dawson too. I loved all the stupid little annoyances of his, his gorgeous face, and the little parts of him he kept hidden from most, but had decided to show me. But I knew it couldn't be *that* simple.

Could it?

"Don't get me wrong, you piss me off too. With your smug little smile, or your bratty fucking attitude, or how you can look sexier in *my* sweatpants than I do," he said, flashing me a smirk.

I was frozen as I watched his eyelashes flutter, and I waited with bated breath for him to finish. Though it sounded like he was listing my faults, which irritated me, as if I didn't already know I was a giant pain in his ass.

The feeling is mutual, though.

"But you also challenge me. Especially when *you* take control. Of the situation, of me..."

The vulnerability that crossed over his expression left my heart aching. I got the feeling that this... this soul-bearing moment was something new for Dawson, and I had to admit it was new for me too.

No man had ever looked at me like Dawson was, had ever poured their heart out to me like that. And the reality of that was scary, but also deeply fulfilling.

"Dawson..." I sighed as I took another step, noting his gaze didn't break mine. He only looked at me like I was a tall glass of water and he was in the fucking desert.

The need to soothe his rough edges, to calm his storms and insecurities was overwhelming. This man ran into burning buildings, saved people, and gave back to so much of this community.

He was a true hero, but who saved him?

Who put out the fires in his life?

Who pulled him from the wreckage?

I wanted to be that person. Dawson deserved someone who could withstand the flames, and at that moment, I found my own inner hero. I charged into his burning building, and I reached for him through the fire.

"I'd never try to control *you*. I was never trying to take that from you. I just wanted to take care of *you* for once. Take one thing off your shoulders."

Dawson reached out, and set his hand gingerly on my hip, which only made his sweatpants slide down bit.

I really need to get a pair of these in my size, they are so comfortable...

Dawson's thumb gently brushed my exposed skin, and I'd be lying if I said the touch didn't make my entire body want to melt into a puddle on the floor.

God, I am in so deep...

Like a puppet on delicate strings, with one tiny movement of his hand, I fell into Dawson, against his chest, effortlessly.

"Damn you, Nolan," he breathed out, his other hand snaking its way up my neck and into my hair.

His touch made me feel alive, the heat of his breath on my lips, the touch of his fingertips sliding into my hair like an out of body experience. I barely had a second to breathe before his lips were on mine, warm and inviting, but not soft in the least bit.

No, there was an edge to his kiss, a roughness that caused my cock to twitch and my heart to race.

I met his harsh lips with submission, wanting nothing more than be burned by this man until there was nothing left.

Dawson pulled away only a fraction, his fingertips on my waist moving up my chest to my neck, the pad of his thumb hooking under my chin to make me look up at him. In his fiery gaze, I could see he was scared.

He was terrified of this thing between us, just as I was, and that was what I responded to as I leaned closer, biting at his lower lip, settling my hand on his hip, pulling him to me.

But inside of me there was still panic, a voice in my head that told me I was bordering on dangerous territory.

Because I wanted to give Dawson everything he deserved, everything I could possibly give the man who gives to everyone else.

But all I had to offer was me, and my racing heart.

Would that be enough?

A startling moment of clarity cut through my thoughts, and I knew I needed to take a step back. I needed to get my head on straight and think things through, away from beautiful calendar gods and addicting kisses, and pretty amber eyes.

S.O. freaking S.

"I need... I need to go," I said shakily, not wanting to leave one bit, but knowing if I didn't there would be no turning back. Because if I stayed in Dawson's kitchen, underneath his touch and kiss, I'd never recover. I would be ruined forever.

Tears threatened to escape my eyes and my heart was in my throat as I gingerly pushed away from Dawson, needing air to breathe.

Except away from Dawson, the air was suffocating.

"Please don't go, Nolan," Dawson's voice shook as his hand gently grasped mine, stopping me.

My back to him, I sucked in a breath, trying to still my racing pulse and heart as I felt the heaviness of his words.

He almost sounded heartbroken.

I was at a crossroads, torn between self-preservation and losing myself completely.

CHAPTER 31

Dawson

THE FIRST DAY on the job at the firehouse, I was terrified. The training I'd endured, all the stories I'd been told, none of it would hold a candle to the first time I'd run into a burning building, nothing could truly prepare me. It was a baptism in fire, so to speak.

However, like most of those big moments in my life, I faced the fire with courage, and I refused to let my fear control me. I needed to learn how to use it to my advantage, and I had.

But that was nothing compared to the ledge I found myself on, tethered to Nolan's hand like he was a life raft, and I was in water over my head.

"Please, don't go. I... I need you." I said the words slowly, tasting them on my tongue for the first time.

I hated that I sounded so fucking desperate. So weak.

But it was the goddamn truth, and the levity of that truth hit me like a ton of bricks as I grasped Nolan's hand. He turned to face me, and I expected to see pity, or judgment even. But that wasn't what I saw at all.

In fact, the glaze in Nolan's eyes looked as *pained* as I felt, and as if he was going to cry.

Please don't cry, champ.

"I don't want to leave, I..." His voice shook, but he took a step closer. "Why is this so fucking complicated?" he said, his voice cracking like the edges of my heart.

I took a step closer to him, feeling as if the earth beneath me was moving, shifting us toward one another like tectonic plates.

"Things don't have to be complicated, you know," I said, rubbing my thumb over the edge of his knuckles.

Nolan let out a sigh.

"They just have to be honest."

Nolan squeezed my hand tightly. The silence between us felt like an eternity until he'd spoken.

"In all honesty... I think I'm falling in love

with you," he said softly, his voice barely a whisper.

My entire body softened at his words, a strange sense of relief flooding me.

I moved closer, catching his gaze. He looked as terrified as I felt, and something about that made me feel emboldened, ready to take on a new kind of fire.

The one that was spreading between us.

And I didn't want to put it out. I wanted it to consume me, consume us.

"In all honesty, Nolan... I think I fell in love with you when you beat me at that fucking race," I said as he closed the space between us.

I reached out to push his hair behind his ear, a motion that made his frames a bit crooked, but I couldn't deny it wasn't sexy.

Nolan stared up at me with glassy eyes, pouty lips, and love.

And that was all I needed.

I leaned in and kissed him, letting the fire within my blood spread. Nolan's hands slid over my hips as his fingers dug into my sides, his lips moving slowly against mine in a torturous fashion that only made me want more.

I wanted all of Nolan fucking Harding, and I didn't care how complicated things were, or that we worked together, or that he knew how to get under my skin.

I only cared about the fact that the thought of *not* having him made me feel like I had the day I faced my first fire.

Scared.

I didn't want to lose Nolan. I'd fight like hell to keep him, and the way he touched me, kissed me, tugged at my shirt, told me he needed this too.

He needed *me* just as much as I needed him.

So, I let him pull my shirt off, let him run his hands over my muscles as I slid my hands down the waistband of *my* sweatpants he seemed to favor wearing.

I guided us through the kitchen into the hall-way, the two of us hurriedly trying to undress one another as if we'd die without direct skin to skin contact.

My back slammed against the wall just outside my bedroom, pieces of clothing littered along my hallway like breadcrumbs in a forest. His lips caressed mine before moving to my jaw, and I couldn't help the groan that escaped my throat, or the involuntary thrust of my hips against his rigid cock.

"I'm sorry," I moaned into his neck, my fingertips shoving at his sweatpants and underwear.

"I'm sorry, too," he purred as his fingers quickly made a go at unlatching my belt. My cock throbbed beneath the constraining fabric, anticipating his touch.

The words that came out of my mouth belonged to me, but they were foreign to my ears. I'd never said them to anyone before.

"Guess you could say I've been a bad boy, huh, champ?" I murmured.

Nolan stopped his ministrations and looked up at me from beneath his glasses.

There was only a moment of hesitation in his eyes, before the sparkle of understanding and the spark of lust took hold.

Please punish me with that big beautiful cock of yours... Make it hurt.

"Yes, you have..." he growled, licking his lips, his entire demeanor shifting. "You have been... very bad." He said the words as if they were another language, one he'd only just started learning.

We'll have to work on the delivery a bit.

"How bad?" I purred as I grabbed him by the hips, pulling him into my bedroom, shaking myself out of my pants. Nolan did the same, stepping out of the sweatpants, the light illuminating his cock like the true gift it was.

Nolan pushed me back against the bed, bringing his lips down to my ear. His breath on my skin was hot, causing my cock to twitch against his as he pressed himself against me.

"Bad enough I think you need to be taught a lesson," he whispered, his voice a little more comfortable.

I could feel myself starting to leak already just from the sheer magnitude of his weight, the lust in his voice... and the reality that I was giving him control in *this* situation was not lost on me.

But I trusted Nolan. I loved him, and that was all the courage I needed as I let my guard down completely.

"My safeword is ice cream," I said.

Nolan raised an eyebrow. "What?" he asked in surprise, completely breaking character in a way that was somehow just as endearing as it was humorous.

"I don't like ice cream," I said, as if it were the most obvious thing in the world.

"You are a disgrace. Everyone likes ice cream," he chortled.

I pulled him closer as we fell back onto my bed, wrapping my leg around his hip as I thrust my cock against his.

"Just add it to my list of things you hate about me," I whispered.

Nolan smirked. "It's a long list, Dawson," he said, and he brought his lips to mine.

"Then start tallying up my punishments, baby," I breathed into his mouth.

Nolan smiled devilishly as he broke away.

"And you say I'm the one who's a brat," he teased as he stepped away, leaving me exposed on my bed.

I leaned back on my elbows, planting my feet on the edge of the bed as I stared him down. My heart thudded in my chest so loud I could hear it like an echo in the otherwise silent air.

"What are you waiting for?" I asked, impatiently.

"To wake up from this dream any minute," he murmured as he took his palm to his cock.

I watched as he lazily stroked himself, his gaze on me heated and full of fire. "I'm waiting," I said, egging him on.

Nolan shook his head as he kneeled before me, looking as innocent as ever as he dove between my legs, taking my cock in his hand. His gaze sparkled with mischief.

"Oh, I'll teach you a thing or two about waiting, Dawson. I've waited for *this moment*, for two fucking years."

Before I could speak, Nolan took my cock into the back of his throat in one, swift motion, his tongue sliding along my shaft. Within one motion, he slid right off, and my cock throbbed, irritated to high hell that the warm mouth we'd just been in was no more.

"Fucking tease," I growled.

Nolan slid one finger in his mouth suggestively, licking and sucking as if he *wished* it were my cock, which only aggravated me. Then I watched him do the same to another finger, moaning and making a show of it as I reached for my cock, but he only used his other hand to smack me away.

Then he smacked *my* cock.

The bounce of my damn cock felt the sting, but I wanted more.

"Is that all you got?" I taunted him.

Nolan took me back in his mouth at the same time he slid one finger into my tight hole. Even though I expected the burn, it still hurt. I wasn't nearly ready enough, but I wanted it.

I wanted to be owned by Nolan, and then I wanted to own him in return.

Mine, mine, mine.

The familiar feeling of my orgasm started to swell, and I fought to thrust myself into Nolan's mouth.

"Fuck, I'm close..." I breathed out, and that's when Nolan stopped. He removed his mouth and his fingers, leaving me tingling, thrusting into the air.

Oh no...

"Good boys get rewards, Dawson. And you haven't been very good," he said haughtily as he straddled me where I lay. My cock ached, wet and ready to come.

Nolan slid his cock against mine, taking hold of both of us in his fist, squeezing. His fingertips smoothed my precum over both of our heads, and I groaned in agony. I tried to thrust, but his legs held me down.

"Please, please... I'll be good, I promise," I huffed out indignantly.

"You promise, huh?" he taunted me.

I wanted to come so bad, but I couldn't deny I was loving every minute of this.

I was loving Nolan in this role, and I didn't want to end the experience.

Nolan slid his fingers back into my hole, building a rhythm as he ground his cock against mine, making me sweat.

"Yes," I huffed. "I promise, just let me come, please..." I begged.

This feels so fucking good...

I'd never been in this position before. Usually, I was the one in charge in the bedroom and my former lovers preferred it that way, and for a long time I did too.

But there was something freeing about being at Nolan's mercy. About giving him this control over me and my body.

Which is probably why in the wild state of my lust I said what I did next.

"Fuck me," I whined like a goddamn porno.

Nolan slowed his thrusts, his eyes meeting mine with surprise.

"I mean... unless you don't want to," I said rapidly.

"Ummm... I want to, it's just... I've... never done it. Topped someone, I mean."

Of course, we probably should have had a conversation about this, but hell... Nolan and I seemed to be born in the fire.

"Well, if it makes you feel any better, champ, I've never bottomed," I said, licking my lips. "I never wanted anyone to top me, until I met you."

Nolan's eyebrows furrowed for a moment as he let go of my cock, pulling his fingers out of me, and for a minute I thought he was going to say no.

He nodded, his eyelashes fluttering as he pursed his lips.

"What if I'm no good at it?" Nolan said with a raised eyebrow.

I sat up for a moment, pulling him between my legs, letting my fingers trace over the flesh of his ass, of his seam.

"I think you'll be *very good*, Nolan," I said softly. "Just channel all that hate and waiting and I think you'll be just fine." His cock was right at my mouth level, so I didn't waste the chance to lick the salty liquid gleaming at his slit. I enjoyed watching his entire body shudder.

"Okay..." he said as he took a breath, his eyelids falling shut from my tongue swipe for a moment before he opened them, peering at me with a boldness that only made me want his fury more.

"Lube?" he asked, his voice bolder.

I sucked at the head of his cock before answering, eliciting a tiny whimper from him.

"Top drawer," I responded, before taking his entire cock in my mouth.

Nolan pulled back, the sound of the cap popping echoing in the room.

"Okay, lean back," he instructed methodically.

I obeyed without question, my nerves starting to circulate as reality hit. Right before two cold, wet fingers wedged themselves in my hole again, this time sliding in with ease as they built a rhythm. My head fell back instantly as ecstasy coursed through me, and then Nolan slid a third finger in. The stretch was good, but I needed more.

I needed Nolan and his big, beautiful cock to fucking own me.

"Are you ready?" he asked, his voice full of desire and anxiety.

I nodded, my eyes closing in ecstasy.

"Yes," I said. "Teach me a goddamn lesson, Nolan."

There was a brief moment where I thought he might have reconsidered, but when I felt the tip of his cock pressing against my slick entrance, nothing else mattered.

He took it slow, inch by inch and the stretch felt fucking amazing. And then he slid in the last few inches and my insides *clutched* him like a vice. A deep groan escaped both of us, and immediately Nolan's head buried itself into my shoulder.

"Fuck that feels good," he whined. "*You* feel really good."

I slid my legs around his hips, the motion driving him in deeper.

"*You* feel really good, champ," I said through my teeth, and I fucking meant it.

I felt so fucking full.

Of excitement, of relief, of love... and cock.

Nolan's chest rose and fell against mine as he gently bucked his hips, the movement shooting pleasure through my damn spine. I needed more. I was so freaking close to coming.

"Look at me," I ordered, sliding my hands in Nolan's silky locks. He followed my touch as I turned his head toward me.

Nolan rocked his hips into me a little faster, and I lost myself in the feel of him filling me to the brim, the weight of his body on mine, and the way he was looking at me.

The words fell out of my mouth of their own volition.

"I love you," I said, my cock sliding against his abs torturously, leaving sticky trails on his skin.

Nolan leaned down and took my lips like a damn prayer.

"I love you too, asshole," he whispered, both of us toppling over the edge into ecstasy. His thrusts halted as warmth spread within me, his hot release filling me and spilling out of me as he drove his tongue down my throat.

My cock pulsed as I came hard and fast against his abdomen, painting his skin in my sweet release.

I wrapped my arms around Nolan and held onto him for dear life as we came together like a well-oiled machine.

And when we'd finally disconnected, I'd never felt more whole.

CHAPTER 32

NOLAN

"YOU DON'T HAVE to get up," Dawson whispered in my ear, tugging me closer to his chest.

I guess I didn't mind being the little spoon once in a while...

I groaned as I grabbed his hand, threading my fingers through his as I tried to hold on to sleep.

"Yes, I do. I have a bunch of stuff to catch up on at work," I whined.

Dawson kissed me below my ear, before nibbling on the bottom of my earlobe like a starving man. The feel of his tongue and teeth on the sensitive skin there gave me goosebumps and ignited my fire, but I knew neither of us had time to waste.

It had been a week since we had unofficially-officially sealed the deal. One week since Dawson and I had been honest about our feelings. One week since I'd been staying with Dawson while my apartment was being renovated, and one week since I'd submitted paperwork along with the Bradish re-eval to my higher ups in an escalated claim.

While Karla had given me the option to take a few days regarding my fire situation, I hadn't taken her up on the offer. I knew I'd need to get to work sooner or later.

Regrettably, I broke Dawson's hold, and we both did the adult thing and got our asses moving. I made breakfast while Dawson showered, then took my turn when he was out. I'd just started buttoning up my last button when Dawson stopped me.

"What?" I asked, noting the look of mischief in his eyes.

"Your glasses are crooked," he said, flashing me a smirk.

"What?" I asked as he reached out to adjust them, the motion putting his fingers above my ear, giving him access to slide them into my hair and pull me close.

I wasn't sure I'd ever get used to being *loved* by Dawson.

I'd been used to being tormented and pissed off by Dawson, but being loved by him far outweighed everything else.

It was a feeling I hoped I'd never lose.

"Personally, I like it. But, we can't have you looking like you just rolled in the hay with *Mr. March* when you walk into work,"

"Mhmmm. But you can walk into work with a hickey on your neck and no one says a word?"

Dawson blushed as he craned his neck, the faint markings still visible after a few days.

"Oh, they'll say words. And I'll tell them all the sordid details if they do ask," he said, grinning ear to ear.

I twisted my lips. "That sounds like very bad behavior," I teased him.

"The worst. Definitely worthy of punishment, if you ask me."

I shook my head in defeat. There was no use fighting Dawson when he'd made his mind up about something, and that something was me.

Or more accurately, my form of discipline.

But I wasn't complaining. I was more than happy to explore this new side of me, and Dawson seemed to enjoy reaping the benefits.

And he also had no problem putting me in my place either.

"I'll take that into consideration," I said, and I pressed my lips to his.

"You still good for M's Place later?" he asked as he finished my last button.

"Yeah, good as I'm going to be, I guess," I answered honestly.

It felt stupid to hide the fact we were together anymore, and neither of us wanted to feed the gossip mill, so we'd decided to be upfront and honest with everyone that mattered. Our jobs, and our friends.

I'd officially be meeting Dawson's friends tonight, as his boyfriend, which still baffled my mind.

Hearing him call me that made me blush, made my heart race, and my lips turn up in a smile.

Because the way he said it was like I was the fucking sun.

My boyfriend.

The feeling was more than mutual.

CHAPTER 33

NOLAN

"THAT SHOULD JUST ABOUT DO IT," I said as I shook Jonathan Bradish's hand, just as I heard the rumblings of Dawson's truck.

"I really appreciate everything you've done, Mr. Harding," Jonathan said with a sigh of relief. "This check is going to take care of a lot of stuff and then some," he said appreciatively.

"Please, you can call me Nolan."

That was the moment Dawson walked in.

"Everything okay?" Dawson asked as he looked between us.

Jonathan smiled. "Better than okay. Mr. Harding here went above and beyond," Jonathan said with a chuckle.

"Is that so?" Dawson said, raising an eyebrow at me.

"Because of the error in the initial report, not to mention the initial findings—" I raised an eyebrow back at Dawson, who only sheepishly blushed. "I was able to file a complaint along with my re-eval and I escalated the claim above my supervisor so it would get pushed through faster, being as there were extenuating circumstances and someone's livelihood at stake." I smiled smugly.

"Breisinger cut me a check for thirty grand, Daw," Jonathan said grinning ear to ear.

"Thirty grand? That's... that's more than—"

"It's what he deserves. This place is his business, after all," I said firmly.

Dawson didn't waste a second. He swooped in and hugged me tight, then *kissed* me with such appreciation I found it hard not to wrap my arms around him and do the same.

When we broke apart, his brother was shaking his head.

"I should have known," he said as I fought to regain myself, steadying my blush and my glasses, which had gone crooked from Dawson's prince charming moment.

"What do you mean?" Dawson asked, clearing his throat, casting me a sly grin.

"I mean, the tension between you two when

you last showed up here was thicker than a fucking poundcake.”

We both laughed, and I could see I was not the only one blushing.

“That obvious, huh?” Dawson asked with a chuckle.

His brother rolled his eyes. “Well that, and you’ve been talking about the guy for like, two years.”

I turned to raise an eyebrow at Dawson. “Really now? I hope they were only good things,” I teased him.

Dawson grinned devilishly.

“Actually they were terrible things. Long list of grievances.”

I bet they were.

“Mhmmm.” I fought my own smile as Dawson wrapped his arm around my shoulder and pulled me tightly to him, pressing his lips to my forehead.

EPILOGUE

DAWSON

"IF I RECALL CORRECTLY, I believe your words were, 'not if he was the last dick on earth,'" Mitchell said with a grin.

Nolan turned to look at me with judgment. "Really, Dawson?"

"To be fair, you were quite infuriating..." I scoffed.

Nolan rolled his eyes. "Says the asshole whose sole desire in life was to make my job a living hell."

"Maybe that wasn't his only desire," Cade said with a smirk.

"Obviously," Weston chimed in as he pulled Cade close.

"I'm surrounded by idiots," I huffed, throwing my hands up in the air.

The waiter came with our drinks and a basket of wings, and I noticed someone kicking me under the table. I didn't have to look to know who it was, since it was coming from the seat beside me. I shot a wary look to Nolan, who was smugly shaking his head.

"You are an idiot," Nolan teased.

"But you still love me," I teased him back.

Nolan shook his head.

I licked my lips as I dove in for a wing as the karaoke singer exited the stage.

"Don't worry you can get your revenge later," I said, flashing him a wink as I ate my wing.

"I'll hold you to that," Nolan promised, taking a sip of his beer.

"I'm counting on it," I growled wickedly as I leaned in and kissed the man of my damn dreams quickly in front of all my friends, in the glow of the bar where it all started.

The karaoke singer who'd taken the stage actually sounded really good, singing Ozzy's *Bark At The Moon*.

"I'm going up," Nolan said as he jumped off the barstool beside me.

"Really now? Since when do you like being the center of attention?" I scoffed.

Nolan stood straighter, adjusting his glasses and looking at me with that bratty cockiness I'd come to fucking love about him. He may have been hot as hell when he was in charge, but God Almighty did I love it when he turned on his brat charm.

I wasn't sure what I liked more, to be honest, stuffing my cock down Nolan's throat to teach him a lesson, or him edging me and fucking me into oblivion.

He placed a hand on his hip and with the utmost attitude said, "You can't stop me." And like the little pain in the ass he was, he stuck his tongue out for good measure.

As if he trusted I wouldn't bend his ass over my damn lap and smack it right here.

Pain in my ass.

"Oh yeah?" I asked as I left my wings and beer and sauntered over to him, holding him in my stern gaze.

"Yeah," he taunted me.

I grabbed him by the waist, pulling him to me. His eyes widened in surprise for a moment, but his body melted in my hold like butter.

Nolan slid his hands in my hair, staring up at me with bright eyes from behind crooked glasses.

I set my palm against his neck, using my thumb to tilt his chin up, and took his lips against mine without warning. I could taste the hint of hopps on his tongue, and just like all the other times, he fell into my hold with ease, groaning as I coaxed his tongue with mine. I was aware my friends were hollering and bitching at us to get a room, but I didn't care. It was all in good fun anyway.

Nolan broke apart from me for a moment, and I watched the blush creep over his nose and cheeks, relishing in the way his glasses had gone crooked from our kiss.

"You'll pay for that," he whispered, his voice full of lust, his cock twitching against mine.

"I'm counting on it, champ," I said as the fire in Nolan's eyes shifted, and he took charge, and kissed *me*, making all my wildest dreams come true.

Thank you for reading Dawson and Nolan's story.

If you enjoyed this book, please return to your favorite retailer and leave a review. Even a few words could mean the world to an author.

Continue the series with Drew's story, Book 3 in Jasper Springs!

DREW

AN MM BAD BOY ROCKSTAR ROMANCE

Drew
An MM Enemies To Lovers Romance
Jasper Springs
Book Three

Copyright © 2024
Evie Riley
Second Edition
ISBN: 978-1-77357-719-7
Published by Naughty Nights Press LLC
Cover Art By Willsin Rowe

DREW

**A wounded heart. A shared love of music.
A whirlwind romance with the power to heal.**

Drew Axel is ready for a change after his famously public split from famed actor, Rozen Lane. When he stops to perform in his childhood town, getting back to his roots, the last thing Drew expects to find is love. Especially with a fellow Swiftie.

Taylor Meade has two loves in his life: His floral shop and his favorite female singer.

Despite being in the business of weddings, Taylor has given up on finding the perfect man to fit into his Swift-inspired dreams. That is, until he wakes up hungover in rockstar Drew Axel's tour bus.

As fate draws Drew and Taylor closer, they both soon discover music isn't the only thing they have in common. Will Drew give up a life of glitz and glamor for his wildest dreams? Or will

Taylor find himself fighting more than just Drew's bad boy reputation?

Readers seeking a bad boy rockstar romance with forced proximity set in a cozy little town may find this story ticks those boxes. While Drew and Taylor may have cameos in future stories, each book in this series can be read as a standalone.

CHAPTER 1

Drew

It's good to be home.

I sighed as I parked my bus at the edge of the parking lot of *M's Place*, a tiny little hole-in the wall bar in the small town of Jasper Springs.

It'd been nearly twenty years since I left the quaint place, after scoring my first big time record deal. Though it was home, it didn't feel like home anymore, not without my parents who no longer lived here, or with the new buildings and shops that replaced the old ones I once remembered.

I sat for a moment and appreciated the view of the sunset behind the trees, the way the light kissed the pavement, glinting off the metal of my *Axe 2 Grind* lanyard hanging in the window.

While my bandmates and I were on hiatus so we could focus on our solo projects, I was excited at the idea of traveling to more local spots to perform instead of the bigger venues the band normally played at. Which meant I'd be taking the bus across the country to hit all the little dives, diners, and practically dungeons in my path from LA to Pittsburgh.

The fresh air and change of scenery would be good for me, or so I told myself.

Though perhaps it wasn't just a need for a change of scenery that had me chomping at the bit, ready to jump on a bus by myself and head for the hills. If I was being honest, it might have had something to do with *America's Sexiest Man Alive*, Rozen Lane. My cheating bastard of an ex-boyfriend.

"You gonna just sit there like a fucking lump, Axel, or are you gonna get yourself checked in?" The grumble of my long-time friend and manager, Helena "Howler" Dryfuss bit as she stopped just behind the driver seat.

I sighed, flipping the key to turn the engine off, then turning in my chair to look at her. Okay, maybe I wasn't taking this trip just by myself. Howler would be with me no matter where I went, like a bad case of poison ivy.

"Can I just have a minute, Howler? Christ, I haven't been home in like, a lifetime. Maybe I just want to, you know, process shit?" I growled.

Helena shot me a scathing look, her bright blue eyes full of disdain and annoyance.

"You had sixteen hours to process, baby. Therapy time is over. Now get your ass in gear, and let's get set up. The show must go on."

I dropped my hand from the steering wheel, letting out a sigh as the door opened, deciding perhaps Helena was right.

Sitting in my bus moping was not doing me any favors at the moment, and if there was one thing that I was capable of doing that would take my mind off Rozen, it was performing. So, I grabbed my white electric guitar from the couch in front of the door, flashing Helena a bright, white-toothed smile as I cocked my head, shedding my inner homeboy and channeling the man people paid to see. The man I'd been for the last twenty years.

"Right, of course."

CHAPTER 2

DREW

M's Place was fairly packed for a Tuesday night, but then again, it wasn't like most of the inhabitants in this town had a lot of options for nightlife. Not unless they got in their cars and took off for the city, of course.

While I'd been used to crowds pretty much everywhere I went, being the frontman of my band and boy toy to *America's Sexiest Man Alive*, I had to admit the atmosphere of M's Place was a breath of fresh air. No one bum-rushed me at the door for an autograph, or tried to break into my bus. It was almost as if they didn't know who I was, or if they did, they just didn't give a shit, and a part of me was engaged by that. It reminded me of those first years I'd been on the road with my boys, trying to get my name out there. Trying to get people to notice me, to pay attention to a skinny-jeans clad skeleton with a mop of hair who looked like the boy next door instead of a fucking rock star.

At least until I'd started to invest in my ink.

Now, I'm a hell of a lot bigger, thanks to a steady diet of protein shakes and grass Rozen had me on for the last year and all the workouts in between. I wasn't exactly small potatoes before I met the man, but I bet I couldn't even get my leg in the top of my old skinny-jeans now.

I tuned up my guitar for my first song, watching the crowd who barely seemed to notice me standing there on stage.

I sucked in a deep breath and grabbed the mic, introduced myself as Drew Axel from Axe 2 Grind, and thanked them for letting me perform for them, something I used to do a hell of a lot more in the beginning when I used to play places like this. Nowadays, Axe 2 Grind was on a tight schedule. I barely got to do meet and greets anymore, something else I appreciated having the ability to do on this tour.

While a good bit of people turned to face me, intrigued enough likely by the name, I could see I hadn't captured *everyone*'s attention.

I will soon enough.

I caught Howler's gaze from the other side of the room, giving me the thumbs up to start my set. I strummed my guitar, the vibration in my fingers a welcome sensation as I struck the chords. The opening riff of Taylor Swift's *Blank Space* echoed in the air as the music from sound check accompanied me. It still felt weird to perform with my guitar without my bandmates, but there was a sort of rush to it too. It was just me.

And while that would have been scary in any other situation, on stage... that's where I was at my best. That's where I came *alive.*

Helena had tried to get me to stick to the formula and perform mostly *Axe 2 Grind* hits, but quite honestly, I was tired of performing the same old songs day in and day out.

I wanted something different, something new.

Covering Taylor Swift's pop songs was definitely not what A2G fans will expect.

I scanned the crowd, looking for one person in the crowd who I could pick out to perform to.

Most people didn't know that was my trick. The magazines always talked about how good I was live. When I was just starting out, I made it a point to find one person in every crowd, and I played for *them.* Usually, it was cocky assholes who thought they were too good to be there, dragged by friends or partners against their will to put up with my "noise."

If I could sway them, if I could pull them in, then I did my job.

And it seemed to work for the last twenty years.

My gaze settled on a man off to the left who was about two rows away. He looked visibly uncomfortable, which was perfect for me. If I could get this guy up and dancing, or at least nodding to my music, then I did my job.

It also didn't hurt that he was pretty attractive, despite his deer in the headlights look.

Actually, if I'm being honest, it only adds to his appeal. I'll give that man something to look wide-eyed about, that's for sure.

"Nice to meet you, where you been?" I drawled as I made eye contact. He looked back and forth, as if I could be singing to someone else, so I zeroed in my gaze as I straightened my back, squaring my shoulders as I continued to sing. "I could show you incredible things," I sang, channeling the persona I usually took on stage.

Bold, confident, sexy, and maybe a little reckless. That's who Drew Axel was to the masses.

I crooned through the lyrics as I let my

fingers slide over the frets, closing my eyes as the rhythm took me. My mind wandered as the words poured out of me of their own volition and I sang on about forever and going down in flames.

Like always, there was a hurricane of emotion swirling in my stomach as I felt the depth of the lyrics I covered.

My own songs didn't turn on the faucet anymore, they'd become less about me and more about what sells. I can't remember the last time I wrote a banger that really accessed your fucking feels.

But Taylor Swift did a really good job of that. Accessing my feels, I mean.

Plus her love life is about as sordid as mine, so if the shoe fits...

As I opened my eyes, I saw my target staring back at me with a look that was some cross between awe and lust, and I know I have him.

I crooned on about the high being worth the pain as I stroked my chords, spinning around as the music fills me. My legs opened as I took my trademark cocky stance, my dark hair falling in my eyes as my whole body practically convulses as I covet the guitar in my hands.

"Got a long list of ex-lovers," I scream-sang as I met his gaze. My cock twitched behind my guitar, which only fed my drive.

I rocked my guitar as I spun around, the heat of the lights spreading like wildfire through me as I ripped out the bit about players and the game. When I was facing the crowd again, I saw Mr. I Don't Belong Here staring at me like I was the only man in the room.

I smirked as I continued to play my heart out, never breaking my gaze.

Because as far as I was concerned, I was only playing for him.

CHAPTER 3

Taylor

The last thing I wanted to do after a long week of back to back orders was go out for a drink. I knew most of the guys my age would be all about shirking their responsibilities and jumping at a chance to get their drink on, especially with someone like Giselle.

Whether she's taken or not...

But me, I wasn't most guys. I knew that sounded cliché, but it was true. I'd much rather curl up on my couch and watch cringey rom-coms or scroll through florist TikToks while I have a self-care night instead of going out. But Giselle, bless her heart, would not take no for an answer.

Especially because her favorite rockstar, Drew Axel, was performing tonight at the local dive bar everyone in Jasper Springs flocked to.

I didn't grow up in Jasper Springs like Giselle, though from the stories she'd told me, I am not sure I'd have wanted to. The town of Jasper Springs itself was pretty small. The high school was built up of Jasper Springs, Deer Park, and Paradise residents, but the graduating class was still barely two hundred people. I couldn't imagine being that close to my classmates.

When I was in a senior in high school—a whopping seven years ago—I was a loner. I had a few friends, but after my break-up with my ex, when I moved to Jasper Springs, I lost contact with them. Nothing like moving to prove who your real friends are.

But I was determined to do this adult dream thing on *my* terms—and a small town like Jasper Springs was perfect for my ultimate dream: to own a flower shop that would put the Hallmark movie flower shops to shame.

I was still a long way from my goal, but I was here. I was the proud owner of *Taylor Made Bouquets*. I was living my dream... sort of.

The wedding scene wasn't as lively as I'd hoped in a small town, but despite that, I still kept the shop open, even if most of my sales were for funeral arrangements or graduations.

When I moved to Jasper Springs, Giselle was one of the first people I met. Long, leggy, and tanned with her dark hair swept back into a ponytail that screamed "Hamptons Honey", she'd taken it upon herself to bring a literal plate of cookies to my doorstep. Which technically, was across the street at the time.

I won't lie, I was worried she'd take our polite interaction the wrong way. Most women mistake my politeness for interest. Giselle said it was due to my lack of assertiveness, and my shyness. People didn't just *assume* you were gay.

But it wasn't something I advertised either.

What was I supposed to do?

Wear a sign that says "This Machine Only Takes Dick"?

No, thank you.

Not to mention, it wasn't like I had a ton of experience with men. Probably not as much as I should have for a twenty-five year old gay man.

My list of ex-lovers was pretty slim. I'd dated a couple guys in high school, but clearly I'd put more into the relationship slash situationship than my partners, including my longest relationship, my ex Zack.

Who left me for bigger, better things.

Though it might also be because I wasn't *assertive* enough in making my interest and affection clear, according to Giselle, who next to my other friend, Julie—who I also met when I moved to Jasper Springs and hit it off with immediately—was probably one of the smartest individuals I knew. I'd never been able to talk about my love of cock with anyone until I met them. Both women just had this comforting air about them. It was easy to open up to people when you weren't worried you were going to be judged or left behind.

I'd been trying to work on the assertiveness thing. I'd listened to audiobooks. I'd meditated. I'd even done those stupid exercises in the mirror. And I thought I was shifting my mindset, that I could most certainly tell people *no,* or walk with faked confidence into a room, if only because I thought if I made that sort of change in my life, my business would prosper too.

Fake it till you make it, right?

But somehow I'd caved like a wilted sunflower when Giselle *begged* me to come with her to M's Place so she could see Drew Axel perform tonight.

I knew who *Axe 2 Grind* were, if only because it was Giselle's and Julie's favorite band. I preferred Taylor Swift, the most prolific artist of our fucking generation.

I bet Drew Axel doesn't write his own songs like

Taylor does. Probably too busy partying on his big tour bus or making an ass of himself in the public eye.

Giselle curled close to me as I took a sip of my wine. I didn't expect top shelf vino at a place like M's Place, but I had to admit the rosé wasn't all that bad.

We'd managed to score a seat close to the stage, as Giselle insisted it was pivotal we arrived early because she thought the show would be sold out, and the place wasn't all that big to begin with.

I hated to admit she was right. The place was packed with the karaoke crowd prior, being as M's was well known for its karaoke and bar bingo crowd that met once a month, and naturally they'd booked Drew Axel's show immediately following their signature event. Many of the regulars stayed through the rockstar's set, mixed in with fans like Giselle, and I'm sure several other significant others and gay besties who were dragged against their will to this show.

But the moment those lights dimmed, and Drew strummed his guitar, something in the world shifted.

I recognized the riff, albeit it was faster, and darker sounding than I was used to, but when he opened his eyes, bright green framed by thick black eyeliner, and looked at me—no, *gazed* at me—like I was the only person in the room, my entire body heated like a flame.

Not to mention my overzealous cock decided that was a good time to remind me no one had looked at me like that ever, and he liked the attention as much as I did.

I shifted in my seat as Giselle removed her arm from my shoulders, standing instead and moving to the music. I was thankful for her move, if only because the last thing I wanted was for my friend to discover my surprise erection in public. We were close, but not that close. I nonchalantly adjusted myself, feigning the façade of comfortability as I shifted in my seat, crossing my legs, and squeezing tight to try and rein in my burgeoning hardness.

What the fuck is wrong with me?

In my peripheral vision, Giselle swayed, but I couldn't focus on her. I could only focus on the way Drew Axel held his guitar, on the way pink and blue lights drew highlights along the curve of his ass in his ripped jeans, on the way his hair fell in his eyes, and the way he kept fucking *staring* at me like he was undressing me with his damn eyes.

My cock twitched in my khakis, all too eager and excited.

The entire set was like that, from his

opening cover of *Blank Space* to his ending cover of *Wonderwall*.

Finally relieved that the show was over, I stood up way too fast, suddenly dizzy, no doubt from all the blood rushing from my head to my... other head.

Fucking hell, why won't you just go down!

"Well, that was fun. I——"

"Sweet G, is that you?" A deep, smooth voice cut through my words, and suddenly there was a rush of people knocking into us.

"Only in the flesh," she chirped excitedly as I turned to see who she was talking to, my eyes widening as I realized it was the man himself.

Drew fucking Axel.

I did a double take, looking from one to the other. I knew she liked the guy, I mean *Axe 2 Grind* was her favorite band, but she'd never once said she *knew* the guy.

Just how did she know a rockstar?

Was my friend keeping groupie secrets?

Drew pulled Giselle into a hug as several other women tugged at the holes of his muscle shirt, clamoring for an autograph. When he pulled back, he grabbed their photos, signed them—and a couple stomachs too—and took his pictures.

Giselle didn't seem put off, but the longer the guy stood there, the longer I stared, which wasn't helping my current situation. In fact, it only made me more focused on *leaving* this seventh circle of hell.

When the girls had scampered off, he turned his attention on Giselle again, who was now threading her arm through mine, squeezing me once again with excitement.

"It's been what, at least twenty years? You still look as gorgeous as the day I met you," he said, flashing her with a smile that was far too cheesy for my liking. A strange pang of jealousy ransacked me as my cock twitched, remembering how he'd looked at *me* like that.

But I knew it was all for show. Men like Drew Axel didn't like guys like me. We were just numbers and figures to them, and they'd sell whatever they needed to in order to get their hands in our wallets.

"Giselle, I think we should——"

"And you look ten times better," she teased, and the man actually had the audacity to laugh like they truly were old chums.

"Let me buy you and your man a drink," Drew said, sliding his hand in his pockets.

"Oh, I'm not her man," I said reflexively. "I'm just the poor soul she held against his will to come here."

I watched as Drew's lips curled into a smirk, and my cock twitched.

I really need to get the hell out of here.

Giselle poked me in the ribs. "Oh, don't even start, Taylor. You know you loved it," she teased.

Drew cocked his head to the side, his gaze appraising me with interest.

"Taylor, huh? Not a fan?" he asked, clicking his tongue.

"Don't take it personally, *Drew*," I said, a strange sense of confidence rising up in me. "You're just, not my type," I said.

His green eyes sparkled in the light as he chuckled darkly, and I realized all at once I hadn't said music.

"Of music, I mean," I clamored, trying to cover up the weird flirty-not flirty dig I'd just taken at a damn *celebrity*.

What the fuck is wrong with me tonight?

"Your words wound me so, *Taylor*." The way he said my name, made my literal hairs stand on edge, goosebumps pricking my skin.

And then he turned from me, shunning me no doubt for my stupid comment, focusing his pearly white smile on Giselle.

"So how about that drink, G?" he said. "You and *Taylor* up for shooting the shit?"

And like the little minx she was, Giselle decided to really make my night a living hell, when she answered, "Taylor and I would love a drink, wouldn't we, Taylor?"

CHAPTER 4

One drink for Giselle and Drew turned into three drinks, and I was not quite drunk enough to deal with either of them.

The two went on and on about their time in school together—apparently the rockstar was from the area—droning on about a catch up like a badly written episode of Reunion before it was canceled.

I'd debated leaving the two of them to stare into each other's eyes for the rest of the night, convinced neither would notice I was gone.

Which is why I'd taken it upon myself to get up and go to the bathroom, when really I just needed someone to commiserate with.

So I called Julie, naturally.

"Hey," I said when she answered.

"Hey," she said, clearly surprised by my late night call. "Are you okay?"

"Yeah, I'm fine. You'll never guess where I'm at," I said.

"The shop?" Julie teased.

"Nope, Giselle cornered me into going to this stupid concert tonight at M's Place," I said dejectedly.

"You mean Drew Axel's concert?" Julie's voice elevated, and I could hear the faint echo in the background from the depth of her excitement.

"Yeah, that concert. Apparently, they know each other, like went to school together. We're having drinks, and—"

"Shut up, Taylor! You are *not* having a drink right now with my teenage dream," she gushed, completely guffawing over what I'd just said.

What was everyone's deal?

Yeah the guy was hot, but what else did he have to offer?

Why was everyone so into this guy?

Maybe it's the tattoos.

Maybe it's the way he holds his guitar.

Or the way he looks at you when he sings.

I forced away the thoughts threatening to bring my cock back to life. I'd only just gotten myself to soften, no thanks to thoughts about the most mundane shit possible.

Thoughts of taxes and funeral arrangements will kill any erection.

"Not really. It's pretty much just the Giselle and Drew show right now. I doubt they even notice I've left to call you."

"You *have* to get me an autograph. I will love you forever!" She squealed.

"I thought you already loved me!" I said, teasing her back. Though a part of me was incensed at her words.

"I do... I didn't mean... I just... I'm stuck here working overnight, and you're drinking with my idol, and I'm having major fear of missing out right now, Tay."

I rolled my eyes as I slowly sauntered away from the bathrooms, my gaze falling on Drew where he sat at the bar. The fans had mostly gone, and the bar itself looked to be clearing out, likely because it was nearly one in the morning, and last call would be soon.

I watched as Giselle smiled, and as Drew ran his tattooed fingers down her arm, smiling in return.

Something about the gesture felt intimate, sweet almost, and the way he looked at her like she was the brightest star in the room, stirred an ache in my own heart.

I wished someone would touch me and look at me like that. Like the way he'd looked at me when he sang *Blank Space.*

"I know, I'm sorry, it's just... I'm having an off day today. This isn't really my scene, you know?" I said as I turned around, leaning against the wall.

"Newsflash, you know you *are* allowed to have fun, right?" Julie said.

"I don't know if drinking and rock music are my idea of a good time," I admitted.

"Rather be one with your flowers and reruns of Gilmore Girls?" she teased.

"You know it," I said. My gaze flashed to the clock on the wall that read twelve forty-five, before settling on the door of the bathroom, and I figured now was as good a time as any to do my business and wrap up this night and collect my date. We'd definitely stayed long enough, and I needed to get home so I could get some sleep before work tomorrow.

"I've got to go, Jules, I think its time to pay the check and peace the fuck out," I said as I hung up, making my way into the bathroom.

Surprisingly, at that time of the night the bar was thinning out, and there wasn't anyone else in the space except me. So, I took my time. I'd just unzipped my pants when the door opened.

The sound of clamoring boots made my body tense.

But when I saw familiar ripped jeans and a handful of tattoos, my body relaxed.

"Apologies if I'm boring you to tears," Drew Axel drawled as he slowly unzipped his pants.

I gripped my cock a little tighter, shaking off the remains of my piss if only because I was far too tempted to focus on other things.

And I didn't want Drew to get the wrong idea.

Why do I care what he thinks of me?

I barely know the guy.

"You're not boring me," I said.

Drew smirked, his green gaze sparkling with mischief.

"This just... isn't my cup of tea, that's all," I said.

Drew scoffed, his gaze dipping to where I held myself, and I felt my cheeks redden. It certainly wasn't abnormal to check out the dick of the guy next to you, but what was abnormal was the way my cock instantly hardened under Drew's gaze.

I shifted my stance as I tucked my hardened cock back in my pants.

"It's not mine either, you know. It's just part of the job," Drew scoffed, his gaze traveling back up my body to my face once more.

A mixture of mortification and excitement coursed as I did exactly what I knew I shouldn't.

I looked down. So sue me.

I watched as Drew's hand stroked his shaft, slower than a man who'd just taken a piss probably should. I swallowed harshly, not because of feelings of inadequacy. There were plenty of assholes out there with bigger dicks than me, and that never really affected me in any negative ways.

But it wasn't Drew's size that had me spiraling.

It was the piercings.

He had a fucking Jacob's Ladder.

Why was that hot?

Why was I still looking like a fucking perv?

"Yeah, well, we all do what we have to do, right?" I said, probably a little too harshly as I zipped my pants and headed to the sink.

Drew grunted in response, before answering, "Right."

And with that, I was off to collect Giselle, and get the hell out of that place. I needed my bed in the worst way.

"Hey, you ready?" I said as I reached the bar, my words forcing Giselle to look at me.

"Oh... but we just got started..." Giselle pouted.

"It's like, one in the morning, Giselle. You

know we both have work, and a life to get back to," I said as I signaled for Miguel to bring the check.

"Yeah, I should call it a night too," Drew said, approaching us from behind. He leaned his hand against the bar as if to steady himself between Giselle and I, the motion knocking his legs right into mine, almost knocking me down in the process.

I grabbed the bar for steadiness myself, as I flashed a glare at him.

What the hell?

Miguel presented me the check, and I sighed, reaching in my pocket for my wallet if only to hurry this along. So, I was quite surprised when Drew literally plucked it right out of my hands—his fingertips brushing the back of my knuckles as he did so, which only relit the fire I'd felt earlier watching him. And moments ago during our weird tense moment.

His fingertips on my skin were surprisingly... soft, slightly cold from the fresh washing in the sink of the bathroom, smooth with the faint sheen of bar soap.

"Absolutely not, this one is on me," Drew said, flashing me with a smirk as he autographed the check.

"Thanks," Giselle said as she clutched my

arm, her warmth radiating through me as my gaze caught Drew's.

"Don't worry about it. Knight in Shining Armor here can get it next time," he said with a wink as he pushed away from the bar.

Heat threatened to flush my cheeks once more, so I turned away from the rockstar in question.

"Goodbye," I growled, much harsher than I'd meant to.

I sped out of M's Place toward my car, toting a clumsy Giselle like a child on a leash.

"Why do you have to be such a killjoy?" she pouted.

I opened the car door for her, helping her inside.

"I'm not a killjoy, I just... I'm trying to take care of you," I said. "Make sure no one takes advantage of you," I said.

Giselle laughed. "Drew was right, you are a knight in shining armor," she giggled.

"No, your knight in shining armor is Aaron, remember?" I said as I rounded the driver's side of the car.

Giselle sighed. "Aaron would understand catching up with an old friend," she said, as I started the car up.

"Mhmmm," I said as I looked in my review mirror.

"Besides, I'm not Drew's type. Not by a long shot." She laughed.

"He's a rockstar, I'm pretty sure everyone is his type," I chirped.

Giselle laughed again.

"You know he is into men, right?" She chuckled.

I nearly hit the brakes on the car.

I knew he'd been in the tabloids about a supposed break up with Rozen Lane, but I didn't believe most of the stories. In fact, most of the tabloids reported on him leaving clubs and houses of *women* of all professions, actresses, heiresses, models. One random rumor of being with the hottest man alive did not make the man gay.

Right?

I shoved down the part of me that wanted to believe a man like Drew actually preferred dick.

My luck is never that good.

"I think you are drunk and not thinking clearly," I said as I drove along the quiet drag toward our neighborhood.

"I think you're just afraid to admit you like him," she teased.

"His show wasn't bad, I'll give him that. But you can't *like* someone you just met. Life isn't a romance novel," I said as I pulled up to her driveway, behind Aaron's car.

I shifted the car into park, and she shot me a soft smile before reaching for her door.

"Thanks, Taylor. I'll text you in the morning," she said softly.

I waited until I'd watched her head into the house, until the door had closed behind her and the lights were turned on.

I sighed in the quiet of my car. I hadn't meant to sound so disillusioned, but it was the truth. No matter how badly I wanted to buy into the fantasy of a hot, sexy rockstar who would literally rock my world, I knew that life didn't work like that, and even if it did...

Even if it did, those sorts of stories were far and few between, and they never happened to a twenty-five year old gay florist with confidence issues living in Small Town USA.

I put my car in reverse, and I decided to put all thoughts of Drew Axel and tonight's events out of my mind.

CHAPTER 5

Taylor

My alarm went off like it always did, at six fifteen in the morning, blaring like a siren. Most of the time, I was in bed by ten, and thoroughly rested, and I'd rise, stretch and be about my normal routine. But after getting less than a good six hours of sleep, I was not in the mood for my alarm and it's havoc this morning.

I reached for the phone, fumbling to grasp it and shut off the maddening sound. Just as I managed to do so, the phone vibrated in my hand, pinging with a sound I knew too well.

Why on earth would Julie be texting me at six fifteen in the morning?

How was she not asleep right now?

In fact, how is *anyone* awake at this hour today?

I swiped up to read her text, my eyes adjusting to the bright display screen.

Did you get my autograph?

I rolled over in bed, groaning in response, though I knew she couldn't hear my disdain through the phone.

No, I texted back, throwing my phone on the pillow beside me before letting my hand fall over my eyes as my entire body tried to wake up.

I felt sluggish and tired, not at all like myself.

Probably because I tossed and turned all freaking night.

Though I was also harder than a slab of marble at the moment. Instinctively, I let my free hand find its way in my boxers, if only to adjust myself for the moment. A nice shower session would take care of my morning wood, no doubt.

I grumbled and groaned, removing my hand from my eyes as I swung my legs over the side of the bed and stumbled to my bathroom.

The light was blinding to my eyes, as was my disheveled reflection in the mirror. I didn't waste time, removing my boxers quickly, my cock springing forth, free from its restraint.

Within seconds, I had the shower running

and stood there waiting for the spray to heat up. The minute my feet hit the cool tile floor, I felt a wave of relief. I ran my hands through my hair, getting it wet first as I closed my eyes, letting the warm water sluice over my skin.

I reached out, bracing my palm against the tile as I let my free hand travel to my erection, the relief of my touch flooding me almost instantly. I let out a groan as I tightened my grip around my dick, slowly building a wet, warm rhythm.

My mind wandered like it always did, the familiar fantasies filling my brain. Fantasies I'd never share with anyone, because I had no one to share them with. It wasn't like I imagined an idol or a celebrity, or even one of the hot firemen that graced the calendar in my kitchen.

No, all I ever imagined was a man, a tall, dark, tattooed man, who was every bit the alpha type—large and in charge, cocky. I'm sure most people thought of such men, usually in the dominant role, owning them, making them beg for more. But in my fantasies, that big, strong, beautiful man got on his knees for *me*.

My cock throbbed as expected, clearly familiar with this song and dance. But my brain threw me for a loop, when the man I imagined staring up at me, licking his damn lips wasn't the generic, tall, dark and handsome I usually imagined, no.

Instead, I saw deep, mischievous green eyes, dark hair falling in them like shadows.

Tattooed hands perched palm flat against his tight, ripped jean-clad thighs, Drew Axel stared up at me like a devil, and I was powerless to push the thought aside.

Not when my cock throbbed, my fingers brushing over the burst of precum that had started to form at my head from the thought alone.

I was alone, in the privacy of my own home, so what did I have to be embarrassed about?

It wasn't like I was ever going to see the man again.

"I'll give you a fucking axe to grind," I grit out through my teeth, my hips picking up their pace as I thrust myself into my warm hand.

I knew it wouldn't be long from the tightening in my balls, the pulse of my cock as I imagined *shoving* my weeping cock in between those pouty, perfect lips of his. Just the thought of those lips wrapped around my cock, of his tongue along my shaft while I thrust myself into the back of his throat was enough to make me blow.

The muscles in my thighs and ass clenched

as I squeezed myself, letting out a desperate moan as I opened my eyes. I came hard, and fast, my abdomen clenching as my body worked to dispel the culmination of my orgasm, watching as rope after rope circled the drain, taking with it my sanity and leaving a fresh wave of guilt in its presence.

It wasn't like I hadn't ever jacked off to the thought of a celebrity before, but this felt different, even though I couldn't explain why.

So instead of dissecting that, I decided to just put all thoughts of hot Drew Axel fantasies out of my mind.

It's just fresh in your mind, that's all.

Doesn't mean you actually like the guy.

I told this to myself, I think because I wasn't ready to accept the truth, and that truth was that my life would never be the same now that Drew had shown up on his rock and roll horse like some ripped-jeans savior.

I tugged at my softening cock, the feeling of elation leaving my muscles feeling loose and like Jell-O. Using my thumb, I brushed the last drops of my release over the tip, noticing the warm water had started to run cold.

Shit, I better get a move on.

I don't want to be late!

And with that, I pushed aside all thoughts of

good boys on their knees, of sexy rockstars, and of melodic voices away, choosing to focus on what I knew was true, and not fantasy.

And the truth was I, Taylor Meade, had a job to do, and that was the most important thing.

CHAPTER 6

Drew

"Finally. I thought I was going to have to peel your ass off the barroom floor again tomorrow morning," Howler said as she looked up from her Rolling Stone magazine, her bare feet perched on top of the bus's steering wheel.

Gross.

"Get your feet off my baby," I said as I swatted at her ankles.

She only had the audacity to stick her tongue out at me like a kid.

"She ain't your baby, D. She's the label's baby. Which technically makes her mine."

I grunted in disapproval as she brought her

feet down, closing her magazine as she looked at me with a wary gaze.

"You're in a mood. What happened? You drink the worm from the tequila again?"

"No," I huffed as I collapsed on the couch.

"Just... being home is always... a thing, you know?" I said.

Helena stood in front of me, hands poised on her hips.

"I do know. I also know that I've been waiting for the last hour on you to get your ass back here so we can get cleaned up good in a proper hotel."

"I don't need a hotel, I have everything I need right here—" I gestured to the bus, the disarray of clothes and merch sprawled about between guitars.

Howler huffed a sigh of her own as she helmed the steering wheel.

The four rum and cokes I'd had weren't doing me any favors. Once upon a time, I could drink anyone under the table, but not anymore. And especially not after my year long detox from alcohol while I'd been under Rozen's roof.

The man was very strict about his diet, and therefore *your* diet was just as important.

Can't be banging a bag of toxins without getting poisoned, right?

"This isn't negotiable, Drew. Civilization

beckons us," she said as she turned the bus on, and headed off toward the Paradise Hotel.

Growing up, the Paradise had always been this epitome of wealth and success, at least to most of the inhabitants here. To have your wedding there was like having it at the fucking Biltmore. It meant you were somebody *important.*

I'd always wanted to get married, and maybe when I was young, I could imagine myself walking down the aisle in the Paradise greenhouse in the courtyard, with some polo-wearing debonair Prince of Monaco-wannabe, but those dreams would never see the light of day. Because life had a different path for me, one that included rock shows, interviews, and bright, shiny lights.

And I was happy with what I'd built myself, what I'd built for my bandmates.

Wasn't I?

"Come on asshole, let's go," Howler said as she parked the bus.

"Do I have to?" I asked mournfully, staring up at the prestigiously lit mansion turned hotel from the privacy of my tour bus couch.

"The hotel is much more secure," Helena said, her voice steady.

I hadn't had a stalker encounter in years, but the levity of the truth hung in the air like sour apple jolly ranchers hang around after you've eaten them.

Sour, and still present.

"Fine," I lamented, hating that even in my hometown, I couldn't just... be.

"Jorge and Jager are already set up. They left right after the show. Everything is to your liking, and if you have any issues..."

"I know, I know, you'll take care of it," I grumbled as I got up.

Helena looked at me with a softness I didn't know she was capable of. "Right. I'll take care of it. You just do what you're good at," she said.

"What's that?" I asked as I opened the door, letting the crisp air in.

"Smile and be pretty, of course," she teased as she held open the door to the Paradise for me.

It wasn't anything I hadn't heard before in the twenty years I'd been performing. Smile and be pretty.

My mind wandered to my brief moment in the john with Taylor. *It's just part of the job,* I had said, and there was a truth to that.

So why did it make me feel so... empty?

Howler waltzed up to the front desk, whizzing past me.

I slowly followed her stride and by the time I

got to the front desk, she was already handing me keys.

"Thanks," I said as I took the plastic from her manicured fingers, the sheen of white plastic shimmering like a freshly waxed chest.

The crisp, bright white and grey with gold interior of the hotel wasn't quite as I remembered, though I'd only been in here once. On Prom night.

My mind wandered back to those memories. I'd gone with Giselle, my cover. I'd really wanted to ask Brayden Lowell to prom, but I didn't have the guts. Though somehow, I'd ended up leaving with one of the other football players that night, holing away in a room his parents no doubt paid for. It was the night everything changed for me.

Because when Brayden told me to get on my knees and suck him off, I didn't have to be told twice.

Something in me clicked that night, and I just knew. That was what I was meant for; that was what I wanted.

For a pretty, suave man with more class than me to boss me the fuck around and let me be who I was, who I really was in the dark spaces I didn't share with anyone else.

But in the daytime, the sins of prom didn't exist, and I soon learned that it was better to keep my sexual preferences under lock and key, until I'd found the right person.

Someone who would be more than happy to tell the world they loved me, and not give a shit what other people thought.

I thought Rozen was that guy. For a little while anyway, but I knew now, Rozen only wanted a project. He didn't want *me*. He just wanted to mold me into everything I wasn't, everything that he wanted in a perfect partner, and when he couldn't do that...

He fucking cheated on me.

I brushed past Howler as I headed for the elevator.

"Good night, Drew!" she called as I hit the elevator buttons, relishing in how quickly the doors opened so I could escape the awful memories plaguing me at the moment.

God, I hope they stocked the bar in the room. I need a fucking drink.

Maybe this trip, this tour, was a bad idea.

I didn't waste time as I stumbled out of the elevator, intent on finding my room as quickly as possible. The hallways were lit with an amber ambiance from the sconces on the beige and white wallpapered walls, casting an eerie glow on the long hall, like something out of Stephen King movie.

When I finally found my room, relief rushed over me.

The bar was fully stocked, not just with alcohol, but with a basket full of snacks. Though upon further inspection, it looked to be all *health* snacks, aka the ones I'd been filling up on for the last year that Rozen had recommended I eat, which only made me sad and disappointed. Maybe Howler didn't get the memo, or maybe the lines crossed somewhere. Still, my stomach rumbled as it had been hours since I had anything substantial before the show.

I fiendishly grabbed the box of whole grain crackers, pouring myself about two fingers worth of whiskey.

Dinner of champions, of rockstars.

I kicked my boots off, sequestering my snacks and drink as I got on the bed. I tossed the box beside me as I took a long drink before setting the glass down on the pristine, glossy surface of the nightstand. The linens were soft, almost too soft, but it felt good. Pillowy, comfortable. I hated to admit Helena was right, it was better than the tour bus.

But even as nice and comfortable as everything was, it didn't make me feel the way I felt when I was curled up on my couch on the tour bus, writing songs no one would ever hear.

Mostly because no one wanted to hear

power ballads anymore. Especially by someone like me.

Briefly, my mind wandered to thoughts of Giselle and Taylor. Giselle had always been comfortable. It wasn't a secret in school that her family was loaded, but unlike the other students I went to school with, she never acted like she came from money. In fact, she was the opposite. She never treated anyone like they were beneath her, and she was friends with practically everyone. And she never once made me feel inferior or bad about the fact I lived by the tracks, the part of Jasper Springs that was reserved for trailers and low-income housing.

That's why I always loved Giselle. She didn't see privilege the same way the other rich assholes in Jasper Springs High did.

Money never mattered to her, only character did.

I wondered if Taylor was the same way or not. Clearly his put together style suggested that he cared about appearances, and he was friends with Giselle, so I knew he must at least be an interesting, good guy.

Is this his scene?

Swanky hotels and mini bars full of champagne?

My cock stiffened in my pants as I thought about him and his judgmental, dark blue eyes.

The way he'd locked eyes with me as I sang, I knew I had him. I'd done my job and rocked his world, in terms of music anyway.

I'd hoped I could have gotten to know him a bit more over drinks and catching up with Giselle, but instead he only seemed to be intent on ignoring me, as if I wasn't interesting enough to give the time of day.

Normally, I wouldn't care. I know I'm not everyone's cup of tea. But damn straight I know I am someone's shot of whiskey, and I'm fucking interesting.

I'm Drew Axel. I've had seven albums go platinum, and I've played sold out shows across the fucking world.

But Taylor didn't seem to give a shit about any of that.

Which was... refreshing, actually.

My mind wandered to that weird tension that had formed between us, as if we were waltzing some forbidden, unknown dance, waiting for the other to strike.

I knew it was a weak move, but I couldn't help myself that I checked him out. I'd been oogling the man all night, and it wasn't just because it was my job.

He was perfect. Tall, dirty blond, handsome and clean-cut, like a shiny new toy.

Taylor Swift's lyrics about being handsome

and looking like a devil perked up in my psyche. I sighed, pulling my phone from my pocket as I queued up *Cruel Summer*.

The opening rifts reverberated in the open air as I took another sip of my drink, my cock twitching, needing attention.

Maybe that's what I needed. A good drink and a good nut.

I set my drink down, deciding perhaps that would cure all my ails.

A nice, hot knight in pretty polos to own me and take away the pain.

But the reality was that I was alone, surrounded by the comforts of a life I'd built, with no one to share my healthy Cheez-It knock offs with.

Shame fell over me as I let my cock spring out of my unzipped pants. I'd barely even thought about eye-fucking Taylor, or his perfect cock—which I'd noticed was visibly erect before he'd shoved it back in its cage. While I didn't like to assume any man was gay, I like to think as a non-straight man myself, my gaydar was pretty functional. It hadn't served me wrong the last twenty years.

"Fuck," I groaned as I slid my hand over my shaft, my thumb teasing the stud at my already swollen head.

The thought of his gaze as it held mine,

while I strummed my guitar, or the way he'd blushed when he checked out *my dick*, made my desire spread like wildfire. I increased my pace, stroking haphazardly as I chased my elusive orgasm.

And in the space of my psyche, no doubt thanks to the drinks and my weird headspace of being back home, my fantasy took new flight.

I imagined myself right back in this hotel room, on my knees, my shirt unbuttoned, waiting for my punishments, like the dirty little brat I was.

I thought of Taylor in a fine tailored suit, staring down at me with that same intense gaze I'd seen earlier, his hand stroking his cock as he readied himself for me.

For me. It was all for me.

"Oh fuck!" I said as I came without warning, my cock pulsing. I forced my hand over the head, if only because I didn't want cum stains on my brand new shirt.

I fought to catch my breath as I rode out the euphoria of my orgasm, feeling a mix of shame, guilt, and remorse. And as I softened, I breathed a sigh of relief, and swore to myself I'd put all thoughts of Taylor and tonight out of my mind.

Tomorrow would be a better day.

I was sure of it.

CHAPTER 7

TAYLOR

FINALLY, after a morning full of nothing but issues—my floral tape not sticking, the flowers all looking a tad bit wilty, since apparently the power went out last night—not to mention, my iPad register not working correctly because of said power outage, I was in desperate need of a break.

I reached for my large iced coffee, which I'd barely had time to drink between answering the phone, trying to get my flowers to perk up, and working on a funeral arrangement, when my cell phone rang.

It was Julie calling, again.

I half-contemplated not answering, because I wasn't truly in the mood to deal with anyone who wasn't a paying customer. I still felt off after my restless night, and my guilty masturbation session this morning, and wasn't necessarily having the best day. But I knew if I ignored Julie, she'd only keep calling until I eventually picked up, so I figured it was best to get things over with.

"Yes, Jules," I said as I sat down in my office, swiveling in my pale blue office chair like a child with ADHD, sipping on their go juice.

"Oh my God, Tay, you will *never* guess what just happened!" She squealed, her voice pitching to a sound I was sure wasn't even human.

I held the phone from my ear.

"You met Drew Axel?" I drawled, my voice full of disdain and sarcasm.

"No! I wish, but..." She caught her breath as I took another sip of my drink. "Giselle just called me," she said between breaths. "Aaron proposed!"

Instantly, I sat up straighter in my chair. "What?" I asked in awe.

Honestly, I wasn't sure the man was ever going to propose. Giselle and Aaron had met in college nearly eight years ago. It seemed even though Giselle had made it more than evident she wanted to get married, Aaron didn't seem all that interested in marriage. He'd noted on more than one occasion, he was happy with how things were. They'd been living together for the last six years, both had good jobs, and seemed content to just... be. It was rather refreshing, actually. And in the last year or two, Giselle seemed to think that was enough, and had given up pushing the idea.

So to say I was surprised... was an understatement.

"She said yes, right?" I asked, panic overtaking me.

"Of course she said yes!" Julie nipped. "Why wouldn't she say yes? Aaron is a dreamboat! He's like, perfect husband material, plus they've been together since like, the dawn of time."

I rolled my eyes. "Eight years is not the dawn of time, Jules."

"Details, details. Did you not hear what I said? Giselle is getting *married*. As in, planning a wedding..." Julie enunciated rather well her wording of wedding.

And I knew what she was getting at before she said it, mostly because my own heart fluttered with the idea.

"Oh, I heard you," I said as I spun around in my chair.

"Which is why I'm calling you. Obviously, as a good friend and bridesmaid—"

"Has she asked you already?" I said, sucking down my drink, if only to quell the panic building inside me.

"Well... no, but I know she's going to! Hell, Giselle and I have been friends since like, the third grade. I know her better than anyone," Julie touted.

"Still..."

"So, I'm doing her a favor while she calls all her relatives, gets the news out there... I'm scheduling some local appointments to help get the ball rolling with the planning. Because time is of the essence, as you know," Julie said matter of factly.

"Uh huh," I said as Julie continued.

"I know you are busy with the Anderson's funeral arrangements, but maybe you could squeeze a quick appointment in?"

"Of course, anything for a friend," I said, my smile widening.

"When were you thinking?" I asked.

"Today," Julie squeaked.

Shut the front door!

"Today? It's like eleven thirty, Jules. What time were you thinking on such short notice?"

Julie chuckled nervously. "Well, she said she was free this afternoon around two, so..."

I looked around my messy floral studio, which looked like a bomb went off.

Booking a wedding would be ideal, but Giselle wasn't just a wedding. She was my friend, and while I would work my ass off to give her what she wanted, a part of me had to acknowledge that maybe I wasn't what she deserved.

Giselle's family was more than well off, and I knew her wedding would be a black tie affair. The kind of wedding worthy of Instagram hashtags and social influence.

I was just a little flower shop in Jasper Springs, with barely enough equipment for a wedding of one hundred and fifty people, let alone one like what Giselle was probably to be a part of. I could have bet the farm their guest list would be over three hundred. At least.

I picked at the finish on my Ikea desk, which had started to peel after one year of installing it.

It was a long shot, right?

But maybe, just maybe it was the shot I needed to take.

Fake it till you make it, right?

"Yeah, yeah, two is fine," I said, forcing a smile as I watched a roll of tape roll off the counter, hitting the floor with a thud that echoed my anxiety.

Julie squealed once more.

"You are the best, Tay! Thank you so much! I promise you won't regret this!" she said, making kissy noises before hanging up and leaving me to marvel in my caffeine and anxiety alone, once more.

What have I gotten myself into?

CHAPTER 8

Drew

"If you need me to come pick you up later, just text me," Helena said, her bright eyes rimmed in thick eyeliner staring at me over her lowered window like she was nothing more than a Soccer Mom dropping her kid off at school.

I slapped the roof of her rental, a silver Saturn, doing my best impersonation of a troubled youngster.

"Yes, Mom, I promise."

"Fuck you," she snapped, but I didn't miss the grin hiding beneath her sourpuss expression. "Sound check is around four fifteen. I need you to be at Darby's no later than quarter to four," she retorted, flipping me off.

I nodded. "Understood. Thanks for the ride."

Helena appraised me with a judgmental look. "Don't mention it."

It wasn't like I *needed* to be chauffeured around like Miss Daisy, I was perfectly capable of renting and driving a car myself, but my manager was, if anything, a control freak, and insisted on being around pretty much all the time except when I was performing, and a part of me actually did like having her around so much. If only because it meant I wasn't quite as alone as I often felt. I watched as she sped off, feeling a sense of relief.

How boring is my life when my best friend is my freaking manager?

Staring through the coffee shop window on the side of the street felt foreign to me. I rarely went anywhere in LA without a camera shoved in my face, so the fact I was able to just stand on the sidewalk by myself without security, without *worrying* that I'd be mobbed by fiendish paparazzi was nice.

I caught sight of Giselle sitting at a table inside, smiling while she played on her phone, and a part of me didn't want to disturb her. She looked so peaceful and content, her ponytail spilling over her shoulder, her perfect smile.

She was bright like a moonbeam, lighting up the night.

I slid my phone out, taking a picture, adding a note with the lyric as I often did when I was inspired.

The problem was, I couldn't finish a song, not since...

Since the breakup.

But if I was being a hundred percent honest, I'd been stuck in the writer's block loop for longer than that.

I used to love writing songs, but the songs I wrote that I performed over and over with the band, they didn't feel like *me* anymore.

Rather they felt like a distant memory of a person I barely knew.

Sick Little Games, Ricochet Heart, and *Electric Sexxx* were great songs, but I was long past fucking around for the sheer fun of it. I wanted more.

But I wasn't able to define what that *more* really meant. Not at that moment anyway.

So, I decided to shove down my thoughts and put on a happy face, which wasn't so hard given the fact I was meeting up with an old friend—an old friend who had the unmistakable quality to light up a room no matter where she was.

"Morning, beautiful," I drawled as I pulled up a chair across from her, popping her bright little bubble.

"Good Morning," she said, her smile huge.

"I hope you had a good time last night," I said.

Giselle nodded. "The best. But this morning..." Her grin widened, her eyes sparkled.

Before I could even ask, she thrust her hand in my face, and I would have had to be blind to miss the gigantic rock on her finger that was most certainly not there last night.

Sweet baby Jesus.

I gingerly took her hand, inspecting the specimen of a diamond that could only have come from a man with supreme taste and high standards.

"Congratulations," I said, mustering all the excitement I knew was needed for a moment such as this, but I'd be lying if I said it was genuine.

Not that I wasn't happy for her, but...

Giselle pulled her hand back, giving me a look.

"I'm sorry but this trumps *everything else*," she said poignantly.

"As it should," I responded, my tone much grumpier than I intended.

"I know it's sudden, but I'm already heading

into planning mode," she said as she sipped her coffee.

"What have you been engaged for like, twenty minutes?" I teased.

Giselle smirked. "More like four hours." She giggled.

"You mean your future husband proposed to you at like, eight in the morning? Who does that?"

"Over breakfast before he left for work, yeah," she gushed.

I didn't want to begrudge her happiness like a Debbie Downer, but that didn't sound at all romantic to me. It sounded spontaneous, sure, but not romantic.

I'd always imagined if someone proposed to me—not that that would ever happen with my track record—it would be somewhere special.

Maybe in a castle or something in Scotland.

Or the Paradise at sunset.

"You guys been together long?" I asked, feeling slightly uncomfortable. Not because I wasn't happy for her, but because despite that, I still felt like *I* was the one who had gotten fucked over again.

Seeing folks legitimately enjoy one another, getting engaged, married even... it was like salt on a fresh wound when you were single and knew you'd probably never have those things.

Plenty of guys were interested in getting married, but the ones I'd met clearly weren't interested in marrying *me*.

"Yeah, eight years. We met in college, knew each other for a minute before we started dating about eight years ago." She beamed.

"Oh," was all I could muster, because I could feel the fear of missing out starting deep in the pit of my stomach again.

I needed to get my head out of the clouds and back on Earth. Focus on my music, the one thing that would never truly leave me alone.

"My friend, Julie, even made me an appointment with the florist. You should come with!" she said excitedly.

"I don't know about that. Don't you think you're jumping the gun at least a little bit?" I asked.

Giselle waved at me, dismissing my obvious disdain.

"Absolutely not. A woman can never be too prepared when it comes to wedding preparations. Unless of course, you have other plans..."

The way she said "other plans" hit me in the chest like a baseball bat.

I didn't have sound check until at least four, and the concert didn't start until nine.

Aside from our meetup, I hadn't really planned on doing much else other than mope around my fucking hotel room, doomscrolling, and trying to avoid anything and everything that had to do with Rozen, who was promoting his newest movie, some sci-fi alien thing I hadn't bothered to learn the name of when we'd been together.

With his new boy toy and co-star, nonetheless.

I shrugged.

Maybe getting out was what I really needed. To put myself outside my comfort zone and distract myself. Maybe it would even inspire me to write some more.

My heart melted a fraction. "I don't," I said.

And because I have the worst luck imaginable, that was the time Rozen came across the screen with my replacement project, Cedric Harlow, both men wearing fine suits, looking hot as hell on daytime television, yapping about said film.

"Fucking figures," I mumbled as I looked away.

Giselle glanced at the tv then at me, her eyes going wide. "Oh! I am so sorry, I didn't think... I mean, if you're anti-wedding, I wouldn't blame you if you didn't—"

"I'm not anti-wedding," I said with a sigh. "I just don't think it's in the cards for me, ya know? I haven't really had the best luck, haven't exactly met Mr. Right. Everyone I meet is Mr. Right

Now, and being famous doesn't really sweeten the dating pool like you'd think."

It was actually quite the opposite. Everyone I had ever really been interested in, or thought about long-term seemed to only see me as a flash in the pan. Something to mess around with in hopes I'd write a song about them and elevate them.

Kind of like a tattooed male version of Taylor Swift.

Giselle's gaze softened as she reached out for my hand. Her palm against the back of my hand was soft and warm, and damn if it didn't feel nice. It felt like old times, to be honest.

"Did you love him?" she asked genuinely.

"What?" I asked, shaking my head.

Seeing my ex, acting as if nothing had happened, as if I didn't even *exist* anymore...

It hurt.

Her question was expected though, honestly. Plenty of people asked that question, especially in the aftermath, personally at parties or even in interviews.

And I'd told everyone what they wanted to hear. I played my part. Mostly because Howler and the record execs had given me specific talking points I was not to deviate from. And I hadn't.

I'd played the scorned lover easily, because I was scorned.

Publicly humiliated on TMZ, no less, being thrown out of *our* home. The same home he still got to live in, with Cedric now in my place like the cookie cutter boyfriend he is. All sugar, no substance. Easily pliable for Rozen to mold into his dream boy.

"I don't know," I said honestly.

Giselle frowned.

"He... he was like this force that just pulled you in. Unrelenting, unstoppable. Made you feel like the center of the universe," I said as I squeezed her hand. "Until he decided on a new universe, that is."

"Cedric?" she asked, and I could tell even if she didn't want to admit it, she kept tabs on me. I wished I could say I was surprised.

"Yeah. Came home from a concert and found them in bed together," I said, worried I was divulging too much. But I trusted Giselle, even though I hadn't seen her in twenty years. I just knew my secrets would be safe with her. They always were.

And even though it'd been twenty years, she was still the same sweet, caring, warm woman I'd buried my secrets with long ago.

"I'm sorry, I didn't mean to be so insensitive," she said. "You don't have to talk about it if you don't want to."

"You're not being insensitive. Actually, I... I

think a change of scenery might be good for me ya know?" I responded. "Surround yourself with positive things, and maybe you will start to attract positive things, right?"

She smiled at that.

Fake it till you make it, right?

CHAPTER 9

DREW

AS WE WALKED UP to the blue awning of *Taylor Made Bouquets*, I couldn't help but feel like maybe this trip was what I needed.

Normally, when I did shows with the band, we didn't stay in place long. As soon as one show was done, we'd be packed up and ready to go by the next morning. Between tours however, I relished being home.

Eating secret Doritos and catching up on Netflix when Rozen wasn't around.

But until he had very publicly thrown me out, I hadn't really given a thought to what home was.

For me, home was the road.

Or technically, now, it was my LA condo, which I only really visited a few times a year. I'd been traveling since I was fresh out of high school.

Being back *home* though, in Jasper Springs, where I grew up, made me realize that maybe that was what was missing in my life.

A real home. The kind of place people actually wrote songs about.

Just a small town boy, living in a lonely world.

Maybe after this trip I'd consider looking for an actual house. The kind with a wrap around porch made for lazy days where I could just sit on the deck and play my guitar while the damn sun went down.

Hell, maybe after all of this was said and done, maybe I'd even look for something in Jasper Springs, where people knew me, but where I was still left alone without a camera in my face twenty-four seven.

I opened the door for Giselle, my senses immediately hit with the onslaught of flowers.

The shop itself was nice, modern. It reminded me of some of the swanky boutiques in LA; all white and grey with sprinkles of pastels and jewel tones. I half-wondered if the ivy wall behind the counter that housed a bright neon sign that read "Good Vibes" in fancy script with a heart was actually real or not.

But my blood instantly ran cold the moment the owner of the shop came out of his office, sucking loudly on his straw from his iced coffee, wearing a pale blue button up that was rolled up to his elbows. His sandy hair hung in his pretty blue eyes that widened when they saw me.

Taylor *Made Bouquets.*

What were the fucking odds?

I guess pretty good when you lived in a town as small as Jasper Springs.

"I... didn't think you'd be bringing *him* with you," Taylor said as he blinked, instead focusing on Giselle who hugged him.

Giselle laughed. "When in Rome, right, Drew?" she said, flashing me a wink.

All I could do was nod because I was speechless. That we ended up in Taylor's shop, but also because...

Damn, he looks good all dressed up.

His pants hugged his ass nicely—I couldn't help but notice when he hugged Giselle—and he looked like he'd stepped out of a Calvin Klein ad back in the day. Timeless, attractive.

And my cock more than agreed, despite his attitude.

In fact, if I was being honest, the attitude certainly helped.

Bad idea, Drew.

Bad, bad idea.

You just got out of a long public relationship.

You're supposed to be focusing on yourself!

"I suppose," he murmured, his gaze flashing to me before focusing back on Giselle again. "Congratulations," Taylor said as he held her hand in front of him, marveling at the bling on her finger.

"Thank you, and thank you for seeing me on such short notice," she said, tucking some hair behind her ear.

I slid my hands in my black jean pockets, taking that moment to waltz around the room so I could focus on anything other than the grade A specimen in tight khakis and a button down.

Fuuuuuck.

My cock twitched as I added that sight to my future spank bank.

Just the thought of popping those pretty pearly buttons on his shirt, at getting an eyeful of the bulge in those pants, was enough to make me feel more than engorged. I shifted my erection, trying to be as nonchalant as possible as the two of them chatted.

"Are you coming?" Taylor asked, the words going straight to my groin.

Fuck me sideways.

I cleared my throat as I turned my body halfway, so as not to draw attention to the massive erection in my pants that I'd sprung because of Tempting Taylor over there.

"Uh, yeah, of course," I said, probably a little too quickly.

Taylor narrowed his gaze, pursing his lips as if he knew.

Suspiciously aware that I didn't want to cum, I *needed to.*

"Okay, well, let's get on with it then," he said abruptly as he wrapped his arm around Giselle and corralled her into his office, leaving me and my damn hard on alone in the showroom feeling guilty as all hell.

The saccharine melody of my girl Taylor carried through the shop speakers like a whisper, lamenting my own thoughts about being enchanted to meet him.

She sang on about sparkling nights and not letting it go, and I had to take it as a sign.

So I sucked in a deep breath, tried to think unsexy thoughts, and followed the man of my literal dreams and my friend into the unknown.

CHAPTER 10

TAYLOR

OF ALL THE people in the world, the last person I expected Giselle to bring into my shop was the rockstar.

I mean, we were just out last night, shouldn't he be off on his way to the next show or something?

After the morning I'd had, I was already all over the place, and a distraction—even a *hot* distraction—was bound to throw me off.

And I didn't want to fuck up the chance to land a job doing exactly what I opened my shop for.

Weddings.

I'd always been in love with the idea of

being in love, I guess. Not to mention there was just something about the idea of walking down an aisle adorned with rose petals toward the man of your dreams, all dressed up in a fine suit... with the look on his face when he saw you...

So I'm a hopeless romantic. Sue me.

I watched as they both curled into their respective chairs. Giselle looked poised as always, like the quintessential bride-to-be; glowing, not a hair out of place, spine straight.

Drew, on the other hand...

He barely fit in my modern gold and velvet chair. He crossed his legs, resting his ankle on his knee as his larger frame spread out in the small space. The motion drew attention to his black jeans, and I had to look at the screen, if only to prevent myself from blushing as I remembered our awkward moment in the men's room the prior night.

Bad idea, Taylor.

Don't go down that road...

"Okay, so I'm thinking orchids and monstera, perhaps some exotic lilies..." I watched as Giselle's eyes widened in excitement.

"What about roses? Aren't roses your favorite flower?" Drew asked as he shifted his weight in the chair.

Giselle smiled, nodding. "I can't believe you remember that, but yeah..."

Drew shrugged. "How could I forget? You wore them to prom."

Giselle fell back in her chair with a giggle. "I did, didn't I?"

It was my turn to raise an eyebrow. Sitting next to one another they couldn't have been more different. Giselle and her perfect manicure, shiny, silky ponytail and her all around aesthetic against Drew in his black jeans, ripped tank, his arms lined with all those tattoos.

I swallowed harshly as my gaze traveled up his arms, over the intricate linework and the muscle. Even underneath all the ink, I could see the swell of his biceps, see the pronounced vein running through them. My cock jumped at the sight of his exposed hips, that delicious hip bone cutting my vision to where it certainly shouldn't be.

Focus, Taylor!

"Taylor?" Giselle pulled my wandering thoughts from the ether, and I realized at that moment I'd been staring.

At Drew and his large... presence.

I cleared my throat, shaking my head as I brought up some designs in the computer.

"Yes, well, I'm sure we can add some roses to the arrangement, if it is something the *bride* requests," I tutted as I shot Drew a scathing look. He only had the audacity to look offended, as if I had done something wrong. As if he wasn't offsetting the entire vibe of my workplace.

God he smells so good.

What is he wearing?

Just as I turned to address Giselle, I noticed Drew was staring.

At me.

Oh shit!

Do I have something on my face?

Did I spill my coffee on my shirt again?

"Take a picture Drew, it'll last longer," Giselle said coyly as she shoved him.

"What?" he responded, completely dumb-founded.

Perhaps I was wrong. Maybe he was just bored. After all, I couldn't fathom the drudgery of this town compared to everything he'd probably seen.

Hell, who was I kidding, what he probably saw on a daily basis.

"The flower arrangement..." she said with a twist of her lips as she pointed to the screen where I'd brought up a selection of arrangements.

"Yeah, uh, well, it's not *my* wedding, so..." he scoffed as he sat up straighter.

"I can email you the arrangements and you can look them over if you'd like. Take your time, get back to me if you have any questions," I said as I broke my impolite staring.

The man in black sitting in front of me almost sounded... sad.

Jealous, even.

But what on earth would Drew Axel be jealous of?

"Oh, that would be super!" Giselle said with a squeal as she rose from her seat. Drew grunted his opinion, and I nodded.

"I'll walk you out," I said as I rose from my chair, walking around my desk and skirting past the lumbering rockstar in my presence. But due to his size, not to mention the size of my office, there wasn't much space.

In fact, as I rounded my desk, my damn shoe caught the corner and upended me smack in the middle of Drew's lap.

Face first.

Directly against his...

Hardness.

Fucking hell!

I scrambled to my feet as heat rushed up my neck and into my cheeks.

"I'm so sorry," I said as I brushed myself off, even though I wasn't covered in anything but shame, and no amount of detergent would fix that.

Drew set his hands on my arms, steadying me as he rose, and I noticed how warm his palm felt against my exposed skin.

Giselle only laughed as she scooted past us.

"Don't mention it," Drew said with a smirk.

I realized he hadn't let go of me, and I didn't hate it. In fact, I kind of liked how his palm felt against my skin. Warm. Friendly even.

I regrettably stepped away from his touch and slid past him to the door, following Giselle out.

When we'd gotten back in the shop workspace, Giselle regaled me with a hug and air kisses as she touted about her next shindig. I'd expected Drew to leave *with* her, but instead he just stood there, looking at all my display flowers, my chaotic space with shreds of tissue paper, floral blocks, and ribbons.

"Is there something else I can help *you* with, Mr. Axel?" I said poignantly as I crossed my arms. I really did need to get back to work, to email those files of arrangements off to Giselle like we'd discussed. I could have ignored Drew, but as I said—I was all over the place.

I noticed Drew was tapping his fingers on his thigh, quite rhythmically, mumbling something almost incoherent.

Ah, so he's certifiable too.

All the best musicians are, right?

"What?" He turned around, the light shining through the window on him like some Halo as the notes of *Teardrops On My Guitar* chimed over the speakers.

I forced a polite smile as I tried to focus on *anything* but him.

What the hell was he still doing here?

I took two steps forward, noting he didn't move. His bright green gaze settled on me as he continued to hum, and I realized he was singing.

He was *singing*.

I thought the performance of *Blank Space* was a one off, but he knew the words to one of the earliest songs of Taylor's career.

I slid my hands in my pockets as I stopped in front of him, raising an eyebrow.

"Didn't peg you for a Swiftie," I said, probably harsher than I meant to.

Drew shook off his weird aloofness, the motion making some dark hair fall in his dangerously dreamy eyes.

My gaze caught on the tattoos on his neck, noticing the black and white snake with red roses and a very flourished word I couldn't make out, crawling up his neck.

He licked his lips, running his fingers—also covered in black tattoos—over where my gaze hovered, and I noticed the *13* on his middle finger.

It's just a number.

It could mean anything.

The way his fingers moved over the expanse of his exposed skin caused my cock to twitch, and I murmured a slight curse under my breath.

Why was just that one touch so fucking hot?

God, I am a mess today!

"Didn't peg you for a florist," he said, flashing me a smirk.

"I've got to get back to work," I huffed, feeling quite on the spot, my own voice betraying me. "So, if you're not going to buy anything..."

"I don't think I can legally purchase what I want," he said with another aloof smile, one that reached his eyes.

I could feel the beginnings of sweat forming on my brow, and I knew I needed to end this— whatever *this* was before I lost all my marbles and dropped to my god damn knees for this man.

Which was *insane* because I barely knew him.

Maybe it's just the rockstar vibe.

Drew nodded behind me, at a small vase of cut pink and yellow roses.

"I'll take those, then," he said with a grin.

I huffed out a sigh, as this man was obviously intent on becoming the bane of my existence.

He'll be gone soon enough, and then you can forget him, his gothic gym-tan-laundry getup, and…

I grabbed the vase, practically sprinting to the counter to check him out.

"Fine," I bit as I set out to pack them up.

"Are you always this prickly?" Drew said as he leaned across the counter, the motion drawing attention to his exquisite arms.

I snapped the water vial on the stems, trying my damndest to focus, but it was hard.

And so was my unruly dick.

Now is not the time!

"Only around cocky rockstars who think they're God's gift to men," I said, realizing a split second later that I'd slipped up.

"And women," I hurriedly added.

I knew from Julie and her obsession with the man and his band that Drew was tied to both men and women in the media, but I'd never paid much attention to tabloid gossip.

Drew laughed, and the sound was smooth. Like a double malt whiskey on ice.

"Noted," he said as I finished wrapping the flowers in their plastic, snapping the gumband in place as I rang him up.

"Thirty-five dollars," I said as I held my hand out.

Drew smiled and the sight was downright sinful as he removed his wallet from his back pocket, taking out a silver AmEx card.

No, not silver.

Platinum.

I ran the card with shaking hands, because at that point I wasn't sure if I was going to be able to hold my cool much longer. It was nearing three thirty and I needed to get the shop cleaned up and closed by four so I could work and get a head start on the Anderson arrangements in peace, and I was also erring perilously close to needing to rub one out in my damn office like a frustrated teenager.

What the hell is wrong with me?

I hurried through the motions, ripping off his receipt from the printer, and searching amidst my messy counter for a pen.

When I finally found the floral-taped, felt-rose pen, I passed it to him, and our fingers brushing for a moment, like in the movies.

Like in my dreams.

Like in a romance novel or something...

I pulled my hand back with haste as he jotted down his autograph, sliding the receipt back, his dark sapphire eyes staring at me like he was challenging me to a bar fight or something. I didn't miss how the heat in his challenging gaze made my cock throb, and it was all I could do to lean on the counter, my hardness pressing against the acrylic backing to try and stifle my god damned erection.

"Have a nice day," I said as I all but shoved the flowers across the counter to him before excusing myself to my office where I could lock the door.

Where I could escape the damn rockstar who was so far out of my league.

When the door chime rang, I let out a deep breath, and adjusted my cock before heading out to lock up the shop. Just as I flipped the lock, my phone rang. I turned around the corner, making a beeline for my office.

"Jules, now is seriously not the time," I nipped as I slumped down into my chair, trying to catch my breath.

"Oh, I'm sorry. Are you still with G? Is she there?"

I sighed as I unbuttoned my pants, if only because the strain against my unruly cock was starting to mar on the side of painful.

Think unsexy thoughts.

Think unsexy thoughts...

I tried to focus on my conversation, hoping that would be enough of a distraction.

"No, she just left a little bit ago, but it's been a chaotic day," I grumbled. "You'll never guess who she brought with her though." I sighed, running my hand over my face.

"I swear to all that is holy, Taylor, if you say she brought—"

"She did. She brought the rockstar."

Julie squealed again at a frequency I was sure would make a dog or cat deaf, as she clamored on with excitement. I pulled the phone away from my ear.

"Oh my God, Tay! I need all the details! Please tell me you got me an autograph..."

"I don't know, does his John Hancock on a receipt for flowers count?" I chirped. My cock was still throbbing, twitching at the memory of him leaning across the counter, those delicious muscles...

Fucking hell.

I swallowed harshly as I brought my hand to my cock, adjusting myself once more, but it only served to be a nuisance as my cock sprang forth from the slit in my boxers like a damn Jack-In-The-Box.

"You are seriously the worst wingman, ever!" She huffed furiously. "At least tell me what he was wearing," she said.

My cock twitched again as my memory filled in the blanks.

This was a bad idea.

I squeezed my cock, taking a deep breath as

I tried to combat my sudden horniness and focused instead on strategically answering Julie, who was waiting with bated breath.

"He was wearing black jeans, frayed at the knees, and studded boots. I couldn't tell the brand. They didn't *look* designer, but who the hell knows. I don't follow gothic fashion," I huffed as I closed my eyes, trying to catch my own breath.

"And he was wearing one of those awful muscle shirts like he was a rejected cast member from the Jersey Shore, which did nothing to hide his obviously tailored physique," I added with disdain.

Or the thick vein running up those biceps.

Christ, this was torture!

"But he was a total weirdo," I quickly added, needing to get my train of thought anywhere but on the thought of Drew Axel's exposed skin, his sexy muscles, or the those fucking tight pants and tattoos.

Or the way he ran his hand over his tattooed neck.

"How so?" Julie touted with surprise, as if this man she didn't even know could do no wrong.

"Well, for starters, he was lumbering around like a Deatheater in my salon, and then when we actually sat to discuss Giselle's concepts, he kept staring at me. And then I caught him humming Taylor Swift while he gaped at the salon after she'd left and——"

"Maybe he thinks you're cute, Tay." The pure joy in her voice was unmistakable.

My cock agreed with her notion, but I was not about to let that convince me of anything.

After all, I was... me.

I was the furthest thing from a spicy hookup.

I sighed as my thumb lazily stroked the head of my cock, feeling the wetness that had already started to bloom, cursing myself silently.

I huffed indignantly, if only to try and hurry the conversation along, but I didn't want to be rude.

"You read too many romance novels, Jules. I am not the least bit appealing to a man who has literally been with *the hottest man alive.*"

Julie sighed. "Sexiest Man Alive, actually. But in all honesty, Tay, you don't give yourself enough credit, you know that."

"I know," I said with heavy breath. "But I need to go, I have to——"

"Work, I know, I know," she said, before chiming in brightly with, "Oh! I should totally call Giselle and see if she and her new bestie are available! We should all hang out and get drinks! Celebrate!"

"That is a terrible idea," I growled.

Julie only had the audacity to laugh.

"Well, you owe me, Tay. That's *twice* I've asked you to hook a girl up, and you didn't deliver," she tutted.

I groaned, in part because she was right but also because the *need* to take care of myself was driving me up a fucking wall.

"Fine," I huffed, and then I hung up without warning.

I banged my forehead against my desktop, panicking because of what I knew I'd just agreed to. And as if fate had a better sense of humor than I did, I noticed that by doing so, the tab on my Internet browser had shifted to reveal an article I'd pulled up about the concert last night.

With an image of Drew on stage at M's Place, holding his guitar in between his legs, his bright eyes staring at me like he truly was challenging me.

Involuntarily, my hips thrust against my sweaty palm, needing the friction, needing the release.

I was so fucking hard, and he was so fucking *hot*.

So, I did the only thing I could think to do, despite knowing it was wrong on so many levels, and I'd sworn I wouldn't do it again. I leaned back in my chair, resting my head on the back as I stared up at the ceiling and closed my eyes.

I imagined those delicious muscles, the weight of his toned body on top of me, those tattooed fingers gripping my thighs as my cock filled his melodic little mouth. I imagined my fingers tangled in his sweaty, long locks as I shoved my dick to the back of his throat until I...

I came with a strangled grunt, once again hovering my hand over my head to collect my guilty release, my toes curling in my brown leather Sperry's as my orgasm ransacked me like a drunken concert goer in a damn moshpit.

"Fuck," I hissed, praying that by the sheer grace of God, Drew Axel would be out of Jasper Springs soon, so that I could get back to living my normal, boring, mundane life.

CHAPTER 11

Taylor

I'd just finished wiping the counter around seven pm when I heard a rapping on my door. I'd fully intended on leaving the shop earlier, but halfway through cleaning I realized I hadn't done inventory yet, and thus, the work of a small-town entrepreneur never ceased.

But a part of me was glad for the distraction, to work off the boundless energy spurt I seemed to have fallen into ever since Drew Axel showed up. Not that I was complaining, I didn't mind a productive boost once in awhile, but this was different.

Because I knew if I let myself walk down

Drew Axel lane, it wouldn't end well for me or my cock.

One look out the store windows and I immediately regretted *having* wall to wall windows in the front of my store, as it meant Julie was peering in with a look on her face that told me ignoring her would incite the apocalypse.

I sighed, throwing away the paper towel in my trash on the way to the door. I opened it to see Julie in all five foot four of her glory, her blonde hair perfectly highlighted and curled as if she'd recently been to the salon.

Dressed in a black form-fitting dress with a choker attached, her eyes rimmed in black smoky liner, she looked like she was either on her way to a showing of The Craft or she had come here to sacrifice me for not getting her the autograph she asked for.

"The Satanic Cult is that way," I said dryly as I pointed to the left.

Julie rolled her eyes as she waltzed into my shop as if she owned the place.

I closed the door quietly and she apprehended me with a gaze that was practically Steve Harvey level judgmental.

"Don't tell me *that* is what you're wearing tonight?" She clicked her tongue against her teeth, her disdain more than evident.

I crossed my arms.

"I was not aware we were going anywhere," I said coldly.

Julie raised her eyebrow. "I told you I was going to call Giselle…"

My blood ran cold as I remembered what I'd stupidly agreed to in haste, because my feeble brain couldn't focus on anything but my need to sate my cock with a mind of its own.

"Yeah, but I assumed it was a no-go because you never called me back," I said as I headed back behind the counter to turn off the neon light.

"And give you enough of a chance to come up with fabricated bullshit about why staying at home is so much better? I don't think so," she said as she followed me.

I groaned in response. "Jules…"

"Nope, you're not getting out of this one, champ. You owe me," she said, pointing one long, coffin-shaped black nail at me.

Where the hell did she pull this look from? Eighth grade?

"And just where, pray tell, do I have to pay for my sins? And to what cost?" I narrowed my eyes on her.

She shrugged. "Drew Axel is playing tonight over at Darby's. Giselle suggested we all go, and hang out after."

I didn't miss the sparkle in her eyes at her words.

"Ah, so when I didn't bow to your request you pulled her strings, instead."

"What are well-connected, newly-engaged, and deliriously happy friends for?" she said, flashing me with a sly grin. "Besides, *I* did get her an appointment with the hottest florist in town. At the last minute."

It was my turn to cast her a look of doubt.

"I'm sure she would have come to the conclusion herself eventually," I said, but even I knew it probably wasn't true.

There were a hundred florists in the city, outside the realm of Jasper Springs that would be far better suited to the pedigree of Giselle and her no doubt, black tie, top of the line wedding.

Which reminded me just how badly I *needed* her business. While I didn't want my friend to feel like she *had* to choose me only because of our friendship, I wanted her to *want* me. I wanted her to see what I could do to make her dreams and her visions come true, and I wanted her to tell her friends.

But most of all, I just wanted her to look back on the beauty of her day and feel *happy*. I wanted to contribute to that happiness, because damn it I was a sucker for weddings and happy endings.

Like a lovesick sadist.

"There's no way out of this, is there?" I asked, pressing my lips together to stifle my burgeoning anxiety.

"Nope," she said, standing her ground.

I sighed as I grabbed my keys from the office. "Fine, but I need to stop home first, and shower." I was remiss to tell her the reason was because I'd busted a nut to her favorite rockstar in my office like a horny teenager.

I'd take that to my grave.

"Fine. But if you are one minute late past nine o' clock..."

"You will feed me through the woodchipper. I know," I said as she rolled her eyes.

"Please, if I was going to murder you, I would choose something a lot less messy," she said with a grin, and I couldn't help but laugh.

I politely set my hand at her back, leading her out of the shop gently, and she relaxed against me, turning her face to stare up at me with pleading raccoon eyes.

"It's okay to have a little fun, you know," she whispered, even though there was no one within earshot who could hear us. The Christmas lights spread out through the trees on the sidewalk twinkled, casting an amber light against the setting sun.

I looked at her, feeling strangely seen. And perhaps it was because I'd had an off day, but I couldn't help but dispel my thoughts to the little witch.

"I know, but..."

"But what?"

We stopped as I approached her car.

"The last time I had fun, Jules..." I could feel my stomach twisting in knots as his name made its way on my tongue. I couldn't stop it.

"You know what happened... Zack happened. He was... in a band," I said breathlessly.

Julie's eyes widened, her mouth forming into a tight little o. "How long..."

I'd given the TLDR version to both her and Giselle, but I'd never told them about *why* Zack left me high and dry. To chase his musician dreams.

"Two years. High school. He left to pursue more *fun* things. And perhaps, more fun *people*."

Julie looked at me with sadness, and I hated it. Immediately, I regretted my words, running a hand through my hair.

"I think you're a lot of fun, when you're not overthinking," she said quietly. The crickets chirped, and the orange and gold clouds drew my attention.

"You have the prettiest voice," she said with a smile. "When you sing."

I rolled my eyes. "Everyone can karaoke, Jules. That's hardly a skill."

"Everyone can karaoke, Tay, but you can *sing.*" she said, flashing me a smirk.

"And you've got an amazing eye for art, you are one of the best shade throwers I know—"

"I do not throw shade," I said, letting out a laugh as I leaned against her car.

Julie fidgeted with her keys as she smiled back.

"You are the shadiest motherfucker I know," she said with a chuckle.

I sighed, feeling marginally better.

"All I'm saying is..." She sighed, before continuing. "It's okay to have fun, you know. I promise if you do I won't tell anyone," she said softly.

"I know," I said, feeling strangely emotional.

"Go home, get showered, get dressed, and be at Darby's no later than nine," she said, her tone changing to something much brighter than what she was wearing.

"Yes, sweetheart," I said, nodding in response.

Perhaps she was right.

Perhaps I did need to let loose, to have a little fun.

I watched her drive off before heading to my car, turning on the radio immediately. The beginning lyrics of *Style* graced my speakers.

And all at once the memories came flooding back.

Zack in his ripped jeans, practically bathed in sweat and beer from the night before. The night he'd stayed out all night.

Watching him throw his guitar into the back of his pickup truck.

His words that cut me to the core.

Taylor Swift was blaring in my car as he looked at me, and I didn't even think to turn it off. The words about just asking someone to leave hitting me in my chest.

I'd stupidly thought he loved me.

The 'it's not you, Taylor, it's me,' speech. About how we were too different.

About how he couldn't breathe with me.

About how we just didn't work anymore, and he didn't want to be tied down to one dick forever.

About how he wanted more. Big lights, big cities, and crowds cheering his name.

He didn't want to hear me calling his name.

Not anymore.

I thought being together for a while meant we were a sure thing.

But I wasn't enough, and I'd never be enough.

Because I wasn't *fun*. I didn't like to get wasted at parties. I preferred curling up on the couch and watching romantic movies to staying up all night and being too blitzed to remember any of it.

I wanted a simple, romantic life of drinking coffee and doing the fucking crosswords together. I wanted to go wine tasting in Napa and spend my summers on the lake soaking up the sun with a man who made me feel like I was more than enough.

Like I was *his*.

I sighed, checking my clock.

Seven thirty.

Perhaps she was right.

Perhaps I did need to let loose, to have a little fun.

What was the worst that could happen?

CHAPTER 12

Drew

"WHAT DO YOU WANT?" Howler said as she glared at me over her bouquet of roses.

"Can't I buy you flowers *just because*?" I said as I grabbed my amp, heading into Darby's.

"You can, but you don't," she said as she set them on the passenger seat of her rental.

"Well, let that be a memo to me to shower you with flowers more often," I said as I kicked open the door to the restaurant.

"If you're going to buy my love, Axel, you should know by now I prefer booze and things that go buzz buzz."

I shot her a look, but I didn't miss the grin on her face.

"Buy your own sex toys, Howler. Your pussy is not my problem," I teased.

"That's not what I meant, and you know it. Fucking ass," she growled as she shouldered past me with the wheeled speakers.

After all, I'd bought her her last "buzz buzz." A custom green Ducati replica of the Green Ranger's Power Ranger bike when *Axe 2 Grind's* last album, *Sick Little Games* went Platinum.

I don't even have a custom Power Ranger bike!

Darby's wasn't necessarily a classy establishment, but it was definitely a leg up from M's Place.

True to form, my manager had everything delivered except me, my guitar, amp, and speakers. Helena might have been up my ass ninety-nine point nine percent of the time, but she was thorough, and the number one reason why my life ran on schedule.

The stage set up wasn't half bad either, and I didn't mind the open space.

M's was quite packed, but at least in this place I had room to move in the crowd.

I browsed my phone, waiting for Helena and the sound guys to finish setting up and fine-tuning their equipment so I could test my mic and guitar.

I propped myself on a stool, scrolling absentmindedly over Giselle's Facebook profile, which I'd added under my secret profile, AJ Andrews. I'd actually been born with the name Axel, because my parents were metal-heads, but very few people called me by my given name.

Axel James Andrews.

I'd garnered the nickname of 'Drews' my senior year because a substitute teacher accidentally read my last name as my first.

And the entire student body latched onto it, effectively erasing any existence of AJ Andrews.

When I'd signed with the record label pretty much out of high school, I'd undergone a "branding" initiative, basically a corporate record label makeover that turned me from AJ Andrews into front man Drew Axel.

Guess there was only room for one AJ in the biz, and that guy's been crooning hits since before I was born.

Howler had advised against any personal social media that wasn't tied to the brand, but all I really did on my profile was scroll for memes and periodically look up my classmates when I was drunk and depressed, so I wasn't sure what the big deal was.

I'd just come across a photograph of Giselle and a group of folks at what looked like Sunday Brunch, at a long table full of mimosas and croquettes and suddenly a pair of familiar blue eyes stared back at me. Taylor sat smirking in the corner of the photo like he knew I was checking him out.

Or rather his picture anyway, since clearly I'd proven to be a step above babbling earlier in his shop.

Real smooth, Drew.

I nonchalantly glanced up at Howler, who was berating one of the sound guys about wiring.

What crawled in her cornflakes this morning?

She'd been in a mood ever since we arrived.

Though I took the momentary break to indulge myself as I hovered my finger over the names tagged in the photo. Julie Bartnett, Riley Evans, Giselle's brother Grayson, Aaron Evans, and...

Taylor Meade.

I'd clicked on his profile faster than I could blink, scrolling through his feed. There were plenty of photos of his floral arrangements—all striking, and beautiful, by the way—and Instagram posts from the shop, but not many of him.

Except the few photographs Julie and Giselle tagged him in. Brunch photos.

I scrolled past his feed until I hit what looked like an older image. Taylor was dressed in nothing but a pair of blue jeans and a white shirt, standing barefoot in front of a town home that looked like something out of a literal movie set. His sandy hair fell in his blue eyes and the smile on his face was the kind of smile you got right before you realized the world was fucked.

I recognized the smile, because I'd had it once too.

When I moved to LA, into my shitty little apartment while I jumped through the label's hoops.

The more I think about it now, the less I know, the caption said, with a lifetime event showing *Moved To Jasper Springs.*

I checked the date, noting it was posted seven years ago, which would make Taylor... twenty-five?

"Earth to Drew!" Howler barked as I was literally whacked in the head by a Koosh ball. The squeak it made as it hit my head only added to the insanity of the moment.

"What the fuck, Hel—"

"If you would have been paying attention instead of swiping right on your next rebound, you would have heard me say, *testing!*" she chastised as she crossed her arms.

I shut my phone off, sliding it back in my pants pocket as I pushed all thoughts of Taylor and foolish innocence behind me.

It was clear that Taylor was a private person, and kept a low profile, and I knew that of all things meant I should stay away.

Let him live his perfect life in peace.

All I ever do is bring chaos wherever I go...

"Right." I slung my guitar strap over my shoulders, taking my stance in front of the microphone like I'd done so many times, and sucked in a deep breath.

Helena walked back to the back of the room, turning to give me a thumbs up.

I picked up my guitar. I didn't know why the first song that popped into my head was the song I'd heard in Taylor's shop but I went with it.

I sang about it being enchanting to meet, strumming the strings. The lyrics about wondering if they knew echoed in the space as I tickled the strings, closing my eyes and feeling the words as I always did when I sang a song by my favorite girl.

I covered the chorus once more, my voice echoing through the room, the guitar chords hitting deep in my belly. I opened my eyes to see Helena with her thumbs up, nodding vehemently.

"Sounds great, Drew! You should totally cover that one tonight!" she belted out through her microphone.

I continued to strum the melody, even though it was much more somber than what I usually liked to play.

"Okay, try something a little louder..." she ordered.

I strummed out some beginning chords of a darker progression, one of *Axe 2 Grind's* more recent hits—*Sick Little Games.*

"Tonight I'll be the monster and you can be my prey. Honey, I'll be the match, and you can be my flame..." I sang the words easily, my fingers dancing along the frets as I picked up the speed.

"Sounding good, baby! Now give me some screams!"

I rolled my eyes. She knew I didn't have any of my scream-o songs on the set list, but that didn't stop her from busting my balls once in a while.

I shook my head, playing right along, instead opting for one of her favorite songs, an MCR classic, *I'm Not Okay*.

"I'm not okaaaaaay," I screamed. I went on and screamed the next line too. And with a final strum of my guitar, I shot her a raised eyebrow.

Howler flipped me off, while touting into her microphone. "Drama Queen."

My phone vibrated in my pocket, pulling my attention as I held up my hand, making the cut motion to tell her to take five.

Giselle: Aren't you playing in Deer Park tonight?

Should I be concerned you've learned my tour locations? You're not going to turn into a stalker are you? I tapped back.

Giselle: Haha, you would be so lucky. No, I can promise you no stalking. My friend slash bridesmaid is a huge fan, and I thought maybe we could come see you play. You put on a hell of a show last night!

I eased up a little, though I shouldn't have been surprised that Giselle would want to bring her friend to meet me now that we'd hung out again. It wouldn't be the first friend of a friend...

Giselle: Taylor's coming too.

My eyebrows instantly rose as I thought about the little mouthy, khaki-wearing devil.

I'm performing at Darby's, nine o'clock. I tapped back instantly, punching the send button.

Giselle: Sweet! Maybe if you're not too busy being the hottest man alive, we can all get a drink. I think Taylor still owes you. She'd added flirty kiss emoji.

Oh Giselle, you haven't changed a fucking bit.

"Sometime today, Axel!" Helena called over her microphone.

Sure. I'll have my manager get you guys some backstage passes. It would be the last text I sent, because Helena pulled the phone right from my hands mid-text.

"Hey!" I nipped.

She raised an eyebrow at me, casting me her best expression of a dejected soccer mom.

"What or who is texting you?" she said as she started scrolling through my texts.

I sighed. Better to just tell her and get it over with, besides I did have a favor to ask.

"She's a friend, from high school," I said calmly.

Helena shot judgmental glares at me as she twisted her lips.

"So what, you're back to pussy now after one dick turned out to be a—"

"No, it's not like that. I promise," I said hurriedly, feeling quite queasy at the idea of Giselle in that way.

Gross.

"She's engaged," I rushed.

Helena cursed. "Jesus Christ, Axel. I get rebound but seriously, don't make me have to print out an NDA," she whined. "I *hate* printing out NDAs."

"They were at the concert last night, her and her friend, Taylor. He's a florist, and—" I sighed, knowing it was just best to be direct with Howler.

"I, uh... they're coming to the show tonight with another friend, and I thought maybe we could do like a backstage pass sort of thing for them."

Howler huffed as she handed me back my phone.

"So that's what this is about, huh? High School Musical wants the Drew Axel experience?"

"It could be worse," I nipped.

"How so?" Helena said as she pulled out her phone, no doubt sending off a text to whoever she needed to contact to get those passes to me as soon as possible.

"I could be out making a scene... getting drunk, flashing my junk all over the internet," I teased.

"If I ever have to scrub photographs of your dick from the Internet, you will buy me more than a new buzz buzz," she said, her tone quite clipped.

"I will buy you all the flowers, and a garage full of buzz buzz's, baby," I said, pouting for added effect.

"Done. Now get back to work. We have a show tonight!"

CHAPTER 13

Taylor

"This place is pretty packed too," I said as I set our drinks on the high top.

We'd managed to get a table close to the front—again—despite my protests. Still, I was intent on actually *trying* to have fun with my girlfriends, even if that meant I needed a little liquid courage to do so.

Lord knows I won't be able to get through this show in one piece otherwise.

The girls had already started celebrating the occasion with a bottle of champagne, which was apparently compliments of the talent, as his *manager* had come by not even five minutes after we'd taken our seats, with a bottle and three glasses, as well as some lanyards with giant printed badges that read *GUEST*.

I'd barely gotten a protest out when Julie stepped on me, drawing all my attention to the sharp pain of a heel cutting through my Ralph Lauren leather shoes.

No doubt on purpose.

I dispensed the drinks—after we'd killed the champagne rather quickly. Just as I handed off Julie's vodka Redbull and Giselle's glass of pinot, the lights dimmed, and the crowd roared.

I hadn't spent much time in Deer Park, but the crowd the prior night certainly didn't hold a candle to the crowd at Darby's. My gaze scattered the crowd, full of women like Giselle and Julie, who had also dragged their boyfriends and SO's—and probably some gay besties like myself —to this show, which should have made me feel less alone, but instead, it did the opposite.

I slid my hand in my jeans pocket, running the other one through my hair as I avoided watching Drew Axel coming on stage like the plague.

"How you doing out there tonight?" he called into his microphone, the crowd hollering in response.

Kill me now.

"My name is Drew Axel, some of you might already know me," he said, his voice lilting with charm that was smoother than melted chocolate.

Low, deep, sexy.

I grabbed my beer, if only to drown myself in it, when Julie literally grabbed me, practically squeezing the life out of me. Her movement forced me to turn around as she jumped up and down like a kid on Christmas, while Drew strummed his guitar, looking out into the crowd with a bright smile as everyone cheered.

"So... you guys want me to play some songs for you?"

Talk about edging, this guy is killing me.

"Okay, okay, well, let's start it off with one you *might* know. This one is called, *Sick Little Games.*"

Julie and Giselle both hooted and hollered as Drew's deep, gravely voice opened with, "Tonight, I'll be the monster and you can be my prey, honey. I'll be the match, and you can be my flame. Pour some gasoline on it, baby. Let's play some sick little games..."

Something about the way he held his guitar, the growl in his voice, and the literal way he actually *played*, his tattooed fingers sliding over the frets and strings, made my cock *ache.*

My gaze settled on said fingers, on the number 13 on his middle finger, the stars on his pointer and ring finger, the motion of his thumb.

The definition on his biceps as he held the beast of a guitar.

This was a bad idea.

This was a fucking terrible idea.

"Baby, you can run but you can't hide. I know you like the chase. I know you like the ride. So I'll hunt you down, baby. I'll show you how to slay, when you and I play our..."

The crowd chanted his words, the telltale sound like witchcraft.

Sick little games.

Baby, you can run but you can't hide. I know you like the chase. I know you like the ride.

I'd never been much for rock music, but something about the way Drew Axel *sang*, the way his voice turned dark and smooth when he closed his eyes, the way the lyrics sounded on his tongue... *fuck.*

The night prior, he'd performed mostly covers, and a few *Axe 2 Grind* songs, according to Giselle, but he hadn't played *this.*

I couldn't take my gaze off of him as he *shredded* his guitar, singing about playing sick little games.

And maybe it was the two glasses of champagne and a glass of beer, but both me and my cock found ourselves wondering just what kind of games Drew Axel liked to play.

"Tell me you want it while mascara runs down your face. Tell me you want to play sick little games," he crooned as the crowd went wild.

Including Julie and Giselle, who were now both practically screaming the lyrics.

It was hard to imagine the man on stage was the same man who'd been waltzing around my shop humming along to *Teardrops On My Guitar*.

And I think that was the moment I knew I was a fucking goner.

Because when he strummed his last note, he looked out into the crowd, and his gaze settled on me, as he sang, "Stay, stay, stay, so we can play our sick little games."

I took a long drink of my beer as I turned from his fiery gaze.

Its just a performance, Taylor, it doesn't mean anything.

Just like last night.

It's his job.

It's what he does.

The crowd roared as Giselle leaned in close to me, yelling in my ear as Drew strummed the opening notes of his next song.

"You okay?" she hollered into my ear.

"Are you gonna stay the night?" Drew sang

in the background, his guitar roaring above the music from the speakers.

"Doesn't mean we're bound for life... so-oh-oh-oh-oh are you gonna stay the night?"

I pursed my lips, feeling warm all of a sudden as he sang a melodic, rocking cover of Paramore's song, *Stay The Night.*

I shouldn't have worn this fucking flannel.

I pulled at the collar, rolling my sleeves up to try and find some relief from the heat.

"I'm fine," I lied, but Giselle raised an eyebrow.

"I just can't believe you like... know this guy. Like *know* him," I said with disdain as I reached for my drink. "He's just so... so..."

"Magnetic?" Giselle said with a smile.

Not the word I would've chosen, but...

"I was going to say... edgy." I wrinkled my nose.

Giselle threw her head back and laughed.

That was when I heard the crowd roar with excitement, the sound of Drew's singing getting louder, and louder.

"Oh my God," Julie squealed just as Giselle started pointing next to me.

I watched as Drew made his way through the crowd, from one side of the floor to us.

Making a beeline directly for *me.*

My blood chilled, and I froze, my beer

halfway to my lips as his bright green eyes met my gaze. I could see the sweat on his brow, my gaze falling over his snake and roses tattoo. I still couldn't make the word out, but my gaze hovered there, just above his Adam's apple, along the pronounced thickness of the veins running up his neck, and underneath the skin of his sweat-slicked biceps.

Fuck, I was so hard.

And almost as if he *knew* the effect he had on me—on everyone, probably—he brushed past me, his thigh colliding with mine as he grabbed Julie, singing, "Are you gonna stay the night?"

But he didn't *look* at her.

He looked at me, and I didn't know how to feel about that, so instead I swallowed my beer and shifted my stance, trying to quell the second erection I'd sprung today for this devilish creature.

I watched as Julie followed him on stage, as he held her hand and crooned the rest of Paramore's song to her, telling her they weren't bound for life as he danced with her.

I watched as he spun her in a circle, knelt before her as he strummed his guitar, his gravelly, dark voice *pleading* with her.

And I watched her eyes sparkle, her smile widen like she'd just won the lottery. I wanted to be happy for her, after all he was her *favorite* rocker, and this experience probably beat out any autograph... but I was jealous.

Not that I'd ever been one to command attention. In fact, I was the last person who ever wanted to be lavished with attention in public. I hated being sung to on my birthday at a restaurant, and I never went out of my way to stand out—unless it was making TikToks for my business.

Maybe it was the alcohol.

Maybe it was the fact that despite my better judgment, this man did things to my cock, to my psyche, that I couldn't control.

Maybe it was because I was already halfway drunk, and perpetually single.

But I wished it was *me* on the stage, looking down at him on his knees.

I drained the rest of my beer, giving Julie and Axel my back as I leaned in to Giselle, yelling in her ear, "I need another drink."

CHAPTER 14

DREW GROWLED on about being drunk in a car and crying like a baby into the microphone, belting out a rather heavy rendition of Taylor's *Cruel Summer,* the sound making my stomach flip.

He leaned forward, his dark, wet hair hanging in his eyes, the spotlights shining on the sweat that flung from his strands in the colored light as his voice crooned on about secrets.

I couldn't remember the last time I'd really been that level of drunk.

Probably after Zack left me.

Sometimes, I wondered what would have happened if I'd chased him.

If I'd had the guts to throw caution to the wind and go after him...

But when he left, as hurt as I was, there was also relief.

What kind of monster was *relieved* when someone left them for fortune and fame?

"Thank you!" Drew said as he finished, and the crowd collectively cheered.

"That was amazing!" Julie said as she hugged me too tightly for my own good.

Giselle drained the last bits of her wine, smiling wide.

"I think even *Taylor* had fun," she said with a wink.

I steadied Julie in my arms, wrapping mine around her waist so she wouldn't knock us both over. My legs only wobbled a bit.

"Yes, yes, I *did*," I said as Julie threw her arms around my neck with a giggle.

"I told you..." she said, her breath smelling of strong vodka.

"The fun isn't over yet," Giselle said as she pulled out her phone.

I turned to see Drew, who was bounding over to us from the stage. I could practically smell his sweat as he neared us, and I didn't hate it.

In fact, I kind of... liked it, if I was being honest.

Julie squealed with excitement as he stopped in front of us.

"You guys like the show?" he asked, running a hand through his wet locks, slicking his hair back.

Fuck yes, I liked it.

"You were amazing!" Giselle said with praise as Julie bounced up and down, still attached to me.

"I am like... your biggest fan," she said with hearts in her eyes. Giselle laughed.

"Somehow, I doubt that, Jules," I said much harsher than I'd meant to.

Julie scowled at me as she removed an arm from my neck, smacking me in the chest.

Drew smiled a sly, devilish smile as he took a swig of the water bottle in his hand before nodding at us.

"You get my gift?" he asked.

"Yes, thank you!" Giselle said as she tapped away at her phone.

"We killed it before you even went on. After all, how else is anyone supposed to view your *show* without being intoxicated?" I bit out.

What the fuck?

Why did I say that?

Drew grunted a sound that went straight to my protesting cock, his tongue flicking out to slide over his lips.

"Taylor!" Julie scolded me.

Giselle didn't seem to notice, and if she did, she didn't seem to care. Whoever she was texting was taking priority at the moment, and judging by the look of hearts in her eyes, I'd bet it was her now fiancé, Aaron.

"I am so sorry, Mr. Axel," Julie hurriedly rushed.

Drew shrugged. "It's okay... Julie, is it? It's like I always say, I know I'm not everyone's cup of tea," he said smoothly as he looked at me. "But I guarantee I'm someone's shot of whiskey." He flashed me a wink.

"Whiskey is horrible," I spat.

Drew only had the audacity to roll his eyes as he motioned for us to follow him.

"Come on kids, the real party's this way," he said, ignoring me.

I followed him and Julie, Giselle trailing behind us, through the back of Darbys into the parking lot, which was crawling with fans and security. On the way, Drew stopped to sign photos and take pictures, naturally.

Once we finally made it to the bus, his manager—Helen or something—met us at the front of the bus. Her piercing blue eyes looked us over like we were an alien experiment, scowling at us before regaling Drew with her disapproval.

"NDAs..." she said as she looked at him with fire in her eyes.

"Don't need 'em, Howler. These guys are *friends.*"

Friends.

I certainly didn't see myself as Drew Axel's friend by any means. Acquaintance was stretching it.

"I'm holding you to that." She hushed as she turned to us, pretending she hadn't just scolded a grown man like a child in front of his *friends.*

How dare she talk to him like that!

I followed everyone onto the tour bus, surprised at how *big* it actually was. I'd always seen these things on television, and thought they looked huge, and I was right. Though it wasn't nearly as messy as I expected it to be.

Drew dropped his guitar off on the couch, waltzing up to the kitchen... er... bar as he grabbed four glasses.

"Who's drinking?" he asked as he went straight for the whiskey.

"Me!" Julie bounced.

Giselle nodded her head. "Does the day end in y?" Giselle said as she walked past me, joining Julie.

I ran my fingertips along the soft micro-suede couch, feeling on the edge of a precipice.

My words betrayed me as I caught Drew's gaze, his eyebrow raised.

"Fine, peer pressure and all," I muttered, straightening my stance and blowing some stray hair out of my eyes. I was *hot*. "But I want something *harder* than whiskey. Lord knows, I won't be able to make it through this drudgery without something to knock me on my fucking ass."

Julie and Giselle giggled, but Drew only smiled.

"Noted. Taylor likes it *hard.*"

I DIDN'T KNOW what time it was.

I barely knew *where* I was.

All I knew was I was having the literal time of my life.

"Come on, Tay, just one song..." Julie pleaded as Giselle giggled, her head in Drew's lap as he ran his fingers through her hair like he truly wasn't some famous rockstar. Like he was just some guy she hung out with all the time.

Like he was her best friend.

I rolled my eyes. Drew raised an eyebrow at me.

"It's okay baby, we all know who the talent is here, anyway," he said with a smirk.

His words started a fire within me.

Was he... challenging me?

Was he... flirting with me?

I was too drunk to process either, and too drunk to say no.

"Fine, if it will shut you up," I said, as Julie screamed, "Yes! "

CHAPTER 15

DREW

GISELLE PLAYED ON HER PHONE, her head in my lap keeping me warm as I trailed my fingers through her hair, wishing she was someone else.

In a lot of ways, it was like we'd never left high school. Like the two of us were just back twenty years ago, trading Louboutins for Chuck Taylors, and football players for hot florists.

I couldn't remember when Taylor lost his flannel, but I didn't miss it. He looked hot as hell in his tight-fitting, white tee shirt, dark blue jeans, and socks, his sandy hair taking on a sheen of sweat from all the drinking, dancing, and laughing.

I was no stranger to liquid courage. Lord knew I'd been in enough situations to require my own. But the moment he grabbed the karaoke microphone, something in him... shifted.

I barely had time to register the beginning notes as he closed his eyes. He opened them, staring right at me as he swayed his hips, grasping the microphone tightly, his bright blue gaze fixing me to my spot on the couch.

He drawled out the Taylor Swift song, going on about compliments and getting drunk and making fun, his voice something between smoky and seductive.

He closed his eyes, singing about a magnetic field being too strong, moving his hips and hands in that flourished, dramatic, over-confident way alcohol makes you move.

My blood ran cold, as the words about a boyfriend caused my stomach to flip.

I shifted Giselle in my lap, if only because my cock decided that was the moment to voice his opinion of Taylor's Taylor Swift Karaoke.

His pitch and tone was absolutely fucking perfect as he belted out the lyrics.

So the florist has some pipes.

I sang the next line about looking at his face, of my own volition, completely possessed by the moment.

By *him.*

Taylor returned with the next lines about being so furious and the way it made them feel, running a hand through his sweaty, dirty blonde hair, his sapphire eyes burning with intoxication, his words hazy and sexy.

Julie hollered, cheering him on.

Giselle shifted into a seated position, turning to look at me. I could see her out of my peripheral vision, but nothing mattered.

Nothing mattered except the most perfect man I'd ever seen in my goddamn life, singing his heart out for me.

The embers of my heart caught, igniting back to life what I thought could never be revived.

The embers of my heart...

The potential lyrics dissipated in the air as I moved forward, leaning my arm over my knees, pulled into his performance.

Ignited.

Captivated, I murmured the following line about them being gorgeous as he sang the words.

When the song was over, Taylor took a bow and threw the microphone back to Julie as he stumbled toward my bathroom, shutting the door. I wanted to go after him, to check on him, but Howler stepped in front of me.

"Jesus Christ, Axel, you know this isn't a high school party right?" she said with disdain.

I sighed, running a hand through my hair. "I know, Helena, I—"

"We should get going, Giselle said as she attempted to stand, but stumbled back to the couch with a giggle. I turned to look at Howler, who sighed, pulling at the skin underneath her eyes.

"Can you—"

"Yes, pain in my fucking ass, I can get the High School Musical Cast a damn hotel room," she nipped as she leaned down to help Giselle up.

"Come on, Jules, I think that's our cue..." Giselle said between a fit of giggles with a grin.

"Awwwww, but I'm not—"

"Come on, Scream Queen, that means you too..." Howler said as she literally corralled the girls like sheep, which was saying something given the fact she was smaller than both of them. Like a gothic sheepherder.

Cute, drunk sheep.

Make all the stable sheep go baa!

Laughter erupted from my chest uncontrollably as I imagined Howler in a long black robe corralling sheep. Howler shot me a look I can only describe as annoyed, realizing that I was laughing at my own jokes, my own internal monologue like some lunatic.

"We'll talk about this in the morning," she said pointedly as she led the girls off the bus.

"Does this mean I owe you a new buzzzzzzz buzzzzzzz," I said, my z's running away with me.

"Fuck you, Axel!" she barked, flipping me off as the doors shut.

I found my way back to the karaoke machine, the remainder of Julie's song finishing its last notes. I shut the system off, removing my shirt as I surveyed my bus. It wasn't completely trashed like it had been in the old days when I toured, but it was definitely a mess.

I collected the glasses, setting them in the sink, heading back to the main drag, when the bathroom door opened, nearly taking me out. I stumbled, as did Taylor, and due to the mess, both of us ended up crashing against the couch. I braced my arms around him, shifting my weight to cushion his fall.

His body was heavy against mine, and...

Fuck... is that...

"That a microphone in your pocket, Taylor or you just happy to see me?" I teased, flicking out my tongue to moisten my dry lips.

Taylor grunted an annoyed sound, but did

not move otherwise, certainly not as I expected him to.

The feel of his hard cock against mine had me gasping for breath as my gaze fell to his lips.

"Shut up," he said, his gaze dark and full of heat as his hips *thrust* against mine, eliciting another deep groan from me.

I was acutely aware of the hazy blur surrounding this pretty little devil, just as I was acutely aware of all the blood in my body rushing to one focal point, a hazardous sign pointing directly to the man above me.

"Excuse me," I said as I breathed a shaky breath, rocking my own hips against him, my hand slowly sliding against the small of his back, against his soaked shirt.

His sweat was warm against my palm, and my heart was racing. My gaze flashed to his pristine blue eyes, waiting for encouragement.

Permission.

Taylor squirmed on top of me, his hands grasping the couch cushion to ground himself.

To keep him upright.

"I said, shut your pretty little mouth," he said.

I was aware the line we balanced was thin, but I was drunk, and so was he.

So I didn't think twice about pushing his obvious buttons.

I always was a sucker for a man on top.

"Make me, Taylor," I growled, sliding my hands into the waistband of his jeans, feeling his warm skin flush with mine.

I expected him to make some quip, but instead he *crushed* his lips against mine in a fashion that made me wonder if he'd leave a bruise.

But my entire body reacted like a livewire to his touch, my cock twitching, straining against my jeans at the feral heat of his tongue in my mouth, of his teeth biting my bottom lip.

"Fuck..." I whispered into his mouth, his hands finding their way into my hair, gripping my locks.

I scooted back on the couch, pulling him with me haphazardly, knocking my guitar onto the floor with a thud, my hands pulling at his wet shirt. Taylor leaned back to remove it, shaking his head, sweat dripping onto my lips from his movement. I licked the spot, tasting the saltiness, which only made my cock *throb*.

"Fucking hell..." he swore, the curse on his tongue a sound that was both hot as hell, and indicative of the alcohol in both our systems.

My gaze roved over him, now shirtless, his perfectly golden skin glittering in the light, down to the rather noticeable tent he was pitching in his jeans.

Fuuuuuuuck, I want that.

He must've caught my gaze, because he smirked, looking down at me as he grabbed himself, his lips still swollen from kissing me.

"Is this what you want?" he asked, his tone dark and inviting. I grabbed myself, if only because I needed to be touched.

I needed the relief...

But my touch wasn't enough.

"Yes," I said hurriedly, watching as Taylor ambled backward, stumbling a bit but making his stance on two legs as he stood in front of me. I watched his fingers fumble with the buttons of his jeans, his fingernail catching.

I rose from my couch, closing the gap between us as I reached out a shaky hand, shoving his away. I settled one hand around his hip, holding him in place as the other flicked the button open, my gaze never leaving his.

I didn't miss the shaky breath that left him, or the way his cock twitched when my palm brushed over his denim trapped mound.

Fire blazed in Taylor's eyes as I slowly pulled on his zipper, sliding my hand between the waistband of his boxers and jeans, over the smooth surface of his ass, pushing them down around his ankles. His fiery gaze met mine, his swollen lips trembling as he stood his ground.

"Then get on your fucking knees," he

breathed, his words settling on me like a steel beam.

"Yes, sir," I breathed as I stumbled to my knees, the animal inside of me ready to obey his command.

CHAPTER 16

Taylor

My head was spinning, and I was certain it wasn't just because I was wasted off my ass.

I took a deep breath, my heart thudding in my chest so loudly I wondered if Drew could hear it.

I closed my eyes as his hot breath kissed my sensitive flesh, his fingers wrapping around my shaft as he licked me from throbbing head to base before taking me into the back of his throat in one fell swoop.

"Fuck..." I cursed, my voice full of desperation as he rolled his tongue around me, sucking with a tension that was so warm, so tight, and so good...

I feared I might blow my load right there.

I opened my eyes, my vision still a little blurry, but when I looked at Drew it seemed to sharpen.

Instinctively, I grabbed him by the back of his hair, my fingers tangling in his locks as I held him in place.

It had been so long since *anyone* had sucked my dick, and I was drunk.

The desperate sound escaped my mouth as I came without warning.

My knees ready to buckle, I thrust myself into Drew's mouth, riding out the waves of my orgasm like a merry-go-round.

I focused on the way Drew looked up at me, his eyeliner smudged at the corners of his eyes. His fingernails dug into the flesh of my ass as I watched him swallow me down, his gaze never leaving mine.

When he pulled away, my heart beating inside my chest, I attempted to speak.

"Get up," I said, palming my cock as I brushed away any remains of saliva and cum.

Drew met my gaze, his smudged-mascara around his green eyes doing a number on me.

Fuck, he was so damn pretty.

He slowly stood, and I moved toward him, backing him against the couch.

I could barely speak, my brain and body

coming apart at the seams. So, I spoke in the only way that seemed like a viable option at the moment. I pressed my lips to his.

Drew stumbled backward onto the couch, pulling me with him, his tongue lavishing mine. I could taste myself on his tongue, and I didn't hate it.

I didn't hate it at all.

I slid my hands over his chest, finding his belt buckle as I groaned into his mouth.

My fingers fumbled with his pants, and from our proximity on the couch, I was only really able to get his pants down halfway to his knees.

I watched hazily as his cock bobbed free. The light glistened off his steel piercings, and my softening cock was already protesting being spent.

"Fuck, that's hot," I murmured as I worked my lips over his neck, over his snake tattoo, while my fingers played with his stiff nipple.

"Taylor..." His voice was all screwed up, the steel of his piercings cool against my warm skin as he thrust his wet, weeping cock against my abdomen, seeking the friction. I let my free hand wander slowly down his chest before settling at the base of his cock, taking it in my hand as my thumb ran over the piercings, one by one.

"I can't... I don't know how much longer I can—"

I sucked his nipple into my mouth, nipping at the sensitive peak, and Drew practically arched right off the couch.

"Fuck, fuck, fuck..." he cursed, thrusting himself against my belly with haste.

Despite the alcohol in my system, it seemed my cock had not gotten the memo. I removed my hand from his dick momentarily, grinding my surprise hardness against his, feeling the sting of the cold metal of his Jacob's Ladder against my sensitive shaft, trailing over the opening of my slit.

The sensation of his cock against mine, mixed with the heat and the metal was driving me crazy. I laved my tongue around his nipple, grinding myself against him as my thighs tightened, as I chased my own release.

"Fuck, Taylor..." He groaned.

I wasn't far off, and I could tell he wasn't either.

"That's it, come for me," I commanded, my voice not my own.

Drew intertwined his leg with mine, pulling me closer, and I couldn't hold off any more. I came again, covering his cock with my release, a litany of curses and his name leaving my lips even as he growled in desperation. His cock pulsed against mine, wet, warm spend slicking my abdomen, mixing together with mine as he let out a string of curses amidst my name.

I shut him up with fervor as I swallowed his moans, his growls, and his ecstasy.

Mine, mine, mine.

Drew collapsed against the couch, and I against him as the alcohol hit its peak along with exhaustion.

I laid my head against his warm chest, listening to the sound of his beating heart until slumber befell us both.

TAYLOR

My head was *KILLING* me, and my stomach roiled like I'd ridden a rollercoaster one too many times, but that was nothing compared to the weight holding me down, pressing against my sore, tired muscles.

I opened my eyes, and panic immediately flooded my body as I found the source of said weight.

Drew fucking Axel laying on top of me, mostly naked, his perfect ass in the air.

His pants were still halfway attached around his knees, and I was...

Also naked.

One hundred percent naked.

Panic and anxiety swelled within me along with the sourness of all the alcohol I'd consumed, and I didn't think twice about scrambling out from beneath him, and making a sprint to the damn bathroom. I barely closed the door before the urge to spill my guts hit me, my head throbbing as reality compounded my psyche.

Holy hell...

I leaned my head against the toilet seat, the coolness a stark contrast to the heat I felt as I tried to process what happened. What I could remember, anyway.

And what I remembered was for the first time in years I had... fun.

A little too much fun, and we...

The bathroom door swung open, and I turned slightly to look up at Drew, now dressed with his pants around his waist like a normal person, but still shirtless. I could finally see the majority of his tattoos. Both his arms were covered in intricate sleeves, and I could finally read what was covered before.

Reputation.

The snake that curled around the letters, with its bright red roses was written in the same vintage style text as Taylor Swift's phenomenal album art.

Big reputation, all right...

"You good?" he asked calmly, staring at my naked ass curled around his toilet. The guilt and shame mixed with strange feelings I wasn't sure how to process.

Like the part of me that *liked* the way he was looking at me right now, even though I was certain I looked an absolute mess.

I caught my breath as the nausea passed, my head still throbbing.

"Yeah, I'm just peachy keen over here," I grumbled as I stood up, flushing the toilet, feeling more than vulnerable standing in Drew Axel's bathroom, naked as the day I was born. His gaze met mine, softening as he leaned against the door.

"Listen, Taylor..."

Oh no, I wasn't doing this. I was not about to do the awkward morning after thing with this man. *I never do this sort of thing*, I wanted to say, but what came out of my mouth instead was, "I can't believe I, that we..." I mumbled as the memories came crawling back

Of his tongue in my mouth.

Of his sinful mouth wrapped around my cock.

I didn't miss the way his shoulders fell as I brushed past him, needing to move, to find my...

Where the fuck are my pants?

Drew sighed. "If memory serves me correctly, *we* didn't get that far," he said, flashing me a smirk. "Though the experience was more than satisfying, at least for me," he said shakily, his stare making my body heat.

I stopped to meet his green eyed gaze as the reality of his words covered me in truth.

It was all a blur of steel piercings, of warm tongues, soft hair and hard abs. I covered my abdomen with my hand, feeling the dried evidence of just how satisfied he'd been, like armor on my skin.

The memory of my own satisfaction, and the shame of just how fast Drew's expert mouth had brought me to release, surged through my brain, causing my stomach to flip all over again.

Panic laced through me as I recalled just how long it'd been since I'd been with *anyone*.

Seven fucking years.

After Zack had left, I hadn't had the heart to even look at another man, and over the years, any attempt to even try and work my way out of the shell I'd built just ended up disappointing me in the end.

I didn't *know* Drew Axel, not really. I didn't know anything about him except that being in the same room with him drove me crazy, that he was apparently a closet Swiftie, and he and Giselle had apparently grown up together. But I had no idea what his favorite food was, or if he preferred coffee to tea, or if the rumors about him and his long list of ex-lovers was true, and if it was...

That was a lot of pussy and dick the man had seen.

My entire body tensed as I wondered about the sexual health of a man who'd been linked to at least twenty people in the media.

"I don't even know if you're—"

Drew crossed his arms as he watched me pull blankets, toss pillows, looking for my clothes.

"Clean as a whistle," he drawled, his tone solid, smooth, but a little... sad? "I'm assuming you are..."

I huffed as I shot him a pointed glare.

The audacity of this man...

"If you must know, I've only been with one man in my short twenty-five years of life, thank you very much, so yes, I am sparkling," I nipped. "Where the fuck are my clothes?" I bit, feeling more than flustered.

Drew tossed my *fucking underwear* and pants at me.

"Well, I'm glad we cleared that up," he said.

Finally, I found my shirt practically buried in between the cushions, and I pulled it out.

I glared at him as I dressed myself.

"Where are the girls?" I asked bitterly.

"In the hotel. I had Howler get them—and

you—a room, but, uh... obviously you crashed here."

I zipped my pants, angry that despite everything going on at the moment my cock was already semi-hard, just from the sight of this man standing around in nothing but a pair of jeans, looking every bit the bad boy rockstar he clearly was.

"Just another day in the life of Drew Axel, right?"

Dark hair hung in his face, tattoos on display, and sad green eyes with streaks of mascara smudged around the corners.

Now is not the time!

You need to get your shit together and get home where you can freak out and process all of this, and get back to your normal, mundane life!

I hopped into my shoes, ran a hand through my hair. Standing tall, I took one look at the sinful man in front of me, my heart twitching in my chest as a strange feeling of *longing* tugged at its strings. As much as I didn't want to admit it, I didn't *want* to leave. But I was a realist, and I knew one drunk blowjob did not equate to anything substantial.

"Taylor..." He sighed.

This... it was a mistake, and it would never happen again, because Drew would be leaving on his giant tour bus, off to perform in some other town and suck some other asshole off with his sinful mouth, right?

"Thank you for your hospitality, but I think I've overstayed my welcome," I mumbled as I shouldered past him, all but running off the damn bus.

Drew did not chase me.

Instead, he let me storm my way off, onto the pavement before he called out, "I think you forgot something."

My dignity?

My morals?

Perhaps my fucking brain...

I turned to see him slowly sauntering off the bus, wearing a loose muscle tank that I wasn't entirely sure was clean, and waving my phone in the air like a beacon.

Of course, how could I have been so stupid...

He stopped in front of me, the rays of the morning sun lighting him up like some sort of dark angel.

I didn't want to look at him, but I couldn't help myself.

"I think this belongs to you," he said softly, licking his lips as he held the phone out for me to take.

I reached out to take it from him, my fingers brushing his knuckles as I did so, and I noticed on his left hand, his knuckles were tattooed with the number 1989, with a heart on his pinky finger. My thumb brushed the smooth skin, the tattooed *1* slowly as my breath caught in my throat.

What the hell was wrong with me?

"Thanks," I said, swallowing harshly.

"It's early, Taylor. The girls are probably still sleeping," he said quietly, even though there was no one in the parking lot but us and a few cars.

His tone settled something inside of me, for a moment.

I pulled the phone from his hand, sliding it into my back pocket.

"I know you need to go, but... not on an empty stomach. At least..." He sighed, running his hand through his hair, the motion undeniably sexy as the sun lit him up. "At least let me buy you breakfast," he pleaded. "Soak up some of that alcohol."

My stomach decided to protest at that moment, giving me away.

My head still throbbed, and I was starving.

"Let me take care of you, and then... then you can grab the girls and leave, and I won't stop you," he said, his voice full of sadness that pulled at my hardened, bitter heart.

How could I say no?

CHAPTER 18

DREW

TAYLOR'S INSINUATIONS couldn't have been further from the truth, but I guess I couldn't blame him for thinking such things. It wasn't like my public image helped matters, when I was constantly photographed at parties, or leaving said parties in LA mansions.

The truth was, I wasn't the playboy the tabloids made me out to be. I'd never really put a label on my sexuality, which only fed into the public's assumptions that I was some hard-edged fuckboy who would put his dick in anything with a pulse.

But in reality, I was a one-man kind of man. I *never* took men back to my bus. Even when I was young and touring with the band, when they were constantly bringing girls back to party as I had last night, I never did.

Because stupidly, I just wanted someone to myself. Someone who wouldn't give a shit about my celebrity status and just wanted to fucking sing some karaoke.

Walking through the Paradise with Taylor was a surreal experience. As a teen with a dream, outside of Prom I'd never been capable of walking into the Paradise, because the price tag that came with anything in there was more than I could even dream of.

But walking in there with Taylor, the both of us looking the furthest from *elegant* at the moment, was enough to make my stupid heart skip a beat. I imagined Taylor in his normal preppy attire—those tight fitting khakis, rolled button ups, hair slicked back—and I could see him perfectly there, sipping a mimosa.

But there was something insanely hot about his disheveled hair, his flannel rolled up to show his toned arms, and his perfect ass in those dark wash jeans, sitting at the table drinking a steaming cup of coffee, which I'd watched him put two sugars and a boatload of cream in.

"You didn't have to do this," he grumbled as he looked up from his menu.

"I know, but I wanted to," I said with a shrug.

"I don't get you," he said with a sigh, putting down his menu.

I peered at him over mine. "What do you mean?"

"I mean, for starters you're... well... you," he said as he gestured to me.

Raising an eyebrow, I couldn't help but smirk.

"Are you always this articulate, Taylor, or has the coffee not settled in yet?"

He furrowed his brows, twisting his lips as he nipped, "Fuck you, Drew."

"Only if you buy me dinner first," I teased, flashing him a wink.

He sighed in exasperation. "You are insufferable, you know that," he said as he picked up his menu again, just as the waitress came by to take our orders.

When she'd gone and we'd ordered half the menu, he spoke again.

"What I mean is... you waltz around here like you're nobody, like you're just some guy and not the front man of a band that's gone platinum like, twelve times."

Ah, so does know more than he lets on.

"I told you, *Axe 2 Grind* is my job. It's not who I am." The words were true, but somehow they felt heavier than all the other times I'd said them. "I mean, you aren't your job, right? There's the you that you reserve for work, and the you that you reserve for other people, your friends."

For the person you love.

Taylor sipped his coffee, his shoulders loosening as he closed his eyes and let out a groan of satisfaction that went straight to my cock.

Not now...

I stirred my own cup of coffee, if only because I needed to focus on something else other than the sound of his satisfied moaning and my cock that was lamenting its own memory of the sound.

"Yes, but my job isn't nearly as... glamorous as yours. I'm not jet setting across the world to play sold out shows and dating *America's Sexiest Man Alive.*"

His words cut through my heart like a knife, and I bristled at the title, as well as his insinuation.

"*Was* dating America's Sexiest Man Alive. Until he fucking cheated on me with his co-worker."

I watched Taylor's eyes widen as my words settled on him.

"You're not—"

"No. I'm not. And I haven't been with

anyone since we broke up." I felt like I needed to say that. I'm not sure if it was for my own belief or if it was for Taylor, for him to understand that what happened between us wasn't just some drunk rockstar party bullshit.

I liked him. I could admit that, but I got the feeling that Taylor admitting he actually *liked me* wasn't quite an easy thing for him to confess. But the way he looked at me when I said 'no, we are not together', was full of relief and understanding, and I knew despite his outward behaviors, his bite, he did in fact *like me.*

"And we are never, ever, getting back together," I said with a smirk, if only to alleviate the tension that had befallen us.

Thankfully, Taylor got my reference, letting out a small laugh.

"Even if he calls you up like, 'I still love you'?" he said with a smirk of his own.

I couldn't help but smile. "I mean, this is exhausting."

Taylor shook his head, rolling his eyes. "Like I said, insufferable."

"Well, well, good morning you two." Giselle's voice broke the energy that formed between us, pulling us both to where she and Julie stood, looking just as put together as they had last night before things got...

Messy.

They looked ten times better than I suspected they felt, if Taylor's hangover was just as bad.

"Good... morning..." Taylor spoke, his voice far away.

"I hope Helena took good care of you," I said, flashing them with a bright smile and I watched Julie's smile widen.

"Very," she said, shooting Taylor an accusatory glance.

While I hadn't given Taylor an NDA, or the girls, I didn't worry that he would divulge what had happened between us, from the sheer fact he seemed to want to do the very opposite under Julie's gaze.

"Rough night, Tay?" she said with a smirk.

Taylor took a sip from his coffee cup before answering.

"You could say that," he drawled, shifting his stance in his seat like a scolded child.

"Join us," I said, noting the other two chairs set at our table.

"Oh, I couldn't intrude..." Julie said sweetly. "Not after everything else you've already done."

"Absolutely," Giselle said over her friend, pulling up a chair with a smile on her face. "But this one's on me," she said as she got comfortable.

Taylor looked as if he wanted to head for the hills as Julie pulled up a chair next him.

The three of them together in the space, looked absolutely perfect. Like they were some serialized modern version of *Three's Company*, complete with the successful woman who has it all, the gay bestie, and the *fun* one.

Sitting in Paradise, watching you shine like a star.

The lyrics came to me almost instantly as I watched Taylor sip his coffee, Julie wrapping her arm around him in a hug while Giselle cracked a smile.

I hummed the words as I slid my phone out to record them. Just before I went to put it away, on a whim, I decided to encapsulate the moment, if only to provide me with more inspiration later.

"Say I'm hungover," I teased and the girls laughed. Taylor rolled his eyes, but the girls squeezed in and he smirked.

Click!

I couldn't help but smile too, because for the first time in a long time I felt like I was finally *happy*.

And when Taylor caught me staring over a fresh plate of eggs, bacon, and avocado toast, the sparkle in his eyes led me to believe even if he denied it, he was happy too.

CHAPTER 19

Drew

I watched, feeling sadness as the trio headed off through the lobby to pick up the Uber Helena had called for them.

Truth was, I had more fun singing karaoke and drinking on my bus with Giselle, Julie, and Taylor than any party in LA.

I wished in that moment, as I watched Taylor turn to wave goodbye, that I could stay.

That things could be different for me.

"Should I be worried about that one?" Helena said calmly as I waved back.

"No," I said smoothly. "I don't think we have to worry about him, or the girls."

"Good. Because I have a last minute cancellation, and the Brisby Ballfield has an opening tomorrow night."

I raised an eyebrow as I looked at her. "I thought we tried to book Brisby and they were filled."

Howler smiled wide. "We did, but they had some sort of corporate event. I guess the event was canceled because of some corporate bs, so they have an opening tomorrow night and called me just this morning and wanted to know if you'd be able to fill in."

"That's not even enough time to sell tickets."

Howler shrugged as she pulled out her phone, taking a photograph of me before sweetly replying, "Come hang out with Drew Axel at the Brisby Ballfield, tomorrow night for a *free concert* at eight pm!"

"You said yes already didn't you?" I asked, knowing the answer. No one knew my schedule better than she did, and she booked all my appearances, even the ones on the sordid talk shows.

"Maybe..."

I sighed as I nodded. "Guess I don't have much of a choice then," I vented.

"Oh, stop acting like I busted your Legos, Axel. You've been going on and on about how much you *loved* this place and missed it, and how you wanted to just kick back for a bit, so I thought you'd appreciate us staying in town a little longer to give you a little bit of time off."

"Working three shows almost back to back is the exact opposite of time off, Howler."

"Psssh. You ain't forty yet, baby. Plus, you know you love it." Her eyes lit up as she got an idea. "Oh, maybe you can do a total cover show tomorrow night. Sing some of those Taylor Swift songs you think I don't hear you humming all the time," she said as she pushed me in the shoulder.

"Yeah, because the masses will *love* that."

"I mean, she is trending *all over* Instagram and TikTok right now, it couldn't hurt to join the Taylor train. Might get us some good likes and publicity."

Just what I wanted. More publicity.

"Tomorrow, huh? So what's on the agenda for today then?" I asked.

She shrugged, flipping her hair over her shoulder.

"I don't have anything on my calendar since it was originally supposed to be a travel day, but even with the Ballfield event tomorrow, we don't have another main show until Tuesday next week, so... maybe you could actually relax today? Curl up in your bed with some Doritos and watch movies. I know how much you love watching movies in fancy hotels," she said, flashing me a grin.

She wasn't wrong, but something about the way she said the words made me feel sad.

Alone.

I used to love venturing out into the cities I played in, but ever since I'd been with Rozen, I stopped venturing out, and spent most of my time at the gym or at health retreats with him. And when I did get time to myself, all I wanted to do was everything I *couldn't* do with him.

Eat junk food.

Watch dumb rom-coms.

Chill the fuck out and just sit on the porch and play my guitar.

Alone.

Hope blossomed in my chest that maybe... just maybe, I could see if Taylor wanted to hang out.

But I didn't even have his number, not that I couldn't find it but...

A text notification popped up from Giselle.

Hey, I just wanted to let you know we all got home and are good, and I sincerely appreciate you putting us all up last night. I can't believe how messed up we got. I haven't drank that much since college.

I texted her back, as a plan formed in my brain.

Glad to hear you guys are good, and it's fine. I'm

glad you had fun, and we had something to celebrate. Taylor okay?

"Sure," I said, as I smiled at Howler, who was giving me a suspicious look.

"Mhmmm. Just be on your best behavior, yeah?" she said, her voice carrying a hint of excitement.

Taylor is fine, why?

A devilish grin spread on my face.

Because I still have his flannel and I wanted to return it to him.

It seemed an eternity until she answered.

He left his shirt on your bus? Damn, that's classic!

I rolled my eyes. I doubted that he'd left it *on purpose*. After all, it was quite a bit chaotic this morning, but a part of me, the hopeless romantic, dared to dream it was purposeful.

Because it would mean he wanted to see me again, too.

I'm going to be around at least until tomorrow, got a last-minute gig, so I thought I'd pop by his shop later and drop it off.

Giselle texted me back his shop address and number with several heart eyes emojis.

It's not like that, I swear. Even though I desperately hoped it was, or that it could be.

She only sent me a string of eggplant emojis and more heart eyes, followed by a kissy face, and I couldn't help but laugh.

You like him.

It wasn't a question as much as a statement.

I knew I should deny my feelings for the snarky, hot florist.

I knew I should put what happened between us out of my mind.

But something about the way Giselle, even after twenty-some years, could read me like a book made me feel seen and heard, and I didn't want to fabricate the truth anymore.

It's... complicated.

Giselle's eyeroll emoji stared blankly at me as she typed away.

Did you... she sent me an eggplant emoji.

I thought about lying.

But this wasn't the first time Giselle and I played this game, and I knew better than to lie to one of the only people on the planet who could see through all my bullshit.

I don't kiss and tell, G. You know that.

A steady string of hearts fluttered across my screen with very large caps OMGs.

Like I said, it's complicated.

Whatever you say... AJ Andrews. Followed with a winking emoji.

I smiled at the use of my name, laughing, if only because it was apparent she had caught me creeping on her profile with my secret profile.

But if anything, her use of my childhood

moniker only solidified my confidence that my secrets truly were safe with her, so I slid my phone back in my pocket, excused myself from Helena's sights, and headed to my tour bus in search of Taylor's flannel.

CHAPTER 20

"I NEED ALL THE DETAILS, Tay. Come on, pleeeeease," Julie whined as we walked up my sidewalk.

I'd told the Uber to leave, and offered to take Julie home myself, after I'd showered of course. I passed her house on the way to work every day anyway.

"Nothing happened," I lied.

But like the super sleuth she was, Julie only called my bluff.

"Really? Then where's your flannel? Still hanging on Drew's bedpost, I take it?" she teased.

My cheeks instantly flushed at her words, which was a dead giveaway.

Damn it!

All at once, I closed my eyes as I realized in my hurry to leave his tour bus, I had almost left my phone, and I'd been in such a mood, feeling like shit I hadn't even *looked* for my flannel. I'd just thrown the rest of my clothes on and tried to get as far away as I could.

Because I knew no matter how I felt, how sexy and intriguing I thought Drew was, that things could never work between us.

For starters, I'd already moved once because of a man, and I wasn't intent on moving again. I'd worked hard to set up my life in Jasper Springs, to build my shop from the ground up. It might not have been much, but it was *mine*, and I was damn proud of it.

Not to mention, Drew had his own life. Sold out shows and photoshoots, and rubbing elbows with Hollywood.

In what world would someone like him want a lazy, small town life where nothing exciting happened?

Well, nothing exciting until a hot rockstar comes to town.

"Doubt it. We didn't make it to the bed," I grumbled under my breath. "More like just the couch." My cheeks flushed as I realized I'd slipped up.

Oops, guess the cat is out of the bag now.

Julie squealed as she pulled me close on my porch, her body practically vibrating.

"Oh my God, Taylor! I knew you had it in you!" she said, letting out a laugh.

I sighed in defeat, bringing my arms up to hug her. The relief that came over me was somewhat cathartic.

"Thanks but, I don't exactly feel all that great," I said.

"Why not? Was it... not a good experience? Did he get like... whiskey dick? Or did you? I mean, we were all pretty drunk and—"

"No, that's not the problem," I said, feeling flushed again.

Julie steamrolled through my discomfort like a dog with a bone, intent on getting the full story. Her blue eyes glittered with the promise of sordid details.

"Then what is?"

The fact I couldn't articulate exactly *what* was bothering me about what had happened, or how I felt about it, was gnawing at me.

I unlocked my door, focusing on my key as Julie pressed on.

"Because if this is some 'I don't deserve him

because he's a big star and I'm not' bullshit, I'm going to smack you."

I opened the door, waving her in with a scowl.

"It's complicated, okay?" I said as I closed the door, Julie finding her spot on my couch as I headed for the fridge to grab a bottle of water.

"It's not. You just need to realize not every man you're attracted to is *Zack*," she said softly.

Just hearing his name out loud made it feel like I couldn't breathe. I stopped, looking at Julie's watery blue eyes as she held my gaze.

I'd been heartbroken to start out my life in Jasper Springs, alone, and the camaraderie I felt with Giselle and Julie was too addicting to refuse. I'd told them about my ex, not in great detail, but they knew the gist. That we'd broken up and I moved to Jasper Springs.

That he wanted to chase his dreams, and I wasn't one of them.

"I know that," I said, swallowing harshly, but even I didn't believe my own words.

"Did it ever occur to you that maybe he actually does you know... like *you*?"

I rolled my eyes. "You've known the man for less than twenty-four hours and you know every-thing about him, right?" My words sounded bitter even to me, but I couldn't help the anxiety swelling in my stomach.

Julie shrugged it off though. "I know that he was looking at you like a fresh serving of apple pie," she said, flashing me a smirk. "And that was just during the show. When you were singing... Hell, I wish *any* man would look at me like that."

My shoulders fell, and hope threatened to blossom in my heart.

His words filled my brain from our breakfast, how he'd told me that he hadn't actually been with anyone since his break up, and quoted my favorite singer. How, despite my bristly attitude toward him, he'd been nothing but kind and sweet.

Which I didn't deserve in the least.

I've been such a fucking asshole.

"Yeah, well, I haven't exactly been the sweetest peach, so don't get your hopes up," I said as I tossed a bottle of water to her.

"Taylor..."

"I'm getting a shower, then we'll head out," I said, avoiding the conversation, the feels, like the plague.

Once I'd popped some Advil and gotten in the shower, I felt like I could finally relax. Under the steady stream of hot water, I felt like I could breathe, could process everything that had happened in the last forty-eight hours.

Showing up to M's Place and seeing Drew for the first time.

Drew showing up to the shop with Giselle, and him singing Taylor Swift.

The taste of his lips against mine, the feel of his cock against my own.

The way he looked hurt at my insinuations.

The look of sadness on his face as he waved goodbye to me.

I braced my hands against the tiles, letting out a shaky breath as his memory filled my consciousness.

His *reputation* tattoo, among all the others, stood out to me as familiar lyrics filled my brain.

About having big reputations, big enemies, and that being a big, big conversation.

I doubted Taylor Swift was singing about her own self-destructive resolve.

Maybe Julie was right. Maybe I was being too guarded, too closed off. But I didn't know *how* to open up after I'd spent so many years protecting my heart. I didn't know how to let anyone in, especially a tall, dark, and hot rockstar who I just couldn't seem to stay away from.

Which is why I planned on focusing on the things I *could* control today, and that was work. Perhaps sorting and designing the arrangements for the Anderson funeral I hadn't gotten to last night—because I'd agreed to close up shop early and go out with my friends for a night—would help me feel better about the fact I was probably never going to see Drew Axel again, and I'd been a complete asshole.

Not to mention there was no way I was getting my flannel back now.

CHAPTER 21

TAYLOR

I'D OVERESTIMATED the amount of orders, not to mention while I was gone, between the hours of last night and this morning, someone had put through *four* online orders for the Anderson event, and they weren't *easy* arrangements.

The shop was a mess, I was out of iced coffee, and I was sorely cursing myself for not being a responsible adult and just not getting wasted last night.

With a hot musician.

Who you're probably never going to see again except in your fucking dreams.

So, imagine my surprise when the door swung open to reveal a dark figure, clad in ripped black jeans and a Ouija print muscle tank, carrying two iced coffees with my flannel draped over his right biceps; the one with the hot, thick vein...

You're hallucinating.

You have to be.

It's probably the stress of everything, of this fucking day...

"Hi," he said awkwardly as he looked around the room.

"Hi..." I said, feeling rather on the spot. There were a hundred things I wanted to say, but instead I said, "Do you need something, or..."

"I... oh, uh... right," he said as he scowled at the messy studio. "Is... is this a bad time," he asked.

I sighed, waltzing up to him, both irritated and relieved to have a caffeine fix.

And maybe because he truly was a sight for sore eyes.

"What do you think?" I said as I crossed my arms, glancing down at the coffee. "You trying to buy my silence?"

"Oh, uh... no. No, shit. I didn't mean—"

All at once, Julie's words came back to me and I had to wonder if she was right. My heart dared to hope maybe there was a sliver of truth to her words.

Maybe this lumbering tower of sex appeal

actually *was* just a nice guy under all the tats and abs.

And here I was, again, being a complete dick.

"Don't you have like, employees to help you?" he asked cautiously.

I scoffed at his remark. "Not for this sort of thing. I'm a one-man show," I huffed as he handed me the coffee, our fingers touching as he did so.

"I mean, Julie has a key, and sometimes she helps me out when I get really backed up, but she's working today and the kid who usually runs my deliveries isn't picking up his phone, and—"

"I can help," he said, heading straight for the counter, setting down my flannel and his drink in the process.

I couldn't help the surprise in my voice as I gasped, following him like a moth to a black flame.

"You? Help? What do you know about floral arranging?" I scoffed. I took another pull of my iced coffee, relishing in the sweet taste on my tongue that made me feel a bit more relaxed almost immediately.

Drew cast me a smirk as he started lining up the long-stemmed flowers I hadn't cut yet for a wreath arrangement.

"I had a girlfriend in high school. Her mom used to make all the arrangements for the local dances and stuff. I used to help her out sometimes, even after we broke up."

My mouth opened in surprise, and I realized I must have been staring when he looked at me puzzled.

"What?"

"Girlfriend?" I asked, feeling strangely on the spot. As if the reality dawned on him, he shook his head.

"I mean, I tried pussy. Like, a lot, and its not bad, sometimes, but I *prefer* dick," he said, flashing me a mischievous grin.

"So, all the women you've been... er... linked with, you've..."

Drew pushed some things around on the counter, before I asked, "Are you looking for something?"

"Clippers. I need to trim these stems," he said, looking at me as if I should have known.

The sight only made me want to put him in his place.

And his comment about preferring dick, well...

I handed him the scissors, and he set to work.

I was impressed that he actually trimmed them perfectly.

"Not all of them. Just a few. Like I said, I prefer—"

"The tabloids tend to depict you as a bit of a manwhore," I said.

Drew shrugged. "I prefer the term *experienced*."

"There are levels of experience you know," I grumbled. "So that doesn't actually convey what you think it does," I said.

Drew laughed. "I mean, you didn't seem to complain too much about my *experience* last night when I made you come. Twice, if I remember correctly."

You are insufferable," I said as I started working on the arrangement he was laying the flowers out for.

"So I've been told," he said, following with a sly grin that actually made me feel at ease.

I took my spot behind the counter as he trimmed the flowers, making a pile that I could easily pull from as I worked to arrange the wreath to the picture.

Silence befell us but it wasn't awkward. In fact, it was kind of peaceful once we'd found a rhythm, a system, working like a well-oiled machine.

Like he'd always been there with me.

My heart lurched as I stole a glance at him. Amidst all the pastels and light filtering in, he looked almost ominous, every bit like a rock and roll demon or a bad boy straight from a romance novel.

But there was a softness to him too; in his thick eyelashes and the way they contrasted his pale skin, the way the corners of his eyes bore the sight of slight creases. The rough definition of his long, calloused fingers covered in tattoos.

For a man close to forty—thirty-eight, if the Internet was indeed correct—he had an effervescent youthfulness to him that was difficult not to notice.

And maybe that was why I decided to break the silence, why I decided to turn over and bare the one thing I'd protected for so long to him.

"Drew, about last night..."

"It's fine, I get it. You don't have to say anything," he said quietly as he clipped another carnation stem. "I'm used to being a regret, so you don't have to—"

"No, I was... I was a dick to you. Not just last night, but in general. I haven't been the most welcoming individual. Honestly, I don't know why you give me the time of day at all considering I've practically roasted you at every turn."

Drew cast me a wicked smile that I suppose would have melted any panties in my vicinity if there were some.

"*Experience* has taught me I have a bit of a

degradation kink," he murmured haughtily, the sound of his voice immediately causing my cock to twitch and my cheeks to burn scarlet. "And maybe I'm developing a kink for grumpy, hot florists."

Somebody fucking pinch me!

"Tell you what," he said as he slid over the last bundle of cut flowers. "Why don't we start over? A fresh start."

I looked at him across the table as I set my hand over the bundle, slowly pulling it toward me.

"I guess that wouldn't be a terrible idea," I said cautiously.

"How does dinner sound?" he asked, shifting his weight.

I moved around the corner with the completed wreath, toward the side door where the delivery van waited for me to load the last few arrangements.

"That sounds nice but, I, uh, have to get these off to the funeral home, but I'm free after seven?" I said, swallowing my nerves.

"What's good around here? I, uh, haven't really gotten to explore much since I've been here," he said sheepishly as he followed me toward the van with another arrangement.

Once we'd loaded them in the van, I turned to face him, the sunlight falling over him, and making him look every bit like the man of my dreams, gold halo and all.

"Well, not much unless you like pizza, BBQ, Chinese, or cafe food."

"Pizza does sound really good, actually. I can't remember the last time I had a good, cheesy, hot slice," he said thoughtfully.

"Okay, so, seven at Jasper Springs Pizza?" I asked nervously, my palms already starting to sweat.

Drew cracked a smile as he nodded. "It's a date."

CHAPTER 22

I PACED BACK and forth in my townhouse, feeling my nerves getting the best of me. I couldn't stop thinking about Drew or what he called our *date.*

It wasn't a date though, right?

It was just two guys starting over, starting fresh, hanging out over pizza.

Right?

So, I did the only thing I could think of that might actually make my stomach calm down, and I called Julie.

Who picked up on the first ring.

"Hey, Tay, what's—"

"I'm meeting Drew Axel for pizza in a half

hour and I think I'm going to pass the fuck out," was all I managed to get out of my mouth.

"You what? Oh my God, Taylor. What... How..."

"He, uh, came by the shop earlier to, you know, uh, drop off my flannel and some coffee, and well, things just kinda—"

"I knew it! He likes you!"

"I mean, it was left on his bus," I mused as I caught a glimpse of myself in the mirror. Despite the heat and panic I felt, I didn't look like I was having a mental breakdown, so that was a plus.

I'd gone with a more casual look, since I wasn't all that sure my usual khakis and fancy button down wedding-esque attire would match the small town aesthetic of Jasper Springs Pizza.

Instead, I'd opted for a simple blue tee shirt, a pair of dark wash jeans, and my black and white Converse that I never really wore anymore. Combined with my casual, just brushed hair, I looked like someone else. Someone I hadn't seen in years.

I looked like the Taylor Meade I was when I'd arrived here, in Jasper Springs.

Young, hopeful.

"Yeah, and that smitten kitten brought it back with coffee, and asked you out? So, I'd say whatever you're doing is working and I might need to bottle some of it up for my damn self," she teased.

"I just... like, what if it's a bad idea?" I said as I collapsed on my oversized livingroom chair.

"I beg your pardon?" she blurted.

"What if... I mean, it's not like he *lives* here. He's just... he's a rockstar. Traveling is like, his job, and he's just going to leave in a day or two, and—"

And I don't want to get my heart broken a second time.

Julie sighed. "Taylor," she said calmly.

I closed my eyes as I tried to fight through the panic and anxiety flooding me. "Yeah, Jules?"

"It's okay to have fun. It's okay to just enjoy the moment. With a guy you like, who obviously likes you."

"But—"

"Nothing is certain, Tay. All we have is *the moment.* So, do as your patron saint would, and be *fearless.* Live in the moment. Just for tonight, okay?"

I sighed as Julie's words hit me, knowing just the song she was referencing.

Fearless.

I glanced at the clock on my end table, noting I had less than twenty minutes.

"Are you still there, Tay?" she asked quietly, and I nodded, even though she couldn't see me.

"Yeah, I, uh, gotta go, Jules. Thanks," I said, and hung up.

I sucked in a deep breath, and left the comfort of my humble abode, venturing into the unknown with a thudding heart, and a wish that maybe Julie was right.

Maybe tonight would be the best night ever, but I'd never know if I didn't make it there, right?

CHAPTER 23

Taylor

I found Drew in the corner of Jasper Springs Pizza, alone in a corner booth, looking quite different than usual. For starters, he was wearing *clothes.*

His ripped jeans had been replaced with simple dark wash jeans like mine, and he'd traded in his muscle tank for a simple, understated, black fitted tee. The shirt alone drew attention to the definition of his muscles, making his myriad of tattoos much brighter.

His dark hair was swept back casually, just a few kamikaze strands hanging in front of his bright green eyes. When he looked up at me, the hint of a smile pulling at the corner of his lips, whatever ice had surrounded my heart instantly melted.

He wasn't even wearing any eyeliner, and I could see his thick, full lashes on display, making him all the more endearing and... seductive.

He looked...

Beautiful.

"Hey," I said, my voice cracking as I caught his gaze.

"Hey," he said as I slid into my seat.

"Everything go okay with your delivery?" he asked as he reached over to grab his glass, which looked like Coke.

"Yeah, for the most part," I said as the waitress came over to take our order. "What about you? What have you been up to for the past five hours?" I asked, trying my hardest to sound coherent, since I hadn't really flirted or gone on a date in seven years.

God, take me now.

"Set up the set list, did some TikToks. Howler added a show at the Brisby Ballfield tomorrow. Kind of a last minute thing."

"Oh," I said as the waitress dropped off my drink of Root Beer.

"Is that something that happens often?" I asked, not wanting to ask the real question on my mind.

Julie said to just live in the moment, don't worry about the future.

Drew shrugged. "Sometimes, yeah. Less likely when I'm with the band, but this solo tour is kind of different. It's more about small towns. Back to my roots, sort of thing, so it's kinda fitting I'll be playing at the ball field I used to hang out at. Twenty years ago, anyway."

"I'm not really all that familiar with every-thing around here," I admitted as I stirred my straw in my drink.

"Transplant?" he asked as he scooted closer to me in the booth. I pretended not to notice, even though my cock very much noticed his proximity.

Down boy!

That's not what we're here for!

I moved an inch closer, if only because I couldn't help myself. Drew... er, Axel, just had this magnetic field to him that seemed to suck me in no matter what, and I hated to admit, I kind of liked it.

It made me feel safe.

Like as long as I was with him, I could just let my guard down.

"Yeah, I, uh, moved here about seven years ago, after..." I held my breath as the words caught in my throat.

Aside from Julie and Giselle, I didn't really

have friends, and even though I had told them the basics, I'd never really talked about what happened in detail. But sitting in Jasper Springs Pizza with a gorgeous man sitting beside me, I felt compelled to tell him.

I knew trusting a rockstar was dangerous. Hell, giving up any part of myself to anyone was dangerous, but I also had the startling feeling Axel, of all people, would understand for some reason.

"After my ex left me to go to Hollywood. To be a *star.*" I glanced up at Drew, noting the wistfulness in his eyes as my words settled on him.

"A star, huh?" He huffed, pursing his lips.

"Yeah, he, uh, had this dream that he was going to be like, the next Adam Levine or something, and I guess I was just holding him back." I sighed.

"Dreams don't mean anything if you don't have someone to share them with," he said as he moved closer, setting his palm on my thigh.

My heart was racing, thudding so loud against my chest, like a drum, I wondered if he could hear it. Nervously, I thought about Taylor's words. About being led headfirst into the unknown, and I bit my lip as those words fueled me to take a chance.

To set my hand on top of his.

I intertwined my fingers with his, feeling his

warm palm against my fingertips, and I let out a heavy breath.

"Sometimes, dreams are all we have," I breathed. "And I don't regret it, staying here in Jasper Springs to build *my dream*. It led me to Giselle and Julie, and…"

To you.

To this moment in time.

Drew squeezed my hand, and I hoped he could feel what I didn't have the courage to say.

"Oh my God! Drew Axel, is that you?" A high-pitched squeal shattered the overwhelming tension between us and I quickly slipped my hand away, my gaze flashing to a woman bouncing up and down with her camera in her hand.

Drew slid his hand back to his lap, his gaze shifting, his smile brighter.

I watched as he turned off himself, shifting into the man the world knew as Drew Axel right before my eyes.

And a part of me hated it.

Because I wanted *him* all to myself.

"You bet your ass, sweetheart," he said, and he stuck his tongue out at her.

I watched as she blushed, squealing some more.

"Oh my God, can I get a picture? Please? I'm a huge fan!" she gushed, and he smiled at me, though his eyes weren't as bright as his smile. He turned to her, nodding in approval as he scooted out of the booth.

"Of course!" he said as she positioned her camera for a selfie, making a kissy duckface and throwing up a peace sign like a basic bitch.

I rolled my eyes.

"Under one condition," he said as he smiled and she clicked.

"Oh my God, of course! Anything!" she said as she took another, before sliding her phone in her pocket.

I watched as Drew slid his phone out, swiped it open and handed it to her.

"Can you take a picture of me and my friend here?"

Friend.

The word made me feel a complex mixture of emotions, everything from anger to satisfaction. Because he saw me as a friend. Someone worthy of helping out, someone he could have coffee and pizza with.

But at that moment, I knew I loved him because I didn't want to be his friend.

I wanted to be more than *friends*.

I wanted to be unequivocally *his*.

"Of course!" she said with another high-pitched squeal as Drew held his hand out to me. His bright eyes shone with warmth and I looked from him to his hand, feeling like this was some sort of test.

Some sort of threshold into the unknown.

But damn it if I wasn't a glutton for wanting things I shouldn't, for flying too close to fire.

I set my hand in his, letting him pull me up.

"Stand right here..." he said as he set both his hands on my arms, shifting me into place in front of the table.

"Oh... okay..." I said, swallowing nervously.

"Perfect," he said as he trailed his fingers down my arm before taking his spot next to me. He threw his arm around my shoulders, pulling me close.

So close I could smell his musky cologne, his spicy hair product, and get a nice, close up of the word that taunted me on his neck.

Reputation.

Boy, you and me would be a big conversation.

I hesitantly settled my hand around his waist, hovering my hand just a hair above his hip.

Drew tightened his grip as he leaned his head against mine, flashing a smile for the camera. But I missed it.

Because I couldn't take my eyes off of him.

"Can we get one more?" he asked, flashing the fan a bright smile. The happy blonde nodded in approval as he whispered in my ear,

"You are the prettiest thing in this room, you know that, right?"

I couldn't help but blush at his words, his hot breath on my neck stirring my unruly cock once more, making my stomach tie in knots.

I knew it could just be words. That Axel was *experienced* and knew his way around flattery probably as much as he did a dick, but I also felt the strangest hint of sincerity in his voice at his words, and couldn't help the shit-eating grin that crossed my face.

"I know," I said as I adjusted my stance, aiming my gaze at the fan who clicked the button.

She handed his phone back with another squeal, scampering off to leave us be.

The momentary boost of confidence I had settled as our waitress brought our dinner, but I still felt the pang of uncertainty, the sting of anxiety poking me.

Because this... this is who Drew Axel was. This was his life.

And that would never change, even if I wanted it to.

Even if I believed for a moment, he wasn't some rockstar, that he was just a deliciously hot, tattooed Swiftie who liked to sing and knew how to arrange flowers, and looked hot in a muscle tank or with a guitar between his legs.

"Well, uh, thanks for everything," I said as I finished my last slice of pizza, knowing that this almost perfect moment in time would soon come to an end, and it was better to cut things off before I fell over the hill and into the point of no return.

"What? You think this date is over already? Are you Cinderella? Do you turn into a pumpkin or something if you're out past your bedtime?" he teased, his lips pulling up into a scandalous smile.

"No, I just, uh, I wasn't aware this was an actual *date,*" I said, hurriedly adding, "I mean, I haven't like, been on a date in awhile and..."

Oh my God Taylor, just stop talking.

Don't make it awkward...

Drew smiled as he signed the receipt, which I'd vehemently tried to pick up, but he refused to let me.

"Nonsense," he'd said. "Let me take care of you. I mean, I kind of had a whole thing planned..." he said as he slipped his hands in his pockets.

"You... did?" I asked, dumbfounded.

He nodded in response. "Yeah, and you know, I'd really hate to go to *SLAM!* by myself," he whined, pouting at me with exaggeration like a small child.

I couldn't help but laugh as I shoved him in

the arm. "Does that look really work for you, Axel?" I retorted.

He grinned wickedly. "Yes, as a matter of fact it does."

"You are insufferable," I said, shaking my head as he walked ahead of me.

"Come on, gorgeous. This night's just getting started."

CHAPTER 24

DREW

I COULDN'T REMEMBER the last time I felt like myself, not the way I felt when I was with Taylor.

Since that very first night, where I'd picked him out of a crowd to perform to, he'd treated me like I wasn't anything special, which for someone of my celebrity was saying something.

I knew most A-list celebs like Rozen would have scoffed at such behavior—not to mention stirred up enough heat in the media to keep the press talking—but for me, it was actually kind of a relief.

I'd spent the last twenty years of my life

being someone else, and perhaps at times, I truly believed it was who I was.

But being home, in Jasper Springs, walking around with Giselle, singing karaoke on my bus, and hanging out with Taylor was more than a breath of fresh air for me.

It was *cathartic.*

And I wanted more of it. I never wanted my time with the grouchy, *endearing* florist to end.

I almost worried that I'd fucked up when I took that fan's autograph in the pizza shop. Granted, most of my time in Jasper Springs had been pretty low-key, but it was bound to happen sooner or later. But right before it did, Taylor had done the unthinkable. He opened up.

To *me.*

The fact was not lost on me, as I got the impression both from his profile, and just from the time I'd actually spent with him—when his cock wasn't being shoved down my throat—that he wasn't the type to wear his heart on his sleeve. Not like me.

No, Taylor bravely showed his true colors to me, and I was hooked.

As if I hadn't been before.

"What is this place?" he asked as we exited the Uber.

"They're running a show tonight on Georgia O'Keefe's 'secret' paintings," I said with a shrug.

"Thought it might be up your alley." I flashed him a smirk. "You do know who she is, right?" I teased, and Taylor took my bait. I swear I loved to push his buttons, get that grumpy attitude going.

Like I said, it's a bit of a kink.

"Of course I know who she is! Only an uncultured swine would question such a thing!" he said as he shoved me in the arm.

He's so perfect.

"Then by all means, lead the way," I said as I waved toward the entrance.

Taylor took off, and I followed, adjusting my shades as we entered the swanky *Rhodes Gallery*. I'd never been one for art shows, but the fact the place was showcasing paintings of a famous floral painter, I knew I couldn't pass up the chance to bring Taylor.

The gallery itself was next to *SLAM!*, a poetry cafe, and it was open mic night, so I thought some dinner, some art, and maybe a romantic poetry reading would be just the sort of thing to get Taylor to open up, and have some fun.

Okay, and maybe I wanted to get back to my roots too.

After all, I started out writing poetry before I moved to writing my own songs.

The light in the gallery was bright, and it lit

up Taylor like some sort of angel. Dressed in his dark jeans and a dark blue shirt, with the light kissing his sandy hair, his blue eyes stood out like O' Keefe's painting of a morning glory, aptly titled *Morning Glory*.

I slowly followed behind Taylor, who was looking at everything with wide eyes and wonder, and I couldn't help but feel like I was seeing something rare.

For a moment, I felt like an observer rather than an icon, and I liked how that felt. To just blend in between the walls of paintings.

When he finally stopped, I did too, taking a quiet stance beside him. He stared at the painting in front of us, a close up image that I couldn't really make out. The long brush strokes and shapes gave it a feminine shape, the stamen in the center poised with a little, yellow bead that reminded me of...

"It looks like a vag," I whispered, leaning against him.

Taylor shot me a dirty look. "Well, you would know, I suppose," he quipped, before adding, "But, that's kind of the point. O'Keefe was known to push the sexual connotations with a lot of her paintings."

"I knew that," I said nonchalantly. "I was just, you know, testing you."

"Mhmm. I'm starting to think degradation

isn't your only kink, Axel. I think you just like to be a pain in my ass."

"Maybe I want you to be a pain in *my* ass, *Tay*," I said as I walked away, leaving him to stand there gaping at me.

"You are…"

"Insufferable. Yeah, I know, so you say. But I'm not the one who's following me through a room full of pussy paintings," I teased as I scampered off in the other direction.

Taylor shook his head as he jogged to catch up with me. I tried my best to not run, after all, I didn't want to get thrown out of the gallery, but there was something freeing and fun about dodging Taylor through the other visitors, around walls and in tiny crevices.

When we finally found each other once more, in a secluded corner that boasted a painting that looked like a sort of sunset and not a flower, he was grinning ear to ear.

"I was going to say, you are something else, Axel," he said as he backed me against the wall. He pressed his body against me, not harshly, but with just enough pressure to show me he meant business.

Well, kinky business anyway, since I knew there was no way in hell Taylor wanted to hurt me.

I set my hand on his hip, nudging him closer,

pressing my twitching cock against him. When I felt his reciprocated hardness, I smiled wickedly.

"I know," I said, my gaze dipping to his lips.

Taylor shook his head as he set his hand against the wall by my head, letting out a deep breath. For a moment, I could see the excitement, the same wonder and awe in his eyes when he looked at *me*, like he had when he looked at Georgia's paintings.

I leaned in just a hair, parting my lips, and that flash disappeared as someone rounded the corner, causing both of us to detach, to stifle our probably inappropriate hard-ons.

"I, uh... think we should—"

"Mhmm, couldn't agree more," I said as I grabbed his hand without thinking, leading him through the rest of the exhibit.

CHAPTER 25

DREW

"Well, that was..."

"Enlightening?" I asked as I led us next door to *SLAM!*, stopping just in front of the cafe window. Inside, the world was shades of amber and ochre, and there was a rather decent sized crowd filling the floor and tables.

"I was going to say unexpected, but enlightening works too, I guess," he said as I nodded at the cafe.

"Fancy a... iced coffee, is it?" I said, cocking my head to the side.

"Sure, why not," he said, flashing me with a grin.

"I like to see you smile," I said like an idiot.

Real smooth, Drew.

"I am actually having a great time, so..." Taylor said with a blush creeping over his cheeks.

Overhead, I could hear the familiar lyrics of my favorite Taylor Swift ballad, *Wildest Dreams.*

I looked at Taylor in the light of the cafe's entrance, as gallery goers spilled out of the Rhodes Gallery behind us, and I couldn't deny the truth in her words.

It was getting good.

And I didn't want it to end.

I moved to open the door for him, waving him in.

"It's only the truth, baby, promise," I said, following with a flirtatious wink.

Taylor found us a table near the front, and it wasn't long until someone came to take our orders.

"It's, uh, open mic night tonight, so if I'm correct, in about five minutes, they'll open up the stage."

Taylor leaned back in his chair, crossing his jean-clad legs as he raised an eyebrow.

"Which means you're going up there, right?"

"Am I that transparent?" I asked, running a hand through my hair.

"Can take the man out of the music, but not the music out of the man, right?"

I cocked a smile at his relaxed humor. I liked seeing him undone, unraveling for me.

And I certainly felt inspired by such things.

By him.

"You could go up there too, you know. I'm not the only musician on this date, you know."

Taylor smirked at my words. "Well, that may be true, but I'm not a performer. I don't... I sing for me, you know? Not other people."

"I get it. You like to keep some things to yourself," I said as the waitress brought our drinks.

"Yeah, I do," he said, and he took a sip of the foam on his Americano.

I noted that the brave souls who wished to be on stage had started to line up, so I excused myself, and Taylor only waved me off. But I could see the smile peeking at the corners of his lips as he did so, which only fueled me to do what I initially came here to do.

Because I hadn't felt this inspired by anyone since...

Since ever, really.

My relationships fueled my songwriting, sure, but it wasn't like I wrote songs about the beauty of love, or the levity of those feelings. No, like Taylor Swift, my flames all ended in catastrophe's, with Rozen throwing me and my shit out on the lawn as the biggest one. I knew the world was waiting for our 'break up song', but didn't have it in me to put any more emotion, any more energy, into Rozen fucking Lane. I wanted to move on from what had happened and I wanted more than ever to give Rozen the biggest *fuck you* of all and be happy.

Without him and his so called love.

I slid my phone out, pulling up my notepad as I anxiously awaited my turn to take the stage, my nerves starting to flare up.

I couldn't remember the last time I'd gotten nervous before I took the stage. I did it so often it was like breathing, but this... this was different. I wasn't singing, or performing covers. I was going to read the first poem I'd written in probably twenty years. And suddenly, the levity of that hit me just as I was called on stage.

Oh fuck!

I walked out, took my seat on the stool, the bright lights hitting me even though I was wearing shades. I opted to keep them on, if only to keep from going blind, but also because I truly felt it hit the beatnik vibe.

I took a deep breath as I looked at my phone, my palms sweating.

"He looks pretty under the moonlight

A fire burning bright

Petals that only bloom in the dead, dark night

He looks pretty against the dawn
Surrounded by the light of the sun
Vines and petals closing, waiting for the one
He looks pretty in the rain, when all the other flowers drown
Because he was born in a thunderstorm, and lightning is his crown
My pretty little flower."

I breathed out the words as I searched the crowd, feeling more vulnerable than ever, and it was both exhilarating and terrifying, but it made me feel alive.

And when my gaze fell on familiar blue eyes, I knew exactly who I'd written it for.

When I'd taken my seat back across from Taylor, I pushed up my shades on top of my head.

"Okay, be real with me, was it cringe?" I asked.

Taylor shook his head. "No, not at all. It was..."

I took a sip of my coffee, finishing the last bit.

"It was beautiful. I had no idea you wrote poetry," he said, dumbfounded.

"There's a lot of things people don't know about me," I said as the waitress came by with the check.

Taylor snatched it out of her hand before I

could even look at it, regaling me with a stern look that immediately had my cock hardening again, and fixed me to my seat like a scolded child.

"You have done enough, let me do something for you," he said sternly.

"You already have, Taylor," I said, my heart in my throat.

Did he not understand that it was him who drove me crazy?

Inspired me to write again after so long?

That he was the reason I didn't want to end this perfect date, this perfect night...

This perfect few days.

"Not negotiable, Axel," he said as he placed his credit card on the dish, the waitress collecting it and scampering off. "Besides, you did say I could get the next one, and then you'd steamrolled me and the girls with a bottle of champagne and a night of binge drinking, so... consider us even, now."

Even, huh?

"Is that so?" I asked, a slow smile spreading across my face.

"Because I rather like it when we're... unbalanced." I chose my words wisely.

I queued up my Uber, calling us a ride while Taylor signed his receipt, taking back his card.

When we'd finally gotten back to the pizza

place, I'd fully intended to part ways and take the Uber back to the hotel, when Taylor suggested he could drive me.

A part of me, the celebrity part of me, had alarm bells going off left and right. Aside from rideshares, Helena usually transported me everywhere, and even when I was in relationships, my partners and I usually carpooled in limos or private cars where neither of us were driving.

The reality that I'd be alone in a car with a man I was heavily attracted felt like the most right thing in the world, but self-preservation made me nervous.

But I trusted Taylor, even though I knew it wasn't logical to.

So, I said yes.

And the entire ride back to the Paradise, I couldn't take my eyes off of him, how the moonlight really did light him up as we drove through the quiet streets of Jasper Springs.

That was the moment I knew.

That this wasn't just some wild mid-life crisis moment, not some mental breakdown, and not some song-writing fodder for my next album.

I was falling in love with the small town florist who loved iced coffee, Taylor Swift, and who made me feel like in a room full of people like I was the only one in the room.

But I couldn't find the words to speak.

Instead, all I could do was string them together in my head like little melodic puzzle pieces.

Driving in your car, watching you sing

Wrap a ribbon around my heart baby, it's a god damn scene

I think I love you and I don't know what that means

For me, for you, for the future unforeseen.

When we finally pulled into the parking lot, neither of us moved. We sat there for what felt like an eternity until one of us spoke, and it was me.

"Well, thanks for the ride, I hope you had a good time," I said, reaching for the door.

Taylor's fingers gripped the steering wheel. "Wait," he said, turning the car off, and climbing out. I did the same, coming around to the front of the car to meet him.

"At least, um, let me walk you to the door?" he said softly.

I could tell by the way he held his shoulders, by the tone of his voice, something was bothering him, but I didn't want to press. Maybe he just didn't want this perfect night to end either, and I couldn't blame him.

He looked pretty in the moonlight, a fire burning bright

Petals that only bloom in the dead, dark night.

I didn't want to waste another moment, so I took the moment and made it mine.

I set my hand on his hip, pulling him close, and to my surprise, he relaxed, his entire body *sinking* into my hold like it was home.

"I'd like that," I said, my voice full of breathy desperation. "I like *you*," I said, the words heavy in the air between us as I leaned my forehead against his.

Taylor's fingers found their way into my hair as he pulled me closer, bridging the gap between us with finality as his lips took mine.

He kissed me with a feral heat, a hunger that only stirred my insides, my blood, like a hurricane.

I kissed him back with my own feverish need, relishing in the taste of his tongue in my mouth, a deep groan escaping my chest as he gripped my hair, his free hand settling on my hip, squeezing it.

I could feel his welcome hardness against my own, the crisp wind chilling my skin as heat blossomed between us.

When he broke away, he whispered, "I like you too."

Though this whisper was full of fear, of uncertainty, and all at once, I wrapped my arms around him, holding him close as I tried to quell the pain he felt.

Whoever had hurt him, hurt him good, but I didn't want him to hurt any longer.

"I wanted to do that all night," Taylor whispered, biting his lip, which was pleasantly swollen from our kiss.

"Me too," I said as I took his hand in mine.

Taylor smiled under the artificial lamp light as we walked slowly to the underpass of the Paradise, the bright lights of inside calling me.

But I didn't want to venture into Paradise alone.

"Stay," I whispered as I pulled him into my arms again, running my hand through his silky hair, gazing into his sapphire eyes.

He looked at me, biting his lip as he nodded. "Okay."

CHAPTER 26

Taylor

My heart beat like a thunderstorm in my chest as I followed Axel up to his hotel room.

There was nothing to blame my actions on now, no alcohol, no 'it's not me its you', bullshit.

And after everything that had happened, after a night that was so unbelievably perfect, after I'd watched him spout fucking poetry over coffee... I couldn't deny the truth any longer.

The truth was I didn't just like Axel.

I *loved* him.

I loved how he held a guitar, how his eyelashes stood out against this pale skin, that he had covert Swiftie tattoos, wrote poetry, and I really, really loved how he could push my buttons in just the right way, to make me feel alive and wanted.

But falling for anyone, musician or not, was terrifying for me. I was worried I'd end up broken hearted again, and this time I might not be as easily mendable.

But I also knew that I didn't want to go home alone. Not without him, but I was acutely aware that this moment was going to change everything.

Because I knew what I wanted, and for the first time in my life, I felt like I could reach out and touch it.

Like I could truly *have it*. Even if it was just for a night.

The familiar words of Taylor's *Wildest Dreams* about seeing me again and wildest dreams echoed in my brain as I followed Axel up the steps, down the hallway, and into his hotel room. The door closed and not a moment later had the storm commenced.

I pulled Drew to my lips once more, savoring the taste of him.

He wrapped his hands around my waist, pulling me closer as we stumbled through the hotel room like two drunken idiots, only this time we were the furthest thing from drunk.

We were both stone cold sober.

"We don't... have to..." he breathed into my mouth as I tugged at his shirt.

"I know," I breathed back as he removed his shirt to reveal his slick, defined chest with the smattering of tattoos stemming from his shoulders. "But I want this," I said, taking in the sight of him.

The next words to fall out of my mouth were the final crack in my armor.

"I want you, Axel."

Something shifted in his eyes, the moment the words were in the air.

All the air was sucked out of my system as he took not one, but two steps closer, placing both his inked hands on the sides of my face, kissing me with ferocity, and passion as he whispered, "I want you too, Taylor."

Fire roared within me, ignited by his words, flipping a switch no one else ever could and I suspected, never would again.

"Oh yeah?" I said haughtily, his hands making quick work of unbuttoning my pants. My dick twitched at the sudden movement, the feel of his palm against my cockhead as he slid my boxers and pants down to the floor.

"Is this what you want, Axel? Hmmm?" I asked as I thrust myself against his hand.

"Yes," he breathed desperately, his hands

settling on my hips as he ground his own hardness against me.

I ripped at his buttons, his zipper, finding his steely cock hard and ready for me. I stroked the velveteen shaft slowly, letting my fingers tweak the steel studs, watching his entire body shudder as I did so.

"Yes, what?" I said as I squeezed him tight, feeling emboldened by his words, his reaction to my touch.

He was so responsive to me, and it was addicting.

"Yes, sir," he purred as he pulled at the hem of my shirt, thrusting himself in my hand.

I could feel the faint beginnings of his precum coating my fingers, and I groaned in response as my own cock twitched.

I pushed him back against the bed, watching as he fell like a domino against the stark white sheets. He gazed up at me, long eyelashes fluttering, his heavy, sizable cock on display bouncing back and forth. Though he did not touch himself, not even once.

He only stared up at me with wonder, watching, waiting for my next move.

For me to instruct him.

For me to take control.

I didn't have a lot of *experience* in that department, being as my sexual partners weren't into much else other than the basics, but a part of me wanted to explore this new side of me.

The side only this man was capable of bringing out.

I grabbed my own cock, stalking closer. If Drew liked me... *degrading*... I could channel my inner grouch. Or at least I could try.

"What makes you think you deserve this cock, huh?" I said as I gave my length a long, lazy stroke. I didn't miss the way his pupils dilated, how his swollen cockhead glistened in the light, how his thighs tightened as he tried *not* to thrust against the air.

"I don't..." he said, biting his lip. "I really don't, but..."

"You're right... you don't, you... you..." I searched my brain for the right word, settling on it, but it still felt awkward to say because I wasn't used to it.

A steady pause filled the space as I licked my lips and let out a steady breath.

"Manwhore," I said, my gaze searching his for approval, understanding. Drew's eyes sparkled, and I felt a breath of relief as I knew I was on the right track.

So far so good...

"I am a whore," he responded darkly, his wicked smile causing my cock to throb. "I'm your whore," he said, his voice full of lust and darkness.

I leaned on the bed, bracing my knees at his sides, straddling him so our cocks were both front and center. The bed creaked with my added weight as I grabbed both of us in my hand.

Drew's head fell back in ecstasy as he cursed.

So, I kept going, because it felt good. Cathartic even.

His cursing, the feel of his skin against mine, the sense of power washing over me that I did this to him.

I made him come undone.

"That's right, *Axel*, you're mine," I breathed, the words like a spell I never wanted to break. I stroked us both in my fist, building a steady, torturous rhythm.

"But I want you to show me just what an *experienced* little whore you are," I grunted, high off the ecstasy of this new power dynamic.

All at once, I released him, pulling him against me as we rolled so that I was now underneath him, his steel-piercings grinding against my leaking cock. The feel of his weight against me, of his piercings kissing my sensitive skin, of my hands running over his muscles just felt so... right.

Perfect.

I wrapped my legs around his hips, locking my ankles together as he braced himself with his elbows on the sides of my head. He ran a hand through my hair, green eyes ablaze with wonder and love.

And I was overwhelmed by him, by the sight of such illustrious, precious things.

"Are you sure?" he asked shakily, breaking character.

I shifted my hips, using my heels to dredge him closer to my entrance, knowing full well what I was asking and that this was it.

There was no going back after this.

But a part of me wanted to break, to know I'd been touched by such a force.

I nodded, my breath catching in my throat. "I'm sure," I said, and I pressed my mouth to his, stroking his tongue with mine as I ground my leaking cock against his firm belly.

Axel leaned back on his knees for a moment, unlocking my grip around his hips. He leaned over swiftly, grabbing a bottle of travel lube from the drawer, and I watched with my heart in my throat as he poured it in his hands, rubbing it all along his fingers, all over his length. When he leaned forward again, he kissed me, welcoming my legs back around his hips as his fingers breached my tight hole, slowly, coolly.

I gasped from the sensation of the coolness,

the sudden intrusion. It'd been a long time since I had anyone's fingers in my ass but my own.

"Breathe, baby. Just breathe," he whispered, his voice catching.

I let out a slow breath, my body adjusting to him as he built a slow and steady rhythm. In, out, in out.

"That feels good," I whispered, closing my eyes in ecstasy as he slid another finger in.

My legs tightened around him as I started to rock against him, my cock throbbing with need at that point as it rubbed against his hard abs, leaving wet, sticky precum trails along his skin.

Drew pulled me back in for another fiery kiss, his fingers vacating me.

There was a steady pause as he lined himself up, his thick, slick head pushing into me slowly, inch by inch.

My body opened up to accommodate him, but the stretch was more than noticeable, and once he was in...

My insides clenched around him as I adjusted to his girth, and his steel.

It seemed like an eternity that we laid there, still and unmoving, locked around one another, me holding onto him for dear life, nothing but the sounds of our labored breath in the silent forever.

He moved slowly, and I arched my back to

meet him as we both found uncharted territory, together.

"Mine," he whispered against my lips as he kissed me, slowly thrusting himself inside me.

My mind and my body splintered into a thousand, broken little pieces as his steel dragged over my sensitive nerves, making me see white. I nodded as I kissed him back, my right hand seeking purchase in his hair, my left settling at his back, pushing him further into me as he bottomed out, a deep unrelenting growl escaping his lips, pushing me over the edge into oblivion.

I thrust my cock against his stomach, coming without warning as he pulsed inside me, filling me with his own searing release. I moaned into his mouth as my orgasm ransacked me, making my entire body shiver and convulse around his pulsing cock.

My fingers dug into his back as I made my way to the heavens and back down again, into the safety and sanctity of his arms as he held me tight against his warm chest.

And when he finally vacated me, the last bit of me shattered along with his escaping release, and I knew I was surely doomed.

Because without a doubt, I was in love with Drew Axel.

And that changed everything.

CHAPTER 27

DREW

Twenty minutes until show time.

For an impromptu concert in an outdoor setting, I was impressed with the turnout. It seemed Howler's social media "Drew Axel Uncovered" flash concert campaign featuring my covers was actually something folks showed up for in spades.

I'm sure the fact it's a free concert probably helped too.

I strummed a few chords, making sure everything was a go, letting myself get carried away.

All day, I'd been humming the unrecorded melody in my head as lyrics danced around.

Like a flower in the breeze, like coffee with just the right amount of cream
    Baby, I was made for you, and you
    You were tailor made for me...

I slid out my phone, noting the chord progression, smiling as the words came so easy now.

But that wasn't the only reason I couldn't stop smiling.

It might have had something to do with waking up next to Taylor as he curled into my chest, or it might have had something to do with the hot shower we'd both ended up in that morning, which turned out to be the dirtiest shower ever. My skin might have been cleansed, but my ass was still a little on the sore side.

But I had to admit, *Sir* was a good persona for him, and I didn't mind his taking control one fucking bit.

In fact, I kind of loved being at his mercy. I got the gist that the role was a pretty new experience for him, and I was intent on providing as much support and encouragement as I could, because damn, did he do it *well.*

Though there was the impending departure dampening all my wishes and dreams, as I had at least two more scheduled shows to perform before I'd have to be back in LA to meet up with the band and discuss our next album together.

I knew it would be a long shot—and after Taylor's opening up to me, I knew that this was territory I'd have to tread lightly. The last thing I wanted was for my new...

Were we dating?

I knew it was more than fucking around, but we hadn't really discussed labels or exclusivity. But I knew that what we had was undeniably something more than friends with benefits. I wanted us to be a thing. I hoped he wanted that too.

You miss one hundred percent of the shots you don't take, Axel.

For some reason my high school Prom fuck's words echoed in my brain. I'd taken my shot with him, in the back of his pickup truck, but he'd shot me down because he was too scared for anyone else to know he was into dudes.

I'd always been one to take a chance, to take the risk. If I would have played things safe all those years ago, I would have never left Jasper Springs, and I'd probably still be here.

Which made me wonder how different my life would have been had I not signed that record deal.

Would Taylor and I have met?

Would we still have ended up tangled up together in my bed if I wasn't a traveling rockstar?

Would we both be shacked up together in a little cozy cottage, making floral arrangements together?

I pushed the thoughts from my mind, knowing I needed to get my head focused on the task at hand. The concert.

Afterward, Taylor and I had planned to meet up for drinks at M's Place, and I figured then we could talk about us.

Or rather, how to proceed with the *us*, given my current schedule. I didn't expect the guy to uproot his life or anything, but I wanted to give things a real shot.

People had long distance relationships all the time, right?

I had just set down my American Vintage II amber and white stratocaster, when I heard footsteps behind me. Figuring it was one of the stagehands, I didn't bother to turn around until a voice called my name, making my blood chill.

"Hello, Drew." The sultry, pretentious tone pulled me from my thoughts, and I turned around in a rush.

Standing before me was America's Sexiest Man Alive, decked out in his shiny new Jimmy Choo's and his deep gray Balenciaga suit. He looked less like a businessman and more like a mob boss, but his stony gaze and perfectly golden complexion made him look like a poor replacement from those Fifty Shades of Gray movies.

"Rozen," I said, my tone clipped. "What the fuck are you doing here?"

True to his nature, his expression was unreadable as he cocked his head to the side, amber eyes making me see red as he looked at me like I was some imbecile.

"I see you are still upset, over our last meeting," he drawled with all the finesse of a snake.

"You mean when you threw me out of our house amidst a sea of reporters because I found *you* in bed with that half-brain co-star of yours." I crossed my arms. "Yeah, I suppose any man in their right mind would be salty about being thrown out of their own damn house."

Rozen took a step closer to me, and I tensed. His eyebrows furrowed, and he must have taken my flinch as something more desperate than what it was.

"We all make mistakes, darling. Surely you know that," he purred, reaching out to run his fingers along my cheek.

I swatted him away as I took a step back.

"Axel, darling..."

"No," I said. "You don't get to play these games, Ro. I'm not some suit you can wear whenever you fucking feel like it. I am a person, with needs, with—"

He grabbed my wrist, a sliver of his suit cuff bristling against my skin as his thumb stroked the underside of my wrist over my veins. His grip was firm, deliberate, and once upon a time, I'd lived for it.

For his order, his dominance.

But not anymore. If our split taught me anything, it was purely how naive I'd been to think Rozen Lane actually cared about me.

He only cared about the control—which was why I was on a strict diet, had damn near all the clothes in my closet pre-selected, and was constantly prepped on what to say and what not to say any time we made an appearance together.

And despite what others thought about our sex life, it was always one sided.

But I'd thought that was what I needed, at the time. I thought that was love.

Now, I knew better.

He pulled me closer with just one motion, and I hated it. He set his free hand on my hip, like a vice holding me in place.

"I miss you, pet."

"I can't do this, not now, not—"

The steel grasp of his hand on my chin turning my head happened so fast I barely had a second to process before he pushed the crushing weight of his lips against mine.

I'd kissed this man a hundred times over the course of our relationship—if you could really call it that—but those kisses had always left me wanting, waiting for something he was never truly capable of giving me.

But now... I felt nothing.

Nothing except the bristle of his dry lips as he tried to force his tongue in my mouth, and it made me want to throw up.

This isn't what I wanted anymore.

Rozen may have been America's Sexiest Man Alive, but as far as I was concerned he was America's Biggest Asshole, and he was no longer welcome in my mouth, or my life.

The audible gasp I heard sent a shiver up my spine as my bearings caught, and I pushed Rozen away.

My gaze fell on Taylor, dressed in his Sunday best khakis with a black button down, the sleeves rolled up. In his hands, he held a bouquet of all black roses, before he'd thrown them down on the dirt of the field.

"Taylor, wait..." I said as I reached out for him, shoving Rozen aside with a force I didn't know I possessed.

But it was too late.

I was too late as I watched Taylor's beautiful blue eyes water, as I watched his heart break before my eyes, just as he turned around and hightailed it out of there, leaving the black roses in the dirt along with his fragile heart.

"What the fuck are you doing here?" Helena said as she careened around the bend, looking between an escaping Taylor and a smug looking Rozen.

"Taking back what is mine," Rozen said coolly as Helena held up a hand to him. She took her stance between us, like a goblin against giants as she flashed her dark gaze at him.

"Last I checked, Drew Axel was a free range chicken, Old MacDonald, so that means you're fucking trespassing on a farm that no longer belongs to you."

Rozen slid his hands in his pockets, raising an eyebrow.

"Are you threatening me, Helena? Because one word to my assistant and I could have half of America raining on your little Black Parade."

I stepped in front of her, my eyes ablaze, my soul on fire.

"Get. Out," I growled. "Take your fucked up shit and destroy someone else, because I'm done, Rozen. With us, with you, and everything you stand for. If you don't want me to punch that million dollar face of yours square in your uninsured jaw, I suggest you turn around and walk out of here real fast and never ever speak to me or my team again. Do I make myself clear?" I said as my ear mic chirped with the warning for five minutes to show time.

Helena slid her arm around my waist, squeezing me.

"Crystal," Rozen said sourly, scowling at me in disdain. Once upon a time that look would have brought me to my knees, but not anymore.

I was worth more than the bullshit Rozen Lane told me I was worth.

And as I watched him leave, my heart shattered because even in our death he'd managed to rip apart the one thing in my life that had given me any semblance of salvation.

My eyes watered as I looked at the black roses, their dark petals blowing in the cool breeze.

"Axel, hey..." Howler's voice called me from my spiral, and I glanced up at her.

"The show must go on," she said, her voice solid and even.

"Helena, I don't know if I can..."

"You can. You can and you will, because you're Drew fucking Axel, and you have an axe to grind."

I looked in the direction Taylor had run off, my heart in my throat.

"And I can't think of a better place to lay your heart out than on that stage, where thousands of people can see it for what it is."

But there was only one person who I wanted to see my heart for what it was.

"So you're gonna dry those eyes, you're gonna stand tall like the motherfucking badass I know you are, and you are going to knock them all dead. And then you're going to go after Little Shop Of Horrors, and you're definitely making him sign an NDA this time," she said with a smirk, and I couldn't help but laugh.

"What if he doesn't——"

"He will, Axel. But first..." She handed me my stratocaster, her gaze soft and understanding. "First you *sing.*"

I did as she said, wiping my eyes of my threatening tears, the countdown in my ears much slower than usual.

Ten, nine, eight...

And when I ran out onto the ball field, the bright lights shining on me and the roar of the crowd welcoming me once more, I knew I needed this.

I needed to put my pain, my words to the mic, to broadcast my feelings in a way I could never truly speak.

"Hey, how you all doing tonight?" I asked, forcing forward my Drew persona I'd crafted so well over the years, hiding behind his mask for just a moment in time.

And I sang my heart out to every Taylor

Swift cover I'd planned to sing, hoping that somehow, somewhere, Taylor could hear them too.

Enchanted, Teardrops On My Guitar, Gorgeous, We Are Never Ever Getting Back Together, Wildest Dreams...

And when I took my final bow, I ran to find Helena, knowing exactly what I needed to.

CHAPTER 28

I JUMPED INTO MY CAR, my hands shaking as I turned the keys in the ignition. My fingers gripped the steering wheel as I stared at the passenger seat where only a night ago Drew sat, sharing the space with me.

The lyrics of *All Too Well* blared through my speakers as Taylor crooned on about sweet dispositions and wide-eyed gazes while my heart thumped rapidly, my throat tight.

How could I have been so stupid?

Hadn't I learned my lesson the first time?

I smacked the steering wheel with frustration as the lyrics about translation and tearing up masterpieces blared from the car speakers.

I shut the radio off, because I just couldn't handle Miss Swift and her words that cut far too close for comfort right now.

Instead, I called Julie as I pulled out of the parking lot, wiping the tears that started to seep out of my eyes.

"Hey, Tay, how did it go at the concert?" she asked sweetly, and though I wanted to speak, all I could do was sob like an idiot.

"What happened?" she asked, her tone immediately shifting.

"He... I..." I couldn't even find the words, but I knew I needed to try.

"Rozen was there, and they were kissing... and..."

"Oh my God, Tay! I'm so sorry..." she said, going into damage control mode. "What do you need, honey?" she asked.

"I don't know, I just... it hurts, Jules. I thought—"

"I'm coming over," she stated definitively.

"No, I—"

"Not negotiable, Tay. I'm coming, and we're going to get through this, okay?" she said, and she hung up.

The melodies of Taylor started up again, as she cried about being a crumpled up piece of paper lying on the ground.

When I pulled into my driveway, Julie was

already there, standing on my front porch with a tote bag full of food by her feet.

I climbed out of the car and walked slowly up the driveway.

She pulled me into her arms, and I couldn't help it. I cried like a fucking baby.

A part of me didn't want to believe what I saw was true. That it was all some misunderstanding, some romance novel trope where the two leads end up at the wrong place at the wrong time. But life wasn't some romance novel, and I knew better than anyone that relationships were complicated.

Drew might have told me he didn't intend on getting back together with his ex, but the darkest parts of my insecurity told me my anxiety was right.

I wasn't enough.

I was just some small town whim, not the Sexiest Man Alive.

I was just some hopeless romantic who'd fallen for a rockstar.

Julie's hands slid up and down my back as her voice soothed me.

I hugged her as I let the tears flow unchecked as we stood there on my porch for what felt like forever.

We spent the rest of the evening watching Netflix, the cheesiest, dumbest romantic comedies that didn't take much brainpower, while gorging ourselves on ice cream. Though it was more me watching than anything, since Julie and Giselle seemed to be in a deep texting discussion half the night. But that was fine, since all I really wanted was to just... be. But company still helped make me feel less alone.

As I curled up under the blanket, my stupid heart still dared to dream about the man who'd crushed my heart, wondering what he would look like on my couch, sitting at my kitchen table with a cup of fresh coffee.

And just like that, the pain hit all over again.

But maybe this was what was meant to be. I never expected us to have a future, anyway.

I knew he'd get on his tour bus, leave, and I wouldn't be more than a memory.

"You really like him, don't you?" Julie finally asked, her voice calm and even.

"I fell in love with him," I said the words, for the first time out loud, and my heart skipped a beat.

Damn heart.

"Maybe you should talk to him. Get his story?"

I cast her a hopeful, sad glance. "Why, so he can tell me I'm not enough to my face?"

Julie scooted closer, throwing her arm around my shoulders.

"Tabloids are notorious for taking a picture and running with a narrative. All I'm saying is, maybe there's more to the story than what you saw."

"Maybe," I said with a sigh as I ran my hand over my eyes.

"All I'm saying is... don't pack up your heart yet, Tay."

I sighed. "Okay," I said, if only because it was ten thirty, and I was exhausted. "I think, I should turn in. Thanks for coming over, but I'm beat," I said as I shut the television off.

It wasn't a lie, exhaustion had hit, and sleep seemed like a peaceful avenue to avoid the hope blossoming in my heart that Julie was right.

Maybe I'd been too quick to judge, but what did it matter now?

It wasn't like Drew was long for Jasper Springs. After this concert, he'd be off to the next one. So, I vowed that I would put Drew Axel out of my mind. I had a job to do, and I had a life to live, no matter how mundane or quiet it was, and I would find solace in that the same way I found solace when Zack left until I'd managed to put myself and my heart back together.

You're on your own, kid.

CHAPTER 29

Taylor

After a near sleepless night, I was surely not running on enough coffee.

I parked my car outside the shop, taking a deep breath as I climbed out. I slid my key into the front door, but it seemed to already be unlocked.

A steady string of panic raced through me as I wondered if I'd left the place unlocked after I'd made Drew's black bouquet, cursing my inattentiveness because of the gothic heartthrob.

I pushed the door open, my eyes going wide at the sight before me.

Every surface, from floor to ceiling was covered in flowers.

Wreaths, vases, standing arrangements in a variety of flora, from hibiscus to roses to peonies and orchids...

Except for the slim, small path from the door that wound through the sea of flowers.

What the hell.

In the center of the room was a large heart-shaped arrangement made of Morning Glories.

Attached was a note. I walked up slowly, the sea of flora making it seem like my shop was a wonderland.

The lyrics of Taylor Swift's *Daylight* were scribbled on the paper, spots of ink blurred and smeared as if they'd been shattered by tears.

The soft strings of a guitar pulled my attention as I turned my gaze to see Drew standing against the door to my office, ripped black jeans and a white fitted tee with a flannel that was blue.

Like morning glories.

"Like a flower in the breeze, like coffee with just the right amount of cream. Baby, I was made for you, and you... you were tailor made for me..." he sang softly, his vibrant green gaze catching mine as he strummed his guitar.

The sight of him amidst all the flowers, dressed down as he was, only made my heart lurch, made tears prickle my eyes.

I was frozen in place, staring at him like

some fool as he took a step closer and continued to sing.

"And all my demons flee the room the moment I look at you, all the flowers rush into bloom," he sang, the melody soft, delicate.

"If I told you I loved you would you believe me? If I gave you the key to my heart would you free me from the dark? Because love never made me feel like a drowning sailor, love never felt so perfectly *tailored* for me..."

The tears escaped my eyes of their own volition, my heart lodged in my throat.

Drew took another small step, and another until the only thing that separated us was his guitar.

"Like a flower in the breeze, like coffee with just the right amount of cream. Baby, I was made for you, and you... you were tailor made for me..."

His voice wasn't dark or smooth, but instead raw and full of honesty. And in his eyes I could see the truth in the words he sang.

See the sadness and the longing, and my heart jumped, my hope getting the better of me.

"Taylor, I'm so sorry..." he said softly. "I never thought I'd see him again..."

"I know," I said shakily, my sweat sinking into the paper I squeezed in my hands.

"He thought... he thought he could come

back into my life like nothing had happened. But something *did* happen," he said, running a hand through his dark locks. His verdant gaze was glassy, and I noticed his hand was shaking.

"You happened, baby," he breathed out. "I fell in love with you, Taylor."

His words fell on me like a steel beam, crushing me with the levity of their truth.

"I love you too," I said through my own shaky breath, afraid if I blinked Drew and all the flowers would disappear.

That perhaps I was hallucinating.

Can this be a real thing?

He reached his hand out, stroking my cheek, and the touch was warm. He looked at me with tears in his eyes, and hope reared its warrior sword.

All the panic, the anxiety, the what-ifs...

None of it mattered, because when I looked at him I knew.

I knew he loved me, and that was terrifying on so many levels.

But so fulfilling too.

"I don't know how to do this," I said through a sob.

And in that moment, Drew slung his guitar around his back, and in one fell swoop, he pulled me into his warm arms, against his solid chest, and I couldn't hold back my tears any longer.

I wrapped my arms around him, holding him tight so I knew he was real. That he was really here in my shop, holding me. My fingers gripped the soft flannel as I buried my head against his chest.

"I know," he whispered, his fingers seeking purchase in my hair as he gently pulled my head back, forcing me to look at him.

"But we can figure it out. Together, if…"

I watched him lick his lips, his dark gaze falling on me with so much hope and promise, it was difficult not to melt into a puddle on the floor.

"If that's what you want, Taylor. If not… just…"

I pulled his face to mine as I took his lips like a prayer.

I kissed him with all that I was, with every ounce of my being, that infectious hope blossoming like an orchid in the darkest of places.

His lips tasted of salty tears and bitter coffee.

"Yes," I said through a choked sob as he kissed me back, taking my face in his hands, his fingers sliding in my hair as he poured himself into me.

"How the hell did you get all these in

here..." I said as I broke away, both our chests heaving.

Drew brushed some stray tears off my cheek as he smiled, the corners of his eyes creasing just a hair.

"Okay, well... I *might* have had some help..." he said.

I raised an eyebrow, but I didn't move my hands from his hips.

"You mentioned Julie helped you sometimes, so... I called Giselle... who called Julie... who had a key..."

I closed my eyes as a tear-filled laugh escaped my throat.

So that's what had her so distracted.

The little devil!

"And... let's just say I owe Howler a bottle of Jameson and new buzz buzz," he said, flashing me with a sexy grin that could easily have landed him the title of Sexiest Man Alive.

"Do I even want to know what a buzz buzz is?" I chuckled.

"Probably not, but trust me when I say you're worth it."

The way his words penetrated my heart was more than validating. It was worth more than a ticket to the Eras tour.

"And don't you forget it," I said, and I claimed his lips once more.

"Never, Taylor," he whispered over my lips as he pressed his mouth to mine.

I guess happy ever afters do exist after all.

EPILOGUE

Four Months Later
Taylor

M's Place was hopping, thanks to the crowd for their usual Bar Bingo & Karaoke. Though crowds didn't seem to bother me as much as they used to anymore.

I dropped off our drinks at the table, with the help of Giselle's fiancé, Aaron.

With just two months left until Giselle and Aaron walked down the aisle, these wedding party hangouts were starting to become more of a frequent thing. And as Giselle's official florist for the wedding, she insisted I attend every function like I was part of the wedding party itself.

But if I had to be honest, I did actually

813

enjoy it. Hanging out with her and her brother, Grayson, Julie, Leah, and the rest of the party, I no longer felt like I needed to be closed up all the time, which was a nice change, and with business picking up—from a viral TikTok of my Taylor Swift inspired bouquets, everything felt right.

Well, mostly right.

Drew was still out of town, and we hadn't quite nailed down his next visit yet, but thanks to modern technology—and quite a bit of phone sex—the long distance thing didn't seem as daunting as it once did. And despite my paranoia that reporters would show up on my porch any day, they hadn't.

"I can't believe in just two months we'll be walking down the aisle," Giselle gushed, her eyes full of that pre-wedding sparkle.

Aaron smirked. "I can't believe in two months we'll be on a plane to Cabo," he said, and he took a drink of his whiskey. "I'm dying for a fucking vacation after all this wedding planning stuff."

"True that," Julie said with a laugh. "I think we're all ready for a damn party." She giggled.

Leah was crooning out a rather tone-def rendition of Carrie Underwood's *Before He Cheats,* and I couldn't help but slightly cringe.

"I'll drink to that," I said as I raised my

glass, everyone clinking theirs together in time. Then a familiar voice pulled my attention.

"You're getting up there tonight, right?"

I turned so fast, I nearly spilled my beer. Drew stood before me, wearing one of his tight, form-fitting tees with his blue flannel, and a pair of blue jeans, and Converses.

My heart leapt at the sight, and I couldn't help that I nearly knocked over the chair, throwing my arms around him. He chuckled darkly as he set his hands on my hips, squeezing me like he too was afraid I'd disappear.

"I thought..."

"Let's just say I had some well-deserved vacay time coming my way." He smirked.

"How much vacation time?" I asked as I held him in front of me, running my hands up and down his arms, if only because I missed the feel of those hard, smooth muscles under my fingertips.

"Three months worth. Which means..."

"You'll be able to come to the wedding!" Giselle squealed, jumping up and down. Julie bounced with excitement too, and my heart lifted.

Three months.

Three perfect months with the man of my dreams.

Leah finished up her song, bounding back to

the group, a look of excitement on her face as well.

"Pulling some big strings aren't you?" she teased Giselle, winking at me.

"Some of us know what's important," he said, flashing a grin. "Besides, I wouldn't miss G's wedding for anything. I know it's going to be epic, especially those floral arrangements," he said as he dramatically pretended to faint.

I hit him in the chest playfully. "You are insufferable," I growled.

Drew smiled at me wickedly. "Oh, you ain't seen nothing yet, baby." He leaned in, delivering a chaste kiss on my lips as the DJ called out the next singer.

"Taylor Meade? Is there a Taylor Meade in the house?"

I shot my boyfriend the dirtiest look, knowing full well he was going to pay for that later. But I couldn't very well leave him hanging, not after he flew all this way.

"You're going to pay for that," I said as I slid my hand in his, pulling him with me to the stage.

"Is this a duet now?" he teased.

I shook my head as I skipped up the steps with him following behind.

"If I'm going to sing like a canary, you best believe I'm going to need backup."

He squeezed my hand tightly, a dark chuckle escaping his throat.

"So demanding," he said playfully.

The lights were bright as I walked to the microphone, the beginning notes of Taylor Swift's *Mine* filling the space. I shook my head as he slid his hand around my waist.

"Like... so paying for this," I said with a grin.

Drew squeezed my waist. "I'm counting on it, sir."

I turned to the microphone, looking out into the crowd, feeling more alive than ever.

And I sang everything that was in my heart.

Mine.

SICK LITTLE GAMES SONG LYRICS

Sick Little Games Song Lyrics
Axe 2 Grind

Tonight, I'll be the monster and you can be
my prey
Honey, I'll be the match, and you can be my
flame
Pour some gasoline on it, baby, let's play some
sick little games…
Baby, you can run but you can't hide, I know
you like the chase, I know you like the ride, so
I'll hunt you down, baby, I'll show you how to
slay, when you and I play our
Sick little games

. . .

So bounce for me, bunny, show me what I like
Shake your tail feather for me, honey, primed for
the fight
Tell me you want it while mascara runs down
your face
Tell me you want to play sick little games

Sick, sick
Sick little games
Sick, sick
Sick little games
Pour some gasoline on it, baby
Watch us go up in flames
When you and I play our sick little games

It's 3 AM and the demons are awake
I can't stop thinking about you and our
Sick little games
You haunt me with your pretty eyes, and the
blood smeared across your face
Dragging me down with your sick little
Promises you made to me were in vain
You said you lived for our

Sick little games

Sick, sick
Sick little games
Sick, sick
Sick little games
Pour some gasoline on it, baby
Watch us go up in flames
When you and I play our sick little games

Run, run, run away, baby
The midnight hour is close at hand
The sun will come up and you'll leave me again
Run, run, run away, baby, just as fast as you can
911 call the doctor, I don't think I can stand
Losing you, begging you, asking you to stay
Stay, stay, stay
So we can play, play, play
Our sick
Sick little games

Thank you for reading Drew and Taylor's
story.

If you enjoyed this book, please return to your favorite retailer and leave a review. Even a few words could mean the world to an author.

Continue the series with Grayson's story, Book 4 in Jasper Springs!

Jackson

Xavier

Jasper Springs

Cade

Dawson

Drew

Grayson

Riley

Mitch

From The Edge

Shattered

Runaway

Jaded

Rescue

Hidden

Tormented

Gray Vale Pack

His Fated Mate

His Wounded Warrior

His Healing Heart

FOLLOW EVIE

Facebook Author Page
https://www.facebook.com/AuthorEvieRiley

Blog/Website
https://authoreveriley.blogspot.com/

Goodreads
https://www.goodreads.com/author/show/39018597.
Evie_Riley

Bookbub
https://www.bookbub.com/authors/evie-riley

Instagram
https://www.instagram.com/authorevieriley/

LGBTQ+ Romance Books ARC Team
https://booksprout.co/author/25823/lgbtq-romance-
books

ABOUT EVIE RILEY

Evie Riley is a prolific, neurodivergent author known for her captivating MM romance novels. She has gained a significant following and topped the LGBT+ action and adventure best-seller charts with her series.

Evie's writing style often explores dark and gritty themes where her men must overcome difficult obstacles in their search for love, but she has also ventured into sweeter small-town romances, incorporating tropes like enemies-to-lovers, friends-to-lovers, age-gap, and forced proximity. She is known for crafting engaging romantic suspense novels and has a knack for creating interconnected series worlds that keep readers invested.

Outside of writing, she enjoys spending time at the beach and has a quirky personality, described by her partner as ranging from cute to deadly, depending on her blood-chocolate levels.

Evie spends her nights writing bad boys in love, and her days wrangling the sweet boys she loves.